Epic of Hornblood Castle

Siege of the Unfinished Keep

Winter at Hornblood

Branch of the Everlong

Eric Kercher

Paper and Sword, LLC

Copyright © 2024 by Eric Kercher

All rights reserved.

No portion of this book may be reproduced in any form without written permission from the publisher or author, except as permitted by U.S. copyright law.

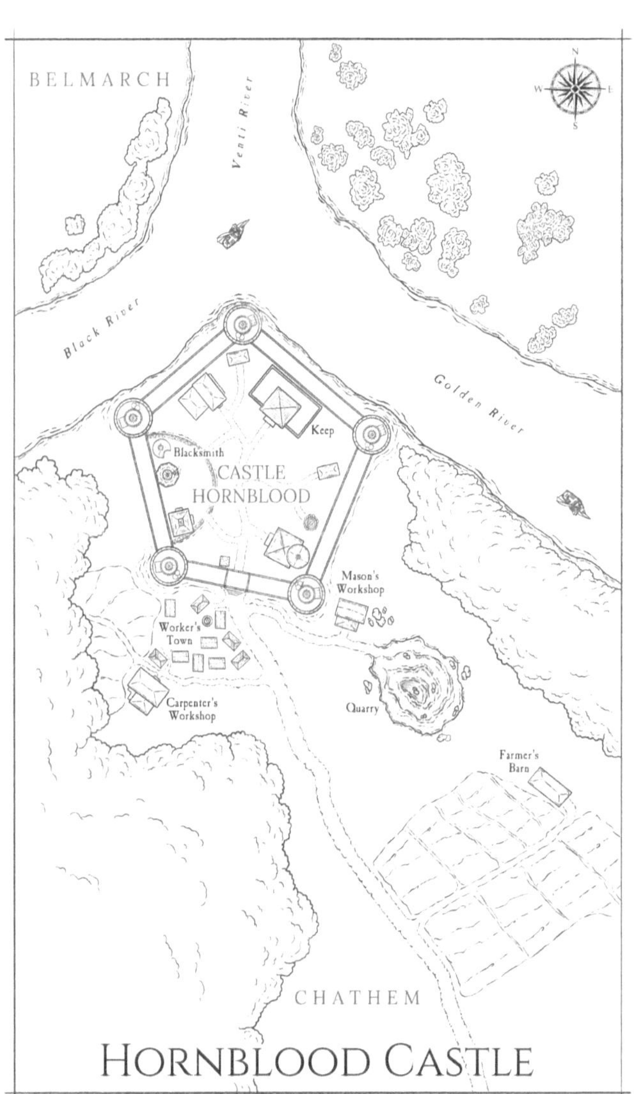

HORNBLOOD CASTLE

From the Author

There are days when we all need an escape from a terrible job, a terrible day, or a terrible life.

Join my newsletter and get an escape from the real world, stories, and lore designed to entertain and delight.

You'll also get *Stories from the Deep*, an exclusive, unpublished anthology chock full of extra epilogues, short stories, and lore from the Patmos Sea Fantasy Adventure Series.

Join now at erickercher.com.

Enjoy the book.

-Eric Kercher

Siege of the Unfinished Keep

Epic of Hornblood Castle #1

Eric Kercher

Paper and Sword, LLC

For Mark and the lessons he taught, the duty he carried, and the love he showed.

1

THE TOWER

Sun poured in the opening, the rock walls rising like sentinels to either side. Sam examined the openings, barely big enough for the beam, and wondered how he was going to do this.

"Can we take out a few stone?" he asked.

"Not on yer life," Bill said. He picked up another stone, wiped his nose with the back of his sleeve, and buttered it with mortar. The haze of the morning had burned off hours ago, but the smell of moisture from the river hung in the air like a blanket. Somewhere off in the distance, a bird called, loud enough to be heard over the sound of masons' hammers and breaking rock.

Thoughts turned over in his head, options to cut it down to size. Aggravation was at the back of his mind, but it was too late to do anything about it now.

The rest of the castle building was hard at work, the early morning breakfast long over. The sun hung halfway up the sky, closer to the noon meal than morning, and soon it would turn and make its descent to the west.

"What are we going to do?" Beside him, Trent wrung his hands. The boy was too full of worry by two hands, but Sam didn't get to choose who his apprentice would be.

Sam looked down, the beam that was to take the main position on the ground beside the wall, and walked around the perimeter of the tower.

The beam was long enough to cover the span, but would need to be cut to size and ends shaped to fit into the strange sized opening that the masons had left him. Sometimes he wondered if Bill did it on purpose, or if it was sloppy work. He opted for the ladder but couldn't rule out the former.

The problem was the cross members. How was he going to get them in? "Take the twine, we'll measure the opening and get to work."

Trent took the other side across the gap, twelve feet up to the floor below. That floor had been easier, they were able to incorporate the big wooden beams into the walls of the keep, but now the circles of the tower left the walls behind and rose above them, leaving him little room to work with.

He tied off the other end, checking both corners, and then knelt back to wait as Trent transcribed the opening size onto an offcut of wood.

When he was done, they left the top of the tower, descending to the dusty ground below. Sam puzzled over the problem while they walked.

They cut the beam to length, carved the end to size, and then had it attached to the crane before the supper meal, with a brief stop for lunch beneath the shade of the walls.

Sam stood up, wiped the sweat off his brow, and peered at the cloudless blue sky. "We'll get this up tomorrow."

"Mortise and tenon?" Trent asked.

"Possible. Let's go back and see how the other beams are coming." He picked up his tool bag, leaving the beam tied up, and together they started for the workshop.

"Oy," Bill called down. "Are you leaving?"

"Yes," Sam cupped his hands and called back.

"I need the crane. Untie your beam."

Suppressing a note of irritation, Sam sent Trent back to take care of it, promising to meet him at the workshop. *He could have told me earlier.*

No doubt Bill was going to blame him for a work stoppage again, and he would hear about it in the morning. Sam tried to relax, stretching his shoulders and arms from the long day hauling the beam around.

The smell of wood shavings and dust entering the workshop made him feel better. Ned stopped his dressing of a beam and nodded. "All goes well?"

"As well as could be."

"Ah, Bill giving you more trouble?"

"Nothing I can't handle." Sam hung his tools on the peg near the workshop opening. It creaked ominously, and he watched it. "Must do something about that..."

Kerien was hard at work planing the beams they needed, his plane scraping across the surface. A ribbon of wood shaving curled up from the opening, before he took it out and tossed it to join the growing pile of them at his feet.

Sam examined the surface, feeling across the grain. It was smooth, a good sign Kerien had sharpened his plane. "Good work. Check for high spots here." He pointed to a rise on the top. "Needs to be smooth for the floorboards."

Kerien looked both relieved and annoyed, the emotions flashing across his face. "Will do," he mumbled. Sam patting him on the shoulder and joined Ned at the water pail, taking a deep draught after him. The old man's eyebrows were long and bushy, and he peered out at him from under them.

"Something's bothering you."

Sam shook his head, taking another drink. The water was warm from being out all day, but still refreshing. His skin had run out after lunch, but he didn't have time to get more. "Just thinking about this connection. We can't just do it like the others, the span is too large."

"What about smaller spans?"

"Will that work?"

"It should." Ned, as excited as Sam had ever seen him, talked him through his idea using bits of stick and offcuts. For not the first time Sam wondered why Ned hadn't been chosen to lead the carpenters over him. He had far more experience, and had worked in fortifications before.

Trent walked in, proceeded to his station to start his next task, and Sam glanced up at him.

His brow was furrowed, and he avoided eye contact with Sam. Something happened.

"How is he?" Ned asked quietly.

"Coming along." It was true, despite his age, the boy was a hard worker, if not the most efficient. Sam could wish for seasoned carpenters all he wanted, but he worked with what he got.

"They denied the request, didn't they?" Ned watched him with clear, brown eyes that hid a mountain of wisdom.

"No volunteers."

Ned snorted. "They'll have to raise pay if they want volunteers." His bushy eyebrows wriggled. "I'll never see that in my life."

"Never say never." They went back to the problem, and Sam wished he had Louis back. He would know what to do, or know faster.

"You haven't put the beam up yet, have you?" Ned asked.

A grip of realization took Sam. They were about to put it up, three stories into the air. "No, we had to take it off for Bill to use the crane."

"Well, that was a help, and he didn't even know it." Ned chuckled, the wrinkles at the corner of his eyes deepening. "Give me a few minutes to think on this."

Sam nodded and moved off, talking to each carpenter in turn. Kerien had fixed one of the high spots, but had torn the grain in his haste. The pile of lumber in the yard caught his eye as he spoke.

Sam shook his head as he moved on. It was getting low. He would have to send out another team to the forest for more raw lumber soon. They were going through what they had on store fast.

Trent was finishing up the beam preparations, using a square to even out the sides. He was slow, only one side was done, and Sam checked his work.

There were gaps in the square along most of the beam, but a few sections were so far out he grimaced. "Here and here," he said, pointing them out. Trent looked crestfallen. "You're improving, boy, don't give up now." He handed the square back.

The smell of dinner was wafting in the opening, brought in with the evening wind. It came from the southwest, the prevailing wind direction. He hurried on to Archie and Stu, journeymen that were almost ready for full carpentership. Bob was working on a door frame, finishing up preparing the stock, and was coming along nicely. He would work on the door next, if they had enough oak to finish it.

They had finished their tasks for the day. "What should we do tomorrow?" Bob asked, hanging up his apron. The dinner bell would be ringing soon. They both looked toward the door. That was a good question. After this section of the tower, they would need flooring. No one had started it yet.

"Take down a few more trees tomorrow. Straight oak is preferable, but anything straight will do."

They nodded. "Go ahead."

Without hesitation they were gone, out of the workshop and straight to the food. The bell rang out seconds later, and the rest of the workshop put up their tools.

Sam stayed behind, thinking about what was left and what was upcoming. The sun was casting its colors into the sky, and he leaned on the workshop porch to watch it.

Castle Hornblood stood imposing before it, a skeleton of what it would be. The great walls of limestone glittered gray in the sunset. It was made of stout, hefty stone.

That reminded him. The quarry asked for another crane. Who he was going to get to do that he wasn't sure, but they had one about to fail. It was there since the beginning and had seen plenty of use.

A few more loads and it might snap in half. Sam sighed, hung up his apron, and joined the others at dinner.

The Square was abuzz with conversation and alive with light. A cheerful fire burned in the center, with the remains of a deer still turning on the spit and sizzling as it dropped fat. The smell drifted over everything and mingled with fresh bread. Sam didn't even mind the undercurrent of unwashed bodies it smelled so good.

He got in line for the food, which had dwindled since he was so late. he was behind a pair of masons talking about the woes they had to deal with.

He made his greetings and listened to the life around them. There was a touch of sadness in his gladness. Families now joined the workers, contributing all the chaos and joy that accompanied them.

Children played and ran in between the legs of their parents in great packs. The women added a touch of comfort in the hard wilderness they occupied, and food was by far his favorite contribution.

"Evening Sam," Twilight said, winking at him. "Some of everything?"

"Please." He took the wooden plate, holding it out over the thick stew that she spooned onto it. A chunk of bread, fresh from the morning, added a garnish besides a slice of venison that still steamed. "Much obliged. You always have a way with food that I appreciate."

"On, get along now," she said, waving a hand at him and blushing, but she looked pleased. He knuckled his brow and went to join Ned at a table, along with a few of the other carpenters.

The masons shot him a look as they took their plates, one mumbling something under his breath to the others. Sam didn't fail to notice.

It troubled him, just another thing to add to the pile of unresolved problems. How could he work with Bill?

The food was good, and hot too, almost too hot. It burned his tongue, so he let it cool. The weak ale that came with the meal helped with the sting, but couldn't remove it.

He let his stomach grumble as his food cooled, making small talk with the others.

"Sam, there you are." The voice boomed behind him, and he winced.

"Overseer Clayton," he said, rising. "Evening to you."

"What is the meaning of holding up the work at the south-east tower? I was told you took up the crane almost all evening." The Overseer brought all eyes to him, silencing the crowd.

Sam cleared his throat. The tips of his ears burned hot, and he fought the anger that bubbled up inside. He thought he would at least have until the morning. "We were unaware that the — "

"Enough of your excuses. How many times do I have to tell you how critical this castle is?" Whispers in the crowd brought his attention, and Clayton rounded on them, shaking a large fist in their direction. "And don't think all of you are free of this, either. I've seen how you sulk and shirk your work. Need I remind you how close we are to Belmarch?"

The Square was silent, except for the crackling of fire and hisses of burning fat. Someone nudged the spit worker and they resumed rotating it, the creaking joining in.

"You'll see me in the morning," Clayton said, turning his haggard eyes back to Sam. "And leave your excuses when you do."

2

OVERSEEN

The night didn't go well. Sam's food tasted like ash in his mouth, but he dutifully swallowed it. He didn't know when they'd have meat again, but doubted it would be soon.

The others gave him a wide berth, letting him alone. He caught a couple glances from the masons, giddy with a hidden mockery, but they didn't say anything outright.

The time came for him to retire, and he bid the others good night. Instead of going back to his hut he went out to the edge of the small town that had been erected and stood at the edge of the farms.

Small puffs of wind tousled the sprigs of greenery and rattled the trees. The wind was dying down for the night, like it usually did, and the sky was half covered in clouds. The stars twinkled above him with a sliver of moon carved out in the eastern sky.

This wasn't the kind of life he was hoping for. He squeezed his eyes shut, imagining what it would be like to be someone else. If Fannon was here...

The chill of the night wore through his clothing, and Sam retired his thoughts and turned back to the simple hut he called home.

It wasn't much, but with his station he was afforded privacy. A bed, a table, and some belongings in a trunk made the majority of the furnishings, with a chair he made himself.

It wasn't the prettiest thing to look at, but it held him up well on three legs. He sunk into it, leaning back against the stiff frame.

What was he supposed to tell him? That he didn't know what he was doing? That he should find someone else to lead the carpenters?

Ned wouldn't do it, and none of the others were even masters. They needed more craftsman here, if the building was going to work, but with the completion of the outer wall there didn't seem to be much desire to finish it.

Day after day they looked for barges and ships coming up river loaded with more recruits to raise the castle. Day after day they were disappointed.

Even the masons were tired, despite the large numbers, and Sam wondered if this wasn't done out of necessity instead of spite.

That wasn't something he thought of before, but he realized it might be the case.

The night was waning, and his body called for rest. Sam yawned and shed his outer garments. After he slipped into bed he decided to go to Bill in the morning and see if there was anything he could do.

This castle wasn't going to build itself.

The roosters woke him. He was grateful to be awake, the strange dreams of a nightmare haunting him.

He had been back in full armor, weighed down and trapped in quicksand, all his family just out of reach. They called to him with gaunt faces and outstretched hands of the palest white, beckoning him on.

He didn't want to go there, wherever it was, and tried to escape, but the sand pulled him closer, trapping his legs and arms and sucking at his neck.

He still felt the coarse grains at the base of his chin and rubbed it. Nothing there.

It was all a dream, too real to be anything else.

Sunlight poured in the slat covered window, another perk of his position. He dressed and pushed open the door to the early morning world.

Others were already out, the farmers and wives in the field, tending to the hardest work before the heat of the day. Gruel was kept warm over the fire and he took a bowl.

It wasn't good, but it filled his belly, and kept him in good enough cheer to keep him alive.

Although, he would have to face the Overseer soon. The man slept in late, so he had some time.

He was the first in the workshop and kindled the remains of the fire with offcuts and shavings to a pleasant size. It was almost time to re-oil all the handles, but he had none to speak of.

He might, if he still had a position after this meeting, be able to beg some from the Overseer. They did still get some shipments from the south, and oil might be available.

But all of this, he knew, was just a distraction. He would have to face the Overseer on his own.

The others were coming in, and he greeted them. They looked at him and slipped by, and he tried to soften his expression, but they got to work and kept their heads down. Little conversation flowed. The sounds of work abounded as the sun rose. He glanced outside and knew any longer would meet nothing but anger.

"I'm off, everyone keep working while I'm gone." He expected something, but was greeted with silence. Even Ned didn't look up.

So Sam turned and left, walking the path up to the castle keep and toward the entrance.

Sunlight still streamed in from above, shining on the first floor, and sneaked its way into cracks down to the bottom level. There were no doors on the main entrance hall, another thing Sam and his crew were supposed to do, so he walked in the large stone arch and down the hall to the first door on the left.

He was inside, talking to someone else, as Sam paused just outside to take a deep breath. The air was dusty and filled with the droppings of the masons far above.

Sam rapped on the thick wooden door, remembering that he helped make it. Vaguely, he sensed a moment of pride before the voice came through it. "Enter."

He didn't sound pleased, although a lot of the bite that had been in the Overseer's voice was gone. Either by a good night's sleep or the dulling of time, Sam hoped it might turn out better than he expected.

Overseer Rhys was inside, with a young man of about twenty. The thick black hair gave it away, he was a Hornblood.

"Come in," the Overseer said, his eyes clouded. He sat behind a paper-strewn desk covered in the plans of the castle. It was oversized to hold them all, and Sam was sure his desire was for a far more elegant desk, for the Overseer was a sophisticated man. Why he ended up here in charge of the production of the building was still a mystery to him.

Silence reigned, and Sam took his spot in front of the desk dutifully, staring straight ahead.

The wood of the Overseer's chair squeaked as he leaned forward and steepled his hands. "Is there a reason why you keep interfering with the mason's work?"

"Not trying to interfere, sir." The room smelled of tobacco and sweat, the trace lingering of a pipe still around.

"Then why do they keep coming to me, saying you're putting them behind?" His voice was calm, for now. Sam wondered if it wasn't due to the Hornblood onlooker.

"I imagine we keep them from advancing from time to time. I'm trying to get everything done."

"Trying." the Overseer scoffed. "I've given you everything you need, and yet you still make excuses." He slammed a fist down on the table, making it jump. Sam kept his eyes fixed on a point above him where an interesting section of stone met. "If it weren't for the deadline, I'd have you removed and sent upriver to the nearest drop off point."

Sam bit his tongue. Better to get it over and done with than worry the man any longer. "Yes, sir."

"I want you to think carefully about what needs to be done and work together, in harmony, with everyone else. Is that clear?"

"Yes, sir."

"I said, is that clear?" Sam met his eyes, fiery behind the puffy cheeks.

"It is clear, sir. Is there any word on recruits?" Sam had to press this. "We could use a few more--"

"Enough!" the Overseer thundered, rising from his chair and toppling it backward. "You'll get what you get," he calmed himself, straightening his shirt and slicking back his black hair. "Dismissed."

Sam dropped his head a small, but respectful, amount and left.

He breathed a sigh of relief as he shut the door. It could have been worse, and it could have gone better. He suspected the Overseer was holding back, but whatever the case may be he still had a place here.

Now, he just had to finish the work. Behind him he heard voices, but couldn't make out what they were saying through the door. He resisted the urge to listen and left, back out the wide open arch to the outside and down the path.

The sun was up in the sky now, burned off the last wisps of morning. Sam whistled in the bright morning air, some of the weight off his shoulders.

Once again, he would live to fight another day.

He glanced up at the tower. Bill watched him with a glower, but Sam just waved and walked on. *No need to upset him now.*

As he walked along the dusty path to the workshop he wondered who the newcomer was. The Hornbloods were set to take residence in the castle, it was their land, after all, but hadn't been seen before now. It couldn't be the Duke, not with him being so young, and he suspected it might be a son or a distant cousin. Maybe a nephew to come see how things were going.

Sam brightened at the idea that they might have another report that would put their situation to light to higher ups. It might be the thing they need, to finally get more workers and more support.

And, if truth be told, more soldiers.

He glanced over, the Ventie River running clear right behind the forest. A few more stones on the tower and they would be above the trees, and with a good view to the other side.

To the Belmarch side.

Which meant they could be seen in turn. He wondered what it was like there, as much as the stories told of death and destruction, he knew it couldn't be that bad.

Although the thirst for war and blood seemed to be real, considering the stories that were told. Invasion, raids, attacks. They had carried them out in spades.

Which, he supposed, is why the castle was being built. Stationed at the headwaters of the Streaming Split, the division of the Venti River into the Golden River on the east and the Black River on the west, the castle allowed for a defensive position at the best river crossing from Belmarch in to Chathem.

It would be where he would have chosen a defensive position, too. Sam shook his head. That life was behind him now, long gone. He was a carpenter, a worker of wood.

He longed for the feel of it, warm and smooth or roughed from a new split, and the smell of it. Fresh, clean, newly felled, or dried and sawn, wood dust brought him to simpler times, a time of peace.

And, hopefully, a time of prosperity. As much as he disliked being Master Carpenter, the pay was better than as a worker alone.

A child waved to him, Netty's girl, he thought, and he waved back. She turned back to her playmates, chasing after one another in the dust.

A low rumble in the distance brought his attention to the sky. Lightning lanced through a thunder head far off. It might be coming this way.

Sam quickened his step and soon found himself back at the workshop. Anxious eyes looked to him, and he smiled. "I'm still here, for the time being."

"We hoped you would be," Ned said, hand on a plane.

"What did he say?" Archie asked.

"Nothing that bears repeating to your ears. Hush now and get back to work. We'll have a difficult time if we don't get that beam up before it rains." Sam looked around. "Where's Trent?"

"Up at the castle. He brought your tools and said he was going to start without you." Sure enough, his tool hook was empty.

Sam checked to make sure everyone had enough work for the next few days and left. A part of him admired the initiative Trent showed. Another part of him wondered what he would mess up.

But by the time he got to the tower, Trent hadn't progressed much past marking up the end of the beam.

Sam stopped, collecting his breath, and examined his work. Everything was laid out as they expected, with two sides marked. He nodded, and Trent took out his saw and started working, cutting away the meat of the wood back to just outside his line.

Sam turned his attention to the middle. After his discussion with Ned, he thought he knew what he was going to do.

"You're in our way," a familiar voice said. Sam turned. Bill, and three of his masons, stood with arms crossed and hammers ready, scowling at them.

3

BEAMWORK

"Good morning to you too." Sam eyed them. Their pupils were dilated and, judging from the smell wafting in his direction, they had found their way into the ale earlier.

"I didn't say it was a good morning," Bill said, deepening his scowl.

"What is it you would like?"

"For you and that sod to stop getting in our way." Bill pointed his hammer at Trent. Sam stepped in between them, causing the other masons to spread out and enter a fighting stance.

Sam held up his hands. "We don't want any trouble."

"You've got it," one of the masons said, a slight slur to his speech.

"Hold on," Bill said. He smiled. "We want to work, that's all. Like he said, no trouble."

"Can we discuss this in a more...private setting?" Sam kept his voice low, hoping that Bill was the only one who had heard.

He scoffed. "I think not. Why don't we help them boys?"

The masons advanced, and Sam stepped back. He pushed Trent away, the boy quivered, and they stepped out of the way.

Bill watched him as they picked up the beam and chucked it down the hill. It tumbled, striking the rocks on the way down, before it finally rested at the base of the wall.

"There. Now we can get to work." Bill walked up to Sam. "Next time you get in our way, we won't be so accommodating."

"We aren't enemies," Sam said. Bill showed him his teeth.

"Just stay out of our way." Bill walked past, shouldering him out of the way. Sam stepped aside, letting him go.

"Why didn't you do anything?" Trent's face was flushed, and his eyes were watery. Sam put a hand on his shoulder.

"Come on," he said. He felt Trent's eyes boring into his back, assuming he was a coward. He felt a touch of it, but there wasn't anything he could do about it. He was here to build, not to destroy. "There's a way to break anything, given the right leverage. It's harder to make."

They trudged downhill to the beam. Sam examined it, running his hands along the dents and scratches it had picked up along the way. The ends were blunted, but they were going to be cut anyway. Miraculously, it was still intact and sound enough to put up.

"Help me with this side," Sam said, stooping down to pick up one end. He gave a count and they lifted it, turning it one revolution, and pulled it up the hill. It had taken the four masons to pick it up, but the two of them struggled.

They stopped to take rests, setting back on the ground every few yards. Sam felt it in his back at the top, the burning of his muscles and arms.

It had taken the cart to get it up here, and at least a half an hour to return it by hand. Trent wouldn't speak to him, and avoided his gaze. Still, Sam went over the cutting with him, instructing him and watching him when he needed to.

He wasn't going to abandon his development over a little tussle.

While Trent cut the ends, he worked on the mortise at the middle. He laid out his sizing and scored along the edges of the hole, about a quarter of the way from the edge of the beam, and then got to work using a chisel to hollow it out.

It was still sharp from when he had sharpened it this morning and made quick work, deepening the hole and creating a pile of chips to each side. He was halfway through when Trent needed to turn the beam and performed the same operation on the other side, but a little smaller to account for mis-measurement.

Slices of wood fell away as he cut. The chisel gleamed in the light of the morning, reflecting the sun and scattering it into tiny shards of light.

Sam leaned down and blew into the hole. Chips and shavings flew out, then drifted down around the opening and ground. He brushed them off, enjoying the smell of the oak as he cut it.

He let himself sink into his work, letting the confrontation slip away. The music of the castle under construction lulled him. Slamming rock, hammer blows, the ring of metal. A rope creaked as the crane hauled another load of rock to the top.

Inch by inch, stone by stone, beam by beam, the castle was coming together. When Sam finished his mortise he stood up and stretched his back, admiring the work they had put in so far.

He hadn't been here for the initial laying of the walls and outlays, but now they towered above him. The keep was well under way, the next priority, before they build the rest of the outbuildings and support structures other than the blacksmith.

Their area was finished, tucked up against the wall. Smoke poured out of the chimney, a fire blazing in the furnace.

He wiped his sweaty brow, glad he didn't have to be there on a hot day like today. The sun wasn't at the peak of its journey and already his clothes were soaked with sweat.

"Done with this side, too." Trent stood over his work, shuffling his feet from side to side. He still wouldn't look him in the eye.

Sam passed his hand over the work, comparing it to the form they had used. He pointed out a few more areas to knock down.

"First, let's move these cross members over. Might as well cut it on the ground."

He had another beam ready, a few yards away down the slope. They went and pulled it from its resting place, setting it up on an offcut to suspend it off the ground.

Sam took one end of the saw and Trent took the other. They started it roughly in the middle, rasps that hit a steady rhythm as each man pulled the saw back and forth.

The teeth cleared out packs of sawdust that puffed out the sides and sprinkled onto the grass. The lunch bell rang just as they finished, the beam falling away into two on either side.

Sam dusted off his hands and left the beam where it lay. "Come on, we'll eat and come finish this after."

After putting away the tools, safe from prying eyes and hands, they walked down the road with the stream of other workers back to the Square.

Up ahead, the movement around the fire seemed more pronounced. When they got there the Square was abuzz with activity and conversation.

"What's going on?" Trent asked, eyes wide, as they reached the table the other carpenters had claimed.

"New lord," Ned said, ripping off a hunk of bread and dumping it into his stew. "Brought a world of trouble, it seems."

"How so?" Sam asked. He waved off a fly buzzing around his head. The soup smelled good. Leftover venison, no doubt, or the bones. He suppressed his hunger to listen to the stories around him.

"Young Hornblood, distant cousin or something like that. Says the Belmarch have rumblings of war and raiding parties."

"I heard they came over the river a few miles down and killed an entire village. Didn't even take them as hostages, just burned the place down. They said the bodies were left all charred and blackened," Archie said. Trent's eyes widened even more.

"Hush now, none of those rumors," Sam said.

"It isn't rumor. I heard the same thing, that the peace isn't holding anymore and they'll be across." Kerien held up a defiant chin.

"These Belmarch aren't that bad. It must be bad blood making tall tales." Sam stood to get in line.

Ned shook his head. "I'm afraid not. I've lived up north my whole life and what they say about the Belmarch is true. A bloodthirsty, horrible people that love fighting amongst themselves more than they do fighting others." He gummed a hunk of bread, some soup dribbling down his chin. "That's the only thing that's kept them from invaded and conquering us so far."

Sam was sobered. He had heard tales about them raiding and pillaging, but had assumed they were exaggerated before. Ned wasn't prone to tall tales, and even less to lying.

"They aren't going to get us, are they?" Trent asked. His hands gripped the bench, knuckles white.

"We've got a wall to keep them out," Sam said before anyone else could open their mouths. "You'd best remember that we have a job to do and can't be distracted from it. Trent, come get your supper."

The line had died down, only two in front of them. The smell of the soup was stronger here, mixed with the smoke of the fire. Sally spooned his portion out with a few kind words, which he returned, and he went back to join them.

The other groups of men and women cast furtive glances around and spoke in whispered tones. Sam met their gaze where they could, seeing something of fear inside.

There might be something more to these tales than he had thought.

Kerien was in the middle of one when they returned, capturing all the attention of the others. Sam picked it up midway through the story. "They took the women first. Did unspeakable acts to them. The men were forced to watch. They begged them to stop, but they only laughed.

"They slaughtered the animals next, forced the women to cook them, and then when they were done with their feast and their...acts." He paused, and the others leaned in. Sam took a spoonful of the soup and blew off the steam. "They killed the men and dumped their bodies into the river. They floated down, discovered by the towns below. A day later, they saw the women. Then the children."

"Horrible," Archie said, face contorted in pain.

"That's not the worst of it. They ate the hearts of the children." The others recoiled.

"Why would they do that?" Trent asked, as white as a sheet.

"Some say they're possessed by demons. Other say it is to grow more powerful."

"Whatever the reason, keep them as far away on that side as possible." Archie shuddered and Trent clutched at his flagon.

"The word is the Belmarch are on the warpath again. That's why they've sent a Hornblood here. They say there's a warlord withing Belmarch that is unifying them."

"A unified Belmarch? God forbid," Bill said.

"We should expect them to attack soon."

"On what authority do you speak?" Sam asked, setting down his spoon.

Kerien paled a little, then dropped his gaze to his soup. "Things I've heard around," he mumbled.

"Rumors then?" Sam arched an eyebrow. "Kerien, I'm disappointed in you."

"We all know they would do it if they could. Why do you think we've finished the walls first?"

"No sense in scaring anyone about it."

"You've right to be afraid of them," Ned said. "They're monsters walking in the form of men." It cooled his head to hear Ned say it.

"Either way, we won't speed up the work thinking on it any."

"That's just it, we're going to be trained to fight." Sam's head snapped to Kerien.

"What?" Bill asked, mouth gaping.

"That's one of the reasons the Hornblood is here. He's brought with him his head guard to train us in combat. No spare swords around, apparently."

This rumor, if true, was the worst. Sam's mind wandered back to darker days. Days he had tried to escape from as much as possible.

Could they be catching up to him?

He steadied his hand on his bowl and took a spoonful into his mouth. He held it there, feeling the chunks of potato and the wetness of the stock, then swallowed.

It went down like a lump of stone and settled in his stomach next to the feeling that had developed.

Fighting was someone else's business. There was no way he was going to get caught up in it.

The others talked about the developments, gossiping about the Hornblood, but Sam let it all wash over him. He didn't even scold them like he would have, his mind was too preoccupied.

Before he knew it, the work bell was ringing again. The workers got up at once, and in a wave went to the castle.

Sam was swept up with them, the others going back to the workshop and Trent and he up the hill with the rest.

His feet carried him without thinking. They were back at the beam already, and Trent was at his side.

"Master Freeman?"

"Yes?" Sam looked down at him.

"Should we get back to work?"

"Oh, yes." he wondered how long he had been standing there without moving. A minute? Or longer? "Take that side, we need to cut these to fit."

As he worked to carve off the tenon, checking his cuts as they went, Sam's mind was on a different time.

And a different place.

4

THE THUNDER THAT WAITS

The sky darkened in the south, a mass of clouds gathering on the horizon. Sam felt the rain before it hit and smelled it on the wind. He frowned and watched the sky, waiting for it to open and pour out its water to the earth.

They didn't get as far as he liked, but leaving it out in the open would have spoiled the timber. So, begrudgingly, he called a halt to the work and they pulled it under a nearby lean-to just in time for a great mass of water from the sky.

It bounced off the rocks and splashed up from the ground to soak his pants. The courtyard was mud in an instant, a chaos of carts and horses and men running to and fro to try and get out of the rain.

"Why don't you tell them to go away and leave us alone?" Trent was hunched in the corner of the lean-to while Sam looked out into the rain. He was hoping it would blow over, but there was too much water for that to be a possibility. This would wear itself out, but not before they needed to get back to the workshop.

The question, however, disturbed him from his thoughts of the past. "It will be better to find a way to work with the masons. We won't be finding ourselves rid of them anytime soon."

"But what they did, what they do..." he trailed off.

"These men aren't our enemies, Trent."

"They certainly aren't our friends."

Sam had to let out a laugh. How naïve. Had he ever been that foolish, that unseeing? "They have a job to do, and they're as low on manpower as we are. But, not only do they have less men than they should, they have far more work."

He spread his arms around him. "All the walls, all the fortifications. They are all stone. Most of their men are in the quarry, and the rest are hauling the stone back and forth."

Trent looked up. His eyes had softened, some of the edge gone out of his shoulders. "I-I didn't think about that."

The air tasted fresh and sweet, the dust knocked down and the tang of it washed away. "There are a lot of things we don't think about." The sheet of rain had turned into a pounding. "It's lightening up. Come on, back to the workshop."

As they left the rain was lessening. It still soaked into his clothes, cold pinpricks that made him walk faster.

"Welcome back," Ned said. Sam shook the water from his back and hands, slicking back his hair.

Trent stamped his feet and scraped the mud off his boots with the side of the porch post.

"Back in for the rest of the day, it looks like." Ned stretched and got up, joining him to look out at the rain. Sam looked down at him. There was an interesting look on his face.

"Yes, I'm afraid. More rain."

"Storm on the horizon. And not just rain." Lightning flashed, lighting up Ned's face. The rumble of thunder came less than a second later.

"Too much. We have too much to do."

"There will always be more to do," Ned said, eyes scanning the horizon. "We must do what we can now, in this time, and let go of the rest."

Sam shook his head. "I wish I had your confidence. I'm not even sure what I'm doing now has any impact on anything other than the few things that are added to the castle."

"We do our part, just as others do theirs."

Sam looked back into the workshop, watching the carpenters at their work. The scrape of a plane, the song of the saw in Kerien's hands. The sound of an offcut falling to the dust. "What am I doing here, in this place?" he wondered aloud.

Ned laughed, making him look in surprise. "That, my boy, is a question we all search for. Even me." He returned to his work with a chuckle, and Sam glanced out into the rain before going to his own workbench.

He had a panel mid carving, a crest of Hornblood with the Tree of Everling embossed on a field of white. He had already carved out the trunk, and most of the branches had come from it, but he had yet to carve the rest.

Taking up his gouge, he sat on the stool, then moved it for better light, and set the tip into the edge of a cut half finished.

The v shaped blade cut into the wood, pulling it away with a light pressure from his hand. He looked back up at his example carving, and traced the branch all the way out to the edge, lessening his pressure and bringing the blade up to a shallower cut.

At the end only a whisper of wood parted from the panel, and he pulled it away to fall to the ground behind him.

He thought as he carved, taking solace in the act as he always did. This was the skill that earned him his master. A steady hand and even pressure with a blade allowed him to work quickly, but precisely.

He had finished most of the tree when the rain slowed to a light patter, then stopped. Drips ran off the roof of the workshop, sloping to the covered porch and falling into puddles below that ran back down the yard and out to the muddy street beyond.

The air was cool now, and fresh. It would have been sweet except for the smell of the mud. Sam kept working, up until the bell of dinner.

"Master Freeman, shall we return to the castle?"

"Not yet," he said, brushing shavings off his work and his pants. "The clouds give me pause. We'll see what tomorrow holds."

Trent turned and walked, joining the others for dinner. Sam let them go ahead, inspecting their work.

Kerien rushed too much, and it showed up in his work. There were plane tracks on the door and saw marks from a careless cut near the tenon. Sam shook his head, another problem he had to deal with. If he would slow down, he would be better than most journeymen, but like this, he could barely be called one.

The paths were muddy as he walked to dinner, his boots squelching with every step. The ground clung to him, refused to let him go.

There was a part of him that was still searching for something, after so many years on this journey. He longed to know what it was, that he could find a way to get there.

Dinner was more of the same, and he kept to himself. He listened to the others talking, then slipped into the shadows to observe.

The talk was muted now, although there was plenty of it. Hushed tones filled the nooks and crannies of the Square as the sun cast its sunset upon the breaking storm clouds.

"More work tomorrow, and what with the winter coming, they'll be pushing us harder than we ever had to work before." The speaker was a mason, one of the older ones on the crew, Danny. He was just off to one side of the lean to Sam had taken refuge in.

"Do you think they'll do it?" That was Rosco, another mason. Sam frowned to hear his voice. He was one of the ones with Bill today.

"It's only a matter of time. You can believe that we'll be the first targets too."

"Well, at least the walls are up."

"The outer walls. We still have too much work on the keep. If they breach those..."

"We'll be dead no matter, even if the keep is finished."

"Come on, let's go get something to drink." Their conversation faded as they went to the alehouse. Sam guessed they would be refused, unless there was someone on the inside letting them have it.

The memory of the morning came back, burning into his mind. Shame came with it, at not being able to do anything, at not fighting back. He suppressed that.

How had they gotten drunk? Sam thought about following the men, but decided it wasn't worth getting in trouble about. They wouldn't take too kindly to him following them and, after the incident today, it would be best to keep a low profile.

Bill would be in his shack tonight. Sam pondered a visit, wondering if it would do any good. He dismissed it, thinking he might be wise to let him cool off a bit, if the rain and weather hadn't done that for him already.

The weather might put him in a fouler mood, come to think of it. Sam chewed on a piece of grass he plucked from a straggly patch growing beside the Square.

It was trying to survive, just like they were, but there was too much trying to choke it out and kill it. Still, despite all that, it was green and vibrant, a small patch of hope in the dust and mud.

Something came over him seeing it. Sam stood up, brushed off his pants, and walked out of the Square.

He turned right, instead of the left that would bring him back to his shack. In a few more moments he found himself outside Bill's place.

He stopped at the door and waited. Voices drifted out from inside. He wasn't alone.

Sam knocked on the hard door. It gave as he did, then went back to its original position. The voices stopped at once.

"Who is it?" Bill asked.

"Sam."

A pause. Shuffling. The door creaked open half an inch. "What do you want?"

Sam spread out his hands. "To talk. Nothing else."

Bill peered at him with a suspicious eye. The smell of ale drifted from the opening. Sam doubted he would let him in, thought he might slam the door in his face.

Then he swung it open and let him in. "Come in." His face was hard, but Sam went in anyway. Another mason, Barry he thought, stood in the corner. Sam entered, then Bill shut the door behind him.

Bill went back to his stool and sat. "I'm listening."

"I've done something to offend you, haven't I?" Sam stopped in front of Bill. He glanced at the table, a few mugs on the corner. Empty, but enough foam in two to be recently full.

A smile blossomed on Bill's face, then he laughed. "Done something? Yes, you've done something. Done nothing but hinder our work is what you've done."

"When have I done that?"

"You drag your feet, take forever with the beam-work, then dare to come in and deny it?" Bill leaned back, but Sam wasn't convinced it was from ease. "Impolite, I'd say."

"I'd agree. Quite disagreeable," Barry said, walking around.

"We've set the beams when you've asked." Sam crossed his arms, trying to suppress his anger.

"So now it's our fault?"

"That's not what I said," Sam said. He was beginning to regret coming. A hint of frustration crept into his voice, no matter how much he tried to hide it. He took a deep breath. "Perhaps we could work together more closely so that I'd know where you need us the most. We don't have enough men right now."

Bill sat up straight, eyes flashing. "You don't have enough men? What do you think we have, men aplenty?"

"I know you don't have enough either — "

"Don't you come in here telling us what we have or have not," Bill cut him off. He was straight on the stool now, practically on the edge.

Barry had edged behind him, and Sam took a look at him from the side of his vision. "I came for peace, not for anger." Although anger is what he was feeling.

"Peace? You came for peace?" Bill let out a snort of laughter.

Rough hands seized Sam from behind. Bill thrust his face into Sam's, his hot, alcohol soaked breath oozing over him. "You came to a fortress of the war for peace?"

———◆○◆———

Torches fluttered in the night, and horses stamped. The Bear stepped up into the saddle, then hauled his hulking frame on. The straps creaked ominously, but held. He swung the black horse around and faced the group of onlookers.

"Tonight we ride for glory and the blood that will flow like rain." Smiles appeared, then a round of cheers went up from the rough-looking group of fighting men. He wished he had more, but a few dozen men would be more than enough. There were enough the torchlight didn't touch the far edge of their numbers. "We will catch them by surprise and make them fear the men of Belmarch once again."

"Like sheep, they would be led to the slaughter and we will leave their bones for the vultures to pick over. You will have your fill of their women and drink the tears of their sorrow." Another round of cheers, and he turned and galloped off into the night. The men followed.

The sound of thunderous horseflesh rose into the night sky, devoid of a moon and black as night. The Bear smiled as he thought of the castle they were to crush, and how easy it would be.

5

UNWELCOME NEWS

The first hit landed above his ribcage, the second in his stomach. His air left, and Sam doubled over.

Barry held him up. Gasping, Sam struggled for breath. When he caught it he stood back up.

"Not so proud now, are you?" Bill snarled. Barry laughed at him.

"Don't hit me."

Bill's eyes widened. "What was that?"

"I said don't hit me." Sam kept his voice quiet, but let the edge of danger into it. It gave Bill some pause, even in his inebriated state.

Barry pulled at his arms, tightening them and hurting his shoulders. His chest hurt, and his stomach throbbed. Bill had strength, he had to give him that.

Their eyes locked. Sam held his gaze and his head upright. There was a desperation in Bill's eyes, and it surprised him.

At last, Bill looked away. "Let him go."

"Boss — "

"I said let him go. He isn't worth it. Just a nobody trying to make a name for himself."

Barry let go after a vicious tweak. Sam rotated his arms. "We're done here."

"It would be easier if we worked together," Sam said, holding hope of one last thing that would let them work together.

Bill thought for a moment, then there was a knock at the door. "Get out," Bill said.

Sam left, knowing it was no use. Men with more mugs brimming with ale stepped aside as he walked out the door.

He brushed between them, ignoring the ugly looks they gave him.

Night was full now, and dark. The lessening light of the Square guided him home, although he walked past his own bed and down the road to the woods.

The sounds of laughter and conversation died down as he walked, replaced with the crickets music. His arms still hurt from being held.

He went to sleep, troubled and wishing he were somewhere else. Had he made the wrong decision? Was he supposed to be somewhere else?

The last thought he had was that he could leave it all behind, go somewhere else, and learn something new.

———◄O►———

The next morning brought strange news. Crowds gathered in the Square as he got ready, the murmuring from their conversation seemed unusual for this early.

Sam walked outside, only to be sucked into the crowd. "What's happening?"

"The Overseer's coming down. Something big is happening," said Luke, a farmer.

Sam looked over to the other carpenters, gathered up beside the cooking fire that smoldered in the morning light. Someone should have been tending it, but it had died down.

Cold food lay forgotten on the tables, and Sam pushed his way through the crowd to take a cake and munch on it while he listened.

"This is too early to let us go. Why are they bringing us together?" Sally said. She was rocking her baby and clutching him to her chest. Her husband tried to calm her.

"We'll find out shortly. Here they come now."

He was right, the Overseer entered the Square, flanked by guards and with the young man Sam had seen in his room. The crowd shouted questions at him, and the Overseer raised his hands.

"Quiet, quiet now. Everybody calm down." The Overseer mopped his head with a handkerchief. His forehead shone. "Now, I've called you all here to introduce his highness Duke Evan Hornblood, the third of his name." He stepped aside and let the young man enter the circle. A hushed crowd watched him.

The Overseer bowed, and the group followed. Appeased, the young man gave a half smile and cleared his throat. "Thank you all for being here and the work that you do. It is so very important that this fortress be completed. Our very way of life is at stake and depends on it. The Belmarch are on the move, no longer content to fight amongst themselves." A murmur rushed through the crowd, and the Overseer gave them a nasty look. It died back down.

"I'm sure you all have worked hard up until now, but I'm afraid I'm going to ask you to work a little harder. This is Captain Yand." He motioned to his companion, a tall, muscular man with a short haircut and a peppering of salt at his temples. "He will be training you all in rudimentary combat."

The Overseer broke in as the crowd started to raise questions. "You will not be expected to fight. This is just a basic precaution. The world is dangerous and we all know what the Belmarch raiders can do, eh?"

The question stuck, and the Overseer again yielded to Earl Hornblood, who nodded in a dismissive way. "No, you won't be fighting," he said, irritated. "But you will be ready to defend her. The garrison takes up residence in the next two months, and will be sent upriver soon. In the meantime, we'll secure the castle and move everything we can inside the walls."

"It sounds like you expect an attack," someone yelled out. The Earl's head swung to the sound, examining the crowd, but the voice was lost.

"We expect nothing. We plan for the worst. The Hornbloods wouldn't have held the northern province this long if we hadn't. Captain."

"At the third bell, you'll be expected to meet me in the castle courtyard. Men, that is," the captain said, gazing over the assembled ragtag group of workers and their families. "We'll work on basic fighting first, then long arms next. Any man caught shirking his duty will be set to the pole and lashed."

His steely eyes looked them over. Not a peep was heard. "Does anyone have a problem with that?" He dropped the volume of his voice to a low whisper. Sam thought he could hear everyone swallowing, but inside, he smiled. This man was hard.

But he also expected him to fight. Sam roiled inside. How was he going to get out of this? Would they take more work as an excuse?

Or maybe that he had to oversee others, that he didn't have time to train.

While he was thinking about this, he had missed more of the conversation, and the Hornblood was talking again.

"There will be rewards for every man, woman, and child for the successful completion of Hornblood Castle. We will be the fortress on the hill, the defender of Chathem, the savior of our people." His eyes flashed as he said it. Sam didn't buy it. "So go forth and do your duty." With that, he swung around, trailing his cloak in a flourish, and left. The captain was at his side, but the Overseer scrambled with his guards.

"Back to work, like he said," the Overseer said as he tripped up the path behind the others.

"Trained to fight, are they mad?" Trent said, rushing up to him. "Why are they doing that?"

"You heard the man, just a precaution," Sam said, taking another bite of his cake. It was cold, but still good. Made with caring hands.

His lack of family was pronounced then, as the men who had them rushed off to talk with them. Husbands led their wives by the elbows, or were led just as much, and they spoke in hushed tones.

Martha practically dragged her husband by the ear, giving him a mouthful. Suddenly, that family situation didn't seem as bad.

Still, the pain in his heart continued, even as Trent followed him to the others. None of the carpenters that remained had families except Archie. "Take some time to talk it over," Sam said, seeing the look in his eyes.

Gratefulness replaced the anxiety, and he left to find his wife Beth and their young girl Nancy. "The rest of us are going back to work. We'll pick up the slack in the line until he gets back."

"I don't want to fight," Trent said, sitting down and crossing his arms.

What was he supposed to say? Sam looked at him, feeling exactly what he was feeling, only without the memories to accompany them.

"Ned, you'll finish the door?"

"Quicker'n two shakes." Ned winked at him and sauntered off with Kerien, whistling a tune to mock him as he went.

"I thought you wanted to fight," Sam said, rounding on Trent. "Or do you just want others to fight for you?"

"That's not fair."

"Neither will the enemy, whoever they are, when they show up here with axe and sword. They'll take your life faster than you can give it up." He softened his tone and dropped to one knee. "I don't like it either. Give it some time, it sounds like it will only be for a month or two and then the fighters will get here. I don't think they'll waste time drilling fighting stances into carpenter's apprentices when that happens."

Trent turned red. "I don't know how to fight."

"You do, in a way. We all do, when we need to." He got back up. "Come on, to work. The first bell's already rung."

They walked side by side through the hardening mud, and Sam watched the sky. The storm had passed and left sunny skies. It would dry everything out and keep it ready to work.

But now he found himself dragged back to fighting. He had come here to escape it, not to get a bigger dose and with less protection.

The others were working, and Sam put on his apron and took up his plane. He stared down at it, a tool of iron and wood.

How was cutting through wood any different than cutting through a man? It bled sap, it was a living creature.

He set it to the plank and pushed. A thin, clean shaving curled up into a circle until his plane went off the end.

Sam's fingers wrapped around it. It was thin, delicate, and smooth. One quick crush and it crackled beneath his grip, then fell as he let it loose.

"Kerien, please come over here." Kerien stopped his work, halfway through a saw cut, and set down his tools. His brows were knit together in a question.

"Yes?"

Sam offered him the plane. "Take a cut for me."

Kerien took it and set it on the board. He pushed, keeping his hand steady under Sam's watchful eye. When he was done Sam rubbed his hand along the cut and sighted down the edge with a square.

There was no gap. "Good." Kerien smiled as Sam straightened. "Now why can't you do that on your own?" Sam kept his voice down, a low whisper meant for Kerien's ears only.

His smile vanished into a frown. The others kept working, seemingly oblivious of the interaction.

"What do you mean?"

"Shall we examine your current work?"

He dropped his gaze, his frown deepening. "No."

"You're a good journeyman when watched. Am I to be here every second of the day to do it?" Sam looked at him. "How many do we have that can?"

"No, you don't need to," Kerien mumbled.

"I didn't think I did. You're on your way to the master's trail, but I'm afraid you'll never make it with the quality of work you have now."

"You want me to work fast."

"I want you to work well."

"But there's too few of us and too much to do."

Sam held up a hand. "Let me worry about who does what and how many we have to work. How many hours of the day do you have to worry about it?"

Kerien shrugged.

"None." Sam ran a hand through his hair, greasy and un-washed. He would need to visit the river soon, if he could ever find time. "I need you to focus on the work you have now, and let me worry about the rest. Deal?"

"I guess."

"It that doesn't work for you we can change places." Sam let a hint of a smile play across his face.

"No," Kerien said with a grimace, "you can keep it."

"Good man." Sam squeezed his arm. "You're getting stronger than anyone in here. I'll have you putting up the beams soon. Go on now, back to work."

Kerien, properly chastened, went back to his bench. He kept his saw straight, paying attention to his line.

Sam hoped it would hold. He wondered if he had done the right thing, but then quickly dismissed the thought.

He would protect all of them, as much as he was able. Sam picked up the plane again and stared down at it. They were his family.

6

MISTAKES

The afternoon sun beat down on them, pulling out the sweat from his body and burning his skin. Sam struggled with one end, the rope creaking dangerously.

"Down now." He tried to guide the end in as Trent unwound the crane. The beam came down, swung wide, then corrected with Sam's guidance.

It set down into the rock, falling within the hole the masons had made for them, and he sighed. "Keep going."

The crane sang, then the beam stopped. The rope went slack. Sam stared down the edge.

One side had gone in well, all the way into the rock and seated exactly where he planned.

This end, as he expected, was stuck halfway in. Over an inch of wood stuck up over the rock, where it should have been under the edge.

"Back up." Trent gave an exasperated look to him, but worked the wheel of the crane in the other direction. The rope pulled taut, then strained and broke the beam free. "Stop."

He looked on both sides, feeling along the edge. There it was, a shiny side and smoother than the rest. A few swipes of his chisel took off the offending wood, and a few steps above for good measure.

When he finished, he looked out over the edge of the castle wall. The green trees covered the edge of the river, but it wouldn't be long until they would be able to see it properly.

From up here you could hear it, a rushing, bubbling noise that was lost unless you really thought about it.

It was the shallowest spot in the Venti for miles, and the best place to cross it. As soon as they were done with the castle the trees would come down on that side, leaving the defenders an easy arrow shot for anyone trying to ford.

The King's men had done well in their selection, although they had torn down an old wooden tower that functioned as the warning for the Chathem defenders in the past.

Masons crawled over the walls of the keep, cutting stone, setting stone, mixing mortar. He couldn't escape the sound of them anywhere, no matter how hard he tried.

Trent lowered the crane again, and this time the beam set in perfectly. Sam ran his hands along the edge, feeling the rise of the stone and the lip that would allow the masons to encase the end in mortar and continue up the next course.

"Now, for the cross members." They were cut and at the bottom, and it meant a long walk down the stairs and through the keep to get there. Trent started lowering the rope of the crane while Sam started down.

The sunlight diminished as he walked down, covered up by the construction above. He paused for a moment in the cool of the corridor below to rest.

Voices drifted from somewhere down the hall. He couldn't help but catch what they were saying.

"We won't get them now. The raiders in the west threaten us more every day. They kill villagers, disrupt trade, and seize as much as they want."

"But even with the Belmarch on the move?"

"The spies tell us they march to fight each other, not us. We'll be safe enough with the walls finished."

"I don't like it." Sam caught himself listening, then moved away, back the other direction, toward the door. The Overseer continued to talk. "You saw them. They aren't fighters, they'll cave the instant someone threatens them."

"Leave that to Captain — " The words drifted away, cut short as he closed the door behind him. That had been the young Hornblood.

Something wasn't right. These men were untested, untried, except for the man they brought with them. Why would they even think about training us?

He didn't have time to think about it though, Trent was waiting. Heat hit him as he left the keep, and the rope was down on the ground and ready.

Sam tied them up, then guided the beam as much as he could until it was too high to reach. He watched it swing for a moment, then went back up the same way he had come down.

The conversation was quieter, too quiet for him to hear now. He felt ashamed that he hadn't left earlier, but even more unsettled by what he had heard.

Trent was swinging the crane into position when he came up, and Sam joined him to push it. It squealed, but gave with enough force, and the beam was soon dangling.

"Line it up first. We've got to get that tenon in the mortise, then set the beam in the wall." Sam picked his way over the unfinished masonry, walking along the thick two-foot wall. Two courses of stone were held together with mortar and connecting spans, which made for tricky movement but thick fortifications.

"Ready?" Trent asked. Sam braced his legs and took hold of the leader rope, pulling gently to swing the wall end toward him.

"Lower it down." The beam dropped until it was about six inches above the wall. "Hold it there."

Sam tipped it up and fought with the end to sight the tenon. It took more effort than he expected, but eventually he hooked it into the mortised hole in the main beam. "Lower it."

Trent let it down slowly, and Sam guided it into the waiting slot in the stone. This time, it slipped in perfectly.

Another test of the fingers, and it was just under the edge. "Good, we'll get the other."

The first had gone well, and he hoped the other would, too. Then he could give the tower back to Bill and the masons to finish, if they would take it.

The next one went up faster, and they were just getting into place when a familiar face showed up.

Trent looked worried. That was his first indication. Sam glanced behind him, checking the last connection to see Bill.

He was alone. That was a good sign. The air hung damp and swollen, not a hint of wind in sight, even up as high as they were.

It was an oppressive heat, and one he was going to be glad to escape. "Afternoon, Bill."

"You finally finished?" Bill walked over to examine their handiwork. "I thought you wouldn't be able to use this after the...fall it had taken."

"Oh, she isn't so fragile as that to be bloodied by a token beating." Sam patted the thick oak. "She's made of sterner stuff. You'll see." A hint of his anger leaked through, and Sam winced.

He had to control himself, if no one else would.

Bill sniffed, then dragged his dirty shoe along its surface. "Too high. You'll have to carve out more for us to work around. Take it out and do it again."

Sam's smile froze on his face. "There's plenty of room for you to work."

"Need an inch or more. You know that."

"That's not-" Trent began, but Sam cut him off with a quick motion of his hand.

"Need an excuse to catch up on some work, then?" He thought about poking him, mentioning something about his haggard look or his unkempt hair. The bags under his eyes might have done it. "Fine. Feel free to blame me."

"The Overseer's patience is wearing thin with you," Bill said, kicking the side of the beam. It didn't move. Sam was hoping his toe broke, but he seemed fine. "One of these day's you'll answer for your shoddy work."

That poked him, and it cut deep. Sam clamped his mouth shut, teeth grinding against one another. He stood and carefully picked his way to the stairs. After a few deep breaths he regained control. "Come Trent. WE have work to do."

"Just going to run away?" Bill stood at the top of the stairs, barring the way. He had gotten there fast, but he knew his way around the stone like the back of his hand. He wasn't the Master Mason for nothing.

"Going to do my job, just like you suggested." Sam tried to step around, but Bill stayed in his way. Sweat trickled down the back of his neck, tickling him. "I can't do it while I'm up here."

"Go ahead, go down. Abandon the work you have to do here. Word will get around." Bill moved in close, mere inches from their noses touching. "I know what kind of man you are. A coward," he whispered.

"Think whatever you like." Sam was cloaking himself now in the old techniques he had learned as a young child. His body was covered in mail, just like he imagined it. Each word was an arrow that bounced off. Sam nodded.

Trent walked past them. Sam stood his ground, matching Bill eye to eye. There was that same look, deep down one of desperation.

Finally, Bill relented. He stepped back, easing the menacing closeness, and waved a hand in front of him. "An early dinner is best for the cowards."

"One day I hope you can learn to trust me." Sam started down the stairs, then stopped and looked back. "First, you'll have to trust yourself."

Without another word, he turned and followed Trent, leaving Bill shocked at the top of the stairs.

Sam had no doubt Bill would tell the Overseer that he had shirked his duty, made a fool of the masons, and failed to give them enough room to work. The Overseer would listen and believe it. What did he know about masonry or woodwork?

He was an aristocrat, fallen out of favor low enough to be sent here but high enough to be treated as a serious man. Whatever he had done in his past life did not lend well to him building a castle, but he was the only one they had.

Sam considered his options as they were swallowed up into the merely warm innards of the keep. He didn't know of anything other than to go about his business as usual.

Going to the Overseer first would seem petty, like he was trying to shift blame from his own actions to someone else. Exactly what Bill wanted.

But on the other hand, waiting for Bill to tell his tale the way he wanted was also a losing proposition.

He was stuck in between a rock and the wall.

"Master, why don't you go to the Overseer and tell him what's happening?" Trent asked.

The boy had picked up on it. Sam wasn't surprised, but he did wish it wasn't as obvious as it was.

"Sometimes you need to pick your battles. Right now I don't curry much favor with the Overseer. Anything would be unwelcome coming from me."

"So why don't you have it come from someone else?"

Sam shook his head. "I'm afraid that's what will happen. Don't worry about this, it shouldn't concern you." But it did, and Sam knew he couldn't keep it from him, nor the others.

He trailed his hands along the stone, bumping over the rough edges and projections of the inner wall. How would he have handled this in the past?

With his fists, probably. But that was a long time ago, and this was a different life. Even now he felt the creature within him stirring, the one that craved blood. Loved it, desired it.

Wanted it more than anything else in the world.

Unleashing that creature would mean going back to a dark place that he had sworn off long ago.

A thought struck him. Trent had mentioned having it come from someone else, but not him.

Was it possible that was the right answer after all?

They reached the bottom landing and entered the hallway. The workshop was to the right.

"Take the tools back to the workshop. I have something I need to do." Sam handed him his tools, turning deeper into the keep.

"Master?"

"Go, do as you're told. And tell the others they need to hurry up with their work, too."

Sam went left down the hall, turned right, then passed the Overseer's room. He kept going until he was at the one room that had been completed.

Sam raised his fist and knocked.

Despite his large frame, the Bear was quiet as he crept on all fours up to the edge of the small rise to the thin man that laid there.

"Over to the right," he said with a rasp, his vocal cords damaged in battle long ago. The Bear followed his outstretched hand, shifting slightly and rustling the leaves. The forest floor smelled of damp and growing mushrooms.

There it was, a slight dark gray protruding from the treetops on the other side. As he watched a man appeared at the top and moved around.

"What are they doing?"

"Building. They've been adding stone all morning."

The Bear grunted. The river was swollen with the rain, bits of trees and other debris floating by. Too high to ford, for now.

"Keep watch," the Bear said, then turned and crept down the hill to the waiting band of his lieutenants. "We're early enough to catch them unaware. As soon as the river lets up, we'll cross and attack."

7

Hung Journey

At first Sam thought no one was in, but a sound of movement inside made his heart beat. Footsteps crossed the room, then the door opened.

"What is it?" The young Hornblood peered out from a crack. "What do you want?"

"I'm here to measure for your room, Sire." Sam gave a customary bow.

"Very well then." He opened the door up. "Come in."

"Thank you." Sam entered. It was the brightest room in the keep, and the best furnished. Most of the furniture had been carted in, but some of it he recognized from the workshop.

Now that he was inside, he wasn't exactly sure what to do. he had to plant some measure of respect for himself if he was going to have any chance of surviving the next few months.

His eyes wandered around the room as he pulled out the measuring stick he kept in his pocket.

The young Hornblood was returning to his desk, and when he got there, he picked up the papers that were on it and slipped into the chair with a heavy sigh.

He put one elbow on the table and held up the papers to the light of the windows, reading.

A few chairs, a table filled with wine and a plate of leftover food, with flies buzzing around it, and a nice carpet made up the rest of the room.

Sam walked over to the window, measuring along its surface. He tried to be quiet and not disturb the Duke, but he would have to talk to him if this was going to work.

But what about?

Two spans on the bottom. Sam checked the thickness of the sill.

It wasn't going to work if he kept this up, not like this. *What was I thinking, coming in here like this?*

He turned back to the door. Why he thought this would work, he didn't know.

Then he saw something that might work.

Sam walked over to the desk and stood in front of it. He waited a few respectfully moments, but when he was ignored, he cleared his throat.

The Duke looked up, a hint of irritation flashing in his brown eyes. "What is it?"

"Where would you like the crest, Sire?"

"What?"

"Your family crest. Would you like it here," Sam pointed to the front of the desk, "or there?" He pointed to the wall above the duke.

The Duke looked, then paused. "Which one would be better?"

"If I may?" Sam waited until he nodded. "The desk would give your visitors something to look at below, but above you, we can carve it much larger and make it more...imposing, if you will. They would be reminded of the strength of the house of Hornblood and the representative that has come here."

The Duke's mouth curled up at the corner, and his eyes lit up. "On the wall then."

"Very good, Sire. Please excuse me." Sam was relieved he never asked why he had to take these measurements now, but he took three spans for the opening, and guessed another three up would do.

A crest that would certainly be imposing. Now, he just had to figure out how to make it.

"By your leave." Sam returned to the door.

Duke Hornblood waved a hand. "Dismissed."

"Good evening, Sire."

He shut the door behind him with a click. A list was running through his mind, and he couldn't produce everything on it.

That meant one person had to be visited.

He set off at a brisk walk, checking the sun as he left the keep. The heat blasted him as he did, pushing away the stuffiness of inside and making him suck in a deep breath of the wet air.

The taste of stone dust came with it. The masons were still at work on the keep, raising the top before they would move on to continue the towers.

But Sam turned right, ignoring the path back to the workshop, and headed for the constant sound of ringing and the smoke rising above a stone structure in the shade of the wall.

Two ends were open, the others made of stone on one side and the wall on the other.

He thought the heat outside was uncomfortable, but as he stepped into the shade of the blacksmith, he was glad he didn't work in there.

It smelled like coal, metal, and oil. The smiths were working, one hammering at a hunk of iron.

"Dale, good afternoon." Sam raised a hand to him.

"What brings you in here?" Dale's muscles rippled as he continued to hammer, turning the chisel over each time. He barely gave him a glance.

"Special order."

"Oh?"

"Call it a favor." Sam leaned against a post and waited for him to finish. When Dale did, he raised an eyebrow and dumped the chisel in the quenching bucket beside him.

It sizzled and raised a puff of steam. That chisel was destined for the masons, to be worn down against rock until it needed to be sharpened once again.

Dale wiped off his hands on his apron, then went over to a bucket of water. He splashed some on his face. "Special how?"

"I need some nails to hang a crest."

"I'll have Brent make you some."

"These aren't normal nails. I'll need them to be three inches long." Sam thought for a moment. "Make that four inches."

"What are you trying to hang, a horse?" Sam didn't realize Dale's eyebrows could go that high.

"Something like that. A whole tree." He would have to find the right wood. Something that matched, didn't overpower the crest, and was strong enough to last. And large enough. "And I need it by tomorrow."

"Now Sam, you know I have too much to do."

"We all do." Sam knew that Dale needed at least three apprentices to keep up with the work. He had two. Another smith would be better. "I think Bill and the masons feel it, too."

"Don't get me started on Bill." The big man's eyebrows dug into his brow now, and his voice took an already deep voice two shades deeper.

Something to think about. Another ally.

"You're having issues with him, too?"

"Only every other day. Bringing me broken tools, chisels so blunted it takes twice as long to sharpen them. Bah." He spit out on the dirt, then wiped his mouth and beard. "I think they break them on purpose, at how bad they look."

"Come to think of it, we've seen an increase in handles lately." Sam shook his head. Another stalling tactic? "Regardless, this would help me out. I'd owe you a favor."

"And that would make how many?"

"Too many?" Sam couldn't help but smile, and the big man laughed a deep belly laugh.

"I'll be calling on you soon, someday. If I can ever get away from this work."

"I hear you. Mayhaps with the Duke in the castle, things might turn around."

"Or maybe I'd mount a hog and ride it into the sunset. You didn't hear that, boys. And get back to work." His apprentices had taken a keen ear and somehow their work had slowed down.

"Let me refit your hammer for you."

"Not a chance. I'll use that until it breaks into driftwood into my hands." Dale gave him a look that made Sam think he was considering breaking him.

"If you reconsider..."

"You're the first one I'll come to."

Dale mopped the sweat from his face. "Go on, leave me to my work."

"I will. Let me know when you need that favor." Sam turned and walked back to the workshop, letting his feet take him as he thought.

He wasn't the only one. Somehow, this was reassuring and aggravating all at once. What was driving Bill to this? And why did it have to be now, when so much was left to do?

The smoke of dinner wafted up over the village and the workshop, meeting him along the way. Baking bread and beans.

Sam was looking forward to one, and not so much to the other. They'd had so much of it before the families had come. It was easy, and fed them well, but day after day they had grown tiresome.

Trent was back, and already hard at work, when he entered the yard. Sam walked among the stacks of lumber, separated to dry out, and tried to find something that would do.

It was difficult to find something so large in span. There were a few that came close, but nothing to what he wanted.

While he thought about it, an eagle circled overhead, screaming as it scanned the farms and fields below. Red as clay, a Firetail Eagle.

A few lazy flaps of its wings took it higher, in a great circle. The tail feathers twisted and fluttered as the great wings held steady, his shadow running along the ground.

Likely scaring away all the other things it was looking for.

Sam let it fly, taking the largest and driest of the sawn planks. It took him a while to dig it out from the bottom of a stack, but soon enough, he had it free.

It had cupped a little, but not much. The heartwood ran down the center, quartersawn.

A few scrapes of a plane revealed the grain. Straight and unobtrusive oak. Just what he needed.

But, it was too small, by just a hair. The dinner bell rang.

"Looking for something specific?" Ned asked as they filed out.

"Yes, a special project."

"How special?" Sam looked to the others.

"Go on, get your food." When they had gone, trudging down the path to the Square, Sam relayed his plan.

"Do you think it will work?"

"It's a gamble," Ned said, rubbing his chin. "But if you think it's worth the time, then I'll support you on it."

"Thanks. Now, if this was a few inches longer, it might do."

"Frame it up." The thought struck him like a thunderbolt. Why hadn't he thought of that? Sam grabbed Ned in a hug.

"You've saved me a great deal of trouble. Here I was, thinking we had to bring down the biggest tree in the forest when it was right in front of me the whole time. That's perfect."

"If you're going for imposing, it won't hurt."

"I'll take this in, go ahead. I'll catch up." Sam dragged the wood into the workshop and muscled it onto his bench. A few hours dressing, another couple of carving, and then some joinery.

He could do it all in a day or two, on top of his other work. It might not be soon enough, though.

Dinner was as he expected, and he chewed the beans without tasting them, planning everything out in his head. Some smaller carvings would work well on the frame, something to stroke the ego, perhaps?

The time went quicker than he expected, and the third bell was ringing. Workers dropped off their plates, but instead of going to their houses, they turned up to the castle.

At first, Sam was puzzled, then he remembered.

The fighting.

They were going up to the castle, to the large training ground that was currently being used to stage materials.

And there they would be forced to learn to fight.

His stomach churned at the thought. He couldn't do it, no matter the consequence.

But everyone else was going, and the other carpenters were looking back at him.

He had an example to set.

Ned raised an eyebrow at him.

"Well, off we go." This would eat into his working time, too. He dropped his empty bowl and spoon off with the washerwomen and followed the others in the fading light.

Each step was heavy, each footfall bringing him closer to a decision he didn't want to make.

But behind him, the carpenters followed. He had to set an example.

The question was, what example was he going to set?

8

TRAINING

They trickled into the dusty yard. Captain Yand stood at the top, watching them. His gaze was steely and his posture was even harder.

Sam slipped to the back once they were there. Bill, he noticed, was leading the group of masons at the front of the pack.

Sam rubbed his belly. The pain had gone away, for the most part, but the bruises remained. Dark, purple welts of a reminder of who Bill really was.

He seemed attentive and watchful. Sam wondered if it was all a ploy to get the attention of the fighter, to use it to his advantage like everything else these days.

"Listen up, boys," Yand's voice boomed, echoing against the castle walls and reverberating. "This is no time for fooling around. I've been given a task to make men out of you maggots." At this, he clasped his hands behind his back and started to stride in front of them in a big loop. "I'm afraid I don't have much time of it either. So you'll have to listen closely. Those who don't will be punished."

At this, he turned. The group, so animated and conversational walking in, was now quiet. Sam thought he could have heard a blade of grass drop.

It emphasized the quiet of twilight that had drawn over them like a blanket. Torches burned around them, spitting and flickering. It cast strange shadows, and the fire mesmerized Sam, bringing him back to the past.

"We will go through the basics first. Now, each man pick a partner and face each other." They paired up, and Yand chastened them to move faster.

Sam took Ned. What was he going to do?

"We will learn to punch, then kick, then throw. First up, the punch." Yand squared up to them, brought his fists up, and demonstrated a punch in the air. "Put force behind it with your hips. Now, you all try."

Sam stood and watched as they punched the air around him. He looked down at his hand, tightening it in a fist.

The world seemed to shrink and lessen. His hand shook. His blood pounded. Breath came in short, quick gasps.

I can't do it. I won't do it.

"You there." The crowd turned to him. The world rushed back to Sam, and he looked up.

Right into the cold eyes of Captain Yand.

"What are you doing?"

Sam's mouth went dry.

"Answer me. Why don't you do what I tell you?"

"I can't." It came out in a whisper. Men around him whispered.

"Did I hear you right? You refuse to do what I said?" Captain Yand stalked up to him, parting the crowd like a blade cutting through flesh. In two more steps, he stood, looming up over Sam.

"I've done what was asked. I've come here by your order." Sam knew he was treading on ice. "I can't fight."

Yand's eyes narrowed. "You'll fight, and you'll do as you're told."

"I will build, I will labor, but I will not fight." Sam dropped his gaze, steeling himself for whatever was to come. "Please."

Snickers ran through the masons. He thought he heard whispers of "coward" in them.

"Keep quiet." Yand turned back to Sam. "Look me in the eye."

Sam raised his gaze and did as he was told. For a moment Yand only looked, examining him, tearing him apart, flaying his mind. He reached into his head and seized his soul.

"Very well then. You all heard this man, he refuses to fight. Well, then, you all bear witness to those who refuse to do as they are instructed." He waved a hand. A man came forward, carrying two pails of on a beam.

Yand snapped, and he put the beam on Sam's back. Sam accepted his fate, took it willingly.

"He'll stand here and bear the weight of his decision." Yand nodded to another. Two men came out, pails full of water. "Not a single drop spilled while we train. To remind you of the weight you bear. The weight of the Kingdom, the protection of it. Not just in how you fight, but in how you build."

One by one, the men added the buckets to the beam. They were heavy, filled to the top. Sam bore the load, glad that this was it.

So far.

"Now, all of you — back to work. Show me your punches, and practice on each other." The men did as they were told, leaving Sam to stand bearing the weight of the water.

Although the water wasn't heavy, it did eat into his shoulders. Sam stood and watched the others as they learned the bare, rudimentary fighting techniques that wouldn't save them in a fight.

If he was going to be serious about this, they should have been learning to use knives and bows. They couldn't stand up to seasoned fighters that would be in a raiding party.

The heat of the day had lessened, but it wasn't gone. Sweat ran down his head, and Sam started to feel the ache of the beam across his shoulders. It bit into him, pressed into him.

It had been a long day already, with hard work. Sam was used to it, though, and he took it in stride.

He breathed and closed his eyes. They kept training, they kept learning. Yand moved on to kicking, then a combination of the two.

"You all need to think about these moves, what you would do in the heat of battle." Yand walked around the heavy breathing men. "When you are fighting for your life you have no time to think, only react. Now, we move on to sparring."

The pairs were faced off, and a few guards that were part of the Overseer's muscle were scattered through the crowd. Sam was feeling the burning in his legs now, but it looked like they had a long time to go.

"First man to get the other to the ground wins. The loser will deal with something unpleasant."

They fought. Grunts, cries, and the sound of men striking other men drifted into the darkening night.

Ned was thrown to the ground by Archie. Kerien tossed a mason about his size. Trent lost badly.

Bill seemed to be doing well, fighting one of his own men. Or, at least, it looked that way.

When the last contestants had finished, Yand brought up the losers in a line. "For failing, you will each receive one strike. Remember this."

Sam looked away as he brought out a club. One by one, he went down the line. Why was he doing this? What good was it to train the men this way?

They sparred again. This time, most of the losers won. The punishment was repeated. Sam's legs were starting to burn. He shifted his stance.

His back would feel it in the morning, and his neck. There would be a bruise there.

He tried to ignore what was going on in front of him, to think of something else. The first thing that came to mind was home and the river.

The coolness against his skin on a hot day, the way it tasted. Fresh, clear. Infusing him with energy after a swim. The fish that swam along its path.

Sam licked his lips, dry. The heat of the sun had drained him, and now he finally felt its effects.

They wouldn't be as productive tomorrow. Could the Overseer see that?

Probably not.

Sam wondered what he would do when he found out they had fallen behind, because they would fall behind. All of them.

Anger, rage. He expected loud outbursts and following chastisements. But there would be no use trying to tell him what had happened.

The training dragged on well into the night. Men were bruised and battered. Not one had managed to win all their fights, even Bill.

Yand had seen to that.

He shifted the pairs, making sure they were matched up in height and weight as much as possible, and if need be, putting one at a disadvantage.

Finally, he called an end to the training. Sam could almost hear the collective sigh that went through their minds.

"Tomorrow I expect you to do better. Some of you may think that my tactics are harsh. Barbaric." Yand loomed over them, looking each in the eye. "I'll tell you this."

He pointed to the north. "Those men won't treat you with respect. Those men won't pick you up from the ground and pat you on the back. Those men are hardened fighters. They will rip out your throat and leave you bleeding on the ground to get to the next one."

Silence. Somewhere an owl hooted. "I'm preparing you for them. For war. No matter how hard I push you, remember that it is for your life. So that you will survive."

Yand waited. No one said anything. "Dismissed. Get some sleep."

They filed out, bent and wounded. Yand came over to Sam, who had been left off to the side. He let the other men go before he said anything.

"You'll need to fight. Those are the orders."

"I've made my choice," Sam said. His lips cracked.

"Shame. Could have been a good fighter. I would have made something out of you."

Sam smiled ruefully. "I don't think so."

"Drop them."

He shrugged, and the weight came off his shoulders in an instant. Sweet relief, as it splashed on the ground. Sam rubbed his shoulders, trying to get some feeling back into them.

"Most men would have dropped those. At least, most not used to carrying them." Yand was giving him a strange look. "You'll fight tomorrow, or we add more weight. You have tonight to think on it."

"You have my answer." Yand froze mid-step. He had turned away to walk back to the keep. "I won't fight. No matter what you do to me."

"Sam, was it?"

"Yes."

"Good night Sam." Yand turned back and walked off into the night. Sam turned and walked back to his own hut.

The night had cooled now, and his hut was the same temperature.

He could leave. Go somewhere else. But then he would be running again. Always changing, always going somewhere else.

He needed to stay, to finish this. There was a promise he had to keep, both to himself and to others.

Sam sat on the edge of his bed, about to get under the blanket, but he stared out the window to the night and stars beyond.

"Remember, move like lightning, strike like a hammer." Bear stood above the group of fighters arranged before him. The moon shone in the night sky, a half sphere of white. The forest was quiet.

Only the creatures of the night stirred.

And the warriors.

"Our swords are strong," one man said.

"For blood and honor," the others joined him. Every man made his last adjustments, checked his equipment one last time.

Made fast his sword and his knife. Axe and bow.

Bear nodded and turned. He took the first step, crunching through the dead leaves and undergrowth of the forest.

The others followed, just as quiet. The smell of pine and oak was strong here, mixed with the undergrowth they kicked up that was earthy and green.

He walked with anticipation and held one hand to the sword on his hip. Bear's eyes shone in the darkness, not a single torch in sight.

They reached the shore of the river within a few minutes. It trickled and murmured, no longer swollen with the rain.

The mud sucked at his boots, but Bear pushed on. A quick splash and he was in. The others followed into the cold, crippling water.

At the deepest point, it went up to their chests. This was the time of most danger. The tower was higher now, and if there was anyone up on top, they would see them.

Bear pushed the limits between speed and stealth.

Then they were on the other side. Dripping and cold, they pushed through the mud and into the forest.

After a quick count, and everyone accounted for, Bear turned them into the dark of the forest.

Not a word was spoken. They went as close to single file as possible, with Bear in the lead.

Up ahead fire twinkled and twisted through the trees. There were voices ahead, and Bear raised his fist.

He couldn't make out the words, but it sounded like two men talking. Guards, perhaps.

His sword whispered as he drew it from the sheath. Dozens more joined him.

9

CHANGE IN THE AIR

"What's this?" Sam looked down, his usual crate gone.

"Moved," Trent said, scooping out porridge from his bowl.

"Where?"

"To the castle," Ned said, shoving a spoon in the general direction. A line of workers trundled up and down the path.

They were pushing barrels, carrying goods, and had packed the carts with as much as they could.

"Inside?" Sam took his seat next to the others, digging in to the porridge. It was plain and needed something to spice it up. A pat of butter would have been nice.

"Orders from the duke. Secure everything, apparently." Kerien looked annoyed. "That's what I heard, at least."

"A precaution, nothing more," Ned said, lowering the tension that had suddenly built. The others seemed to relax, just a bit.

"Which means we won't be able to use the cart today either."

Sam stood back and thought about it. He had planned on bringing up a few beams that were ready, to get ahead of Bill and the masons.

One more day might not hurt, but if things changed then Bill might have another black mark to use against him.

"Looks like a good day to work in the workshop, then." Sam finished up his breakfast, listening to the conversation about the changes and answering at the appropriate points.

"Are they going to move us into the castle?" Trent asked, just as they were all finishing up.

Sam exchanged a glance with Ned. "I doubt it," Ned said. "Not enough room to fit us in there, and I don't suppose the Overseer would be too keen on having us right outside his window."

"No, I suppose not," Sam agreed. He rubbed his ribcage, still a bit tender. "Moving a hundred workers, not to mention their families, inside the walls would take an enormous amount of work." Not that the Overseer or the Duke would do any of it, or their contingent of a dozen or so guardsman stationed to protect them.

Mary stalked by with a countenance of storm clouds. Kerien didn't have the sense to leave her alone.

"Collecting dishes?" he asked, reaching out with his bowl.

She whirled, slapping it away. "Do I look like a maid to you?" Her voice was quiet, and dripping with venom. "Take it and wash it yourself." Kerien pulled back his hand fast, as if it had been bitten by a snake, a look of shock plastered across his face.

"I'm sorry," he managed to get out after a second. Mary glared at him a moment longer, then turned to the others. They backed up a step.

She walked off, grumbling under her breath. Sam caught a few words, some would make a sailor blush. The others were related to walking all the way up to the castle.

"What's gotten into her dress?" Kerien asked, when she was far out of earshot. His confidence had suddenly returned, and Sam had to hide a smile.

"They took the food, too. Now they'll have to bring it back down every night to cook. My guess is that the Overseer told them they couldn't stockpile anything out here." Sam turned and started walking up the path. "Are you coming? I have a feeling today is a good day to start moving supplies out of the workshop. If we're lucky, we'll get a day or two head start before we move everything."

The others caught up to him. "Where do you want to start?" Ned asked.

"The light stuff, tools first. Everything you can't bear parting with you can keep in the workshop, everything else goes into crates and barrels for the journey." The sun was up, but a cloudy sky blunted its rays. It was still humid enough for Sam to taste it and for his clothes to stick to his body.

"And there is a visitor. Wonder what he'll say?"

A guard was waiting in the lumber yard, itching the strap beneath his helmet.

"Morning," Sam said, walking up to him as the others filed into the workshop. "I'm assuming there's an order."

"From the Overseer," he said, nodding. Matthew, his name was Matthew. "You're to move all work inside the castle walls."

"Did he say where we're supposed to put it?"

"Not yet, that will be decided at a separate time."

"We need a dry place to keep everything."

Matthew looked into the workshop. "Don't you have a group of carpenters? I suggest you build one."

"Fair enough," Sam said, suppressing a spike of anger. "Will we get an extension on our castle work, then?"

"Nothing was said to me about it." Matthew furrowed his brow. "Anyway, I've given you your orders. That's all I was supposed to do."

"I understand. Thank you." Matthew walked off. Sam couldn't help but notice how loose the straps on his armor were. If there was a battle it would be easy to slide a knife, or a sword, right through his ribcage and into his heart.

But he wasn't running the guards and he couldn't tell him what to do. "I know you all heard that," Sam said, turning back to the workshop. They all pretended to be working, but the sudden interest in their tools didn't fool him. "Get out the crates."

Sam brushed off a fly, but it buzzed around his head, irritating him.

"They want us to move into the castle walls, that's what I heard," Trent said, leaning over the table and whispering to the group.

"You heard wrong," Kerien said, taking a bite out of his roll. He chewed with his mouth open, flecks of bread spewing as he talked. "There is no way the Overseer is going to let us into that place. Not in nine hells."

"Well, I heard it." Trent sat back, crossed his arms.

"You mean to tell me he's willing to take all of us in?" Kerien swept his hand around the Square. The tables were filled with masons, carpenters, smiths, and every other trade you could think of needed to build a castle. Not to mention their families running around and eating with them. "The unwashed masses?"

"Where would they put us?" Archie asked.

Kerien pointed to him, nodding. "He makes a good point."

"I dunno. We could build houses."

Kerien let out a laugh, loud enough to attract attention. Both Sam and Ned gave him a stern look. "They barely gave us the materials to build this place. You think they want us wasting time putting huts together when we're racing against time as it is? Not likely."

"Stranger things have happened," Ned said. He gummed his roll on the left side of his mouth, the side with his best teeth. Or what little teeth he had. "Strange feeling in my bones. I don't like it."

"You don't like anything, old man," Kerien said.

"Respect," Sam said.

"Sorry," Kerien mumbled. He didn't sound sincere.

"The Duke's brought changes to the castle, whether we like it or not," Archie said. His wife was working the bread line, still handing out food. She would join him soon, when she was done. "Some of those might be forced on the Overseer, too."

Changes. Changes like training workers in the art of combat. Or, in Sam's case, adding weight to his load each night, he refused. His shoulders ached, and the reminder made it worse. He rubbed them as he listened.

"We've had to move half the workshop up there without a good replacement to move it to." Kerien's brows were furrowed. "Now we have to work in the sun, with no protection from the heat."

"I could take you up to the tower with me. Trent could use some time dressing wood."

A ghastly look flashed across his face at the suggestion. "No, thanks." It almost made Sam laugh.

"Time to finish up. I've got work to do." Sam brushed off his hands, dumping the crumbs back onto his plate. At least they had plenty of bread and grain. Meat would be nice, though.

"We still have time," Kerien said.

"Take it. I'll be in the courtyard." Sam bid them goodbye and walked back alone. A shorter rest, but it would be worth it in the end.

Today was cooler, a sign of the change in seasons to come. Summer seemed to be giving way already to autumn, and a cloudless sky helped with the pleasant feeling he felt.

The quick walk back helped stretch his legs, and he went fast enough to shorten his breath.

Underneath the one lean-to they had been given was his project, nearly finished. A few late nights and time stolen as much as he could between jobs had gone a long way.

Now, it was nearly finished. The tree stretched out, splaying as large as he could make it. He was proud of this one, at the lifelike nature the trunk had taken on, and the detail of the leaves.

He sat and got to work, feeling the slope of the carving as he worked the gouge into the wood. The form was in there, hidden by the tree itself. All he had to do was let it out, little by little.

Carvings fell to the ground. He blew out the dust, wiping away the bigger chips, and focused on one leaf. It needed a more graceful curved, and he almost closed his eyes to do it.

There was a feeling in the wood that it enjoyed being worked under his hands. It was warm, and fine grained, seasoned enough to be hard, but not hard enough to blunt his blades.

He sat back, looking over his handiwork. *Better. Much better.*

The others had returned some time ago, and Trent was waiting at his side.

"How long have you been there?"

"A few minutes. How do you do that with the gouge, Master?"

Sam looked at the tool in his hands. Freshly oiled, recently sharpened. "A practiced hand. And a steady one. Ready?"

Trent nodded.

Sam made a final cut, brushed away, and set down his tool.

"Up to the top." Trent nodded, then they went to the unfinished tower.

The masons had worked past the beams already, laying the next course in a heaping hill that bunched to one side. They were working already, and gave them hard stares as they tapped out their stones and built them up.

With a nod, Sam greeted them, but they said nothing in return. The floorboard ledge was already in place, and with the beams set, they could start work on the structure to hold it in place.

They craned up smaller beams, laying them along the edge and cutting them to fit across the main beam. They rested on the ledge, which would be filled by the masons, and left about two feet in between each.

Sam decided to start on the south side and work up from there.

The first cross members were easy to put in place and cut, relatively small, and with the two of them manning the saw, it went fast. Scribing to fit was more difficult, but with a little chisel work it was manageable.

The feeling of eyes on him, however, was another matter. Every time he looked back at the masons one was staring at him. He thought about asking them why, but it wouldn't do any good.

The looks were affecting Trent. He was careless, preoccupied, and kept making mistakes. He dropped an offcut, even though his hand was beneath it, sending it tumbling into the tower below.

It hit with a clatter, and Trent winced. Sam gave him a stern look, but said nothing. All the masons looked at him then, with strange looks on their face.

A too deep cut from a chisel was the next thing. "What do we say?"

"A steady hand and a steady eye. First time."

"Then focus, the first time. Remember, you can't uncut." The lesson that he first learned, and learned with great embarrassment. An older apprentice to a hard man, his apprenticeship had been valuable beyond words.

"Yes, Master." Trent dropped his head but went back to his work, hand shaking.

"Everything else fades away. Everything else can wait. Guide your hand and be confident." Sam watched, partially shielding the boy with his body, straddled on the main beam.

The afternoon dragged on, but by the time dinner rolled around over half the cross members were laid and ready for the planking.

Sam stood, stretching his back and rubbing his neck. The masons had fled with the first sounds of the bell drifting up from below and had given them parting nasty glares. "A few more days and we'll be on to the next thing."

The next thing meant hours and hours more planking, dressing, and finishing timber for the floor. He wasn't relishing the thought, but a few more hours at his special project would help.

Sam gulped down dinner as fast as he could and went back to his carving. He managed to finish all but the border by the third bell, and after another punishment session with more water, went back.

The world slipped away as he worked, into the background. It was him and the wood, an image burned into it that had to get out.

At long last, in the wee hours of the night, he sat back and sighed.

It was done.

A few quick handfuls of sand to polish, and it gleamed bright and bold in the night. He couldn't wait until the morning to put it up, so he grabbed a hammer, and the custom nails delivered the day before and went into the castle.

It was quiet, and eerie. So full of the sounds of construction during the day, it echoed with the sound of his footsteps.

The night air had knocked down the smell of construction, leaving it fresh and woody smelling.

Sam knocked at the Duke's door, then pushed it aside.

After another trip for a ladder, and some wrestling, he had it in place. A few quick taps of the hammer on one side evened out his precarious position, and a minute later, it was in place.

He stepped back and admired his work.

It wasn't the best carving in the world, but it was his best. It was imposing, large, grand, and would satisfy the purpose for what he built.

Of that, he was sure.

Let it be a surprise. Sam yawned, gather his tools, and shut the door quietly as he left.

It had been a long day, but it was well worth it. He hoped this effort would secure what he needed most right now.

An ally.

10

INTERRUPTED

The scream woke him up. Sam's eyes flashed open. The night was cool, the smell like normal, but there was something wrong.

A gurgle of death brought him fully out of sleep.

He sprung to his feet, struggled to put on his boots, and rushed out of the hut.

Blood pumping, Sam turned left and right to see what the problem was.

"Raiders, raiders!" Someone was yelling something from the forest.

He didn't hesitate.

Sam turned and ran, ringing the alarm bell in the Square. If it was a false alarm, he would have to deal with it.

The bell was loud and left his ears ringing.

Workers started to assemble, and their families, asking what was going on.

"I don't know, get to the castle."

Sam looked into the forest, trying to see what was out there. It was dark, and still.

Not even a night bird calling.

The hairs on the back of his neck rose, and he unconsciously clutched at his side.

But there was nothing there. Of course.

He relaxed his hand, stretched it out, and took a deep breath. About half the workers were up or on the road already. Bleary eyes looked at him, children cried.

And guards were coming the other direction. "What is the meaning of this?" One asked. He had a smashed nose and a glare in his eyes. Dawain, Sam thought. Matthew was the other.

"A scream, to the south. An alarm." Sam didn't keep looking at him, but turned his attention back to the forest. "Something is wrong."

"You've woken everyone up, that's what's wrong," Dawain said, irritated. "And you disturbed our watch. If we have to come down every time one of you gets too twitchy, we'll never get anything done."

A movement. Sam snapped his head in that direction. There it was again. Something was moving.

"Get down." Sam dropped, an unusual sound tickling his ears.

"Get — " An arrow struck Dawain, brushing above Sam. He clutched at it and cried out.

"Attack!" Matthew drew his sword. Dawain stumbled and turned, and another arrow hit him in the back.

The gates were a few hundred yards away. "There are too many," Sam said. "We've got to get back to the castle." The stream of workers and families had slowed to a trickle, but they were running now. "Come on."

"Go, I'll stop them." Matthew advanced into the night.

Sam shook his head, then ducked as another arrow flew by. That was aimed at his head. "Come on."

He pulled Dawain over his shoulder. The man was in shock, mumbling something over and over again.

He could still walk, though, and Sam led him up the path. He glanced back.

Fighters were pouring out of the woods, less than two hundred yards away from the makeshift worker's village.

They looked angry. And large. And all of them were bearing deadly looking weapons.

The other guard had seen them too and was sprinting in their direction. Sam pushed harder, breaking them both into a run. The dust of the path got in his eyes and mouth, tasting like dry sand.

He spit it out and kept running.

Ahead of him the screams had started, of pure terror. The iron gate was creaking, breaking free of its position. It had been closed before, when it was installed and tested, but had lain open since.

It looked like they wouldn't have much time until it was shut.

Arrows flew by him now, and he zigzagged left and right as much as he could to try and avoid them, making them as much of a difficult target to hit as possible. It worked, and Matthew caught up to them.

He didn't stop, but ran past. Sam wanted to cry out, but fueled his surprise into his legs, carrying on the wounded man despite the lack of help.

A quick glance told him why the man had run past. Dozens of fighters had flooded the streets of the worker's makeshift town, now all converging on the path up to the castle.

And even worse, there was a party of them rushing the gate along the edge of the wall. "By the wall," Sam cried out. He wished he could point, he wished he had both hands free to signal, but Dawain groaned, reminding him that his life was in his hands.

They weren't moving fast, though, and they still had at least a hundred yards to go.

The workers had made it, all shuffling into the relative protection of the gates, and were milling about the courtyard beyond.

Clanking from the gates, black and shining in the moonlight, called out to him, urged him on.

Finally, someone on the castle walls had seen the other raiders and were firing arrows at them. It didn't stop them, if they could get inside before the gates closed, the defenders would have no chance. This had to be their aim.

Sam's legs were like lead now, weighed down by the full weight of Dawain. Their lead was shrinking even now, and cries of war struck up from the raiders.

They knew they would catch them.

He dug deep inside, finding the part of him he thought best left alone, and touched it. Just enough to raise his strength, just enough to keep him going.

The anger and energy helped, and he sped up. He took the other man's arms on his shoulders and hefted him onto his back, feet dragging behind.

The shift in weight helped, putting his effort into muscles unused in the chase, and Sam ran for all he was worth.

His heart pounded, his lungs burned, and the gate came down.

Now it was halfway closed. The raiders were less than a hundred yards away, sprinting along the wall for cover.

A quarter left. The war cries were closer.

He dare not look behind.

His mouth was dry but tasted like iron, his nose strained with the breath in his body.

A few more yards. What felt like hands reached out behind him, spurring him on to sprint.

He ducked, clearing the gate just in time, and fell forward. Dawain sprawled into the dust.

There were hands clutching him, pulling him.

The gate slammed shut behind him, its iron bands enveloping his hurt and aching body.

Sam fell to his knees, and they pulled him forward. The air tasted sweet, cool in his mouth. Someone forced water into his hands, and he drank of the coolness.

It went down into his belly, a big slug of cold that shivered through his stomach and out to the rest of his body, cooling him.

"Well done," the crowd said. Hands were clapping his back, but he was short of breath and dizzy.

The guards were running through the yard in an uneasy state of alarm. Half were dressed, while others were still in nightclothes, and Captain Yand strode through them, shouting and ordering them to their posts.

"Look after him," Sam said. They rushed Dawain away, careful of the arrows sticking out of his back and front. He was still awake and alive, but the whites of his eyes showed as they rolled back into his head.

Confusion reigned in the courtyard. The night's stillness shattered, broken like pottery on a rock, and voices were talking, shouting, screaming.

Sam tried to stay on his feet, but his legs gave out and he sat down hard. The ground met him, hard as rock.

"Sam, talk to me." Ned was there, at his side, worried eyes covered in bushy brows that were pulled down tight. His arms were on Sam's shoulders, shaking him slightly.

"Fine. I'm fine." There was banging from the gate, the sound of metal on metal.

The taste of iron was in his mouth, and he spit it out. Blood. *Must have cut my lip.*

"They came out of nowhere," Archie said, clutching his wife. Sandra looked wild, her eyes as big as saucers.

"They came from the forest. Probably came across the river when no one was looking." Sam regained his breath, words no longer labored. "They were here without warning."

He could see them gathered at the gate. Sam wished they would shut the big, wooden doors that had taken so long to make, but no one had had the sense to do it.

Captain Yand was directing archers to the front to shoot in between the openings in the iron. "Get out of the way, go somewhere else, behind the gate," he bellowed.

The workers and their families were happy to oblige, and in the scuffle and rush, some semblance of order returned.

They picked up who they had to and moved out of the line of sight. Sam saw a dozen guards.

That was it.

That was all the fighting men they had. To hold this castle from dozens of hardened fighters. He caught glimpses of their faces.

Scars crossed their bodies. Their armor was cut and torn, battered in battles long ago. These were no mere raiders, they were organized.

"You see it too, don't you?" Sam asked, helped along by Ned.

"I do. Evil times have befallen us." They shuffled forward, joining the others safely out of the way of returned arrow fire. "I prayed this day would never come, but now it has."

Stars twinkled above, oblivious to their plight. What had once been filled with the smell of dust and rock, progress on a fortress to stand against attack, had turned to the smell of blood and battle.

"They found out, and sent a force to capture it before it was too late," Sam said, taking a seat and leaning against the hard stones of the keep.

Ned gave him a halfhearted smile. "Too late for them, it seems."

"Well, now we fight back, then wait for them to go." Something orange and yellow was glowing, flickering light through the night.

"What is that?" someone asked farther away.

Sam knew. He smelled the smoke, even from here.

"Fire!" someone else shouted. "The village is on fire!"

His clothes, his bed. The small place he could call his own. It was gone now.

And the rest of the wood would be burned too. All that effort, all that time.

The beams, the timbers.

Oak, ash, cherry. It had taken months to season some of the wood, and now it would be gone, burned to ash.

Sam clenched his hand, drawing it around a clump of dust. He squeezed with all his might, breathing deep to counteract his anger. The sand was hard, bit into his hand.

He didn't care. He kept squeezing until he couldn't bear it anymore. Until that red of anger receded. That thing that resided deep inside him had to stay asleep.

"Trent," Sam said. The young man, eyes wide from the excitement of the night, was at his side in a flash. "Go see if you can tell if they destroyed the workshop."

With a nod, he was off, running to get a better view. He chose the wall, running up the rough steps that ascended to the heights above.

"Why did you send him?" Ned asked.

"I need to know."

"You could have sent anyone else."

"I could have."

Ned stared at him. "Why?"

"He loved that workshop. It was the only one he's ever known." Sam looked down, dropping the sand back to the earth. "He needs to know it's gone. Forever. Needs to see it with his own eyes."

Now that the shock had worn off, the others were stirring. Curiosity had taken some, and they had peeked out from behind the keep wall to see.

Yand was still yelling orders, directing men to and fro. A few yells, a few more curses. Some in a tongue that he wasn't familiar with.

The Belmarchers. Why had they chosen now to attack, after all this time?

They must have been watching them, marking their progress. Any earlier and they would have walked into the castle through the unfinished gate, or the holes in the castle walls.

Perhaps finishing the gate had helped. He looked up at the half finished stone tower. Its top looked like a toothy grin against the night sky, like it had taken half a bite out of it.

That tower would do no good now. The warning was gone and over with.

Sam shivered. The cool air of the night had sapped some of his strength, but the few minutes of rest had helped with everything else. He didn't want to believe it, wished it were untrue. It kept calling to him.

He stood, surprising Ned and the other carpenters who had gathered around. "Where are you going?"

Starting for the tower, he looked back for a moment. "I'm going to see for myself."

11

BURNED

Sam met Trent on the stairs.

"It's burned." Tears streaked down the man's face, tracking through the dust and the ash. Big plumes of smoke were roiling up in the air behind him.

What a fire it would make.

"Go back to the others, get some rest." This was going to be a long night. Sam knew Trent wouldn't be able to sleep. None would, after what had happened.

Still, it was the best he could do. "Why did they have to do it?" Trent asked. Fire raged in his eyes.

The same fire Sam felt in his heart.

"Like any other reason a man does what is evil. Because they wanted to."

Trent looked like he had something else to say, but held his tongue and rushed by Sam on the narrow staircase.

He moved to let the boy pass and continued the long climb to the top. When he got there, he stopped dead in his tracks.

The fires blazed in the makeshift village, the thatched roofs of the hastily constructed shacks lit up and licked by great tongues of fire.

He felt the heat even from the top of the wall and saw its distortions as it wavered and flew into the sky. The workshop was on fire, bodies stuffing burning torches into the wood piles.

They crackled and spit as they burned the fresh wood. All the potential in them was licked away, consumed by flames.

An arrow flew by his head, and Sam ducked back down behind the wall. The fighters were still out there, ready to kill them all.

He had a feeling that if they got in, they would spare no one. They were the advanced party, small but light. Able to move quickly, unburdened by the long chain of supplies an army needed.

Which meant more were coming.

Sam took a deep breath, the fires of rage threatening to burn him away. He had come to this place to escape war, not to be in the thick of it.

Soldiers yelled down below, clashing with each other over the gate. Someone finally gave the order to shut the wood gates, and they were creaking closed.

Still, the fighting went on. Sam risked another look, searching for the archers. They had taken up residence to the left of the village and were peppering the wall with arrows. One saw him and raised a bow, but Sam dropped down out of sight.

He had managed to count them. At least a dozen archers that he could see, and presumably a larger number of fighters at the gate.

They would need to get in. The gate was the weak point, but defenses more than made up for it. Even now he expected they had stoked the fires in the room above the murder holes, ready to drop down burning pitch and oil on the attackers.

But that would only deter them, not keep them away.

Sam felt the cool of the stone against the back of his head, sucking the heat from his head. Smoke hung thick in the air now, on the cloudless, calm night. So thick he could taste it in his mouth and feel it on his tongue. It was oily and bitter.

The others were huddled in a mass next to the keep. The Overseer was out now, dressed and perplexed, walking next to the duke, who looked angry.

One guardsman rushed up to the workers, calling for their help. Sam roused himself and rushed down the stairs, joining a reluctant group of the strongest workers to follow.

The doors were still open, cracked down the middle. Six men were trying to push each side shut, including Captain Yand, but hands and weapons of the attackers held them back.

Arrows flew into the castle from the opening, and the guardsmen urged them in. "Either side now, push for all your worth. Your lives depend on it."

"Put your backs into it," Yand growled. Sam found a spot on the far side, a quick sprint across the opening before any arrows could hit him, and shoved into the wood with his shoulder.

The locking beam was ready, but it was too far open to put it into the iron braces that held it.

Sam dug in, lowering his shoulder and finding his footing. He pushed against the dirt, which gave way a little, and tried again.

"Push, push!" They pushed and strained. The doors closed an inch. Someone on the other side cried out as something snapped. A hand, a weapon, Sam couldn't tell.

He kept pushing, as did the others. Inch by inch, it closed. The opening at the middle narrowed.

"Get the lock!" Yand bellowed. A few men broke off and picked up the thick, stout beam that would lock into place, lifting it over the heads of the pushers.

But their momentary abandonment of the doors allowed the enemy to push it back open, an inch at least.

Arrows flew through the opening, one hitting a man in the arm. He cried out.

Sam pushed, trying to get traction. The locking bar was in one set of braces, but the doors were too much to put it in the other set.

Men gasped around him, groaned, and grunted. The smell of blood and sweat mingled with smoke from the fires. Sam gritted his teeth and pushed for all he was worth.

"Put your backs into it," Yand was on the other side of the doors. Veins stuck out on his forehead, and his face was red.

Something snapped, and the door shut to his left. Sam felt his side give, then it, too, slammed shut.

Hands scrambled, fingers grasped. His own found the wood and pulled down. The locking bar slid into place.

Sam slid down against the door, gasping for breath. Men leaned against the wood nursing wounds or trying to recover their strength.

Yand was breathing hard, but stumbled back, drawing his sword. "To the walls. There's no time to rest." He pulled a guardsman off the door, who stumbled and staggered to the stairs. The others caught the hint and streamed up to the wall.

Only a few men were left at the doors, Sam and a few masons. The enemy forces were yelling and pounding on the door, shudders running into his body.

Sam stepped back. His shoulder hurt from where he had jammed it into the wood, and he rubbed feeling back into it.

"What are we going to do?" a guard asked.

"Keep calm. We have a thick wall between us and them." Sam looked up at it, newly finished. He shuddered to think what would have happened had they come just a few months earlier, when it was still open.

But then, he knew what would have happened.

There would have been no one to dig their graves.

"How can you be so calm?" The man's hands shook. Damien, Sam recalled. "They burned our homes..."

Sam thought about it for a moment. Yes, it was difficult, terrorizing, unthinkable. But it had happened. "I don't know, but I'm too tired to be upset."

It was true, with so little sleep, his body felt exhausted. He needed a break.

The shouts and screams would keep him up. The excitement from the night was too much. On the other side, the sound of splashing water, then cries of pain. They had done it. Sam imagined they would retreat now, far back out of arrow range, and leave them alone.

"Go back to the others, get some rest." Sam turned to go back up the wall, taking the stairs carefully in his exhaustion.

He wouldn't be able to last much longer. A quick glance back showed that the workers and their families were being herded inside the keep. Sam wondered where they were going to put them. The main room? On the finished side wings?

He reached the top, turning the thought out of his mind, and joined the others at the edge.

They were retreating, pulling back through the side of the village, which had burned through most of the shacks and was now a smoldering, festering ruin.

Twangs from the bows of the defenders were few and far between, despite Yand's urging. The enemy bowmen had fallen back too, joining the band of warriors as they set up a distance away.

The retreat was orderly, and they even carried their wounded out with them. These men were disciplined, hardened by battle.

The chances of them simply giving up and going home despite the loss of the element of surprise was going to be low.

"What are you doing up here?" Yand demanded.

"Checking the village, sir," Sam said, turning to face him. The man looked awful, covered in dirt, mud, and blood mixed with ash. Sam wondered if he didn't look the same. The face he wore was one of anger.

"Get down below with the others. This place is for fighters only." There was no room for negotiation in his tone.

So, Sam bowed and walked down the stairs. The smell of smoke was clearing, now just a hint on the fresh night air, but the sounds of panic and terror from the families continued.

He joined them, entering into the great hall that had been finished for some time. It was barren, still waiting on his carpenters to furnish, and was another thing on the list that needed to be done.

Sam almost laughed at the thought. That was gone now. What would his priorities be? To build more doors so that the enemy couldn't come in?

He found the other carpenters huddled near the front. Children were crying, women were trying to calm them, and the men reached out to him with questions as soon as they saw him.

"The gates are shut," he said, raising his hands to quiet them. They rushed around him, peppering him with more questions so that he couldn't even respond. "Where is the Overseer?"

"With the Duke," someone said. Sam furrowed his brow.

"We're safe for now." A great sigh of relief seemed to ripple through them. "Has there been any direction?"

"No, we came in here to get out of the way and be somewhere safe," David said.

"Where are we supposed to sleep? The children are tired." Mary clutched at her two boys. Their eyes were red, and they held onto her legs for dear life.

Sam felt it too. He looked around. There was plenty of space for every family if they spread out. Everyone was looking to him, even Bill cast a watchful eye his way.

"We'll sleep here, behind the walls of the keep. That will put more than a few inches of stone between us and whatever else is out there. Spread out, let every man and family have his share."

They pushed to the back of the room, as far away from the entrance doors as they could. Sam didn't mind and looked out over everyone, making sure it was as orderly as possible.

They divided up by trade, like they always had at meals. The masons and their families, the largest group, took the farthest back. The smiths were next, then the carpenters, and everyone else.

Sam took the spot as close to the door as he could. There was no bedding to speak of, but the children were laying heads on their mother and father.

A hush fell over the room. Outside was quiet, punctuated only by a shouted order here or there. Somewhere an owl hooted, a strange reminder of the natural world that still existed.

He sat down, leaning against the stone wall. Anxious eyes looked out, but the excitement of the night quickly faded away. One by one, they went to sleep.

Sam felt himself drifting off, but still they were all looking to him. he wasn't sure what he could do for them.

He wouldn't fight, and he couldn't save them. They were trapped here, as much as the enemy was kept out, they were kept in.

Not knowing what tomorrow would bring, Sam let himself be overtaken by exhaustion and slipped into a blissfully empty sleep.

12

SECURE

Dawn brought a new day and a painful rousing. His body ached from the strain of the previous day and the rough sleeping conditions.

Dozens of families were strewn about the great hall, and sunlight streamed in from the openings near the top of the ceiling.

Dust motes played in the shafts of light, drifting in the otherwise quiet room. Light snores and heavy breathing were the only sounds.

Sam got up and stretched. A few others were awake, but the vast majority were still asleep. The guards were nowhere to be seen.

He went outside, still groggy from the sleep, but waking with the rest of the world. The sun rose empty, no sunrise to speak of, in a clear sky. Smoke still drifted up from the direction of the village, white wisps that curled up into the air and were taken away by a gentle, rising wind.

Men were on the wall standing guard, two on each wall. The rest were nowhere to be seen. Sam took care of his business in the corner, then walked back over dusty ground to the gate.

From this side the wood looked fine. The locking bar was still in place and seated in its braces. Other than the dust and mud kicked up in the hasty shutting, it bore no evidence of ill use.

He wondered if they would care if he went up to the wall. He longed to look out, see what the enemy was doing. Were they encamped, or had they retreated in failure?

Judging from the hard stares of the sentries, who looked even more exhausted than he felt, it was the former.

Eventually, he decided to risk it, and climbed to the top.

"You shouldn't be here," the guard said. It was Matthew, and his heart didn't seem in it.

"I'll be gone in a moment, just wanted to take a look." Matthew glanced back uneasily, but the keep was silent and there was no sight of the Overseer or of Captain Yand.

"Make it quick."

He was right, they had made camp. A fire ringed by tents was far off in the distance, well out of bow-shot or even sortie range.

It was haphazard, but not undisciplined. The tents were tied down and staked into the ground.

He wondered how long it would take for them to come back. One of the enemy soldiers was tending the fire, adding logs every so often to keep it going.

"Thank you," Matthew said roughly.

"For what?"

"Last night. You carried Dawain. I should have done that."

"You raised the alarm, allowed us to shut the gate in time. I'd say you proved yourself well."

Matthew turned away. "It sounds like he might make it."

"I'm glad of it."

"You should go now. You've been here too long." His eyes searched the horizon, ignoring Sam.

Seeing all he needed to, Sam acquiesced. The wind was picking up, and the sun was getting higher. His legs felt like jelly on the way down, a combination of tiredness and the unsettling oneness of the stairs.

At the bottom, he wondered what to do. Construction would halt, of that he was certain, but what else would they be tasked with?

The others were waking up now, coming out in a long stream to relieve themselves in the corner of the yard. Sam mentally went over the inventory of wood in his head.

There wasn't enough to build housing for everyone, not even for tents. Where would they all stay?

He put the thought out of his mind. That was for the Duke and the Overseer to decide. Not him.

<hr>

"What are we going to do about it?" Duke Hornblood sat in his chair, eyes bloodshot.

"We need reinforcement, Sir," Overseer Rhys said. "We should send for them as soon as possible."

"They have us trapped in here. I have to agree." Captain Yand stood next to the Overseer in front of the desk. His eyes briefly flickered to the crest above the Duke, then back to their steely gaze.

"And this is the advance party?"

"That's what I think," Yand said. He stood with his hands behind his back at forty-five degrees, legs spread exactly shoulder width. Despite the mess on his uniform, he could have been on the parade ground.

"Then we send a messenger, go to my father or the King." The Duke stood up, paced furiously behind his desk. "They'll come with armies and fight back the incursion. They have to."

"Well..." The Overseer shifted his weight. His belly jiggled as he did. His mouth twisted.

"Out with it." The Duke turned on him.

"With the invasion to the east, the King might not have much to send." He hastily continued under the impetuous gaze. "At least until later in the year, after the fighting season is over."

"That assumes they can get here," Yand said. "The passes might be blocked."

"Even with a message we might not see help until when, next year?"

"In the worst case, I'm afraid so." The Overseer flinched as he spoke, expecting the worst.

The Duke stopped pacing and drew in a deep breath. "I was afraid of something like this. We don't have the men or material to break out, do we?"

"Not without significant losses. Even then, we're over-manned." Yand tilted his head down. "Permission to speak openly, sir?"

"Granted." The Duke took his chair again, tapping his foot against the floor.

"We should expect attacks. Often. They'll probe our weaknesses, try and find a way in. They'll add men to their ranks, grow their raiding party into a small army if they can. This was supposed to be a surprise attack. Now that they've failed, we can expect them to come hard and come often until we...dissuade them."

"So, how do we survive?"

"Fight them off. We have supplies, arrows, and food to last. We'll repel anything they decide to throw at us."

"For how long?" the Duke asked.

Yand was silent, but shifted, showing his first real hint of discomfort. "We will have to do an inventory of everything inside the castle. Luckily, due to your grace's foresight and diligence," at that he gave a small bow. Of course, it was his idea. "We brought in as much as we could before the attack. A mere trifle remained outside the castle walls."

"We're stuck here with them?" The Overseer recoiled, the thought just striking him. "Oh, dear..."

The Duke took a sip of his now warm wine. "Whatever do you mean, dear Overseer?" He gave him a nasty smile, and the Overseer paled.

"Nothing," he said, gulping. "I will organize the inventory and come back with my report when it is complete."

"Do that." The Duke stood and stretched, taking a glance back at his crest. It had appeared there quite unexpectedly, if not welcome. He felt better sitting with it hanging above him. It reminded any with him of the magnitude of who they were speaking to.

But, at the same time, it was a constant reminder of the weight of duty and horror that hung above. All things considered, the good outweighed the bad.

He would have to thank that carpenter, it was well made and stout. "Is there anything else we need to discuss?" He yawned. It had been hours since he had any real sleep to speak of.

"I've set up rotating shifts of guard work. They'll raise the alarm if anything happens with our new...friends."

Duke Hornblood nodded. "Good. Dismissed."

Captain Yand snapped to attention. The Duke almost heard the crack through the air as he moved and saluted. With a quick face, he turned right and marched out of the room.

Always a stickler for decorum and ceremony.

"Good day, your excellency." The Overseer bowed, his eyes sunken. He looked just as tired as the Duke felt.

The Duke let them go, then went to the small window that overlooked the castle courtyard below. Men and women were milling about, uncertainty in their faces and their movements.

A great weight had been laid on him, but he never imagined he would be in this situation.

"Trial by fire indeed, Uncle," he said to himself, watching his vassals work.

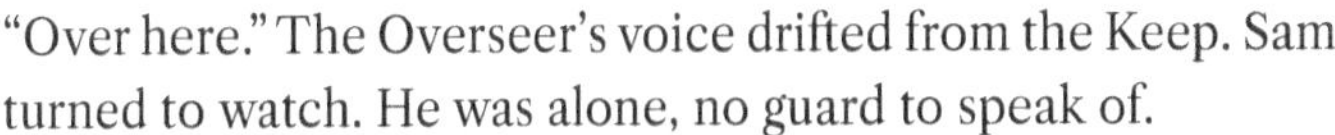

"Over here." The Overseer's voice drifted from the Keep. Sam turned to watch. He was alone, no guard to speak of.

His guards must be occupied on the walls.

The workers turned to watch, and the Overseer beckoned them in.

They milled about at first, but the look of frustration on the Overseer's face brought them in.

The sun was high in the sky now, almost to noon, and they had spent an unproductive morning talking and wandering around. Sam made sure to keep the carpenters working, setting up a temporary workshop, and they were working on the frame for a more permanent home before the meal bell had rung.

The Overseer wiped the sweat from his brow, the sun shining in a cloudless sky.

Sam wondered what the attackers were doing. Why had they pulled back so? Did they not sense they could overwhelm them?

He glanced back to the gate, strong and heavy. The walls had been designed well, sloped gently to allow a full range of attack from anyone above, with no place to hide, and crenelations for the archers to take cover between shots. They must have thought it wasn't worth the risk, and the boiling liquids being dropped on them, to try it again.

Smoke rose from the gatehouse. There would be a fire kept up, and boiling water or oil always at the ready to be dropped down on the attackers stupid enough to get too close.

If he were on the other side he would be making a ram right now, or ladders to scale the wall in the night.

The Overseer's voice brought his attention again.

"Divide up into your prospective trades and take stock of everything we have. Masons, you're in charge of cataloging the foodstuffs, carpenters, the bedding and housing supplies, and everyone else can pitch in where needed."

"What's going to happen?" Someone called out. "We've been here all day with no news."

Others voiced their agreement, causing the Overseer's mouth to twitch. He held up his hands.

"We've been attacked, as you know, by Belmarch raiders. They've taken up camp just outside of range of our arrows."

"What are you going to do about it?" Someone said.

A flash of irritation passed across the big man's face. "They will be dealt with in time. The King's forces will come to save us. We're going to send a messenger to hurry them along, but in the meantime we have some work to do."

"Work? What work?" Bill asked. "We can't get to the quarry to cut stone, so we can't build the walls. We're stuck here with nothing to do and a whole lot of nothing to do it with." His masons agreed.

"Take care," the Overseer said, drawing himself up to his full height. His booming voice rang out in the courtyard. "I still oversee this castle until it is finished. The Duke would not react kindly to those who step out of place in questioning me."

Bill backed down, and his masons grumbled. They outnumbered the carpenters four to one and made up the majority of the workers. With the amount of stone going into the walls, it made sense, but Sam was starting to feel uneasy about it.

Although, now that he thought about it, he wouldn't have to worry about the schedule as much anymore.

Wind kicked up the dust, spraying it into everyone's face, then died down again. Sam spit the gritty dirt out of his mouth and wiped it from his eye. It scratched against his eyelid as he did.

It seemed to dampen the mood on the crowd, and the Overseer glared at them. Hearing more no objections, he said, "Get to work."

Stalking off, the Overseer retreated to the safety of the keep, and the coolness of its walls.

The group split into the respective trades, and the carpenters gathered around Sam. He kept an eye on the masons as they milled around Bill.

"Trent, go back to the supplies and pick up anything valuable you can. The best chisels, planes, and saws. Take it to the keep and lock it into the empty room on the second floor." Sam slipped him a key.

Trent looked down, surprised, then back up. "Why is that?"

"I'm afraid things are about to get ugly."

13

All Day and Nothing to Do

Trent rushed off as fast as Sam had ever seen him go.

"What are you thinking?" Ned asked quietly.

"I'm thinking now is a...volatile time. We've been surrounded by enemies, people are scared, and things happen that might not work out for the best," Sam said. He kept his eyes on his carpenters, but watched everyone else out of the side of his peripheral vision.

Volatile was putting it nicely, this was a recipe for disaster. Idle hands, and a few hours of discussion turning them into a united force.

The question would be, is it a force that would preserve life, or take it?

"In the meantime, we'll do what the Overseer asks. Ned, take Archie with you to inventory the lumber. I'll take Kerien to check on the tools. If we have any luck, Trent will have slipped into the keep by then and we'll have a stash for ourselves."

They worked out the finer details, agreed to meet back near the keep after dinner, and dispersed.

Ned and Archie went to the stacks of lumber, staged for the beams and supports that would have been needed for the rest of the keep. Sam looked up at the tower. He wasn't sure they would ever finish it now.

Kerien, for once, looked nervous. "Bill sounded angry."

"Wouldn't you, if your supply of ale dried up, stuck in a burning village?" Sam strode away, and Kerien ran to catch up. "Men will do strange things for alcohol. Desperate things."

"You don't think they'd — " Kerien swallowed hard, "do something rash, do you?"

"We're stuck in a castle with few defenders and even less competent ones. They sent us the guards who couldn't be trusted anywhere else, disposable, unusable. Captain Yand is the only soldier in this place." *Well, except one other.*

"But they know how to fight."

"Not like the Belmarch raiders do. They'd tear them to pieces in an instant, and spit on their graves afterward." Sam thought a moment. "I think they'll send for help, if they can. A rider, probably, if they had any horses. Of course, since we don't have horses the river would be the next best thing."

"We don't have any boats."

"That might be a problem." They had reached the makeshift workshop. Trent was stuffing supplies into a large crate. "Make sure you take the back way and be sure to be quiet. I don't want anybody seeing you take those in."

"I think I have everything." Trent looked around hastily. Sam peered into the crate, moved a few things around. He'd done well, got most of what Sam was thinking.

"Good," Sam said. "Go." He clapped him on the back. Trent nodded, collected the crate, and took off.

The boy knew how to move, and move quietly, when he wanted. He was always sneaking up behind Sam when he least expected him.

"We'll start at the front and work our way back. You start counting and I'll tally."

"Saws first?" Kerien held up a two-handed saw.

Sam nodded.

The inventory took longer than he expected. They had managed to get more out than he realized. There was enough left to stock the workshop with everything they needed, with the set that Trent had taken with him.

He showed up a few minutes later than Sam expected him, but gave a good report. Everything was locked away and safe.

Evening was coming, the sun halfway down the sky, and the smell of burning ash had finally fallen away from the wind. There was a fire burning in the courtyard, and food cooking over it. Soup, from the smell of it.

They finished everything and went to join the others milling around the campfire. Sam stopped at the well, took up a bucket, and splashed his face.

It was cool and felt good. The dust from the day washed away, and he used the rest of the water in the bucket to wash off his hands.

Bill was standing off to the side, surrounded by his crew. Sobriety had not done him well. Large, black bags highlighted the bloodshot eyes.

They met his, and Sam saw the danger in them.

It made him angry and flared up his rage. After all of this, after the attack, and this man still had a grudge against him.

What have I done to him, other than help him? Sam remembered being overly helpful in accommodating their schedule, trying to get his work ready a day or two before theirs. In turn, they changed what they were doing. He now realized it was on purpose.

His hands dug into the bucket. It was hard, solid wood and damp from use in the well. He wanted to throw it at Bill, chuck it against his head.

But that would accomplish nothing. Sam took a deep breath, letting the smell of dinner fill his lungs. Bill had pushed his way to the front of the line and was ladling out his portion.

Sam dropped the bucket back into place, letting it clang against the stone wall of the well, and returned to join the others at the back of the line.

Ned and Archie came up. "How did it go?"

Ned gave him a side look. "Better than yours, apparently."

Sam tried to relax more, let his scowl drop. "Sorry, not your fault."

"Whatever it is, I'd stay away from you right now."

"How are the supplies?"

Archie scratched the back of his head. "Plenty of oak," he said. "In various sizes and lengths." That was to be expected, as it was the main timber in the area. "A bit of other wood, but I'm sure there won't be enough to continue outfitting the keep with furniture."

"I thought we should have brought the rest up here," Kerien said.

"You said no such thing." Archie's eyes narrowed as they rested on the younger man. "Don't be making up stories."

Chastened, Kerien glowered at Archie. He was a bigger man, and would put up with no sass. "Any word on the attackers?" Ned asked, trying to change the subject.

"Nothing," Sam said, and the others agreed.

"I heard they've set up camp in the village," the man in front of them said, turning their way. His name was Dave, a farmer. "Tore up the fields too. I hope they go home soon."

"Not likely," Ned said. "They're like wolves. Once they've tasted the blood, it would take killing them to get off the scent again. I've heard it before."

"Then there's no hope for us, is there?" Trent asked. He looked forlorn, beaten down by the circumstances. It was the most dejected Sam had ever seen him.

"Look here, don't you think about despairing now." Sam pointed to the walls. "We've got a few feet of good, solid rock between us and them. It'll take more than a few arrows to break our resolve."

But there were some things that could. Walls could come down faster than they go up, given the right persuasion. There was no need to tell Trent that, though.

"We learned to fight and I didn't even get a chance," Trent said. Sam bit back a laugh. The boy might be a promising carpenter, but his martial skills had left much to be desired.

Taking to the plane was a whole lot different than taking to a sword.

What am I thinking? Sam turned back to Dave. "Any word on how many, or if they came alone?"

"I heard there are dozens, if not hundreds, of them. They've hidden more in the trees to try and fool us, to lure us out of the castle." He got to the front of the line and held out a bowl to be filled. "They just wait for us to lower our guard and they'll strike, you'll see."

He probably wasn't too far off the mark, but Sam doubted they had an extra stash of warriors hidden somewhere. Why they wouldn't use them to attack and overwhelm them at the outset was a silly prospect.

However, he had underestimated enemies before. An old scar reminded him of a time.

"Are you telling stories again, Dave?" Martha dipped into the big pot, stirred it around and pulled out a spoonful to dump in his bowl. It steamed from the heat, and a few potatoes slipped inside. "Shame on you."

"I swear I saw them in the woods. Mark my words." He pointed his spoon at her and closed one eye.

"Go along then." She clicked her tongue. "Next."

Trent went first, then Kerien. She gave them the same amount.

"Can I get more than that?" Kerien asked, staring into the bowl. It wasn't filled.

She gave him a long stare and put a hand on her hip. "No. We've decided to ration the food until we know how long it will take to get supplies back in the castle. I'll have no grumbling either."

Kerien said something under his breath, but then smiled and moved along. When everyone else had gotten their food, Sam let his be filled and joined them on makeshift log benches near the outskirts of the fire.

The heat of the day had died, and it was cooler than the day before. Sam stirred his weak broth, searching for a clump of something more substantial. He found it and chewed, the taste of potato exploding with the soft piece.

"We're in here and they're out there," Archie said, staring out over the gate. "I can't believe it. It happened so fast."

"That it did, lad," Ned said mournfully. "Sometimes that's how life goes. Up and out in the sunshine one day and a squall the next."

"We should do something about it then," Kerien said, glowering. He hadn't spoken since his reprimand, and Sam could tell it was behind his eyes simmering. "Why don't we catch them by surprise?"

"Because we're a bunch of tradesmen, not soldiers. That's why." Sam drank a spoonful of the broth after he spoke. It was still good, salty, with a hint of spice.

"We've been training," Kerien said, straightening. "We could fight them if they gave us weapons."

Sam glanced in Bill's direction. One of his masons handed him another bowl, and he took it greedily. It was filled to the brim. Behind him the door to the keep opened, letting out a serious-looking Captain Yand. "Careful what you wish for, Kerien."

"On your feet," the head guard bellowed. Sam stood, and others scrambled. In a few seconds everyone was standing.

Yand strode forward, flanked by guards on either side and the Overseer on his right. "Good evening." His voice held an edge of steel. "I've heard you all have been asking about ou r...situation. Let me assure you we have planned for this very eventuality." He smiled, showing off a row of gleaming teeth. "And these preparations that you found so odious before will allow us to hold out against a bloodthirsty and determined enemy.

"It is true that these are Belmarch, but they are no simple raiders. They bear the standard of the Raltone's." Murmurs ran through the crowd. "I see you've heard of him."

Sam hadn't, and looked around. Some people had gone pale, and there were a few trembling.

"The advantage we used to have, mainly that the Belmarch are a bloodthirsty and strife-driven people, has become quite tenuous. They are, for the moment united, most against their will, and if this unification is completed, shall be a force to reckon with."

"This was an ad hoc attack, carried out before preparations were complete, hoping to surprise us and loose us from the foothold we have in the castle before it was complete.

"Luckily for us, they were too late. Overseer Rhys has informed me that, due to your hard work and effort in the early stages of construction, the walls were completed far earlier than expected." Bill looked satisfied and preened with looks from his fellow masons.

"They've set up a picket line and surrounded the castle." Yand cast a stony gaze around the group. "I expect they will call for reinforcements, a proper army, to counteract any troops the King will send to defend it. They will fail. We will keep hold of this castle and hold it to the last man for, ladies and gentlemen, your very life depends on it."

Uneasy glances. Hands clutched at loved ones, and little children burrowed into the dresses of their mothers. Sam didn't relish the thought of death, and the death of innocents was even worse. These children had done nothing wrong, they were only born to the parents that brought them here.

He had to wonder if it was really as bad as everyone said it was.

Captain Yand cocked his head to the side. "In that light, you have all now been conscripted into the King's service. You will fight under me." Yand's eyes locked on Sam's. "Or you will die."

14

Knight Shift

Sam bore the look and gave some in return. Now he was in the fire, there was no escaping it.

"We will start by dividing you up into squads. Each squad will be led by a guardsman with the proper knowledge of fighting and defense, and all of them will report directly to me."

While Yand was talking, Sam wondered where Duke Hornblood was. He should be out here, not his stand in by proxy. Was he holed up out of fear or cowardice?

Or was there something else going on? He couldn't say one way or the other.

Glancing down at Kerien, and his ashen face, he realized he might have been too hard on the young man. Saying words was one thing, but having to live them out was quite another.

He put a hand on his shoulder. Kerien glanced over, then dropped his head. Sam let his hand slip away, hoping for the best.

"Overseer, if you please?" Yand stepped aside. The Overseer took his place. He cleared his throat and unrolled a scrap of parchment.

"Here are the assignments. First squad to be led by Guardsman Hale. Come up as I call your name." Names echoed along the silent courtyard, bouncing off the walls and tolling like bells.

A song for the dead. Despite the thick walls and the strong defensive position, Sam had mixed feelings about their future.

Would those names be read as heroes who had perished? Or would they be the names of the survivors who fought and saved themselves?

He looked down. His soup had grown cold, and he pushed it around. The others had abandoned theirs as well.

His appetite was gone. The seriousness of the situation struck him then. There was no getting out of it now, nowhere to run.

Kerien was called out of the group of carpenters, and in a daze, stepped forward to join the growing group of men.

The second squad took Ned, and Archie too. His wife clutched at him, trying to hold him back, but he gave her a forlorn look and broke free to join his new squad, standing beside Ned.

There were about fifteen in each group so far, and the Overseer began the next one.

"Sam Freeman." The first name, assigned to Guardsman Heath.

He walked through the crowd, which parted for him. A long string of masons joined him, and the blacksmith's apprentice, Brent. Then it was over, and fourteen men surrounded him.

"Bill, master mason." He strode forward, seemingly careless of his fate, but a slight hiccup in his step betrayed him. Sam watched Bill stand in his group, congratulating masons as they joined him with handshakes and hearty welcome.

And then the Overseer called Trent.

Sam felt his heart drop. The boy walked forward nervously. *This can't be happening like this.*

Bill gave Trent a cool stare, then sent a smirk towards Sam. Of all the men who had to be with Trent...

Sam shook his head. They finished the rest, a fifth squad that took the remaining men, including Dale the blacksmith.

"You'll get to know your squad leaders better."

"First squad will take the first watch," Yand said, taking over from the Overseer. "Watches will be explained to you, and training will be required for everyone. We're at war now. I suggest you act like it."

The Overseer rolled up his parchment, turned, and walked into the keep with Captain Yand to leave them all in the deepening twilight.

Heath welcomed them, but Sam was too distracted to pay much attention. He kept thinking of those days filled with blood and death, how he could never seem to escape them, no matter how hard he tried.

"Sam, are you paying attention?"

"Hmm? Yes, I am," Sam said, registering the question. A few of the masons sniggered.

"None of that now." They were huddled around in a tight circle, and the smell of unwashed bodies and sweat was strong. The masons reeked of mortar and lime. It was in their clothes and on their shoes, if they were lucky enough to have them. Heath continued. He was a competent guard, and a semi-confident man.

Sam felt bad for him, being thrust into this position. No doubt he would prefer to live life as a simple man. He struck Sam that way.

"As I was saying." A quick glance at Sam. "We'll be taking up the next watch. It will be in the middle of the night, so you need to be ready. They'll send a runner around to wake everybody after the night moon has passed."

"We don't get sleep?" Someone called out. Sam didn't know his name, he was new to the castle and worked in the quarry most of the time. Almost all those masons were unknown to him, slaving away all day breaking rock to be carted back to the castle.

"You'll get sleep tomorrow. That is, unless you'd rather have your throat slit in the night?" The comment stopped any comments that might have been coming. "The Belmarch will do it too, given the chance."

"How long is the watch?" Another mason. Sam didn't know his name either.

"A few hours."

"Will we have weapons?" Sam asked.

Heath paled a little, then shifted his weight from foot to foot. "About that... You'll have to call for help if you see anything out of place. I'll be there on the walls too, so if you need anything you can ask me."

"Weapons would be nice, in the event of an attack." Sam kept up the pressure, not sure if it was a good idea. A weapon in his hand might be worthwhile. Another in the hands of those surrounding him... might be a different story.

But it was too late. The words were spoken, the question asked. It wasn't possible to take it back, even if he wanted to.

"No weapons, not until training is complete."

"Training? I thought we were done with that." This one he did know, a weaselly mason by the name of Brough. They were murmuring and whispering to each other now.

Heath brought up his hands. "None of that, everyone will have their say in due time. Captain Yand will be leading the exercises, and we'll be teaching you everything you need to know."

"It's a little late for that." The voice was angry and belonged to a man with an angry face. "If we wanted to be soldiers, we would have signed up for that."

It was uncomfortable to have so much in common with the masons, but Sam felt it. He agreed, but kept his mouth shut. Some of the others, however, didn't.

Looking a bit taken aback, Heath screwed up his face and stood up. "Quiet." He spoke with more confidence and found his footing. "Duke Hornblood has declared martial law. That's why you're under me now, and as squad leader, I can mete out punishment as I see fit." He glared at them. "And punishment will be severe for those who disobey and incite others to disobey. The lash will be waiting for those who don't listen to me, or the gallows. Take your pick, you grubs."

Dead silence.

"Dismissed." Heath turned on a heel and marched off to the guardhouse.

Grumbles and complaints were aired, but not until he was out of earshot, then the group dispersed.

Sam was left to wonder how things were going to change, and if they were going to last long enough for him to taste that lash.

He yawned and shivered. Sam clutched at the cloak surrounding him, surprised at how chilly the brisk night air had become.

A fire burned in the Square. Too far for bow shot, the Belmarch warriors had set up camp right in the middle of the burned shacks and shanties he had called home for months.

He thought about the good things that had happened there. The meals, the dances, the celebrations as the wall was finished. Good food, good company.

And the losses as well. Men he had known for too long, and some too short. Gone, taken away from this world to the next.

He wondered if he was going to be next.

Blinking, he tried to stay awake. The watch had come too soon, the messenger shaking him too quick. He had been groggy, and traces of it still lingered.

Leaning against the side of the wall, he took a closer look down the edge.

It was a long way down, and for a moment he had a quick moment of vertigo. Light from the moon shone down on the cleared land just beneath him.

A ditch was supposed to be dug there, an additional defense designed to make it harder to get a siege tower close to the wall, but, like so many other things, there wasn't enough manpower to do it and it had been put off.

Everything was quiet, and an owl hooted in the distance.

The stone was hard, but it was more comfortable than standing. Sam's eyelids felt heavy, then shut.

He snapped them open, then rubbed them to get out the sleep. A step back took him out of danger. There would already be one man at the whipping post tomorrow, no sense in adding his own flesh.

Instead, he looked up and down the wall. These men weren't cut out to be guards and defenders, and were having trouble staying awake. However, the recent news of the previous watch had put some fear into them and they seemed to be doing well.

A few more hours and it would all be over.

Sam walked some, watching the forms move and turn around the campfire far away.

He couldn't help but analyze them, no matter how hard he tried.

Their tents were up well, but the spacing was off and they could have been more in line. They were haphazard, suggesting that the commander of this group wasn't used to encampments.

Rookie, perhaps. Or more likely, he cared little about discipline and sharp lines and more about death and destruction.

Of that, he had his doubts. He thought he had seen men out gathering wood, but that was before the sun went down and it had been hard to see.

Now, however, they had men away and posted as sentries. *They watch us and we watch them.* He couldn't make out their eyes this far away, but he knew it was true.

If he was in charge of them, he would have posted sentries in the forest too, but he had looked hard and had seen no sign of them. That meant they were either not there or so disciplined they refused to be seen.

Time would tell, and Sam hoped it was the former. They might have a fighting chance were it the case.

He scratched at his beard. He had grown used to shaving in the morning, but with the excitement he hadn't found the time. It was growing in thick and itchy, a time he disliked the most. A few more days and it would be fine, or a quick shave if he could sneak it in.

Someone shifted to his right, and another coughed farther down the wall. He had been assigned a small portion, just enough to walk and keep moving, but not enough to feel comfortable.

Sam did a few laps, trying to bring some feeling back into his legs. His shoes were already worn, and the sole was in danger of holes. It wasn't pleasant on the cold, hard stone.

Something caught his eye in the forest. Sam blinked away his tiredness, then focused on the spot.

A puff of breeze shook the trees, but other than that, all he could hear were his compatriots on the wall. One shuffled his feet, another coughed.

There was something out there, he was sure of it. All his exhaustion fled at once, and he was alert as his heart kicked into action.

Out of the dark woods, as quiet as a fox on the prowl, men slipped out and started the long trek across open territory to the wall.

They were carrying ladders.

"Attack! To the wall." Sam's voice rang in the courtyard, and the enemy burst into a sprint.

15

GRASS ON THE PLAIN

The alarm bell rang in the night, clear and loud. The attackers were at the wall already, and there was no one with a weapon in sight.

The ladders dug into the ground, then started a long ascent up. First one, then another.

Sam looked around, desperate for something to keep them at bay. Swords and blades glinted in the hands of the men below, and they looked ready to use them.

Guardsman Heath was running, buckling his belt, to get to the stairs. He was shouting, telling them to repel the invaders.

If it wasn't so serious, Sam would have laughed. Repel them with what? A chunk of wood?

The thought struck him. Bit by bit, the ladders came closer, pushed by the men below. There were dozens all the camp as far as he knew.

And there were less than ten here, converging on the same spot. "Check the other sides, they might be coming from different directions."

Sam sprinted to the stairs. Heath was at the top, panting. "They're using ladders. We need to push them off, do you have anything that can do that?"

"Spears, down below. They're coming with them."

"That's not enough, and they won't get here in time. What else do you have?"

Heath ran to the edge, then swallowed hard. "There are so many."

Sam took him in his arms and spun him around. "Think. Do you have anything long?"

"No...I don't know."

He let him go and growled. "You two, come with me."

"Go," Heath said, dazed. Sam ran down the stairs, careful not to trip, and ran for the wood. It was farther than he would like, but they were there before the guards started streaming out of the keep.

"Take these." Sam pulled out long, square pieces of wood, almost like poles. He handed them to the two masons who followed, and took one for himself. "Up the wall."

They ran back. Sam's heart was thumping, and the extra weight wasn't helping anything. The night was cool and smelled fresh, but he knew if they didn't hurry, it would be filled with blood.

They beat the guards, who were trying to rush in behind them. Sam took the steps two at a time.

When he reached the top, an attacker was over the wall. Heath was fighting with him, sword drawn and flashing.

It wasn't a fair fight, and before Sam could do anything about it, the wicked-looking blade took Heath across the shoulder.

Desperate, Sam swung the pole as Heath dropped, giving him enough room to go over his head.

The man opened his mouth in surprise, but didn't duck in time. A shudder went down the pole and up Sam's arms to his shoulders. He heard a crunch, then the man flew over the side of the wall to his right.

A clatter next to him distracted him from another attacker as he popped his head over the wall.

"Push it off," Sam bellowed. A guard rushed by him as he stopped to shove his pole against the ladder rung. Grunting and straining, Sam dug into the stones of the wall and pushed with all his might.

It was heavy. Someone must have been on it. Hands took the pole, joining him, and added strength.

The ladder creaked and moved backward, inch by inch. It shook and shivered, and a head appeared.

It reached the tipping point and swung back. The man on it shrieked as it fell backward with a crash.

Gasping for breath, Sam leaned on the pole. "Push them off the wall."

Guards rushed past him, attacking the two men who managed to get up the other ladder. More clatters as another found a perch.

There was shouting, a clash of sword, and screams. A guardsman stabbed a ladder climber, who fell down onto the man behind him.

Sam saw his opening and rushed in, pushing the ladder away.

Shouts from the other side of the wall. There was another group trying the same thing on the west side.

They had all three poles in use, pushing. The guards sheathed sword, rolling the bodies of the attackers away, and joined them in pushing another away.

Another three ladder attacks, and they pushed them all away.

"Take two to the other side." The courtyard was ablaze with activity now. Sam pushed two members of his squad toward the other side of the wall. When he was sure they were going, he handed his pole off to another group and knelt down beside Heath.

He was still alive and coughed as Sam rolled him over.

"Stay with me now." Sam grasped his hand. It was warm and slippery. Blood trickled from the corner of Heath's mouth.

He reeked of it, and fear. "Did we stop them?" His voice was weak and halting. Sam looked down.

There was nothing he could do.

"We stopped them. Thanks to you. You're a brave man, Heath." The only one with a weapon, but brave enough to face a hardened soldier on his own.

"I'm glad." Life was draining from his eyes. Sam held on tight as Heath clung to him. "I don't want to die."

"I know." Sam fought back tears as the last of his life left, and his body gave up its spirit.

The hand went limp, and Sam let it drop from his own. Such a young man, less than thirty summers old. Taken away in the blink of an eye.

Sam closed his unseeing eyes and murmured a prayer over him. The rest of the world came back in focus for him.

Yelling, screaming, cursing, the men fought to keep the ladders off the wall. Arrows were flying up now, and some found their mark.

However, the guards were sending them back in return as well. Even with only one pole, they were able to keep them back, and some threw whatever they could find. Rock, chunks of the wall, they tossed them at the attackers where they could.

Sam knew it would be over soon. They'd had their chance, and now it was gone. If only they could burn their ladders, that would stop them.

For a time.

He had no doubt there would be more attempts, more ladders. They would need more than sticks to defend the castle.

Captain Yand was surveying the fight, blood dripping off his sword.

"Archers to the west wall," he said.

Sam felt his age now. A younger man would have kept up, but he was past his prime.

"They'll be back," he said, leaning up against the wall. "How long do you think we can keep this up without weapons?"

Yand glanced at him, his eyes flashing in the moonlight. "Empty words from a man who refuses to fight."

"And yet they weigh your heart."

"I am in charge of the defenses of this fortress, carpenter, not you." He wiped the blood off his sword on his pants. He must have been the one to kill the attacker. "Will you advise the Duke on matters of state next?"

The momentary image of him whispering in the young Duke's ear brought him some levity, but didn't change the situation they were in.

"It's only a matter of time before they have more troops and more siege weapons. How can you hope to hold out when that happens?"

Yand gave him a cold look, then returned his gaze to the battlefield below. The archers were having an effect now. With a perfect vantage point from the wall, they landed arrow after arrow among the attackers.

Some lay still on the ground, unmoving. Far more than Heath.

This attack had cost them, and would cost them more.

Faced with the continued repulsion of their ladders, the Belmarch were starting to retreat.

"They run now. They will run tomorrow." Captain Yand sheathed his sword and stood against the wall, leaning out over the edge. The ladders were left in the field, splayed out like sticks in a forest.

Yand turned and swept his cloak over his shoulder. He walked past Sam, then stopped. Over his shoulder he said, "You wish for weapons. You may have your wish granted yet."

A chill ran down Sam's back. Memories flushed to the surface of his mind. Unpleasant, horrible memories. Someone groaned from down below, another victim in a senseless war.

Yand continued, walking briskly to the gatehouse. He was probably going to the other side, where the yells and clashes were still continuing. They were struggling to push back the ladders.

There were more over there, and Sam got to his feet and ran down the stairs. A flush crept up his cheeks, even despite the chilliness of the night.

His blood was up and warm. He didn't know why, what had set it off, but it was there. Being called a coward, he could deal with.

Something didn't sit right with him.

Step after step he ran, passed the waiting women and a few children that had been woken by the noise.

They called to him, asked for news, but he ignored it and took the steps up, joining them just in time to add his weight to a pole.

Together, they pushed it off. It clattered on the rocks below with an accompanied scream. Bows twanged and arrows flew.

Another ladder. Another repulsion. A few more and they had had enough. The ladders stopped being lifted, and the Belmarch fled.

Yand had arrived, and was directing the mop up. Sam caught his breath, resting on the edge of the wall.

A few more arrows found their mark, but they were only wounding shots. They ran till they were out of range, then limped the rest of the way, carrying their wounded and leaving their dead.

Regrouping, the Belmarch huddled together in a mass and turned back to their encampment. The defenders on the wall let out a cheer. Sam knew it would be short-lived and let them. They were clapping hands, congratulating themselves on a job well done.

Few wounded on this side of the wall. They must have been slower, for the slope was steeper on this side. Or they had been seen earlier.

Either way, the end of the battle had come and gone.

"Settle down," Yand said, his booming voice echoing. "They may be licking their wounds tonight, but we lost good men. Keep your silence for them."

Smiles faded away, the joy of the evening gone. Hats were removed and held in hands, and everyone looked back to the stairs.

They were carrying his body down, two men at the feet and one at the head. Heath had gone stiff already.

Sam looked back to the enemy, too overcome to try and remain calm. There was a figure in the distance, at the tree line. He was large and imposing, standing off to the side.

He watched them from afar. Sam could feel his gaze, could smell the sweat and hate flowing from him.

He set his chin on the cool rock. It dug into his skin, but he didn't care. It was a feeling, it was real.

It took him away from thoughts he had wished were left far behind, from a past he had tried to escape.

"Everyone not on watch, back to sleep. Take care of what you need to tonight and be prepared for tomorrow." Yand turned to the guardsman beside him. "Squad leaders, take charge."

He strode off, back to the keep. Sam had no doubt he would sleep well tonight, not like many in this castle.

"Third squad, we're taking over," Dawain said. He was in charge of them.

"What do we do? Heath's gone now," a mason said. Sam shook his head. Come and gone, a flash of bright light and extinguished a second later.

It brought his own fire inside, fueling it.

"Heath's squad, you clean up, collect the arrows, then get some sleep. I'll be in charge until the morning."

They scattered, collecting up the groups of arrows that had been brought out by the guards during the attack. Bows were unstrung and were carried back with the rest of the weapons and guardsman to the keep. Sam carried a few bundles with him to store in the armory outside when Trent ran up to him. "What happened?" His eyes were wide and wild. "They kept us inside, wouldn't tell us what was happening."

Foolish. "They attacked, as you can see." Sam walked by, but Trent turned and kept up.

Heath was in the courtyard now, laid to rest, and had been covered by a blanket. "We stopped them. For now."

"How did they do it? Was it difficult to keep them away?"

"Trent, I'm tired. No more questions, please. We'll talk about it in the morning." Trent fell back beside him, still but trailing a few feet. "

His tone had been too sharp. He should apologize.

But all he wanted to do was sleep now, and if a few harsh words had helped that, it was worth it.

"I'll see you in the morning. I can answer your questions, then."

"Goodnight." Trent walked off, back to the keep. Most of the women had gone back in, corralling their children with them. The stillness of the night was coming back as they did.

Sam returned the arrows and looked up into the night sky. Stars twinkled, wisps of clouds obscuring them as they moved across the world.

He would have no peace here.

16

FOLLY OR COWARDICE

Hands lifted the rough locking bar, pulling it out of the braces. Quietly, they moved it and set it down. A few dabs of oil on the hinges made the door as silent as it could be, but it still creaked.

The sound seemed deafening to the workers, and they held their breath. Watching, waiting, they kept going when it was clear there were none who heard it.

The portcullis was trickier. Three men worked to raise it, cloths and linens wrapped around the chain that pulled it up, but there was no way to hide it. The sound rang clear in the deep still of night.

A clap on the back, and the man was out and under in a flash. Hands worked the portcullis back down, letting it shut with a soft bang. The door was next, squeaking shut and locked in less than a minute.

The man was gone, blended into the night with a dark outfit and quiet shoes.

Yand watched from the wall, wishing they had a horse to send with him. He tracked the movement along the wall, in the shadow of the night, until the man slipped into the safety of the trees.

Their hopes rested with him.

———◆○◆———

A haze settled over the castle, creeping into the walls and sticking to the stone. Tendrils of waters dripped from protrusions.

Sam breathed in the late morning air. Wet, heavy, and filled with smoke.

"Any word?"

"Nothing so far," Sam said. Ned nodded, then took a seat next to him on the wall. His joints creaked as he settled into place, legs dangling over the edge.

"It's been three days since the last attack. I thought we'd have something else by now." Sam peered over the wall through the mist. He could just make out the line of trees. They stood as giant sentinels in a line. Sounds of construction drifted across the expanse from time to time.

"The Duke's been out to see the womenfolk," Ned said.

"Oh?" Sam shifted.

"Wants to reassure them something is going to be done. That they'll have a battalion of fighters coming any day now."

"Good news then."

"Well..." Ned turned to the makeshift shacks they had constructed. Families were huddled beneath them, waiting.

For what, no one knew.

"Captain Yand is a fierce fighter. He'll have a plan." Sam checked his bow again, still wondering how they had managed it. Another weapon in his hands.

Could he use it? Other than at practice?

Bales of hay were one thing, a human target quite another.

"How is Trent doing?"

Ned shifted and was silent for far too long. Sam cursed silently. "He's holding up."

"They beat him, don't they?"

"They call it training. Bill's convinced him of that."

Flashes of anger drifted across his vision. The fog lifted for a second, blown by a stray bit of wind, then settled back before he could get a better look at their encampment. "I want to tear him limb from limb sometimes."

"I know what you mean."

"I thought not having the pressure of construction would help, that he would ease off of us." He tightened his grip on the bow. "I was wrong."

"The Overseer protects him still." Ned shrugged. "Even with his thefts of extra rations."

"A punishable offense," Sam quoted. "Who is there to judge the law in this place?" he looked into the sky. Fog obscured the clouds.

"Not us, I'm afraid. It was never us to begin with." After a pause, Ned continued. "I'm too old for this, Sam." There was a weariness in his voice that shocked him. Sam looked to him.

"No one has asked for this."

"You're right about that. No one has. Even though I knew it might happen, I still came. A long life lived, I'm now at the end of it."

"You aren't giving up, are you?"

"Not quite yet."

"The Ned I know wouldn't give up as easy as that. There's still plenty of forest. Wood to work, things to build."

"I've spent my life building to make amends for the things I've destroyed. I thought it would make the world right again." He stood up, brushed off his pants. "It turns out all of life is vanity."

Like a knife in his heart, Sam felt the words bore into him. What kind of damaged had he done? Lives lost, lives ended.

"Is there any cause for hope?" Sam whispered the words, more to himself than anyone else.

"We all have things we're running from." Ned put a hand on his shoulder, gazed into his eyes with sad, drooping eyes, and turned. He creaked down the steps, leaving Sam alone at his watch and alone in his heart.

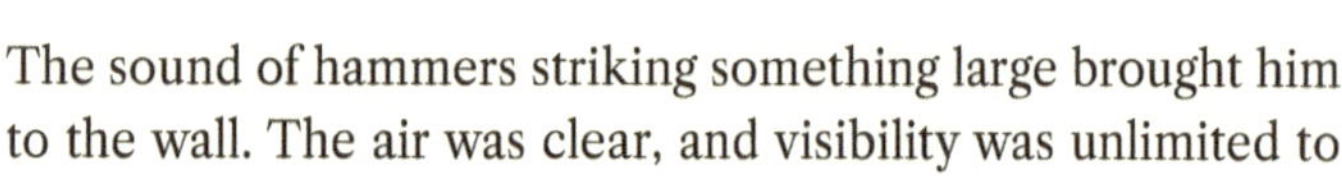

The sound of hammers striking something large brought him to the wall. The air was clear, and visibility was unlimited to the enemy encampment.

The trees were beginning to turn, gold and brown creeping in on the oaks. It was only a matter of time until autumn would come at last.

"What are they doing?" A man sidled next to him, leaning on his bow.

"Don't do that," Sam replied after a quick glance.

"Do what?"

"You'll break the bow, leaning on it like that." The man, startled, let go and stood up. Philip, if Sam recalled right.

"Sorry." Sam was probably harsher than he had right to be, but the long nights and lack of sleep was starting to get to him. The training, too, wasn't as easy as it might have been once. "So, do you know what it is?"

"A catapult." The machine was obvious, even from this far away. The spoon shaped arm, the bracing that led to wheels. They were planning on using it to take down the wall, if he had a guess.

And off to the side, somewhere hidden in the bushes or behind the trees, they had a battering ram. Of that, he was sure.

Crude lines and mismatched joints aside, the catapult looked like it would only take a few more days to be operational. After that, it was only a matter of time before they were using it to batter the walls and bring them down.

Philip sucked in a breath, then let out a low whistle. Absentmindedly, he almost leaned on the bow again, but then caught himself after a sharp look at Sam. "What are they going to do with it?"

"Throw rocks at us, more than likely. They'll be too far from our bows for us to do anything about it." Sam surveyed the courtyard again. All the building materials had been cleared to the side to make room for training.

Stacks of stone ran up against the west wall. Some were cut, others fresh from the quarry. Work had halted on the keep until the siege was over.

Crates, foodstuffs, and other supplies were around the smith, including the rest of his fuel. Their stacks of firewood were dwindling despite the rationing. It was taking a lot of it to cook the food.

That made him glance nervously at their supply of lumber. Good, hard lumber that had been seasoned more than a year already. He had seen the eyes looking at it, devouring it, thinking about burning it next.

A foul taste rose in his mouth, the more he thought about it, the sicker he was going to get.

He wanted them to keep their hands off it, to leave their hard work alone. No one was going to burn the stones of the masons for all the work they put into shaping it and cutting it. Those rocks would be like that for the next hundred years or more.

"Sounds bad," Philip said, recapturing his attention. Sam turned back to the enemy. They were pounding something in place at the back. Something with the arm, perhaps? He didn't know.

It had been too quiet this last week. No attacks, no new arrivals, nothing. They just sat there, waiting for them and pillaging the crops they had planted.

His stomach grumbled at the thought. He would give anything for a fresh chunk of venison right now.

Or a fresh vegetable.

The thought of it, fresh and cool. A cucumber, crunchy with juice dripping down his chin. He pushed the thought away. It would do no good.

"We aren't in the best of circumstances right now."

"Give it time, your Lordship. The messenger needs to get to Whitehall." The Overseer sat in front of the desk while the young Duke stood over him.

"You said it would take a week at most to get there. Surely the King would have sent word by the fastest means possible." His hair was disheveled, his shirt ruffled.

"We had no birds to send with him. We must wait for the slow word," the Overseer said, trying his best to be cool and calm, to infuse his voice with the same. A smile was plastered to his face, stuck there with pure will.

"I would advise patience as well, sire." Yand was standing with his hands behind his back, watching the Overseer carefully. His steely eyes held something behind them.

"I expect the King to send a battalion. How long would it take to get here?"

The Overseer and Captain Yand looked at each other. The Overseer clamped his mouth shut.

Yand held up his chin. "With the...turmoil in the Kingdom at present, aid might be...underwhelming."

The Duke spun on his heel. "What have you been hiding?" He leveled a glare at the fighter, one that belied his station but not his age.

"Hiding? Nothing, sire. News in the Kingdom travels fast, I thought you knew about the raiders to the east?"

"I knew about them."

"And that they have diverted the majority of the King's forces?" Silence. "That the men at arms were raised to march on them and restore peace, but they did not find easy ways?"

The Overseer cleared his throat. "I have heard the same. The brigands fight well, and hide in the hills, harnessing our forces. Rumors are that the King will ride on them himself with his own forces."

The Duke stopped, then sat in his chair. "And there will be enough left for us? To defend against a far greater threat?"

"This threat is an incursion at present, your lordship." A cloud descended on the Duke's face at those words.

"Incursion? A Duke, trapped in his own castle with no way to leave, is merely an incursion?"

"They have no reinforcements as of yet," Yand said. The Overseer breathed a quick breath of relief as the Duke turned on him.

"They kill my men and keep me locked away, is that not enough for the King to send aid?"

"I hope it is," the Overseer said, then added quickly, as the glower was lowered to him, "Belmarch is preoccupied as a whole. Some might see this as a spearhead designed to land more forces, others might see it as an opportune time to raid and pillage. We have walls to protect us, and men to man them. It is possible the raiders will leave, given enough time."

"And when would that be? When they have eaten every-thing in our fields?" Red was creeping up the Duke's neck. "When they have stripped our forests bare, destroyed our quarry? They aim to kill us and take this fortress as their own. They will march an army across and ravage our land."

The other two said nothing. Yand stared straight ahead, the Overseer was locked in his most ingratiating look.

"I can tell you don't agree." The Duke sat back, the anger falling away from him. "Speak your mind."

"We may be on our own," Yand said. "And there may be no help to be had. We should plan accordingly."

"And you, Overseer Rhys?"

"I prefer to be behind well-defended and strong walls. Men who are cautious are bound to lead long lives."

"So this is it, then?" The Duke looked from one to the other. "I must choose between folly and cowardice?"

17

CRAFTING

Sweat poured down his face, stinging his eyes and dripping off his eyebrows in distracting drops. Sam dove left, narrowly avoiding a blow, and countered with a weak attack to the left hip.

Trent saw it and shifted mid swing to twist out of the way. *Better than last time.* He followed up with a strike to the ribcage.

That blow landed and was less held back than the one before.

Groaning, Trent took another step back, kicking up dust and rock as he did. The training ground was emptier than it had been, but still reeked of sweat from the men.

Sam spat away the salty sweat. "You're learning."

"Not fast enough." Trent held his side. Sam chuckled and twisted his sword around. "Another round?"

"Not tonight." He wasn't used to this, and his muscles were telling him. The aches were less than the first few nights, but they weren't pleasant.

Trent nodded and offered a hand to take the practice sword. Sam handed it over and let him take it to the Keep.

"The lad is doing well. I wondered who was teaching him." Bill stepped out from the shadows of the lean-to far back behind the wall.

Sam turned, cursing himself for not noticing earlier. "You refuse to teach him anything, don't you?"

"We teach him enough." Bill leaned up against the wooden pole. Sam's hand instinctively clutched at his side.

At a sword not there.

He breathed, trying to calm his palpitating heart. What good would getting angry do?

Still, he had seen the bruises when Trent hadn't noticed and was taking off his shirt. Well-hidden underneath his clothes.

Not ones Sam had given him in their nightly sessions.

"There are lessons to be given," Sam said, stalking to the right. His eyes slipped over the area, looking for something to defend himself if the need arose.

"Oh, that there are." Bill grinned wickedly. "Lessons to never be forgotten indeed."

"Where are your friends now, Bill? Hiding, waiting to ambush me when the time is right?" Sam couldn't see any of them, if they were in the shadows, they were well hidden.

"Just me. Wanted to hear if the rumors were true. Seems kind of unusual that a carpenter would know how to teach a young boy swordsmanship, don't you think?"

Sam shrugged, continuing to circle. "I'm good with a blade. Must come naturally."

"I think you're hiding something."

"Aren't you?"

"Don't change the subject."

"How is it that Bill, a nobody, manages to become head stonemason building the Hornbloods a castle?" Bill's grin faded a little. "Oh yes, we can talk about rumors if you'd like. About trying to get out of places that are designed for bad people who do bad things." Sam stopped and turned his head. "Oh, how are the dungeons coming along, anyway?"

Crickets chirped in the grass. The night was dark, devoid of moonlight, but the stars shimmered in the black blanket of the sky. It was getting late, he needed to go back to his own bed.

"I suggest you stay away from me, if you know what's good for you, and focus on the problem at hand." Sam jerked a thumb behind him. "A very nasty problem that can slide a blade between your ribs before you get a chance to use that dagger hidden in your boot."

Bill pulled his left leg back. *So that was it.* "I'll remember everything you did to me."

"If that was a problem, I hope you would have a better memory. Goodnight Bill." Sam turned and walked away, going at a reasonable, uncaring pace, despite the man wielding more than a grudge behind him.

He didn't know where Bill went, probably back to his own special hut that he had his masons build, despite Sam's objections.

He, however, didn't care. He might have made things worse between them, that was true, but there were more important things to worry about than a petty feud between two men.

As he slipped through the doors, joining the rest of the sleeping forms in the great hall, he had a momentary pang of regret. How was badgering Bill supposed to make him an ally?

He undressed and slipped into the small covering they called a bed. A few men were snoring, but most were just asleep. Trent was bundled up in the corner, at least Sam thought he was.

The families had their own places now. Rough, unglamorous places to gather, but enough to keep them out of the rain and wind sheltered by the wall on one side.

Now, the great hall was filled with the bachelors, all except Bill, of course, who had his own special place of rock and stone.

That man was infuriating, and more dangerous than everyone else thought him to be.

The thought of how to handle him stayed with him, keeping him up. He stayed awake for a long time.

Sam picked over the wood, turning each piece in his hand. he looked down one edge, checking for twists and cracks. He needed a good, straight piece for this.

Finally, he found one. A thick piece of ash that smelled seasoned and was coated in a thin layer of dust. He knocked it off, then scraped a corner off to reveal the grain.

Straight, and no knots or defects he could see. It would do.

A steady drizzle of rain was coming down outside. Small holes in the ceiling let in drips, and the workshop had been arranged to account for these. Piles of wood were shifted, and buckets were placed in the worst spots. The others dripped into the dirt and made mud.

It had been a while since he had done any work here, being on a rotating shift of watching and training. He didn't know how long he could pretend anymore, and it was weighing on him.

He took the wood and split off the chunk he needed. Long, straight, about two inches thick by two inches wide. Six feet long, at least, and more than enough to do what he wanted it to do.

He prepared the cut piece, shaving off the sides and marking his width. He did the same to the other side. The plane rasped along the edge, a ribbon of broken wood flying from the end of it.

It fell with a whisper, letting out the smell of the wood like a perfume that filled the leaking workshop. The others were gone, leaving him to work alone.

Sam couldn't recall the last time he had worked alone, but he enjoyed it.

The shavings fell, then he turned it on its corner. A few more planes turned it into a flat.

Continuing with the other sides, he carved it into an octagon. He checked it after he was done. It was still straight and smooth. Ready for the lathe.

He set it up, chucking it between the jaws and wrapping around the leather cord that served as the power source.

A few pumps on the pedal got it spinning, and he lightly touched the gouge to the edge, running it along down the length.

Wood peeled off in chunks, sputtering and spraying. When they came out as whole shavings, he moved down the pole.

It took a few moves of the lathe, but eventually that octagon turned into a smooth cylinder.

A few rubs with the fine sand and it was polished, ready for the final step. It was not his act that would finish this piece, but someone else.

Sam laid it across the workbench, then stepped back. A storm raged in his mind as the gentle rain showered outside.

He was confused. He didn't know what to do or how to do it. And, worst of all, he was trapped here.

Trapped, like always. And no matter what he seemed to do, it always seemed to make things worse.

He breathed in the fresh scent of the air, then let it out. Closing his eyes, he repeated a training he had learned long ago.

Release. Breathe. Hold. Exhale.

Over and over again, until the storm settled some. *Concentrate on the breath, let everything else go.*

He thought making something would calm him, but here he was, nearly at dinnertime, and he was just as agitated.

The bell rang, breaking him out of his concentration. He took up his cloak and threw it over his shoulders, pulling the hood up to keep out the rain.

Smoke trailed from the chimney of the keep. The kitchens were working today, of that he could have no doubt.

Which meant warm food. His heart lightened a little. The past few days they were served the remains of what was left uncooked, hard breads locked away into barrels that would break your teeth and tasted about the same, and the rest of the cheeses before they were too moldy.

They had to scrape the rest off. There would be no more milk or cheese, not with the animals left outside the walls.

Sam was sure they were long gone, slaughtered to fill the bellies of the attackers.

"What's good?" He slipped in behind Ned at the back of the line.

"Mush, from what they're saying up ahead." He didn't sound lighthearted, but Sam couldn't blame him for that. Who could, in conditions like these?

"Oh, I thought it would be something else. Something mo re..."

"Cooked?" Kerien asked. Sam nodded. "We might get some bread, if the rumors are true. Martha baked some with flour ground from a mill that the masons cut for her."

"So there is a bright spot." He could remember Martha's bread. Soft, warm, fluffy on the inside and a delightful crunch on the outside, slathered with butter that melted into golden heaven.

Reality was far more different. It was gruel, ground up oats in water cooked until they were mush, and a small roll to go with it.

He pressed a thumb into his. Sam was glad it went in, not as hard as the biscuits had been, but not as soft as he remembered it.

They were good, but would have paired better with butter, or a haunch of pig.

Sam ate with the other carpenters, listening to their tales of woe and pain as he did.

"I can't seem to sleep, with all the waking up in the middle of the night to go to watch." Kerien had bags under his eyes, dark black, and they gazed with a semi-blank look.

"Sleep? My legs are so sore I can't even think about it," Trent said, rubbing them. "There's too much training and lugging stone around."

"What do you have to do that for?" Ned asked.

"Prepare for attacks. Although they keep moving the locations."

"Locations?" Something tickled the back of Sam's thought.

"Last night it was the west wall, but today they said it was the south wall."

"What are you talking about, Trent?" Kerien stared at him.

The boy looked around at them, eyes wide. "The rocks, don't you have to move them during your watch? Well, at night I mean."

"I haven't had to move rocks," Kerien said, then returned to his meal to scoop the last little bit out of his bowl.

"Neither have we," Archie said.

"They have you move piles of rocks in the night?" Sam asked.

"Yes."

"There is no reason to do that. Bill is playing with you again." Ned's expression hardened, but Kerien smiled.

"You haven't been falling for that, have you?" His eyes twinkled malevolently.

"They said..."

"Guardsman Sal didn't tell you that, did he? It was Bill, wasn't it?" Trent looked down and kicked the ground.

Somehow, this made everything Bill had done worse. Toying with a young boy, making him do useless tasks.

Sam was going to have a word with Bill about it, and he would have that word soon.

Had he known this before, the night might have turned out differently last night.

The bell rang, a voice shouting out over the noise.

Everyone went silent and listened to it. They put down their meals and rushed to their assigned areas.

By now, everyone knew where to go, unlike before. It had been chaos, with confused men running around like chickens chased by a fox.

They fell into lines, waiting as the guardsmen rushed out of the barracks, already dressed and ready for the attack.

Yand strode across the courtyard, bellowing orders. His eyes met Sam's, and then they slipped away.

"We've got another fight to take to the enemy, men. Don't let me down now."

18

THE MESSEGE

Enemy torches blazed on the horizon, arrayed in a group around the creaking and trundling catapult. They were geared up and ready to fight, with war paint and gleaming armor.

The entire castle seemed to be out on the walls, including women and children near the back. Captain Yand whispered something to the head guard, and in a few moments, the guards were chasing them down, but let the men remain.

Sam took up a perch with his carpenters, an electricity in the air that he longed to reach out and touch. The feeling of it filled him with shame, but the anticipation was too much to ignore.

"They're going to attack, aren't they?" Trent asked in a hushed whisper.

"It looks that way, boy," Ned said. The rocks were still warm from the sun, and the air shimmered slightly with the haze. Fall may have come, but the weather hadn't turned cold yet.

And it was a good thing too. Sam wasn't looking forward to the freezing rain and blizzards of winter. Not like this, not as unprepared as they were.

"They're doing something there," Kerien said, pointing. All along the wall others were saying the same thing. A buzz went up of conversation, but a quick look from Yand lowered the level to a mere whisper.

They were doing something with it. It had stopped, the men pulling it dropping the ropes to the ground and hammering in stakes to the wheels. The sound drifted across the open ground, a dull, ominous sound.

Men were moving around it now, and there was some shouting. Sam shaded his eyes with a hand and squinted, trying to make out what they were doing.

He caught them loading the bucket with something, but it was small, and he couldn't see any stones around to continue the attack.

They cranked back the arm, two men heaving at the rope until it was loaded and ready.

"Here it comes." Sam ducked down, right at the top of the crenelation. Others followed suit.

An order, and the cord pulled. The great arm swung forward, faster than Sam would have expected, and slammed into the top crosspiece with a crash.

The rock flew at them, crossing yards in the blink of an eye. It sailed over their heads, then landed in the courtyard with a soft splat.

Sam crinkled his brow. "They missed those idiots!" someone shouted down the line. A great roar of laughter went up from the defenders.

"Fools, be quiet." Yand's voice cut through it all, and the cheer died away. "Do you even see what they've done? Bring it to me."

He pointed to the missile.

A guard was down in a flash. He turned when he reached it, a look of horror on his face. "It's a head."

Gasps. Someone from inside screamed, a woman in the keep. It was taken to Yand, who covered it with a cloth.

"See what they've done! These are the men we fight, not men but demons." He raised his bloody package above his head. "Prepare to repel an attack, and realize that there is no safety in surrender."

He walked down the stairs and back into the keep. Everyone was silent until he was inside, then started talking.

"They aren't doing anything." Trent was looking at the enemy.

"This was a message, not an attack." Sam looked back at the waiting troops. There was a man out front, larger than all the others. He would have no mercy, he would give no quarter. Of that, he was now certain.

"They're saying it was Jedediah, one of the fastest guardsmen." Word came down the line, passed from man to man.

"What was he doing out of the castle? Foolish," Ned said, making the sign to ward off evil.

"Not foolish, an act of desperation." Sam breathed deep of the warm autumn air. It brought fresh scents of the forest from across the river.

"What do you mean?"

"I doubt Jedediah snuck out of the castle, which means he was let out." Sam looked back to the keep. Would they be able to hold out without help? The next messenger wasn't expected for another month, at the earliest.

Thoughts raced through Sam's mind, trying to connect everything he'd seen. The conversation around him continued, and he withdrew from it.

What will the Duke do? There they were, waiting for a response. They had no response other than arrows and words, the thick walls of the castle their only real defense.

How long would that hold against a determined enemy and tons of rock chucked through a catapult? Not long, he suspected.

"They aren't attacking, so that means they don't mean us much harm, right?" Trent asked, eyes wide.

"Did you see the head they flung over the wall? They mean us plenty of harm." Kerien pushed him. Not hard, but enough to be uncalled for.

Sam gave him a stern look. Kerien shrugged. "It was a dumb question from a dumb kid."

"Not long ago I seem to remember another dumb child," Ned said, calm. His big, bushy eyebrows lowered, but his eyes were fixed on Kerien. "Fighting each other won't help anything."

"I'm not the one causing all the problems." Kerien jerked his head back toward Bill and the masons grouped around him on the wall.

They were deep in conversation, heads bent toward Bill, nearly at the center.

The ale had gone long ago, and the foul smell that normally clung to them was replaced by simple sweat and unwashed body smell. Sam didn't like the look of them, even considering what lay outside the wall.

If there was a way to just get rid of Bill, to get him out of the castle. *No, I mustn't think like that.*

"We're trapped together here. Might as well make the best of it," Ned said. He reached for his pipe, grabbed it, but then put it back in a pocket.

There was nothing to fill it with. Not anymore. The grimace on his face told Sam all he needed to know.

The bows were out and ready, handed along the squad of men on watch. They were few and far between, and not nearly enough to equip the now fledgling army of castle workers.

"We need more arms, more bows." Sam kicked himself for just thinking of it now. "We can make them with the stock we have."

"I've never made a bow before. I wouldn't know how," Archie said.

Sam looked at Ned, who shook his head. "Only once, and it didn't go well."

"We're carpenters. We work with wood. I'm sure we can make it work."

They were all silent, even as conversation surrounded them. "Do you have anything better to do?"

That got them. Construction had halted with the siege, with no way to get supplies and no reason to continue it. Survival was more important right now than a leaky roof.

"We'll give it our best," Archie said, jutting his chin out.

Sam returned his gaze back to the invaders, watching them watch the castle in return. He wondered what they were thinking, what they were planning.

They had to have a next step, and it had to result in more bloodshed and pain. Like a thorn in his flesh, the thought bothered him, dug into him deep inside.

Why couldn't they leave us alone? He wasn't a Chathem native, but he hadn't seen any aggression to the Belmarchers on his part. No thoughts of invasion, no desire to take their lands. So why is it they did?

The big man out front turned away as the sun started to set. He had given his message, his work was done. The rest of the army turned away, except for a few lone guards, and retreated back to their camp.

Something tickled Sam's mind, like a breeze on a flag.

"What are you thinking?" Ned asked.

"I don't know yet. Meet me tomorrow morning to work on the bows. I've got something I want to look at." Sam bade them goodnight, and they dispersed like the others not on watch. They were going back to their families, if they had them, or to talk amongst themselves down below. The watchers remained ready and alert in case the attackers decided to change their minds.

The Duke's room was lit, and shadows moved along the wall. He had no doubt Yand had gone there to break the bad news to him. He didn't envy the Duke right now, with an unseasoned guard and only one true fighter in the bunch he had a series of hard decisions.

One of which was surrender.

Sam picked his way along the wall, moving around the watchers scanning their areas. To those who were friendly, he greeted, to the ones who weren't he ignored.

The latter group was made mostly of masons, poisoned by the words of Bill, no doubt.

Sam shook his head, and a few moments later was at his vantage point.

It was the eastern side of the castle, the only side that abutted anything but the forest. The Golden River flowed right below, built on the rocks that made up the bank.

It was quiet and calm. The river trickled and moved underneath that top exterior. The wall was over forty feet above it on this side, plenty of space to prevent boats from attacking and scaling the wall.

He looked down. The water wasn't directly below him, that was reserved for the rocky bank. Anything that dropped down there from this height would be crushed and shattered upon them.

But what if they could get a little farther out...

He tried to judge the distance, moving along the wall to find the shortest length of bank. It was about halfway down. The one guard assigned to this side of the castle watched him with a curious look.

A few feet, ten at most. That was all that separated them from the river.

Sam sat, dangling his legs over the side of the wall, and thought. A thin wind blew over him, ruffling his hair and bringing with it the smell of the river and forest. Leaves were starting to change on the other side, hints of brown among the green.

They were in a bad position. With no help on the way, it would only be a matter of time before the Belmarchers would reinforce their numbers. They would get the upper hand eventually, whittle away the defenders one by one if they needed to.

He would never have thought he would be in this position. Sam shook his head. A foolish lack of insight in retrospect.

But now he was here.

He imagined what he would do if he was in charge. If they gave him command tomorrow. Would he sit here, waiting to be slaughtered?

Would he just accept a head thrown over the wall, a challenge that had to be responded to?

His stomach churned thinking about it. A heron swooped low over the water, chasing its reflection upriver. One eye looked beneath the calm surface.

A second later the beak flashed, struck, and water splashed. It never broke flight, but a wriggling, struggling fish struggled in its beak.

It flew off into the gloomy twilight. Sam sat and watched until it was his turn to take the watch.

He went to the courtyard, through the ritual of guard change they had come to learn so well. A transfer of weapons, a count of the arrows. The squad leaders exchanging a few words, then they were sent to their respective section of the wall.

Sam looked over the courtyard on his way up, thinking about how they could use the slope to their advantage. The keep was finished enough to be a defensible position.

He shook his head. This wasn't his job, this wasn't his to think about. Captain Yand was in charge, and Duke Hornblood was in command. They were supposed to see the defenses, to arrange what they had to finish to stay alive.

A part of him knew that they hadn't done a good job. They had barely kept the ladder attack at bay, and a few after it, with little plan to counterattack.

He couldn't help but feel some resentment at it, that he could have done it better. A wave of fear washed over him as soon as he thought it.

He didn't know how to lead a siege, let alone defend from one.

But now he wasn't sure either one of them could either.

19

Councils and Conundrums

The Duke stared up at the emblem of his house. It was enormous, imposing.

At first he had liked it. Loved it, really. A constant reminder of where he came from and where his authority lay.

Now, however, with how things were...

"What do you mean, he came back?" A few flies buzzed around the head laying on his table. He wrinkled his nose at the smell. Decayed. Dead. At least three days, but the stench.

"That's our messenger. A guardsman, Jedediah." Captain Yand was standing at attention behind him. The Duke felt the room swirl. He could see him now, that frown, speaking in quiet tones. It would be worse than anything he had ever said.

And here he was, overseeing all of it.

He closed his eyes, not hearing what Yand was saying. It was like the moment had come and wiped away everything. The world whirled, and he stepped over to his chair, feet jerking unnaturally.

he collapsed in it. The man wasn't staring at him from this side, those cold, dead eyes looking straight into his soul.

He felt sick. His stomach rebelled. He had seen death before, but it was peaceful, quiet. Not like this.

Not like this.

"Your highness?"

"Hmm...?" The Duke turned his head, hand trembling. he pulled it back to the armrest of the chair.

"Would you like something to drink? You look a little bit pale."

"Yes. That would be..." Yand walked over to the bar and poured him a glass of the dark red. he took it with hands that betrayed his condition and pulled a deep drink.

It flooded his mouth, threatened to choke him, but he kept it down. Lukewarm, it tasted like ash before it went.

"So, what do we do now?"

"We could try another messenger, but I doubt it'd have any other outcome." Captain Yand returned to his position.

There was a small knock at the door. "It's me."

"Come in." the Duke managed to keep his voice from trembling, but the sheer willpower it took made him take a deep breath.

"I came -- " The eyes of the Overseer fell on the head, cutting him off. He rummaged around in a pocket, finally finding it, and pulled out a handkerchief, which he held daintily to his mouth. "Foul."

"We were just discussing our...guest." Yand said dryly.

"I heard rumors it was Jedediah." He got closer, then squinted. "I couldn't tell if I didn't at least suspect."

"And now we have come to it. Tell me, Overseer, what would you do were you in my shoes?"

"Cut the rations, of course."

"You wouldn't negotiate?"

The Overseer snorted, sending his belly jiggling. "You'd have more luck negotiating with a rock. The Belmarch have their foothold now, the only thing that will drive them from our soil is swords. They don't leave survivors."

"But surely, a noble of my rank would warrant some ransom?" The Duke licked his lips, then remembered his wine. He took another deep gulp.

"No, you don't understand them." The Overseer shook his head. He eyed the wine. The Duke gestured, and he poured himself a glass. "Take it away, no use keeping it in here to smell up the place."

The Duke nodded, and the Overseer summoned a servant. the head was taken out, albeit at arm's length, and with it the smell diminished.

"As I was saying. The Belmarch are raiders, not occupiers. They will try and conquer us and take the land. They don't need gold, they need food and weapons."

"Surely ransom could be paid in steel?" the Duke looked out the window. Sunlight filtered in, and dust motes danced in it. Normally, he would take pleasure in seeing it, but not today.

Not this day.

"They want our blood." The overseer squinted. "Haven't you been taught our history?"

The Duke burned red. "The Duke has taken to sporting like a fish in water," Yand said, stepping in to refill the cup of wine. "His pursuits have been athletic over almost all."

"Ah." The Overseer looked to his right, tapping his chin. "I believe this invitation to negotiate is a trap. They will try to draw us out and strike at us."

"What good would that do?" the Duke asked.

"We would be leaderless, and easier to overpower," Yand said. "Or so they assume. The Belmarch have always been warriors, and see us as weak. A people to be destroyed and murdered."

"They haven't been able to yet. And, with this castle still standing, they won't. They know that, and they'll do every-thing in their power to get us out of the way," the Overseer said.

"Penned up in here, it doesn't seem like we'd be able to stop them from crossing at all." The Duke turned and stared at the emblem again. He thought about tearing it down, casting it into the fire and seeing it devoured piece by piece.

That would give him some respite of the reminder of what a failure he was. Couldn't even call for help the right way. He shook his head.

"Archers can do some damage, but you're right," Yand conceded. "We aren't in the best position. No one suspected that the Belmarch would be able to send out an army for the rest of the year. We were wrong, and now we have to deal with the consequences."

A sudden weariness overcame him. The lack of sleep, especially the last few nights, and everything that was weighing on him caught up to him. "I grow tired of this talk. We'll ignore the attackers for now. Put more men on the walls though, I want them to think we have more than we really do."

Yand bowed slightly, then saluted. "As you wish, my Lord." He snapped to attention and marched out.

"Leave me," the Duke said, swirling his wine. He took another sip. It was bitter in his mouth, and the aftertaste lingered. It hadn't blunted the headache like he wanted. It hadn't blurred the feelings he had inside either.

He took a bigger swig, then drained the glass. "Leave me."

The Overseer murmured his pleasantries, then departed. The door shut behind him. Duke Hornblood slipped into his chair, feeling the weight of his family upon his shoulders.

The plane scraped down the billet, cutting a whisper thin shaving off. Sam grabbed it and pulled it out of the way. He checked the surface with his hand.

Smooth enough to get away with. "How's this one?"

"Only one way to tell," Ned said. "Archie, do the honors."

Although of average build, Archie held a secret in his frame. He pulled at the ends of the stock, bending it in half.

Sam winced, then looked on. Archie strained, then pushed a little more. Over half a circle's worth, and it still held. "A little stiff."

"I dare not go any thinner." A pile of broken bows had grown in the corner, kept to be reused where they could. Sam thought the best they could get out of them was pegs, but didn't share his misgivings with the others.

"A fresh set of blanks would be helpful," Ned said.

"And where, exactly, do you think we could get those? From the forest we keep hidden out back?"

Kerien sniggered at that, but a quick glance and he was silent and back at work. They hadn't told anyone what they were doing.

Yet.

Sam intended to, when the time was right. He cut in the notches for the bowstring, then rubbed it down with sand to smooth out the worst of the ridges. A few lines of twine around the middle was the best they could do for a hand rest.

A knock on the post. "Who is it?" Sam asked. He hid his bow, then motioned for the others to do the same.

"Master Smith requests your presence, Master Freeman." The voice of Issac, the older of the two blacksmith apprentices, drifted in through the canvas tarps they had put up for privacy. Rain also, but privacy first.

"I'll be there in a minute." The shadow at the door disappeared. Sam doffed his apron and hung up his tools. "Keep working. The more we get done, the better for us all."

"Will we be fletching arrows next?" Kerien asked.

"If need be." Sam ignored the hint of malice in the tone. "Ned's in charge."

He left before Ned could finish his sputtering and protests. The day was nice, not too cool, but with plenty of sunshine.

Wind from the wrong direction brought up the smell of the latrines from the bottom of the walls. It made him wrinkle his nose, but there wasn't anywhere else to put it. At least they had kept it as far away from the well as possible.

A few stretches later, Sam was off. It didn't take long to wander around to the smithy, which still had smoke coming out of his chimney.

Even the Duke had run out of that. It was to be saved for the winter, or used for other things.

Like the bows. If it didn't go well Sam would have some explaining to do. No one authorized use of the wood, and the Overseer had been clear about use of supplies.

Still, it wasn't enough to dampen his spirits, as high as they could be considering the conditions, and he slipped under the roof and into the heat of the smithy.

Greetings were exchanged. Dale put up his tools and apron. "Boys, give us a moment. Take a break up on the wall, if you will."

When the apprentices were gone Dale pulled up a stool for Sam and patted it. "I've done what you asked for. Can't say I'm the best weapon smith around, but it came out decent enough."

He went over to the storage area and pulled out a cloth covered package, the pole Sam had turned sticking out the other end.

A few moments later the cloth was off, and Sam's heart gave a sudden skip of a beat. Dale put it on the table.

It gleamed in the light of the forge, casting rays of yellow and red. The longer he stared, the more it looked like it was on fire.

"Go ahead." Sam reached out at the permission. "I had them polish it to a fine shine."

"You didn't have to do that."

Dale shrugged. "There isn't much else to do. Besides, it takes no fuel."

Like everything else, that too was running out. Wood for the forge, wood for the cook fires. But not enough wood to finish the castle.

"How long do you think it will last?" Sam asked, running his hand along the wooden shaft. He touched the edge of the blade, being careful not to cut himself, then used it to shave off a few hairs on his arm.

They fell, parted as easily as a sharp chisel cuts through pine. He dare not touch the metal again.

"I don't know. Until the end, I expect." Dale crossed his burly arms. "I came here knowing the Belmarch were close. Close enough to kill me."

"You wanted them to come, didn't you?"

"You don't know them like we do, Sam. You haven't seen what they can do." Sam looked up, staring into those haunted eyes. He had always wondered what drove the big man to do what he did.

"Let's hope it doesn't come to that."

"What is your story?" the question took Sam by surprise. He wrapped the spear back up and set it back on the workbench. "We all know you came from somewhere, but never talk about it. Was it the south? Or east?"

"I'd rather not talk about it. That life is gone. That man is dead."

"If that man could help us, maybe it's time to resurrect him." Dale never had been a delicate person. That was something Sam liked about him, how blunt he was. Ore, metal, human. It was all just to hammer into place as needed.

"Thank you for this." Sam wondered why he had done it. The cool, unyielding metal. The warm, hard wood. Why make such a weapon now?

"I hope you'll use it well."

"It isn't for me." Dale eyed him, but could sense the rift that would open if he kept pushing and decided not to ask.

"Consider it a favor for now."

"Am I going to regret it?"

"That depends on how you feel. I haven't decided what to ask in return, but I will ask something."

Sam dipped his head. "Then, whatever it is, when the day comes, I intend to pay it."

20

STICKS AND STONES

Monotony. Day after day, the same. The days grew shorter and the air cooler, and still the Belmarch camped and watched.

Sam almost wished something would happen. They were going to starve them. He wondered what they were thinking, why they hadn't even used the catapult.

It was on the seventh day that he finally found out why.

"They give you seven days to surrender. That's what I heard," Ned told him. They were up on the wall, the brisk autumn breeze chilling him beneath his thin coat.

"What happens if you give up?" Sam saw his breath puff out in white, then caught away. It was early in the morning, and the sun would soon be strong enough to warm them.

Across the field the Belmarch were preparing the catapult for action, or so it appeared. They had found chunks of rock, probably from the quarry, and had stacked up a pile high enough to bring down three castles combined.

"They kill you anyway, but lose less men." Ned was cold, staring at them.

Sam felt the words enter him and dive deep into his soul. What kind of men would do that?

He was starting to suspect he knew. They weren't too different from some men from his past.

And yet, they were. Every day he expected there to be more troops, and every day he was surprised to see about the same number patrolling around the walls.

They were going to try and take them with a force of less than a hundred, and they might do it too.

A few hours after dawn the rocks started to fly. The first one Sam watched get loaded into the catapult, aimed at the gate, then loosed.

It rushed through the air. Men shouted to get down, and it smashed into the wall to the right of the gate.

Sam felt the wall vibrate beneath his feet. His heart was pounding as he watched them load another. The rock they had thrown settled in the field between them.

The cold was forgotten as another came rushing at them. Even though he was well out of the way, he still felt anxious when they came.

The third rock skipped over the top of the wall, almost hitting a man who dove out of the way just in time. It spun and dropped into the courtyard.

Women screamed, clutching at the children and pulling them out of the way. They left everything, the wash, the food, the chores, and ran inside.

Yand was up on the wall now, watching everything transpire. His presence settled the guards and the workers, and he seemed to have no fear of being hit.

"Let them throw their rocks," he said, watching as another bounced off the wall. "These walls are strong, they will hold."

The attack continued through the rest of the day. They were using the leftover rocks from the quarry, of that Sam found out from the conversation of a few masons. They would have more than enough to keep it up.

"How did they get them here?" Sam asked. He took a swig from his water skin, grateful for the warm air.

"I haven't seen a cart or horse anywhere," the man said. It was one of the younger guardsmen, Al, if he remembered right. "Come to think of it, I haven't seen them move them either.

Sam looked harder and saw them moving rocks by hand in the evening twilight. They stopped the attack at night. He guessed it was too dark to see anything.

Before they did, he managed to get a good look at the wall. For the most part, it seemed fine. There were a few chunks missing here and there, and one crenelation now lying in the surrounding field.

Rocks were scattered everywhere, like they didn't know what to aim at. They tried everywhere along the wall, and Sam wondered if they were looking for a weak point.

The gate, however, was unharmed. It had been hit once, but nothing after that. He went down after his watch was fished to check it.

The wood was still solid, still strong. He couldn't see anything wrong with the locking beam, and the braces that held it in place were undisturbed.

"What do you think?" Ned asked, walking up behind him.

"I'm not sure. Why wouldn't they attack the gate?" Ned shrugged at his question.

"They don't want to break it?"

"I thought that would be the point of attacking it."

"They aren't too smart. My guess is that they think it will help them to keep it intact."

Sam realized what they were doing now. "This isn't just an attack to kill us. They want the castle for their own."

Ned cocked his head to one side. "They want to take it over?"

"Yes. They want to use it as a stronghold, an entry point for an invasion, I'm sure of it."

"You should tell the Overseer then. I'm sure he hasn't thought of it, with how un-curious he is."

Sam ran his hand along the rough wood. He had helped build this, it was one of the first tasks he had been assigned when he arrived.

That had been long ago now, it seemed like ages. Despite the change in circumstances, he still felt a distance between him and the Overseer.

"It's just a guess. I don't think it's worth mentioning." Ned looked at him oddly, a cold, searching gaze.

"It wouldn't hurt to tell him."

"Not tonight," Sam demurred. "Maybe in the morning. I feel the day." He yawned, somewhat surprised to feel like he was telling the truth.

How easily lies and deceit seemed to come to him lately.

"Goodnight Ned, I'll see you tomorrow."

"Give it a thought Sam." They shook hands. Ned went to the wall and a long night watch, and Sam went back to the keep.

But it wasn't to sleep, as much as he wished to. Trent was there, waiting for him with practice swords in hand.

Sam took his, after exchanging greetings, and swung it around. "Ready?"

"Yes."

Trent did better than he had in the past, even to the point where Sam had to try and put up a defense to keep away from getting hit by the practice sword.

He was sweating and breathing hard after a few rounds, the chilly night air a welcome refreshment against his skin when they stopped to rest.

The air was clear, but it smelled of refuse and human waste that had built up in the corner near the wall. There wasn't a better place to put it, something they hadn't thought about during the construction of the castle.

Sam caught his breath between bouts, wiping the sweat from his brow. Moonlight glittered against the facets of the wall, splintered by the rough rock surface.

"Has it got any better?" Sam asked when they had finished. "We'll go again tomorrow, I need some rest."

Trent nodded and took the practice sword. He hung around. "You can tell me what's going on."

"What can you do about it?" There was a harshness to his tone, one that surprised Sam.

He was about to reply when he stopped to think about it. What could he do? Ask Bill nicely to stop? Tell the Overseer who already hated him and couldn't stand him? Or go straight to Yand, or even better, the Duke, to put his foot down?

Better to keep his mouth shut than make it worse. But here was Trent, downcast and hating him, and he was right.

Sam searched for the right words, but came up short. "Try your best and that's the best you can do." It was hollow, and he knew it.

He regretted it as soon as it had come out of his mouth.

The chill of the night, now that they weren't moving anymore, had crept into his bones. Winter would come soon, and cold. Cold enough to take away his strength and leave him with nothing.

"May I go now?"

"Tomorrow. We'll meet again tomorrow. Good night, Trent." Trent mumbled something that could have been good night, then was off.

What were they doing to him? Threatening him if he talked to anyone else? He wouldn't put it past Bill, not in the least.

Sam balled up his fists and thrust them down to his sides. He felt the anger, and the thing that he had long since tried to erase at the back of his mind.

It was there, waiting for him to get complacent. To take over when he thought nothing else could make him lose control.

Picturing Bill's face in his mind, he almost did. He looked back to the lean-tos, expecting him.

It was empty. As still as the night. A guard shuffled on the wall above, just out of sight. Here, in the corner of the keep, they were as hidden as anywhere else.

He fought it down. Bit by bit it went away. He tried to relax, to picture himself in the river, drifting and floating with the current instead of fighting against it like the rage he felt.

Deep breaths helped. Slowly, it retreated.

How he longed to be gone from here, from the reminders of a past best left forgotten. He retreated into the keep, out of the wind and warm enough with the bodies of everyone else to banish the autumn chill.

Helpless and a bit hopeless, Sam turned in for the night.

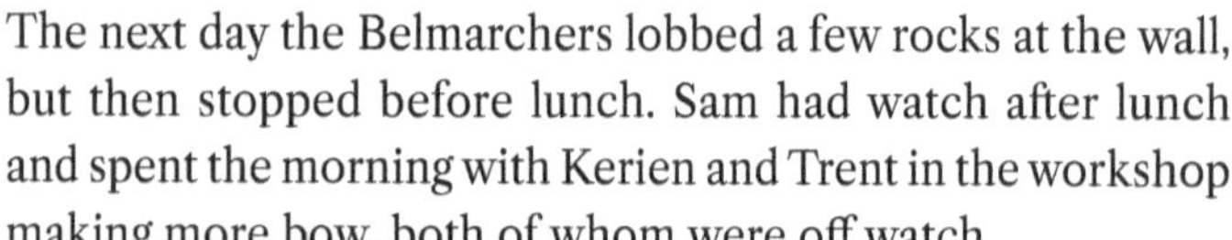

The next day the Belmarchers lobbed a few rocks at the wall, but then stopped before lunch. Sam had watch after lunch and spent the morning with Kerien and Trent in the workshop making more bow, both of whom were off watch.

It didn't go as well as he hoped. The first few bows they made had been fine looking, but after a few shots some of them had cracked and broke.

"Another failure, yet again." Kerien tossed aside his work in progress, too thin to be of any use.

Sam looked up from his, taking light cuts with a chisel around the end where the string would go. He had heard the crack but was too busy to look up then. "Try again."

"I've been trying all day, and all week." Kerien scowled, then crossed his arms. "What good are a few extra bows going to do us, anyway?"

Sam felt along the edge, took another cut, then felt again. It was smooth now, wouldn't cut through the bowstring. He blew off the shavings, then rubbed it with sand. "It isn't what we finish with, it's how we survive. A few extra well placed arrows could help with that."

"So then we should be making arrows."

"If you'd like to try your hand at it, go ahead." A spark of an idea grew inside his mind. "If you're up to it, that is."

"You don't think I can do it." Kerien looked at him with narrow eyes.

"Can you?" Trent asked. His face and voice betrayed a genuine interest, and it was the most alive Sam had seen it in weeks. What scars was the boy hiding underneath that facade?

"I bet I can. It can't be that hard." All of a sudden Kerien's confidence wavered.

"Try splitting first, then the lathe," Sam said. He had seen the young man eying it off to the side.

"Do we have feathers?"

"I saw the children playing with some. Archer took down a few crows flying by." His mouth watered at the thought of the meat, but alas, it was taken into the keep. To the Overseer, no doubt, or the guards if they saw it.

His stomach grumbled remembering the stuffed goose they would have at the new year back home. Moist, succulent, bursting with flavor and covered with dried berries saved from the last summer harvests and piping hot potatoes covered in butter.

Sam ground down on his teeth, banishing the thought. With the reduced rations everyone was hungry, and the reminder made him conscious of the other's need too.

"There's some twine in the supplies. You might be able to use it to tie them on."

"I'm going to do it. You'll see." Sam was glad to hear it. There was something for him to do, and less complaining too. It had started to grate on him, and he knew it bothered the others.

But with so little work and so much anticipation of attack, how else was Kerien supposed to feel?

Kerien took up a stick long enough to get a few arrows out of, then cut it to length. Sam considered asking Dale to make a few arrowheads, then pulled himself back.

There wasn't any guarantee this was going to work. They weren't fetchers and bowyers, they were carpenters.

But Kerien had taken up the challenge, and even Sam perked up at the thought. He didn't know who kept count of the arrows, but he doubted they had enough to fend off an army.

And adding more to that number couldn't hurt any.

Sam watched and looked on as Kerien split the log in half, then halves again. Soon he had a pile of shafts, not quite ready to be made into arrows.

Somehow, just having them lifted Sam's spirits. Perhaps, just maybe, they could find a way out of this siege if they worked together.

21

A Meeting in the Night

The arrows turned out to be easier to make than he thought. Soon they had a bundle of crow-feather attached headless arrows waiting for something to attach to the top.

"Impressive," Ned said, fingering one. He pulled on the feather to see how well it was attached. It held, even with some substantial force. "How many do you think we will need?"

"Far too many for us to make. I overheard some guards talking about how they feared they would run out and there would be nothing left to stop the Belmarch." Sam sighted down one. There was a slight bend, but not too much.

"I've got to go on watch, will you keep working on these?" Sam put the arrow back in the pile. "And don't spread the word. I've asked Kerien not to as well..."

"Say no more." Ned clapped a hand on his back. "We'll take care of what we can."

Sam stroked his beard, now full and long, and thought about a good shave with warm water. How the blade would part the hairs and leave his chin cool, feeling the breeze once again.

The same breeze blew through the workshop, and he was suddenly grateful for the beard again. "Winter's coming too fast."

"We'll manage." Sam didn't see how, with the weak coats and poor coverings they had and no way to get more.

"Sam Freeman," said a voice from behind him. Sam turned.

"What is it?"

"Will you come with me, please?" There wasn't much confidence in his voice, and after Sam exchanged a glance with Ned, turned and followed.

"What is this about?"

"They need to see you."

"Who?" The guard pursed his lips, but kept on walking. A dozen reasons rushed through his head, but Sam pushed them all away.

Better to find out than to make it worse than it had to be.

"I'll find out then." Sam followed the man through the keep and down the side passage to a familiar door.

The guard knocked once, and a voice bade them enter.

Inside was like a different world, with the scent of filth and the outside replaced with rug and wine. The Duke sat in his chair, the imposing crest above his head hanging as a constant reminder of who was in charge.

The guard shoved him forward into the room and Sam stumbled. He caught himself and bowed before the Duke.

Captain Yand was in the corner of the room, standing next to an empty fireplace.

"Sam, may I call you Sam?" The Duke was smiling, his face young and handsome, but strained. These past few weeks had not been easy on him, and it showed.

"Certainly, Sire."

"Captain Yand told me of your quick thinking and you action that led to the repulsion of the Belmarchers."

"It was nothing that any other would have done." Sam bowed his head and dropped his gaze to the floor. Surely there was something else to this summons. That was days, weeks ago. Why bring it up now?

"You showed real courage, if what I hear is true. However..." The Duke tapped on his desk. "You seem to be holding something back, not giving your all, should we say?"

Sam's mouth dried up. How much did he know?

"I want to change that, and I'll need your help. Would you care for some wine?" The Duke nodded and a servant poured a glass. With a quick movement across the room, it was offered and placed in Sam's hand.

He stared at it. How long had it been since he had a good glass of wine? Before he came here, of that he was certain.

It was dark red and smelled wonderful. He caught hints of honey in with the grape, fermented at the peak of the harvest with the juice as plentiful as it could be.

What was happening? Why was he being called here?

"May I speak freely?" Sam asked.

"Go ahead."

"What is it you want of me?"

"What is it I want?" The Duke stood up. He was in full regalia, including a cape. "I want from you what I want from every one of my subjects. To obey my commands and provide the very best they can."

"I understand, Sire. That I have done since the moment I arrived here."

"I've been told of your handiwork, but there are other talents that you have that you have been hiding, isn't that right?"

Sam didn't know what to say. It wasn't right, not anymore. But he couldn't say that, not after training Trent. There would be no truth in it.

He was caught, like a fish in a barrel. Now all they had to do was throw in the spear and run him through.

"Is there anything you would like to share with us?" Yand asked, moving away from the fireplace and circling Sam.

Sam took a drink of the wine, and it flowed to the back of his throat. It was good, some of the best he'd ever tasted. Mellow and smooth, with a hint of oak and an aftertaste of honey just like it smelled.

"We are in a siege, with the chances of us walking away low," Yand said. He went behind the desk and stood next to the

Duke. "Anything that could help would be your responsibility to provide."

"He speaks the truth," the Duke said.

"I swore off that life a long time ago," Sam managed to choke out, his voice cracking. "I'm afraid I'm of no use."

"At least train the men, give them a fighting chance."

Sam shook his head. "I was never that good. Never at the level you are, Captain."

"You don't seem to see the seriousness of the situation." Sam raised his gaze and locked eyes with the Duke. "This isn't a game that you can walk away from if the turn doesn't go your way. There are men out here that need you, that rely on you to survive. Are you just going to walk away from them like they don't exist?"

"I'll do everything I can to help them." Sam unclenched his fist. "Everything I can, not everything you ask." He set the glass of wine down. It didn't feel right with what everyone else had to eat and drink.

Here he was, warm and enjoying something he hadn't had in months, and everyone else was out in the cold, shivering. They were on the walls, they were keeping watch.

Something stirred within him, itching to break free. The thing he feared the most. Coiled, lying in wait. They were calling to it, they were trying to wake it up.

And he had to keep it asleep.

"I can build for you. Give me the men and we'll make something they'll regret invading every step they take within these walls." Sam looked up. The Duke's eyes were widened, and his mouth parted slightly. Captain Yand stared at him. "I can't fight for you, but I can do this."

Duke Hornblood looked to Yand, who came up beside him. The two talked in hushed tones, too soft for him to hear. Yand frowned, but turned to Sam.

"What did you have in mind?"

The Overseer was brought into the room, summoned by a servant, and despite his hesitancy, they planned.

It took hours, poring over the rough maps and schematics of the castle. Sam mustered all his knowledge, all his experience, but still could only think of things to build.

He would need the others to put the plan into action. And one of those was Bill.

"It would be better if you approached Bill," Sam said, turning to Overseer Rhys to broach the topic. He had remained cool toward him the whole time, only responding to Yand and the Duke.

"I suggest if you need something done about your problems, you handle it yourself." The Overseer looked down his nose at him, voice filled with ice.

Sam took a deep breath. There was no sense in getting mad at a man who could throw you in chains at the second he was provoked. He doubted even the Duke would try to contradict an order like that. "I understand, sir. Is there anything you suggest I do to... repair our relationship?"

"I suggest you own up for your past mistakes. You cost this project time and resources, and money, by your inability to plan ahead and complete what you were responsible for. We never had a problem when Luca was in charge."

He wanted to remind the Overseer they had about four more carpenters before they were all killed by the Rotting Sickness, but that too would have helped nothing.

"I've taken full accountability for when we have failed, but I'll not take that responsibility for someone else."

"Do you mean to call me a liar?" The Overseer's eyes were bulging now, his great cheeks puffed up with air. Hot air.

"Gentlemen," Yand warned. His voice carried the weight of command with it, and what he could do to back it up. "Why don't we call it a night and meet in the morning? I could use a good night's sleep."

"Good idea," the Duke said, cutting off the Overseer. "Sam, please leave us."

Sam stood and saluted, then walked for the door. He hazarded one last glance in the room. The Overseer was seething, and his heart dropped, but was that a hint of a smile on Yand's face?

He shut the door behind him. His mind was buzzing from the night and the ideas with even more percolating up.

He thought about going to sleep, but then realized he would be up in another hour or so for watch anyway, and wandered out of the keep and into the courtyard.

The night was calm, the sentries on the wall walking a now well-known route around the perimeter. Sam went to the workshop and looked over the supplies, running his hand over the raw wood to feel its roughness.

His mind wandered to the spear hidden in the corner of the workshop, covered in clutter and not forgotten. Why had he hidden it there, amongst broken projects and broken tools?

And what was it for, if not to give to one of the others. It would be a powerful weapon in Captain Yand's hands, and the other guards would benefit from it as well.

But he hadn't given it to them. Not when it was finished, not days after. He had hidden it here.

For what purpose? Sam brooded on it, couldn't escape it, until the watch bell rang and it was his time to go back up onto the wall.

Throughout the night, as his energy drained away and frustration and exhaustion started to take him, Sam wondered and fought himself.

"What do you think?" The Duke rubbed his temples, the weight settling there. It helped, a little.

"A man who did what he did is either a fool or brave. Like I said before, he is no fool." A servant took away the glasses to wash. Duke Hornblood looked to the fireplace, wishing they had enough wood to make it burn cheerfully. The stone walls sucked the heat from the room in the night, robbing him of the little comfort he had left. Even the tapestries didn't help much.

"I often wonder if I'll ever live up to the expectations of my father, let alone the rest of the family." The words felt strange, but he needed to speak them. There was no one else to share them with, not now. He had no peers in this place. He was utterly and irrefutably alone.

Yand listened and kept his face blank. He had always been respectful that way, never giving any indication of what Duke Hornblood had meant to him.

"I thought this...assignment was going to be the one that finally let him see that his son wasn't a worthless dandy." He smiled ruefully, and stared up at the crest. The urge to tear it down was even stronger now, and he clasped his hands behind him, fingernails digging painfully into his skin.

It was a feeling, though. One not washed in wine or liquor.

"You are no dandy, and you are far from worthless."

"Kind words, Yand, but I'm afraid you aren't the liar you make out to be." He could see it on his face, plastered all over it. Empty words. Like his empty name. "Now I'm afraid I'll always be the son who lost the castle before it was even finished."

He couldn't stand it anymore and swept up the glass, downing the wine in one long gulp. "I'd like to be alone now."

Yand snapped to attention, saluted, and was out the door in a second, leaving the Duke to nurse his cups in the dying candlelight.

22

KEEP YOUR ENEMIES CLOSE

The arrows clattered onto the table. "Can you help us out with these?"

Dale picked up the top arrow, examining the end of it. "Looks like it isn't going to work very well." He held up the headless end.

"Funny." Sam crossed his arms. Dale was grinning from ear to ear and holding in great guffaws. "You didn't answer my question, though."

"I can help. We've got the iron, but I'm worried about the fuel."

"What do you have to do besides this?"

Dale shook his head, smile fading away. "The Duke has me making swords. I'm not a weapon smith, and the spear was hard enough, but I've only been able to make three in the last week."

"Three is better than nothing." The smoke of the forge, smaller than usual but still billowing, drifted through the air. Drips of water fell from the eaves, plopping down into the puddles fresh from the rain.

"Has Bill been by here?" He didn't know why it popped into his brain, but it was out before Dale could answer his question. That made the last of his smile disappear.

"I try to make it clear this isn't a good place for him. He hasn't been by in some time." He dropped the headless arrow back into the stack. "I'll see what we can do about these, in between swords. Arrows would be better anyway."

"I don't know which was better; Bill with all the ale he could drink, or Bill with none of it."

"He's a vicious one. Wiry, but strong. The drink softened him, if he was in the right mood." The thought of it made Sam remember times he wasn't in the right mood.

"I need a way to get him to come around to me."

Dale snorted. "Easier to get a mule to follow your commands, without a thick stick for prodding."

"I'm at an impasse. I don't know how to handle him and neither does anyone else."

"He's afraid of you."

Sam furrowed his brow. "Bill isn't afraid of me. He's afraid of you, not me."

"Not in the same way. He's afraid of me because of these." Dale held up a bulky arm. "There's something else in you that makes him afraid."

Afraid? Of me? He thought back on their interactions about the emotions Bill displayed. He thought it had been disgust, jealousy maybe. Not that he had anything to be jealous of. *But fear?*

Never.

"If he was afraid of me, he wouldn't be doing what he is to Trent."

"I've heard the rumors. Are they true?" Sam nodded. Dale rubbed his chin, his lips tightening. "What a fool. You have your work cut out for you then, and I'm not sure I'll be of much use."

"Well, if you can think of anything I'll be all ears." Sam looked out to the courtyard. "Rain's let up, I need to go." A stone smashed into the wall, and Sam sighed. "They've started again."

"Better get to it." They clasped hands, then Sam turned.

It was time to pay a visit, one he had been putting off for days.

The shack was bigger than the others, made with the best stones and solid. No wind would get through those walls, only the roof was a weak point.

Sam stood for a second, gathering his wits, and knocked. Shuffling from inside, then it opened.

A whiff of something strange came out of the open crack. Sam couldn't put a finger on what it was, but it wasn't unpleasant.

"What do you want? Come to beg for your apprentice?"

"I came to talk, nothing more."

Bill eyed him. He was leaner than he had been, not gaunt, but wiry. It was in his cheeks.

The shack was well furnished, with a bed and a table, and even two chairs. How he had found these, Sam was baffled. Bill was nothing if not resourceful.

"Come in." Bill opened the door. He was alone, for once.

"Thank you." *Now, how to start?* Bill took a seat, but didn't offer him one. "How long do you think we'll last, divided like we are?"

His eyes narrowed. *Good, he was thinking for once.* That was unkind, but Sam felt some unhealthy satisfaction in the thought.

"I aim to stay alive for a few more decades or so." Bill put a hand on the table, but kept the other one beneath it. Sam took note of it.

"May I?" Sam gestured to the open chair. Standing above would be no use, they needed to be on the same level, see eye to eye. Bill nodded after a pregnant pause. Just enough to be impolite. "I know we've had our differences, and I haven't always taken the time to find out why. I want to change that now."

"Very noble of you." It was dripping with sarcasm.

Sam took a seat, put both hands palm up on the table. "As a gesture of goodwill, I will start by admitting something you've suspected but haven't been able to confirm."

Bill leaned in, ever so slightly, but his lips stayed tight.

"With your permission, of course," Sam said.

"Go on."

"I'm not from Chathem. I can pass off easily enough, I have some distant blood on one side of my family, but my homeland is Unarcia."

"I suspected you weren't from around here. Lying about your heritage, what else have you been hiding?"

"Never lied about it, and you know it. Refusing to talk about it I can be accused of, of that I'll admit, and evading any question on the subject. That is fair, but not lying."

"I don't see the distinction."

"You might not," Sam said. "I left a life behind, one I had grown tired of after years. I came to Chathem to make a new life for myself and escape war and death." Flashes of battle, and it pained him to remember. Sam shut his eyes and took a deep breath, banishing it to the far reaches of his mind.

"Why did you run? Cowardice?" There was always a dig, a little knife in the words. He knew it was to set him off guard, to roil his emotions. It was working, but Sam had to stop it.

What had Ned said? That we all have things we're running from. Something changed in Sam's mind, he realized that Bill would be the same.

What was he running from? What life had he left behind? That explained the rough words, the sharp jabs.

Knowing that changed everything. The creases in Bill's eyes didn't mean he was angry with Sam, he was angry with himself.

Sam was the conduit, Sam was the element that brought it out.

"You run from your past, just as fast as I run from mine." Bill's eyes widened, just a hair. His lips snapped shut. "You've done violence, haven't you?"

"You don't know anything about me," Bill growled, setting his head down.

"Then tell me. What am I missing? Were you a brigand, a thief perhaps?" A reaction rippled across Bill's face. *So that was it.* "You've killed, I can see it in your eyes. It pains you."

Bill's mouth wriggled and fought. It opened, then closed again.

"Whatever you've done, I don't care." There was a power in knowing. "You may kill again, for a good cause. You might do violence again, for the weak and helpless. You might change." Were those words for Bill?

He looked away. "You don't know what kind of life I've live," Bill said. The fight had gone out of his tone. It was warm in the room, from their bodies and the heat of the sun warming the stone walls. The table was smooth from years of use.

"Perhaps we have a common enemy, one willing to cut off our heads and throw them over walls without blinking an eye." Sam pressed, leaning forward. "Perhaps we've known each other a few years, and that we have more in common than we think. Perhaps we learn to set aside our differences and fight together."

"I don't trust that you'd fight. You'd turn and run at the first sign of trouble."

"You know that's not true, and I don't think you would either." Bill's shoulders drooped. "I've killed men too, Bill." His eyes snapped to Sam's. "I can't change that fact, and it haunts me to this day."

The eyes. Remembering the eyes haunted him. The fear, the hate, the terror. Seeing the life drain out of them like water from a cracked jug.

It came over him now, caressing the thing deep inside. For there was another fear, another thing he was hiding. That was a secret he could tell no man.

It would go with him to his grave.

Bill's eyes showed his emotions, what he was thinking. Every flicker, every blink. Sam could read it all, could feel it just as bill felt.

"I...I've done things. I'm not proud of them."

"Look at what you've built here. Great walls that keep us safe, a castle to protect us from enemies. That is no mean feat, not done of a little man."

"I'd like you to leave now." Bill cast his gaze to the ground. Outside, a bird chirped. Sam's heart sank. He had been so close. He tried to think of words that would finish what he started. None came.

There would be no reconciliation, no putting away of things better left behind.

Sam stood. "I'll leave, but just remember what I said."

Bill said nothing. Didn't move, didn't even look at Sam.

There was nothing left to say. Sam turned and left, shutting the door on Bill. He wondered, as he walked away, if it was forever.

Stone scraped on iron. Again and again, Sam dragged the chisel across the sharpening stone. The pungent oil, soaked into the stone, kept the temper of the chisel as he cut fine shavings away from the blade.

He thought as he sharpened, letting his mind wander and his hands work free of thought. Scrape. The lantern shivered, caught by a gust of wind blowing through the workshop.

Scrape. The iron was cold in his hands. Scrape. *What to do?*

The first lesson he had learned as an apprentice was to sharpen the tools. Hour after hour, he sat at the sharpening stone. He sharpened until his hands blistered and his fingers stung, stained black from the iron.

He had taken to it surprisingly well, making his master pleased. He didn't tell him why at the time, but these weren't the only blades he had sharpened.

Sam tested the bevel. Flat, straight. Not like the situation he was in right now. If only things would be so easy as this in real life.

He looked to the sky then, the clouds of a fall rain rumbling on the horizon. There was an electricity in the air, sparks from the foretelling of lightning, and the air was thick with the smell of rain.

Back to the spear. It haunted him, followed him.

He had no wish to use that blade, to bring out the thing inside him, but what choice did he have?

Sam sucked in a breath, then let it out. "Control yourself, control the blade." That was the second lesson his master had taught him. He hadn't forgotten it all these years later.

He could burn it. Cast it into the fire and let his desires be devoured once and for all. Sam shook his head. *It would do no good, it would still follow me.*

That only left one option. To use it.

The chisel was sharp now, and a few tests on the end grain of an old chunk of gnarly oak yielded clean, fresh shavings and no tear out.

He returned the chisel to the leather bundle, joining its brothers all in a row. Each one was razor sharp, ready for use.

To build. That was who he was now. A creator, not a de-stroyer. He was here to build, to make, to improve.

So why did it have to be so hard? He tied the smooth, leather thong that captured the roll and set the tools back beneath the bench.

There was no stalling now. Thunder rolled through the workshop, the first drops falling on the thatch roof and dust outside. They puffed up small clouds of dust that were driven down by the next drop.

Sam looked back and walked out into the rain, letting the cold pinpricks fall on his head and shoulders.

The warning bell rang out, cries accompanying it. They were attacking again.

23

SURPRISES AT THE GATE

Men rushed to the gate, and Sam was not far behind. His heart was racing, and he took a bow from the stack, noting it was one of theirs. How had it gotten here?

"How long?" he asked, crouching down beside Ned. A crash of stone slammed into the wall.

"Not long." He winced as, a few seconds later, an arrow clattered against the wall. Sam took a quick peek as Ned nocked an arrow.

They were assembled into rows, and Sam wasn't sure it was the same amount. Had they had reinforcements arrive?

"Who saw them?"

"The western watch." Sam handed him another arrow. The feathers brushed his hands. Ned stood up and pulled back. A few seconds later, he dropped back down. "Too far."

"On the eastern flank!" A guard shouted out from that side. "Ladders are coming."

Another rock smashed into the wall, breaking off a crenelation and falling into the courtyard with a smash.

The sun was out, and the day was warm. The chill of the morning was still in the stone, though, and it bit his unprotected hands.

They were prepared this time, with long sticks that mirrored his first set. They could try and use the ladders again, but it wouldn't turn out well for them.

Sam doubted they would, or that if they did, it was the only thing they would do. Whatever the Belmarchers had done in the past, they learned well.

They were covering their advance with arrows, poorly placed but enough to make the guards on the wall duck down and keep their cover.

It was stupid. They had a better firing position from up here, but it wasn't his place to try and urge them to fight.

Deep inside the thing was growling, forcing him to act. He fought desperately to keep it calm. Sam squeezed his eyes shut.

The sound of the enemy approaching broke through his defenses. There was an energy in the air. This wasn't a feint, a move designed to distract them and wear them down. Hour after hour could pass that way.

This was something entirely altogether different.

"How long do you think it will take for them to retreat again?" Kerien ran up, ducking down behind him. Sam looked him in the eye.

"They won't."

Kerien's grin faded, but Sam couldn't bear to see it. He returned his gaze to the field.

He saw it before the others. Before he heard the creak of the wheels, before he smelled the fresh pine and oak it was made from.

"Battering ram!" The cry went out up and down the wall, punctuated by another rock from the catapult.

"That won't work, will it?" Kerien peered over the wall, then looked back to Sam and Ned. "Will it?"

They were firing the catapult strategically, aiming at the largest clusters of men on the walls. "They've been practicing on us."

That was what all those rocks were for, now scattered throughout the fields of the walls.

"Incoming," Ned said. They ducked down, the rock smashing against the wall just below them. It shuddered beneath their feet, and the crenelation shifted perceptibly.

"Spread out," Sam said.

The guardsmen were up on the wall in force now, and each of the squad leaders was assembling their men at the assigned locations. Ned and Kerien were pulled away, leaving Sam with the rest of his squad.

"Hold your arrows," Matthew said. He was shaking, not cut out for this level of fighting. "Orders are to fire when given the command." His voice was filled with uncertainty, but Sam stood behind him.

"When given the order, make it count." Matthew looked relieved, almost glad. Sam felt sorry for him and wondered if he would live the rest of the day.

He had made it this far, there was always hope. He seemed to be a firm guard on his own, it was the leadership that changed him.

Even now, he looked back at Yand in the guardhouse atop the gate, who was busy giving orders and stoking the fires.

The battering ram was trundling up the road. Few rocks were blocking its way, and the covered roof was protecting the enemy pushing it.

It looked wet. Sam frowned. They had soaked it in water, of that he was sure. Clever. That would stop fire from reaching it.

He glanced at the oak.

It was only a matter of time now. The creak of the wheels rose from its steady progress, men chanting and keeping time within. He couldn't make out their words and didn't want to.

"We need to brace the gate." Sam turned to Matthew. "They'll break it down if we don't."

"My orders were to the wall, as are yours." Fool of a man, choosing this moment to grow a spine.

He needed more time. All the plans, if they got it, it would be for nothing. "Let me talk to Captain Yand."

"Ladders!" The warning run out on their side.

"Repel invaders," Matthew said, turning to the wall. "Archers ready."

"Fire volley!" The order came from the gatehouse, ringing out clear. Guards were yelling to target the battering ram, but it was completely protected.

There was nothing to aim at, nothing to hit.

Sam ran up the line, distributing arrows to the waiting men. They shot at the ladder carriers and made them regret not moving fast enough.

But enemy archers were giving back almost as much in return. A man cried out, pulling back with an arrow in his shoulder.

Another toppled back, falling over with an arrow in his eye. Sam helped the wounded, bandaging them when he could and helping them down to the courtyard below where women waited to care for them when he couldn't.

"Take care of him," Sam said, handing off a young mason to Martha. She nodded and started to work, breaking off the arrow shaft. The man screamed in pain.

Sam looked up at the guardhouse, then at the gate. The stairs were right there, less than a few feet from his own squad. It would just take a few seconds, that was it.

Then, a pounding on the gate made his mind for him. The gate shook, dust falling from the top, reverberating in the castle courtyard.

Sam turned and sprinted to the wooden stockpile, urging anyone he could see to help him. The men were on the walls, fighting and dying now. They tried to push away the ladders, but they kept coming. Sam struggled to pick up the largest beams still in the stockpile, bellowing for help.

No one came from the walls, but there were women and children flowing from the keep. They helped him, struggling to pick it up, but with enough of them and Sam's direction, they were able to drag it across the courtyard.

He set the end of it as high as he could get it. A few men had come down from the wall and were helping now. The gate was buckling, the locking bar cracking and bending dangerously.

He could feel it cracking, could hear the sound and it sent dread deep inside with every click and scratch.

"Brace, there." They set the other end in the mud. Kerien was there, beside him now. "Get a hammer and nails. And you, get more wood."

They pushed one end into the ground deeper, and the methodical pounding continued.

He was breathing hard, the strain of pulling the wood across the yard catching up to him. Blood mixed with the smell of dust and ash, faint but still there. He felt sick, but there was nothing else he could do.

That's not true, is it?

The image of the spear came to mind, but Kerien was there with the hammer and nails. He set a chunk of wood above the beam, hammering it into place.

Each hit from the battering ram drove the new brace deeper. More wood came, more beams to brace. The iron sounded like it was giving way.

The tip of the battering ram broke through, splintering the gate.

"Archer, we need archers down here!" Sam yelled. It was confusion, men were everywhere. The hole grew, the pointed end of the ram widening it.

There were men on the other side, and bowmen of their own. An arrow sailed past Sam's head, stinging his scalp. He hardly felt anything but the blood running down his cheek.

A few bows were there now, and an exchange took place. Water splashed down from above, the murder holes no doubt, but the roof of the ram meant it only trickled under the gate and underfoot, making a dirty scene even worse.

Sam slipped on it, falling against the door. A splinter drove into his hand, and he pulled it out and threw it away.

It would hurt in a few minutes, but he had to keep going. He hammered another brace home. Sweat mixed with the blood, stinging his head with the salt. He wiped it away, but it only made the wound worse.

"Hold fast." Yand was there now, urging the men back into position even as the arrows flew. Another beam went up, driven into the ground.

The ram started again, slamming against the hole to widen it.

It forced Sam back, barely keeping his footing. He came back to the door just as it slammed again, crunching the thick oak and splintering it.

Bows twanged and arrows flew. The hole was noticeable, wide enough to get a man through, but only if they forced it.

"Wood, hand me wood." Sam motioned to Kerien, pointing to the hole. His lungs burned and ached. Something was burning on the other side, sending billows of acrid black smoke through the hole.

Kerien saw and disappeared. The braces were moving, but still holding. They bent with each blow, and casualties were building up.

However, the defenders were keeping up a steady rhythm of arrow fire into the hole. The ram creaked less, the shudders were fewer. For a moment Sam started to hope.

Then he saw the attackers on the walls. They were coming up ladders and fighting on the ramparts.

And these men were fighters. Not like the tradesmen that faced them with minimal training and poor weaponry.

"They're coming up the west side," Sam said, and pointed. Yand followed his direction, frowning.

"You, you, stay here. Keep up a steady fire and feed them arrows until they burst. Everyone else with me."

Yand turned and led the force up the wall, leaving just two men to defend against the battering ram party.

Kerien was back, carrying the thickest planks they had. With a quick duck and few dodges, he was on the other side, sliding the first across the gap.

The archers joined them, dropping their bows to pick up braces. Sam hammered the braces into place just as the battering ram hit them.

They bowed dangerously, but the plank stood up to it. He had a moment of sadness, that would have been a good, sturdy table top, before he finished the last nails.

Frustration welled up inside him. It was the final straw. A symbol of what had come, a relic of his past.

All the hours he had put into this place. The heartache, the late nights. The friendships he had developed, and the grief of those friends gone just as easily as they had come.

He had no need to keep the beast down now. It was asleep, just like his future would be.

"Sam?" Kerien was beside him. "You're hurt." He was troubled, looking at his head.

"This?" Sam touched his head, it came away bloody. It stung. "It isn't bad."

They were still pounding on the gate, although it was weak. They must have lost men, too many to replace. Trying an attack from all directions had been too much.

But, judging from the fighting on the walls, it had been a worthwhile distraction. Yand was up there, fighting and killing with ease and skill Sam hadn't seen in years.

His sword seemed to be lightning, flashing from one man to the next. None could stand against him, and it gave him hope that they could fight this back, survive another day.

One by one the ladders were pushed off the western wall. One by one, the attackers fell to the onslaught of the hulking fighter within the walls of the castle.

Heat flowed through the cracks and splinters of the massive oak gate. Sam leaned against it, watching the flickers of fire come through.

Captain Yand had dispatched the last attacker, his body slumping against the rock. He sheathed his sword as Sam caught his breath.

Yand took up a stick, and with another, pushed at the ladder. It fell back, but then so did Yand, clutching at his face.

Sam watched in horror as Captain Yand slipped on the rock and tumbled into the courtyard below.

24

DEATH OF A GIANT

His heart beat in his throat. Sam willed Yand to get up, but he knew he wouldn't.

The sounds of battle continued around him, but it seemed to fade as he rushed over to the body.

Life had drained from him, the eyes locked in surprise with an arrow sticking out from his neck. Others were there beside him. Hands sought a heartbeat, a breath of air, something.

Martha closed his eyes with a bloody hand. "There is nothing we can do for him."

Finality.

Yand had been taken to oblivion, left them here to experience death and destruction.

Sam closed his eyes. It wasn't his fault, he didn't decide to leave them, but the end result was still the same.

They were left without a leader, without a fighter. Where was the Duke? Holed up in the keep while everyone else fought? Away from the stench of battle, the smell of the dead. Away from the blood and gore that came so easily to war.

Away from everything he had tried to run away from, and failed.

Sam rocked back on his heels. His eyes opened. they were taking the body away now, carrying it back to the keep with the others.

Men still fought on the wall. Arrows were loosed, ladders were pushed. They still came on, relentlessly.

Sam felt like there was a weight on his chest, pressing against him. He gasped. Too little air, he had to breathe.

When he did, he almost threw up from the smell. Men were screaming, dying. Attacker, defender, it didn't matter.

He should have left long ago, when Luca died. How could he not see it?

He knew this could happen. Why had he still chosen to come?

He sat down, ready to go where he needed. But where was that? Not here. He had been ineffective, walked right back into the life he hated.

Someone was calling his name. He looked up at the wall. Ned was shooting his bow, a determined look on his face.

Trent. Where was he? He had forgotten all about him. The west wall. He had been at the heart of the fighting, where Yand had died.

Scanning the ramparts, Sam saw no hint of his apprentice.

Heart sinking, he leaned back on his knees. Another failure in a long line of them.

The sounds of battle faded, and Sam slipped into his own mind.

Flashes of the past materialized, then decayed away, one after the other. Faster than the speed of light, yet as slow as anything he had experienced before.

This would be his grave, his death knell. It would ring out through the ages to mark an insignificant, unknown man who made nothing of a mark on the world.

All his work would be destroyed, cast aside, corrupted. The wood, the stone, the rock. Torn down piece by piece.

He took a deep breath.

There was no point. The Belmarchers would get in, they would fight, and they would kill all of them. The women, the children. Everyone.

He was dead. What good would it do to fight now?

Bill was walking toward him. For what reason, Sam knew not. He stopped in front of him, obscuring his view of the fighting.

There was a strange look in Bill's eyes. Hatred, disgust, rage perhaps?

"You sit there in the dust when others fight?"

The words cut deep, deep into the very heart of him. But Sam knew it was no use arguing with him. Trent was right, Bill was right. He was a coward.

And now he would meet his end, the same way.

"I thought better of you." The words surprised him, shocking Sam out of his thoughts.

"Why?"

"You never struck me as the cowardly type." Sam's eyes opened wide at that. "Pompous, self-righteous, yes. But not a coward."

Anger struck him, the thing deep inside stirring for the first time in hours.

Bill turned. "Stay there in the dirt where you belong. Humbled, waiting for the axe to fall." He looked back at him over his shoulder. "As for the rest of us, we will fight without you. Trent will fight." He flung his head to the east wall.

Trent was there, sword flashing in the sunlight. Ladders stuck up over the wall, but he was leading the charge. Trent, barely a man.

And here he was, wallowing in the dirt like a pig. Sam looked down at his bloodstained hands. Would they ever be clean again?

"Goodbye Sam. You've been chained by your own thoughts for far too long. I hope death frees you of them," Bill said, and then walked away.

Emotions raged through Sam. Anger at being rebuked by the very man who had the least standing to do it, but being right about it. Pride at seeing Trent fighting so hard and so well. Fear, at feeling the old thing coming back to life again, itching to be released.

His mouth was dry, his lips cracked as he opened it. Licking his lips, he got to his feet. His legs trembled from the events of the day. He was so tired. "I'll not stand by and have you take what little honor I had."

Bill stopped.

"You don't know what I've done, what I have tried to forget." Sam's eyes watered at the memories.

"We've all done things we've regretted. Didn't you know that, Sam Freeman?" Bill walked away, a smile playing on his lips.

For the first time in years, a flame of hope flickered within him. How could he let these people die when he had the ability to at least fight to stop it?

He gnashed his teeth and turned, taking the first step across the courtyard. Men died, falling from the walls. Another step. Women tore at their clothes, using them as bandages to stop bleeding. Another step.

Children cried, others faced it stern faced and stubborn. Another step. The thing within him woke up, and he held its leash tight.

Never again.

His feet knew the path, and his hands reached under the cloth, closing around the handle of the spear.

He drew it out and turned back to the wall, ready to face the enemy.

25

ONE BY ONE

For the first time in years Sam cast an eye across the battle-field and analyzed it. Gone were the doubts, banished to the farthest reaches of his mind.

Now was the time to act.

The eastern and southern walls were taking the most in the attack. Somehow, after the push from Yand, the western wall seemed under control.

But the rest of the castle was in utter chaos. Men were running, fighting, retreating without any rhyme or reason.

Sam knew what he had to do. He gripped the warm shaft of the spear and sprinted to the southern wall.

The longest of all the defenses, it continued to be bombarded by rocks through from the catapult. Ned was up there, with Archie by his side, and the rest of two squads.

Smoke rose from the guardhouse above the gate. He would be surprised if anyone was still up there. The gate was still holding, even though flames licked at it.

Sam grabbed hold of the shirt of a boy running by. Scrawny, with eyes darting like a lizard, he knelt down next to him.

"Joseph, do you remember me?" The boy nodded, fear filling his eyes. "I'm not going to hurt you, but those men are. Will you do me a favor?"

"My mom told me to hide in the keep."

"And she's a good woman. Will you go get her and get as many as you can to get buckets and anything else that can hold water?" The boy was still frightened. "I won't say anything about where I met you, deal?"

"Where should we take them?" His voice was cracked with fear, but it held together.

"Captain Yand needs you to fill them and take them to the guardhouse above the gate. You're a very brave young man. I know you'll do well." The eyes calmed, and Sam let him go. He stood on his own feet, not yielding an inch. "Go now, as quick as a rabbit."

The boy took off, headed for the keep. Sam wasn't sure it would work, or that anyone would listen to the young boy, but they needed every fighting age man on the wall.

Trent was holding his own, even rallying the rest of his squad. They were pushing back the ladders, keeping the rest of the attackers at bay.

Another wave of pride washed over him, glad that the young man had taken so well to swordplay. Even though he was rusty, it had never been his strong suit.

The tip of the spear glinted in the sunlight. The lance, on the other hand...

It felt good to hold in his hands. This time, he was less ashamed of it. These were good, honest men and women. They deserved lives free of murder and fear, to live out a simple life in service to their families.

He wanted them to eat, to be loved, to laugh again. The castle had been filled with too many gaunt faces, too much sorrow, for too long.

An inkling of a plan started to form in his mind. It was a wild shot, but he wasn't sure they had any other options.

Fire and water. Balance, and enemies.

"Ned!" Sam reached the bottom of the stairs and started to take them two at a time. His legs and lungs protested, but he ignored them.

Ned's face appeared above him. He was blood-stained and exhausted. One of his arms was cut, and he was favoring his left leg.

"We can't hold them off much longer."

"I know it. You've done well." He reached him, looking down the lines of men. They were sluggish and reacting. Half were resting behind crenelations. "We can't hold them off much longer like this."

"What did you have in mind?" Ned stood straighter, and a smile actually came to his lips. Sam wasn't sure if it was hope or anticipation, but he returned the smile with one of his own.

"A surprise they won't forget."

Sam took Ned's place, a renewed strength flowing through his limbs. A ladder clunked on to the wall next to him. No one moved, so he gave them a glare and faced the man riding at the top of it.

"Are you willing to give up that easily? Are you not men of Chathem?" Sam swung the spear out and stabbed. The man on the ladder, clutching a sword in one hand, ducked.

Sam rapped his other hand on the knuckles with the flat of his spear. Instinctively the man let go and lost his footing at the same time.

He fell, clattering down into the fighters holding it. "You fear death, but death you will eat your fill of if they get a foothold here." Sam swung his spear around and pushed the ladder off with all his might. It fell, and he turned to face the others.

"You built this place," Sam said, swinging his spear around to point to a mason. "Your hands built this wall, a defense in troubled times for your future and that of your kin."

He pointed at another. "You set the crenelations, sweating to move them in place." He grabbed hold of Matthew, who was crouching down next to him. "You kept us safe and guarded these walls."

He had their attention now, and the fear was flowing from them. Now, something else replaced it. They were getting the will to fight back. "Are you willing to lay down your life in defense of your brother, your kin? Or will you let them take us and hang us from a pike for the birds to act?"

Grumblings now, and murmurers. It was starting to work. They were talking at least. "Rise to your feet, and fight."

The smell of smoke permeated the air, overriding all else. There was a respite in the attack as the Belmarchers gathered their strength.

Sam looked over the edge, hazarding a moment in the firing line. More dead and wounded than he expected.

One by one, the men along the wall rose. They got to their feet despite their wounds, their fears, and the enemy.

One by one, they rose to fight.

26

THE BEAR

"What are we supposed to do?" Matthew asked. Sam grabbed his hand and helped him to his feet. He almost slipped on the blood.

"Hold them off as long as you can. Make them pay for each foot they advance with arrow and rock." The Belmarchers were massing again, gathering the ladders for another attack. He ducked, narrowly avoiding another arrow. "Take out those archers."

The western wall was flagging again. Sam picked up a pole and handed it to a middle-aged mason. "Repel the ladders as long as you can."

Something caught his eye in the courtyard. Women, and the older children, were streaming out of the keep.

They had buckets, pans, pots, and even cups. Anything that could hold water.

Sam's heart soared. They could do this, they could repel this attack. They just had to hold on a little longer.

Men were coming over ladders, despite the defenders pushing them back. They were getting a foothold, and, with the distance he would have to run, Sam wasn't sure he could make it in time.

Then, he saw the largest man he had seen in his life. Over six feet tall, with a sword almost three feet long. His armor gleamed, and his eyes glowed.

The defenders fell back as he swung his sword, clearing a way for him to gain a foothold on the wall. Sam could almost smell the hate in his eyes, and his bloodlust. It radiated out like waves in a pond disturbed by a rock.

A brave guard attacked. The man knocked him away like he was a rag-doll, and he slammed into the stone.

Sam took off at a run, as fast as he dared across the uneven wall paving stones. He left the other attackers behind him to push off the ladders and blunt the advance.

The big man cleared out an area six feet wide, cutting through another defender, shoulder to hip. His sword stuck, and he kicked the body away. It tumbled into the courtyard and lay motionless, leaking blood.

This man had to be stopped, and at all costs. In a foreign tongue, he turned back to his men and urged them on, laughing at what could only have been an insult in his native language.

Despite the warmth of the sun Sam felt a chill run up his back. He had heard of men like this, and only had the misfortune of meeting one other in a fair fight.

And that was years ago, in his prime. Now, Sam was older and unpracticed.

But what was he to do? Turn and run? To where?

There was no running from this fight, not anymore.

A moment later and he was at the retreating flank of the defenders, then pushing through, yelling at them to move out of the way.

They had no problem letting him through, scrambling out of the way of the advancing Belmarchers.

Sam's eyes widened, and he drew up short. The man was even bigger up close.

"What have we here?" the man asked. Sam took a fighting stance, and breathed deep, leveling his spear.

Every second he delayed another attacker mounted the ladder. There were four of them over the edged, and a quick glance told him there were more coming.

In fact, the other attackers from the south were starting to round the corner, rushing on.

Sam returned his attention to the big man. There was nothing to say, so Sam stepped forward and attacked.

The tip of the spear shot forward, aimed at the throat.

The man batted it away without blinking an eye. The shock from the parry ran up the spear shaft and into Sam's hands.

It hurt.

He said something else in his language. The other attackers backed up and smiled. Sam crouched down and prepared for the assault.

His first attack may have been a feint, but the man was committed.

Huge, heavy swings of the sword parted the air. Sam had no time to parry them and ducked out of the way. He was fast for such a large man, too fast.

All Sam could do was move out of the way and retreat. Step by step they went south. Sam attempted a counterattack, but a mailed fist punched him in the face, sending him spinning.

Sam swallowed. His jaw felt like it had been pulled out of place.

He knew he was outmatched, and that there was only one likely outcome to this fight.

But there Trent was, still fighting. His leg was bleeding, and he had a cut over his left eye.

He dispatched an attacker with the help of a man from behind, then turned to ward off the ladders, grabbing hold of a pole and pushing.

Sam felt the sword coming and dropped, swinging at the same time and shooting his spear forward.

It caught the big man by surprise, and the spear buried deep into his thigh, slipping in between a plate and under leather.

There was surprise in his eyes, but Sam didn't hesitate. He wrenched his spear free and attacked.

His arms were waking up, remembering the forms he had worked so many times before. Thrust, pull, swing. Every opening he could exploit, he did.

Sam's advantage didn't last for long. With a grunt the big man tuned his spear and swung in a counterattack. Sam stepped back.

But not fast enough.

The sword cut through his shoulder. The smell of iron filled the air. The adrenaline overrode the pain, but Sam knew he would feel it.

the big man smiled at him. "Too weak. You're all too weak."

Sam panted, each lung a painful lance. "We kept you out this long."

"Your time for life is over." The big man's smile turned into a snarl.

His attacks came faster, and somehow stronger. Sam fell back again. He was losing ground too quickly, there wouldn't be enough wall left.

Then Sam felt the hard south wall behind him and knew he had run out of time.

27

Against Rock

Sam was at the south end of the wall. The big man thrust, nearly skewering him. Without room to maneuver, fear choked him.

He was breathing hard, harder than he had in his life, but his body knew what to do. Sam cleared his mind, letting it take over.

There was nothing left but to let go. He would either die here, or he would die later.

"Now is the time of your death, little one." The man cleft the air just above his head, and Sam struck him on the right knee. He pulled back his sword across Sam's right shoulder, slicing through skin to the bone.

He cried out, then ducked out of the way of another attack, turning onto the south wall. A northern wind was blowing, the sun beginning its descent in the western sky.

The big man squinted, and Sam saw his chance. "Over here you big oaf." Blood pouring down his arm, he dragged his spear across the rock and retreated a few steps.

Other defenders had retreated with him, unwilling or unable to help the fight. Sam didn't blame them, but he didn't have time to keep track of them.

The big man turned and roared, squinting and swinging wildly. It was easier to dodge, the weight of his armor finally having an effect.

Sam slipped past his attack, light and free of plate mail. Seeing his advantage return rejuvenated him, energy flowing back to his limbs despite his aches and pains.

Sam got closer, trading a few punches to the head and receiving one in return that sent him flying back and seeing stars.

He caught his backward movement, jaw aching, and had to immediately parry a thrust to the side. It caught his abdomen, cutting through him on the left.

Now, losing blood and feeling the pain through the adrenaline, he set his stance.

The big man was laughing, an unpleasant, grating sound that filled him with dread. His sword came in from the left.

Sam caught it with the tip of his spear, spinning it down and smashing the butt of his spear alongside the big man's head.

It snapped over, and he stepped back.

The man smiled again, spat out a few teeth, and was back on the attack.

They traded blows. Sam was flagging, unable to keep up with the sheer strength of the man. He was like a wild animal that, no matter how many wounds it had, refused to die.

Sam stumbled, the rock under his left side giving way, and scrambled back to safety. He got another cut for the distraction across his chest.

He is toying with me.

Sam panted, heart racing faster than a horse in gallop. Blood soaked his right arm, and he had to tighten his grip on his spear.

The sun was in his eyes again, but Sam knew that would be no help.

Evan winced, hearing the scream cut short. Was that one of his subjects or the enemy? His hands trembled around the cup, splashing wine to the floor in drips.

He couldn't help but notice they looked like big stains of blood.

He should be out there, fighting alongside Yand and the others, but here he was, cowering like a coward.

His sword lay across his desk, his armor donned, and his uniform immaculate. The same could not be said for those outside.

Duke Hornblood stared up at the crest above his desk. He was a Hornblood, and the Duke. He would rule his father's lands someday when he was gone.

So why couldn't he go and fight for them?

Yand had known his character all along, despite his years of teachings and urging. That look on his face as he left.

It stung the young Duke.

He slammed down his wine, angry at himself and the world. He didn't ask for these circumstances, didn't ask for glory.

And he didn't ask to be thrust into battle with no army to support him.

His father would have levied his forces had he known, come marching north to beat back the Belmarch and put them in his place.

Eyes cast to the side, he hung his head and shuffled back to the wine bottle, pouring the last few drops into his glass.

He drank them, then retreated to his chair. He wanted to shut up his ears, to ignore the cries and screams, the clashes. He wanted to ignore the smells, horrible smells that came into his room. Blood and fire, bile and waste.

A knock summoned him from his wine induced stupor. Even that couldn't give him courage.

"Leave me in peace."

"Sire, it is Captain Yand." *Here to give me a tongue lashing, no doubt to urge me into the fight.*

"Tell him to get me when he's won." There was a pause, then whispers.

This wasn't right. Yand should have been pounding at the door himself.

So why hadn't he?

Like a lapdog, he was forced to follow the young Duke around, to be a protector and guide. To satisfy his mother and her suffocating ways.

He had found him in the streets, dressed as a commoner and passed out in the gutter, dusted him off and brought him back.

Not once had he gone to his father with a bad report to bring him under his wrath. No, Yand had done that all himself, with those disappointed looks and refusals to chastise.

Rousing himself, Duke Hornblood stumbled across the room and wrenched open the door.

Two servants, shocked at seeing him, mouths opened, stood before him. In anger, he opened his mouth.

Then, he saw Yand.

"No. No, it cannot be." The Duke took one step back as the servants recovered their composure and shock turned to fear.

"There was no saving him," one said, voice trembling.

Duke Evan Hornblood staggered against the door frame and slipped to his knees.

Captain Yand was dead.

All was lost.

28

OVERTURNING

Trent yanked out the sword and kicked, sending the man flying back down the ladder. It never seemed to help, they kept coming no matter what they did.

"Push." Trent and another man used the pole to tip the ladder back, hands below grabbing it to keep it on the wall.

They managed to push it far enough back it tipped over, but just like before, the attackers picked it back up, repositioning it and tilting it back into place.

He was tired, exhausted. He wanted to sit down and rest, to stop his cuts from bleeding.

But there was no time for that.

Men yelled beside him, urging them to keep it away. Like a beam in place, the ladder snapped in between the crenelations.

Trent took up a pole someone had dropped and set it against the ladder. he pushed.

And slipped.

The pole went between rungs, and he grabbed a hold of it and he leaned left, then toppled over.

The pole caught the side of the ladder, stopping his fall. It shook as a man started climbing.

It moved. It seemed like the ladders always stayed together, lashed by thick ropes too strong to simply cut away. They were resilient, made to stay together.

What was it that Sam had said? There's a way to break anything, given the right leverage.

It had to be thirty feet tall, made from thick trunks split in quarters. The rungs gave it stability, but it was the sides that kept it together.

"Help me," Trent said to the nearest defender, back turned to him. "We need to break these ladders, and I have an idea."

The man turned, and all the blood drained from Trent's face.

It was Bill.

But there was no time to be afraid now, not in the thick of battle. A vicious-looking man was three quarters of the way up.

"Twist it, make it fall over this way." Trent motioned with the wall, then made sure the pole was set.

Bill was covered in blood, but didn't seem to have a scratch on him. Trent didn't stop to think of why. He only hesitated a second, then set down his sword, taken from an attacker, then grabbed onto the pole.

Together, they pulled. The ladder scraped against the wall, but hands at the bottom held it up. It was heavy and took all the strength they had to move.

The ladder twisted, then popped out over the crenelation. "Next one," Trent said, gasping between words. Sweat poured down his head.

They took the pole out and moved it, leveraging again. The ladder resisted at first, but it gave way again.

"One more," Bill said, panting. They moved to the next one.

The ladder creaked and groaned, the attacker almost at eye level. They were out of arrows now. No way to get him off but by pushing or hand to hand combat.

Trent pushed with all his might. The ladder moved, crept over. The attacker took another step, sword in hand and eyes flashing.

That was all it took.

His weight shifting caught, then the ladder screeched against the wall as it started to fall.

One side caught a crenelation, then twisted and snapped. The ladder landed on its side, broken in two.

Others had seen it, and a great cheer went up. They copied the tactic, defenders tipping the ladders over and sending them cracking and crashing to the side.

Within a few minutes the wall was clear, the attackers frustrated and yelling on the ground below.

"Give them what they really want, boy," Bill said, picking up a chuck of rock and tossing it in the air. He threw it down with two hands, hitting the leg of a man with a sickening crack.

Trent slumped against the side of the wall, letting his body recover. The sun warmed his skin. A fresh breeze cooled his sweat soaked hair and brought with it the smell of the river, fresh and light above all the stench of fighting.

The guardhouse was burning, or it looked that way. A long line of women and children passed buckets and pots of water down a line up to it.

The vessels went in full and came out empty. Trent wasn't sure where it all was going, but as he looked closer, he realized it wasn't the gatehouse that was on fire, but something below the gatehouse.

The gate.

The thought passed through him like a ghost, chilling him to the bone. It was still holding, but orange dancing flames were visible through the hole in the middle, made by something large.

Then movement took his gaze to the south wall.

It was Sam.

He was fighting the largest man Trent had ever seen, and it looked like he was losing. The big man's sword knocked away his spear like a sliver.

Trent leaned down and picked up the strange sword. It was slick with blood, still warm but cool to his touch.

Only the east and west were in jeopardy now. Attackers trickled in, fighting to keep their foothold from defenders to the north and on the stairs up.

The guards at the southern wall were stuck behind Sam, unable to do anything but watch and fall back as he did.

"Bill, look." Bill swung his head around, seeing the problem in an instant.

"To the east," Bill said, flicking the blood from the tip of his sword and starting down the stairs.

Trent went with him, anxiously glancing up at Sam. The bear of a man hammered at him, over and over again.

His sword flashed in the evening light, wickedly swinging and drawing more and more blood.

Sam's clothes were in tatters. Trent had to do something.

His eyes played across the wall, looking for something, anything.

What could he do?

Archie and Ned were there, still shooting arrows at the attackers below.

"Ned," Trent said. He kept shooting, the closest to Sam. Trent gathered his breath, then screamed at the top of his lungs. "Ned!"

29

Deathrattle

A hand shot out, wrapping around the shaft of his spear. Sam ducked the sword, pulling to try and free his weapon.

But the big man held fast. He gave a yank. Sam tumbled forward.

The man reeked. Not only of death, but of a foul odor from those that wallow in filth.

Sam twisted, trying to get out of his grip. The big man squeezed him tight, crushing him.

There was no air in his lungs. The armor poked into him, an unyielding mass that threatened to break his bones.

The world started going dark. Sam tried to breathe, fought for air. He didn't know when it had happened, but there was a hand around his throat.

I'm going to die.

It was all he could think. He tried to picture his sister, his mother. Someone.

But he couldn't. Thoughts had fled. The darkness closed in.

Then he was gasping for air at the man's feet as he laughed above him.

Sam struggled to his feet. The man punched him. "Put up a decent fight. Not great. I'll enjoy killing you."

Sam couldn't respond. He was still trying to catch his breath.

The big man snapped his spear in two with one hand. It parted like a reed bent by the wind.

The two halves fell to the floor of the wall, and he kicked the spear head off. It clattered on the way down, too far out of reach.

It landed point down in the dirt below.

Metal rasped on rock. Sparks flew, drawing Sam's attention back.

The big man was not smiling now.

His sword was scratching down the wall. It was clear what he intended to do with it.

"Ned!" Trent's voice rang out clear and loud, above all the other sounds.

He was running across the courtyard, a sword in hand.

He had viewed Sam as a coward, watched him refuse to fight.

Now, in his last hour, would he let him see the same again?

The broken spear shaft was between them, right at his feet. Sam searched every inch of him and saw only one place it would do any good on the big man.

He just needed an opening, he just needed some time.

Sam tensed up, prepared to move.

The man raised his sword high above his head. Sam knew he would swing through and would drop to the right.

That might be enough.

Then, an arrow blossomed on the big man's hand. The sword clattered to the ground.

Sam dove, grabbing what was left of the spear shaft just as the man turned in a fury that dwarfed all others.

There was more than murder in his eyes. This man would not stop at Sam, he would continue to the others.

Then the women, then the children.

Sam plunged the jagged, splintered end right into his eye.

There was a briefest hesitation of resistance, then it squelched in.

Bile rising in his throat, Sam pushed as hard as he could, ignoring the scream that chilled him to the bone and touched his very soul.

It crunched deeper, then home.

The scream stopped, and the man fell on him.

Together they tumbled, and Sam hit his head against the wall.

Light. Voices. A tunnel. He wanted to stay asleep. It was so comfortable.

Then, a touch.

Where am I?

Sounds, like someone talking through water.

The light faded. The sounds cleared. Hands pulled at him.

Sam was on his feet. His hands wouldn't move. But that wasn't right.

They did. He tested them.

" — done it. You've shown them. They're running like dogs now!" Matthew was triumphant, pounding him on the back.

He shook his head, regained his senses.

The attackers were being driven back and retreating in full.

The big man had been the one driving them on. And now he lay face down on the wall, propped up by the spear that projected from his head.

"Is he?" Sam asked, mouth full of what felt like cotton.

"Dead. Like a rock." The defenders made quick work of the two attackers who remained, overwhelming them within seconds.

Sam's legs trembled. They felt like jelly. The smell of smoke.

The guardhouse. The gate!

Children and women were passing water to it, and now the men joined in.

They threw the water down the murder holes, dousing the flames. The attackers were retreating now, fleeing across the field.

Sam looked at them, leaderless and confused.

Now would be the perfect time for a counterattack.

To ride out and run them down, ending the siege once and for all.

But he had no army.

"To the gate," Sam said. He stepped forward, then almost fell.

"No, you don't. You'll rest here, with me." Sam looked up, Ned's smiling, old weathered face looking up at him.

"Was that...?"

"Yes. I can put my mark where I need it, given the right amount of prodding." Ned jerked his head over to the courtyard. "You wouldn't be alive if it wasn't for him."

Trent was leading the others at the well. He was passing out water, dunking the bucket as fast as he could and pouring it into the waiting containers.

Sam embraced him, partially supporting himself on the old man. "I wouldn't be alive if it wasn't for you."

"We aren't safe yet." Sam released the embrace, and Ned followed his gaze. He sat down on the wall, leaning up against the crenelation.

"You don't think they'll leave?"

"No. They fought like animals to kill us. Predators that persistent won't let us go." The smoke was lessening now, the water having its intended effect.

The sun was setting, casting a golden hue on the world. The sky was soft red, unlike the harsh color of blood, and yellow and orange.

The wind was blowing away the smoke, and the accompanying smell. It turned black, then white, then faded as Sam watched the enemy retreat to their encampment.

"We've done it. We've beat them." Ned stood beside Sam, making sure h didn't fall.

Sam closed his eyes and rested.

They'd beat them, for now.

Epilogue

The castle was quiet now, the still of night descending like a blanket. Only the vultures talked, breaking the night's stillness with their quarrels and fights.

There were so many dead, and many more wounded. Archie was found in the courtyard, and his wife refused to leave his side.

She cried bitter tears and cursed the castle for taking her husband.

Sam cried with her. For the man that Archie was and could have been.

His body joined a long line that started with one, then two, then grew to fourteen.

And Captain Yand among them.

Duke Hornblood had come out of his room, briefly, to look after the men. He had turned and fled back into his room when they started moving in the bodies.

Sam helped, muscles aching and body torn, or tried to. He had to stop often and catch his breath, bandages covering his body.

"You need to go lie down and rest," Martha said.

"I'll rest when the work is finished." Sam knew there was a long road ahead, and more tears and sadness.

Trent came up to him after they were done, each man covered in a blanket to hide his face from the world, for they would never look upon it again.

"Thank you," Sam said.

"I didn't do anything you didn't teach me." Trent was blushing, barely visible in the torchlight.

"You reminded me that I might not be able to pick the battles I fight." A young carpenter, holding his own against hardened fighters.

Trent was going to do fine.

He shifted. "Sam?"

"Yes?"

"How are we..."

The moon sat among the stars, plump and white.

"We'll find a way."

WINTER AT HORNBLOOD

Epic of Hornblood Castle #2

Eric Kercher

Paper and Sword, LLC

To Milo

1

FOG OF WINE

"Still there?" Ned joined Sam on the wall, staring out over the bloodstained field. Winter was around the corner, the winds turning cold and biting when the sun went down. Leaves were falling now, most of the gold, brown, and red coating the forest floor.

"Still there." Sam pulled at his coat, itching his bandages. A few days hadn't done much to heal them. "Shouldn't you be asleep?"

"I should be asking you the same question." Ned's beard and mustache had grown out, just as bushy, if not more so, than his eyebrows. They couldn't hide the gauntness of his cheeks, though.

"Give me a few minutes, I'll be in. Any word from Overseer Rhys?" There was another question to that, deeper.

"That's your realm, not mine."

Captain Yand had left a deep hole, one that Sam hoped the young Duke would fill. So far, though...

"He's young, give him time." *Not that young.* Twenty was more than old enough to be a journeyman apprentice, if not a full carpenter.

The thought reminded him of Archie. His gaze was pulled over to the freshly mounded sections of earth in the corner of the castle. That, Overseer Rhys had done well to execute. The ceremony had been short, the mourners few, but the entire castle had been there. Duke Hornblood included.

Forty-seven. Forty-seven men remained alive within the walls to man and fight. Another thirty-five women and children on top of that.

A heron skimmed along the tree line, then dipped into the river beyond. It was far outside of their line of sight now.

"I'll go inside." Sam stood up, aches and pains twitching at him. Ned clapped him on the shoulder, which brought a sting with it.

"Sorry. Get some rest."

The fires of the Belmarch burned well beyond the arrow range of their bows. Sam had hoped they would give up without a leader, that they would slink back across the river in the dead of the night one day. That hadn't happened. Now, he doubted it ever would.

They had burned their dead on pyres, the bodies that they could. Sam had ordered the others dumped into the river. The pillars that had gone up then were big, and white. The fires burned hot, consumed everything, including flesh and bone. *Whatever they believed, their dead were gone, just like ours.*

Sam limped down the stairs, feeling a pang in his left foot every time he set it down, but eventually made it to the bottom. He went back into the Keep, only to find Bill leaning against the wall, waiting for him.

"Sam," Bill said. Sam was startled by the interruption and almost dropped the door on himself.

"Yes?"

"May we... talk?"

Sam nodded, and Bill went back out with him, back across the yard and into his stone hut. The room was cool, warmer than the outside air, but not by much. Bill offered a chair and Sam took it, sighing as the weight came off his left foot. The small fireplace tucked into one wall was barren and dusty. A spiderweb was strung along one corner. Even Bill couldn't escape the lack of fuel and wood, a prudent rule set by the Overseer. With winter coming, though...

"We need to break free of this siege," Bill said.

"We're in agreement." A long silence stretched between them. Sam was wary. He didn't trust Bill yet. "What do you propose?"

"Kill them all." Bill shrugged. "They won't leave on their own."

The shack smelled of mildew. The floor was damp somehow, even though they hadn't had rain in a while, near the fireplace. Sam shifted in the chair to get more comfortable, easing the way it was digging into his back.

"Easier said than done." His voice was full of sarcasm.

"You know the Duke isn't cut out for this." Bill shook his head. "I don't know where he's been hiding his stash of booze, but I'd love to know where." He licked his lips. "Loves it more than I ever did."

Sam looked into his eyes, the strange look of truthfulness in them. *Was that true, or was it just what he believed?*

"We can't force him to act."

"We have to." Bill pointed out his window. "Or do you want to die here? They'll tear us limb from limb and feed us to the dogs if they could."

He jabbed at the large bandages wrapped around his torso. "Or did you forget the man who gave you that?"

Sam frowned. Mention of it made his wound burn and itch. It hurt, but only grazed his ribcage. "I remember."

"He would have broken you earlier, had he not wanted to toy with you, make you an example."

"He's dead now," Sam reminded him.

"But another will rise in his place."

"How do you know so much about the Belmarch?" Sam squinted at him, examining his face, his hands.

"I've lived near the border all my life. It's impossible not to know them." Bill leaned in closer. "If you did, you'd hate them like I do."

Sam didn't see where this was going, and the look in Bill's eyes made him uncomfortable. The man was small and wiry, but somehow he had managed to escape the fight with a few cuts and scratches. And Trent said he was covered in blood. How he managed to do that, Sam had a burning desire to know, but at the same time didn't.

"We can agree on all of this," Sam sat back. "So, what does it have to do with me?" He crossed his arms.

"You're a fighting man, but not just any fighting man." Bill leaned in more. "You could take control, lead us out of this place."

"That sounds an awful lot like a revolt."

"Revolt? No. Such a strong word. Such a dirty word." Bill held up his hands, as if innocent. "You're not just a fighter, are you?"

"I've seen my share of bloodshed. I want to put it behind me, to leave it where it belongs. No man should kill another."

"Come now, Sam. We both know better. Men must die, either by another man's hands or of old age. Why is it that certain men keep the privilege for themselves?"

"Is that what the Belmarch think? That any man can kill another?" There was something wrong in the words. Twisted, perverted. They made so much sense, but didn't feel right.

A child yelled in the courtyard. It made Sam stop, but the sound of laughter followed, and he relaxed.

"I want to survive just as badly as any other man, but there are some things I'll not do."

Bill's eyes watched him, dark and foreboding. "We'll see how well you keep that word."

Sam stood up, unable to be in the man's presence anymore. "I take my leave of you." His voice was gruff and short. Bill nodded but said nothing.

An unpleasant man. Always had been, always will be. Sam was glad to shut the door behind him, even though the day had faded into twilight and brought with it more chill.

How long had it been? A few months? A few weeks? Weariness overtook him, burrowing deep into his bones. Everything seemed to blend together. He went to bed troubled, not seeing a way forward, no path of survival.

"How do you propose we do that?" Evan took another sip. He turned the goblet in his hand, examining it in the failing light. It was dirty, smudged with fingerprints, and streaked. That was what he could see, in better light he suspected it would be worse. It smelled better than it looked, the aroma of the dark, red wine pleasantly floral. Better than the smell of death and blood, or the commoners that stunk.

"I still have some pull in the capital." Overseer Rhys sat across from him. "Provided I can get to them, there are those who would still listen to me."

He was fat, but not as much as he used to be. Evan's stomach grumbled, but he ignored it. Wine would help with that, too.

"Do you have an army that can sally forth and break a hole in the invader's ranks? Or perhaps a secret passage you've been hiding from me that goes straight to the King's chambers?" Duke Evan rubbed his eyes. He wearied of this topic, which had come up more frequently since...He was gone. Through the buzz in his head, he knew that. He wished he were still here now, standing beside him with that disappointed look.

"No..." The Overseer shifted in his seat.

"Then let us speak of it no more." He was tired and lonely. Even the Overseer was too far below his rank to be called a friend in this place. Even a cousin would be better than nothing. He'd even take Theo, brash and stupid as he was, for a companion than rot away here.

The Overseer clearly wanted to talk more of it, but he cleared his throat and took out a scrap of parchment. "Shall we proceed to inventory, then?"

Evan cringed. "Go on."

"Barrels of flour, thirty-two. Barrels of biscuit, fifteen. Boxes of nails, ten. Quarried stone, fifteen thousand pieces..." The Overseer went down his list, order unchanged from last time. Food continued to decrease, as did everything else.

He droned on. Evan drank more, then emptied his goblet. He thought about filling it up, but the long list was making him sleepy.

Then something caught his attention.

"Casks of wine, three. Bottles of wine, seventeen."

Evan sat up. "Stop. What was that?"

The Overseer licked his lips, wrinkled his brow, and went over his list again. "Oak, seven stacks?"

"The wine."

"Ah. Three casks, seventeen bottles."

"I thought we had over twenty bottles last week." His heart palpitated. It didn't sound bad until he thought back to the first inventory. Double the casks and over a hundred bottles of his own personal stock had accompanied him here.

The Overseer's mouth was working, but no sound came out.

"Answer me," he said.

"We did, sire."

"Then who took it?" Another long pause.

"Wine has only been issued to your Highness."

"What? No." He ran through the week in his head. There was no way he had drunk that much wine. Or was there?

His head buzzed, and he stood up and went to the bar with the bottle. It was almost empty. He opened the case up with his key. A quick count confirmed it, then another count. Seventeen bottles, standing like sentinels.

"It can't be. Someone has been stealing from me."

"Sire—"

"I don't want excuses, Rhys, I want answers. Find the man that did this and bring him to me." He drained the bottle into his goblet. Half a glass, at best. It tasted sickly sweet.

"I will conduct an investigation," the Overseer's eyes drooped. "And I will report all that I can find."

"Good. Carry on." The wine went to his head, made him feel drowsy. The long list of supplies didn't help. He wasn't paying attention, even long after the Overseer had concluded and tucked away his paper. He was thinking about his father and uncle. What would they do if they were in his situation? Would they ride out, breastplate burnished and gleaming, to lead a fatal charge and break the enemy line? Or would they do what he was doing, hide away here in the safety of his walls and wait for the inevitable to happen?

He cursed his luck, and his own stupidity for pushing his father to send him, and for Yand for not stopping him.

Even through the fog of the wine he knew that wasn't quite right. The memory of that night came back, the low conversation, Yand imploring him to wait until the castle was finished. But he had pushed for this, to distinguish himself and prove his mettle.

He stared into the goblet. Was this all he could do? Was this his character?

The Overseer stared at him. Evan realized he had been calling his name for some time.

"Yes?"

"What are your orders, sire?"

His orders? His orders? A spark of anger tried to ignite, but it found nothing inside him to burn. Instead, it smoldered. Evan looked upon Rhys with contempt. What right did he have to demand from Duke Hornblood?

"I grow tired." His speech was starting to slur. "Leave me."

The Overseer clamped his mouth shut and stood. He gathered his robes. "Goodnight, your Highness."

He left. Evan stood in front of his desk, staring up at the crest of his family as tears rolled down his cheek.

2

MEMORIES OF THE DEAD

Swords, axes, and knives were spread out over the floor. Sam rubbed his chin.

"This is what we got?"

"That's everything." Mathew knelt down and touched one of them. The barracks were dark and musty. Dirt was strewn everywhere on the floor, and the beds were unmade.

Sam recalled helping to make some of them a long time ago. It seemed so distant now, even though it had to have been less than a year.

"And what are you going to do with them?"

"That's just it. We don't really know." Mathew stood up and shrugged. He had aged years in the last few weeks. "I didn't know who else to go to."

"You should take them to the Overseer. Have him decide."

"We talked about that..." Mathew dropped his gaze to the floor. Something felt off, but he didn't know what.

He wished he was still in bed sleeping, that the young boy hadn't come to get him. He wished the head guard hadn't been killed in the fighting, leaving a vacant hole for someone to fill.

And, he realized, he knew who they had in mind.

"I'm a carpenter, not a leader."

"We keep the watches, rotate them like we used to. How long will that last?" Mathew shook his head, then grabbed onto his arm. "I'm afraid of the others sometimes, the look in their eyes. Hopelessness."

Sam took a deep breath, then let it out. He told the truth—he was no leader. What experience did he have guarding a castle?

Nights on the picket line tickled the back of his mind, but he thrust them away.

"Pick the man most willing to lead. That's my advice to you."

"Right now, that's me, and I can't do it. I haven't led anything, let alone the defenses of a castle."

The man most able to do that task lay in a grave not a stone's throw from where they were talking. Funny, how life ended up like that.

What authority did he have, though? Just because Mathew thought he was more suited? A man half his age determining the course of the leadership?

Sam couldn't help but let his mind wander back to his conversation with Bill. It had put him on edge, and here Mathew was doing just about the same.

"Talk to the Overseer. He'll know what to do."

"I can't. I'm just a guard, and everyone else is the same. The rejects that couldn't make it in the capital, sent to the boundaries of the kingdom." His eyes were filled with anguish.

"You've survived a battle. You can survive this." Sam patted him on the shoulder, intending to slip away. He had lingered here too long.

"At least come with me. To give me courage and a kind word?"

Kindness isn't what the Overseer showed him. "I don't think that would be a good idea..."

"Please?" It was worse than a cat crying over spilled milk, and almost as pitiable.

He wanted to shake him, to tell him he was a grown man and he needed to fight his own battles. To leave him out of it.

But how can I do that?

"I'll go with you then," Sam said reluctantly.

The relief on Mathew's face made it seem like a good decision.

"Thank you. Thank you from the bottom of my heart." He shook his head. "I've lost so much sleep thinking about this."

Sleep. That was one thing they all needed more of. It seemed like the entire castle was on a knife's edge, everyone underfed and tired. He hadn't realized it until just then.

"When we get out of this, everyone will sleep a lot better." Sam wanted to get out of the barracks, uncomfortable in the cold, unpleasant room. The smells, the taste of sharp iron. He wanted to leave. "Come get me when you're ready. I need to get to the workshop to start the day."

"Can you go now?" The question stuck into him, unanticipated.

He wasn't ready to go now. "I have to meet Kerien to get him started on a new idea I've had," Sam said. "I couldn't be done until next afternoon."

"Afternoon would be good. It will give me the morning to gather my wits. Will you meet me after lunch?"

Sam searched for an excuse. A task, watch? Mathew would know his watch schedule. That wouldn't work.

"That will do fine." Sam edged to the door. A visibly happier Mathew walked him to it.

"I'll be ready. You don't know how much this means to me and everyone else."

Troubled, Sam left the young man. He wasn't sure there wouldn't be a revolt if the Overseer did what he wanted and clapped him in chains.

Cool, distant. That encompassed every interaction Sam had had with him lately, ever since the attack and Yand's death.

He wondered what the man had been doing. What had he been scheming, whispering in the Duke's ear?

The cool winds of late autumn blew across the courtyard, capturing his coat and threatening to pull it off. If it could be called a coat. It was a collection of rags now, cobbled together from garments of dead men.

The others were already there as he entered. Trent and Kerien were splitting arrows, and Ned, looking even more tired than Mathew had, was shaping a new bow.

"Where have you been?" Kerien asked sharply.

"Mind yourself," Sam said. The storm cloud in his heart darkened, threatening to break. Kerien narrowed his eyes, but held his tongue.

Sam felt some pity for him, his leg bandaged up like that.

However, the attitude it gave him was more than enough to quash the feeling.

The comforting smells of wood dust and oil of the workshop helped though. After the outburst, everyone busied themselves with their work, at least until things calmed down again.

Sam went to his workbench and put his hands on it, resting and feeling its weight. He had spent many an hour here, and it was an old, familiar friend. The smooth top was worn and dinged by countless projects, the shelf beneath filled with offcuts and chunks of special wood, even the way it creaked when he leaned against it. It all helped center him in a time of madness.

While he listened to the others work, scraping, cutting, and polishing away, he wondered what it would have been like to lose this too.

So much had been burned in the first attack. His clothes, his shack, even the letters he had been saving. The one, single reminder of his old life had disappeared in ash and smoke. Drifted away, never to return.

In some ways, it was a blessing. Now, he could never go back.

Ned cleared his throat and glanced back. Sam was calm enough now, balanced again. *I need to control myself better.*

"Any word on the guard duty?"

"Nothing."

"What did they ask of you?" Trent was focused on his work, even though he wasn't cutting out another shaft for arrows.

What did they ask of me? To entreat for them, or to spark an outburst?

"They had a question about inventory. I told them I couldn't help them and directed them to the Overseer." All true, but not all the truth.

"Too dumb to count anything. Sounds like our guards," Kerien said. He was moping, taking too long with his work. Another thing to irritate Sam, and he knew it.

"With so few of them left they probably feel the strain all too sharply." Ned took up a handful of sand and rubbed it along a high spot on his bow. "Word is they're recruiting, if you'd like to join them."

Kerien snorted. "Never in a million years would I be caught as a guard."

"There are worse occupations."

"Sure, and there are dirtier pigs in a pigpen, but you don't see me digging in one."

"Our young friend has a way with words," Sam said, winking at Ned. He still wanted to knock Kerien upside his head, but would play along for the moment.

"Aye, but you might see him sleeping in one."

Kerien reddened at the comment. Sam shot Ned a questioning look, but he only returned one with a look of mirth.

Kerien said something under his breath, but not loud enough for anyone to hear. Sam had the vague impression it was aimed at Ned, from the way he looked over at his corner of the workshop.

"Why do we have to fight?" Trent was quiet, but there was a will in his voice that shocked the room.

It was so quiet they could have heard a feather drop.

Trent turned, his face screwed up into a strange expression. "Don't we have enough to think about that we shouldn't be fighting?"

"You're right," Ned said softly.

Sam reflected on this in the silence. Things had been so hard since Archie died. His tools were a constant reminder of him.

And a constant reminder that any one of them could be next.

He was right. It hurt that Sam hadn't seen it earlier, hadn't said something earlier. They were at each other's throats, even though they were surrounded by an enemy army.

Sam couldn't help but hang his head in shame. "We've been together for a long time now," he said when the silence had stretched to the breaking point. "If we work together, we'll make it through this. I know it."

"Like Archie made it?" Kerien asked. His face was away from them, engrossed in his workbench.

What do I say to that? Sam couldn't lie, and turned over words in his mouth. All of them seemed to be empty, all of them insufficient.

Should he comfort them, tell them that everything was going to be all right in the end?

He didn't believe that. It might be possible, yes, but to promise it was another sort of matter.

His mind drifted to the dead. To Archie, and the family he loved so much, left behind. To Yand, how hard and uncompromising he had been, but for good reason.

Forcing him to bear his weight had been a reminder to Sam of his own duty. There were those here that needed him, that relied on someone to lead them.

He felt ashamed. Once again, here he was, cowardly and refusing to do what was right. How many would have survived if he had trained with Yand? Something about it made him sick inside. It coiled in his stomach, made its way to his back, and twisted around him. Archie would have been here, and his son would still have a father.

Sam set down his plane, unused. "We have failed Archie. We haven't remembered what he did."

He undid his apron and hung it on the side of his workbench. "Come, everyone. This can wait. We have more important things to do."

He had put others to rest before, but never like this. Men who had fought and died, spilled their blood on the field of battle.

"Where are we going?" Trent asked, his eyes wide and following Sam across the room.

Sam didn't answer, but threw aside the threadbare flap of burlap that functioned as a pitiful wall.

They set down their tools and left tasks unfinished. Ned was first, then Trent, and finally Kerien.

Something was bothering him. It had to, how his eyes were downcast and his jaw shifted.

"Leave it behind," Sam said. "For the moment, at least." Kerien paused, then limped along.

Sam got back in lead, shoulder to shoulder with Ned.

The courtyard was alive with children, but they didn't play as hard as they used to. Their voices were softer and cracked. Thin arms and legs replaced the plump, full frames they used to have.

The boy who had taken his message watched them. Sam smiled at him, and he held up a hand to wave.

Around the back of the Keep and up to the makeshift cemetery, they traveled in silence.

They formed a line around his spot, a bit of wood stuck at the head of the grave.

Others bore similar indications of their trades, mostly stone.

Sam remembered. He remembered the bright smile, the skillful hand. How he used to shave too much on the right side and skew his boards. It had taken him months to correct it, but Archie persisted.

"He was a father, a husband, and a friend." Sam's voice echoed off the hard stone of the wall, shattering and cracking. "A steady hand, a keen eye. Goodbye, Archie, and thank you for everything."

Sam knelt and put his hand on the grave, trembling with a rage and wave of emotion. He crushed the sandy earth between his fingers.

The others did the same, and together they bade a friend farewell.

3

CHANGES

"We take them at the pass, cut off all retreat to the north." A whisper in the back, a tremor in the front. General Granb's hand traced along the mountain range. "It's a perfect place for an ambush, and they'll never see us coming."

"That's because we can't get there. The roads are already almost blocked, and the mountains are impassable at this time of the year."

"How dare you interrupt, you miserable whelp," Granb said, eyes narrowing and hand on his sword.

Raltone watched in silence, sizing up the situation. Sable wouldn't say anything if he wasn't completely sure of himself.

The young man strode forward, a sneer on his face and his chest out proud. His black hair streamed down his back. "Your time is through, General." His title was dripping with contempt. "And your tactics outdated. I have a better plan."

General Granb turned to Raltone. "Surely you won't listen to this impudent imp?"

"General Granb has driven the unbelievers from their strongholds," Raltone said. The General smiled and turned back. "However, you may proceed." He lifted his little finger.

He had grown too used to leading the men. Whatever Sable's plan, just having it voiced would help bring down the General's ego, and any potential plans for betrayal.

The smirk on Sable's face broadened. He wasn't the most likable man, but his fighting prowess was too valuable to throw away.

He snapped his fingers. At once, the candles in the tent flickered, then some went out.

Raltone couldn't explain it. There they were, flickering and sputtering, doing their best they could to put out their light, but nothing came.

Instead, a gloomy darkness fell over them, and everyone fell into a hush.

"We've bickered and quarreled amongst ourselves for too long." He seemed to grow. From behind the crowd something stirred. Men moved out of the way as an old, wizened figure stepped through them. "But there is another power, an ancient power that has been long forgotten."

The man shuffled to the center of the room and stood next to the map table.

He was entirely unimpressive, but somehow Raltone's eyes were drawn to him. He sat up when the old man produced a shriveled hand from his robe.

"Watch, and see what future awaits us." Sable knelt before the man, who touched him with his finger.

Strange sounds came out of the man's mouth, and the air seemed to suck out of the tent. Raltone sat up, feeling something run up his back.

Sable... *changed*. There was no other way to describe it.

Raltone couldn't look away. Sable seemed to be writhing with pain or pleasure, but the old man chanted on.

Finally, it was done, and Raltone looked upon the man and saw the future incarnate.

When they had made their peace and said their final good-byes, the group of carpenters went back into the workshop, took up their aprons and tools, and stood at their workbenches.

But none of them put tool to wood.

Even the familiar feel of his favorite chisel, warm and smoothed, with a touch of coolness at the blade, couldn't drive Sam to put it to use.

There was a feeling of hopelessness that hung in the air, more prominent now that Sam could put a finger on it.

He had felt it before, but hadn't recognized it until now.

"What are we going to do?" Trent asked.

The sound shattered the stillness and encompassed everything Sam was thinking and feeling.

What are we going to do?

None of them had a family to go to. They didn't have orders from the Overseer to fulfill. Nothing drove them to do anything.

"I'm afraid we wait," Sam said at last, setting down his chisel. His heart wasn't in it, not right now. "Take the rest of the day off. Rest. Relax. Sleep."

It was the sensible thing to do, but they resisted. True, they took off their aprons and put up their tools, but they all lingered.

Sam didn't blame him, he wanted to stay too. To be around people.

Where else could he go? They were trapped within the walls of the castle now. A few hundred yards in any direction would bring them up against an obstacle of stone feet thick.

He felt hot. He was trapped, stuck like a rat in a box. His eyes burned and his neck was on fire.

Sam took a deep breath, suppressing the panic that tried to overtake him. He didn't know what to do. He had never been in this situation, but he wasn't about to lose his head to it.

That would never do, and it wouldn't help at all.

So what was he to do?

He remembered the night in the Duke's chamber, going over plans and constructions. It had been a time of hope, a time of planning.

Perhaps it was time to resurrect those plans, to make his ideas come to life.

Sam turned back to the courtyard. There was plenty of stone left piled in heaps along the wall, but he knew there was little in the way of wood.

His eyes rested on the half-finished keep. It went up two stories, with the third partially complete in two separate watchtowers. They were rounded and projected above the top of the Keep, a place for defenders to rain down arrows if they needed to.

The crane stood lonely, like a lone sentry on the unfinished tower. It hadn't been used in weeks, since the initial attack had halted all construction on the tower. It was still functional, though, and could be used again.

Sam shook his head, remembering the days of sweat and effort that stretched into the long summer days. The work that had gone into that building was overwhelming. Dozens of masons, the carpenters, and the blacksmiths had all helped to make it rise from the dust.

And, with a few tweaks, they might be able to make something of a defense.

But it would take a lot of work. And he would need help.

A leaf fluttered up over the southern wall and twisted in the light breeze. All the trees had shed theirs, leaving the forest bare.

The leaf twirled and danced, then fell into the courtyard to join the few other strays that had come over the wall.

Just like he had. A transplant in a dangerous situation. The fresh smell of the air couldn't help him feel better, and he'd never felt more alone in his life than that time in the makeshift graveyard.

The Overseer was back, standing politely in front of his desk. "What is it?"

"Our daily meeting, sire," he frowned, somewhat ruffled from his normal appearance.

Evan peered out of bloodshot eyes and eyelids that felt too heavy. His head swam. How much had he had to drink?

Two bottles lay empty on the desk before him, and sunlight streamed in the window. The air was stale, and suffocating.

"Already?" It had seemed like hours had passed in a second. Their last meeting had been yesterday, but it felt like the same day.

He smelled bad, and he knew it, but he tried to not be hurt by the way the Overseer's nose wrinkled as he came closer.

Both of him.

"Shall we begin?" He took a seat.

Something in the way he said it made something inside Duke Hornblood snap.

"No."

"Your Highness?"

"No. I'm not ready. I want you to leave, to leave me alone." He clutched at his goblet. It was empty.

He wished it were full, but knew he couldn't handle another drop.

He should be coming up with plans.

He should be walking among his people.

He should be a leader.

Instead, he was here, wallowing in his own filth and drink like a commoner.

How he longed to go back to those days of carousing—staying out late, laughing with the rough and hardy, kissing beautiful women.

Instead, he was here, in the middle of nowhere, surrounded by Belmarch with no hope of prevailing.

"Perhaps in a few hours?" The Overseer was standing now. If he detested the Duke, he didn't show it.

"Curse your hours. Curse your meetings and your supplies and everything else." Evan snatched up the empty goblet and hurled it at him.

The Overseer flinched, but the glass flew well clear of him.

It smashed against the wall, leaving a strange streak to run down the wooden panel.

Anger turned to anguish. Evan stood. "Why do you—" he swayed, the world turning dangerously. He smashed his eyelids together, then opened them wider and clutched at the desk. "Why do you bother me with these trifles? Go train the men."

The desk held him up, if barely, through the outburst. Evan knew he was shouting but didn't care.

He wasn't like his father, strong and stoic, who could turn a man with a soft word. He wasn't like Yand, who didn't need to say anything. Men would snap to attention if he merely walked by.

The Overseer was sweating. "I can't, sire. I don't know how. I'm a courtier, a member of the court, not a fighting man. I haven't picked up a sword in years."

"But you have used a sword." Evan released one hand and pointed it at him, but the motion threw off his balance and he tumbled to the floor.

His head hit the floor with a thud, and pain lanced through his head. Duke Hornblood groaned.

"Your Highness, are you hurt?" Two Overseers swam in his vision.

"Of course I'm hurt, you buffoon." Hands clutched at him, pulling him into a sitting position. He braced his hand on the cold stone.

How long had it been since he had a fire going? A cheering, crackling fire that spit its heat into the room?

Too long.

His head hurt, a dull thumping at the back where he had struck the floor. All his anger was gone. He didn't mind the Overseer helping him into a sitting position.

"I don't know what I'm doing, Rhys," he moaned. "I'm not my father."

"This is true," the Overseer said in a measured tone. He swept the hair from his forehead, looking for blood. "And you aren't Captain Yand."

"Then what am I to do?"

"Be your own man. Be Duke Evan Hornblood, protector of the north and defender of the realm."

"I don't know if I can do it." A momentary vision of himself in full armor, astride Charger, marching into the capitol in victory.

It faded, lost in the gloom of the room. He held out a hand to the sunlight, trying to catch the shaft of yellow.

He would never have that glory. Not in this life. Not now.

Not trapped in here.

"I'm fine." He snatched his hand back into a fist. His head was starting to throb, whether it was the blow or the drink, he knew not. "But we'll have to do this another time."

"I've seen your promise," the Overseer stared at the corner of the room. "I see what your father sees in you."

"My father sees nothing but a disappointment when he looks at me," Evan said bitterly. "A failure. He'll be glad to be rid of me here."

"I don't want to contradict you, sire," the Overseer said softly, "but that is not what your father sees when he looks at you."

The crest stared at him, mocked him. It told the tale of his family, how they grew from nothing to the most powerful clan and vessel liege to the King. They almost single-handedly put him on the throne.

Nothing like him. Nothing like him at all.

The dregs of the night seemed to swirl inside him, sending the world spinning.

He didn't feel well. It was a familiar feeling, one that often led him to strange bedfellows. Like pigs.

What would his father do in this situation? Alone, out-manned, and trapped. Would he lead the host forth in battle? Or would he do something else?

"If you'll excuse me." The Overseer stood and made for the door.

Evan didn't want him to go all of a sudden. It would leave him alone. All alone, like he had always been. No friend, no playmate. Always the Duke and the Grand Duke's son.

"Goodnight, Duke." The door shut with a click.

He was alone. Truly and deeply alone.

4

A Proposal

Belinda, Archie's widow—a pretty girl all of twenty years—accosted him in the courtyard the next morning.

"Sam Freeman, how dare you!"

He turned, only to have her fists hit him in the chest. He backed up, but she advanced, one arm clutching her child and the other swinging.

"Belinda, calm yourself." He didn't try and stop her but raised a hand to intercept the blows. There were tears in her eyes, but a look of rage in them.

"How dare you visit my husband's grave after what you've done?"

"What have I done to offend you?" Her blows were getting weaker, the tears stronger.

"You took my husband from me." Strands of dark brown hair fluttered in her face, then caught in the tracks on her cheeks. "He's dead because of you."

The accusation cut him to the core. Extreme sadness welled up inside him, sadness he thought he had left behind yesterday at the grave.

He caught her hand and held it. She cried out, trying to wrench it away. The baby was crying in her arms, screaming with fear.

"Belinda," he said, catching her up in his arms. She struggled, but then her struggles turned to sobs of pain, anger, and despair.

"What am I to do?" she cried through the tears.

Sam shut his eyes and held them both. What could he say to her? Could he ease her pain any more than his own?

He opened his mouth, dry at the lack of words. Sam licked his lips. "I don't know. I don't know what to do." He whispered the words, looking to the gray, cold sky.

It was unforgiving, just like life. A marriage ended, a future destroyed. A father taken to the grave.

It was his fate too, however he tried to fight it.

The cries of the baby died away as his mother calmed. She was warm.

Then, without warning, she pulled away. "Don't ever go to his grave again." Her bottom lip trembled. "He deserved better." She pulled the ragged blanket around her child, whispering in his ear to calm him.

"Belinda, there isn't anything I can say to help you feel any better." Sam stared into those red-streaked eyes, so full of fight and steel. He hadn't remembered that about her. He had always seen her as a soft, silly little thing, always giggling and unserious. "I miss Archie too."

She sniffed and raised her head. "He was a far better man than you are." A wave of emotion passed over her face again, and he thought she might cry. "I wish he'd never brought us to this forsaken place."

The baby cried out again, his eyes wide. Belinda leaned down and shushed him, rocking him from side to side.

He looked so much like Archie—his nose, his eyes. Sam stared into his little face, wondering how it came to be like that.

The truth is he could have done something for Archie long before. He was asked, but refused. Now, a child was fatherless.

Who was going to take care of him? His mother would care for him, of course, but what about her?

Who would provide food for her? A place over their heads? Clothes to wear?

He noticed that hers were in rough shape, a collection of worn clothes that were approaching rags. His own were only slightly better.

And the blanket she wrapped her child in was used and in tatters, held together only by the wrapping.

"Can I help you in any way?" Sam cringed at the words, how they came out.

Her eyes narrowed at him. "I've told you how you can help me. And make sure no one else gets killed." She spun on her heel and walked off, leaving him to ponder the conversation all the way to the workshop.

He stopped outside, looking back over the courtyard. Just a wall and a gate, now damaged and weakened by the fire. There was no wood to fix it, of any note, and the braces were left nailed to it.

All they had to do was break through that wall and storm across the courtyard. They could be in and through before they had a chance to secure the Keep.

There were so little defenses ready inside the castle that he was afraid any breach would end them.

Bill's shack was just there, across the way, and the plans he had proposed were still sound.

A twinge of guilt took him at not doing more sooner.

"Sam, is that you?" Ned asked from inside the workshop.

"It's me." He had his hand on the flap of the entrance but only slightly parted. Would Bill be willing?

That was a problem for another day. He only had a few hours until the appointed meeting time, if that, and a lot of work to get done.

The others were hard at work, almost exclusively making arrows. The stock of wood was getting lower every day, with no way to replenish it.

Sam went over to them, running his hand along the rough-cut timber. Most of it was seasoned, dry enough to work without much movement after they had moved all the wood that was most ready to be used before the attack.

He breathed in the deep smell of it, letting the oak, ash, and cherry push away his fears and failures.

The others made some small talk, but left him alone. Sam joined them, helping to make arrows, until the flap ruffled and Mathew appeared.

"Sam?" he asked, looking in with a question in his eyes.

Sam was putting away his tools and wrapping up the chisels. "I'm ready." He wiped the dust from his hands and joined Mathew at the door.

"Where are you going?" Trent asked, a touch of concern in his voice.

"I'll be back soon. I'll see you at lunch." Sam slipped out and let the flap fall down behind him.

"You weren't going to tell them?" The gravel crunched underfoot.

"No. I don't want to be there as is." Sam frowned, pulling his cloak tighter around him. Cold days had come in force. Even the warm sun on his skin couldn't keep him warm. "Let's get this over with."

Mathew was quiet the rest of the way, and Sam didn't feel much like talking. There was a storm brewing inside him, a collection of troubles in his mind.

He reached forward in time, thinking of what could happen. The walls were large, but not too long. With the men they had now it wouldn't be hard to keep them manned to repel an attack.

But each loss would be felt more and more. Day by day, their strength would lessen. Attack by attack, they would crumble.

Or were the Belmarch planning something else? He didn't know, but he did know the last attack cost them dearly. They had lost more men than the defenders.

They could be licking their wounds, letting their injured heal, all to prepare for another rush.

They were at the Keep now, the doors opened and shut behind them. Sam felt the thunder rise to a peak in front of the Overseer's door.

He took a deep breath.

Mathew was looking—or studying—the door. Sam couldn't tell which. His fingers twitched and trembled.

Sam put a hand on his shoulder and patted it. "Go on."

"I'm not so sure about this anymore. Maybe we'll get Verith to meet him instead." There were visible drops of sweat on his brow.

Instead of responding, Sam reached out a fist and knocked.

Mathew's eyes opened in surprise, and his jaw dropped. Sam gave him a shrug as they heard the Overseer respond.

"Come."

"Go on," Sam said, giving him a little push. Mathew reached out a trembling hand to the door and opened it.

"Mathew?" The Overseer put down a sheaf of paper, then, seeing Sam, opened a drawer in his desk and dropped it inside. "And... you."

Sam's heart dropped. He shouldn't have come. He knew that now, but the young man in front of him looked so pitiable.

"Overseer." Sam nodded respectfully and stood behind Mathew.

The Overseer's hard gaze lingered on Sam, then slipped to Mathew. The room smelled of tallow from the one candle in the corner and of must. It was unlit now, but Sam suspected it got its fair share of use, judging from how melted it was.

"Overseer Rhys," Mathew stammered, then remembering his place, saluted.

The silence drifted from long to uncomfortable.

"I imagine you had a reason for coming to see me?" The Overseer stared down from his seat.

Mathew's mouth worked. No sound came out. The Overseer tapped his fingers against the desk.

"Get on with it, then. Is there word from the wall?"

"No, Overseer. It... is another matter."

"And what of it?" The Overseer's tone was flustering Mathew, making him even more nervous than he was.

Sam watched on. He had a strange fascination with the whole scene. The young guard, the foppish leader. That this was the best they had to offer made him feel as if they had no chance at all.

He could offer a word of encouragement, give him something to hold onto. However, he knew that might make it worse from the way the Overseer had seen and dismissed him.

Instead, he opted for the least intrusive interjection, merely coughing quietly.

The Overseer's eyes snapped to him, and he gave him a gentle smile. Mathew straightened, a good sign.

"We need a leader, someone to oversee the daily defenses of the castle." The words spilled out of him, rushing all at once and almost joined together.

"Hold on, what do you mean?" The Overseer broke eye contact with Sam, turning his attention back to the guard. "This isn't a message?"

"No."

"Then what are you doing here? I have more important things to attend to."

Mathew hazarded a glance at Sam, who gave him a nod and a look of encouragement that he didn't feel himself.

The boy wasn't ready for this. The Overseer had always preferred to keep to himself and stay in his quarters while they worked on the castle. He would come out from time to time to bark orders and check on things, but he had never been the kind to train and encourage.

It was no surprise he was reacting this way. Sam should have known and anticipated it, told Mathew to expect it ahead of time. He felt shame.

Another list of things he should have done. A growing list, remembering Belinda and her words.

Mathew swallowed, shrinking back from the desk. His feet quivered, as if they were ready to run to the door.

He wasn't sure what to do. Sam wasn't sure either.

"Overseer..." Mathew swallowed, trying to gather his courage. Sam looked on with sadness.

If the man wasn't brave enough to make his case, how could he ever be expected to lead the other guards?

He was young. Too young to be caught up in all of this. Someone else needed to do it.

Looking over the Overseer, a soft man despite the lost weight that had slimmed him down, Sam knew he couldn't do it either. When Yand had died, they had lost more than a good fighter.

"I must entreat you in this matter," Mathew said. In the distance, a child cried, muted by the thick keep walls. "We must have someone to train the men. Someone who can lead them, if need be, in battle."

Sam half-expected the Overseer to start shouting, but what he did next surprised him. He sagged back into his chair, deflating.

"And what would you have me do? Pick up spear and sword? No, I think not."

"No, not have you do that."

"Then what?"

"I ask that you appoint a man for the task." At this, the Overseer rubbed his temples. There was already a man in the castle that was designated to lead, but that man had been shut away out of sight.

Go on, ask him. Sam willed Mathew to do what he came for.

"Will you do this? The men are crying out for it."

"And you are not the first to approach me on the matter. Out with it, ask your question."

Mathew took a deep breath, then spoke. "Put Sam Freeman in charge."

5

DISAGREEMENT

Sam's mouth dropped in surprise. He quickly shut it before the Overseer looked at him.

What was he thinking? This isn't what we agreed.

"Sam Freeman?" The Overseer looked at him now, his own eyes opened slightly in surprise.

"No," Sam said, meeting his gaze. "I can't do it."

"Well, we are in agreement. For once."

"Overseer, he's the only one with the leadership to do it. You've seen him fight. You know what he can do. He trained Trent to fight."

"Is this true?"

Bill. It had to be him. Would Trent reveal his night training to anyone? Sam didn't think so.

"Mathew has the wrong idea," Sam said. "He would be a good choice to lead, and you should make him the head guard."

"We all know that isn't right," Mathew said, hands clenched into fists. It didn't stop the quivering of them.

Sam felt sick. For all the same reasons he knew Mathew wasn't right, he had still said it. His eyes dropped to the floor.

Silence seeped into the room. Sam could feel his own breath in his chest, the hard stones of the floor beneath his feet.

His mind wandered back to the past, to all the other places he wished he'd rather not be. A cold battlefield frozen in the winter. A hot graveyard still reeking of blood under the unforgiving sun.

He didn't hate the Overseer, but he didn't like him either. The man was weak in some respects and hard in others. The wrong things.

But he wasn't stupid, and he knew how to handle himself in situations like these. Sam suspected that might be one of the reasons he was put in charge, despite not having any experience building castles before.

Not that many did. There weren't many castles in Chathem, but plenty of watchtowers.

He doubted that anyone had the experience to build one, which might have been why it had taken longer than expected.

Cloth shifted, rubbing against itself as the Overseer leaned back in his chair. It creaked, protesting the injustice, but stopped.

"We're going to die if we don't know what to do," Mathew said, stealing Sam away from his thoughts. "Would you ask the Duke?"

"I make no promises to you. Particularly this impudent request." The Overseer once again cast his gaze over Sam. It slid off him like oil on water.

"Mathew, he's right. I'm not the right man to lead anything," Sam said. What he wanted was a different life, to build.

"You took a risk, like all of us." The Overseer clasped his hands together. "Striking deep into almost the very heart of the enemy. You knew this day would come."

He was talking to Sam, who wisely held his tongue.

"I wonder why. Would you like to enlighten us?"

"Money," Sam said. "Like the other men here." The Overseer let out a bark of a laugh, incredulous.

"Is that why you came, Mathew? For the money?" He turned his attention to the guard.

"For the chance to advance, Overseer." Mathew hung his head. "And the money."

"Which you, no doubt, have realized is now contingent on our survival. Yes, money can be a great motivator. I'm not sure it is the motivation, though, for all." The Overseer waved his hand. "I will consider your request. Again, I make no promises."

Mathew was going to get out of it without getting in trouble, of that Sam was glad, but he couldn't let this rest.

"I beg you not to consider it." Sam stepped forward, taken by a mood. What was he to lead anything?

"That will be enough from you," the Overseer snapped. He picked up a quill, preparing to dip it into his ink. "You have had your say."

Sam didn't think that he had, and leaned forward, putting his hands on the desk. The way the man spoke to him, like he was filth, dirt on his shoes, angered him.

A word, a little phrase spoken, could end this for him. Sam knew it and locked eyes with the Overseer.

They were cool, calculating. Gone was the bubbling old fool hidden in the folds of fat. There was something else in there.

Something dangerous.

I can end any chance now. He never liked me. He hates me.

"If you have something to say to me, say it." The Overseer spoke in a whisper, weight behind his words.

He had something to say.

"Good afternoon, Overseer." Sam let go of the desk, feeling the blood rush back to his fingers, and stepped back.

He turned and walked out of the room. Mathew hastily bid his farewell, maintaining his decorum, and followed.

He caught up to Sam in the hallway, grabbing his arm.

"Sam, I—"

"That isn't what we discussed." Sam spun around, advancing on the man, who shrunk back.

"There is no one else." There was pain in Mathew's eyes. "I'm sorry."

"There are plenty of men."

"Not in this castle. You have to understand what we're up against. It isn't a game."

"No," Sam growled, "it isn't." He didn't know why he was dumb enough not to see it before. This was always Mathew's plan.

"What chance do we have without you?" Mathew looked in his eyes, searching for something.

Sam turned without answering him and walked away.

He was a mixture of emotions. Anger, fear, loathing. Most of it was directed at himself. The rest was directed toward Mathew.

"I'll tell you what chance you have. None. Even with me, you have no chance." Sam waved his hand. "Look around you. Do you see anyone coming to help us? Do you see an army marching to the rescue?"

He couldn't see, but Mathew shrank back as if hit.

"If you want my help, then I can give you some advice. Make your peace, and prepare for death. That's what you'll get in this place. That's what you'll get with me."

Before Mathew could answer Sam spun on his heel and took off as fast as he could. His feet clattered on the stone floor, a soft sound in the long hallway. He didn't hear Mathew try and come after him.

Sam left the Keep, fleeing to the north wall and away from as many as he could. It was more peaceful up here, to the tower he climbed, and in little fear of attack.

The Golden River churned below him, the river running over the rocks at the base of the wall.

Sam leaned against the wall, letting the cold wind bite through his coat. The first snowflake of the year drifted down from the white, puffy clouds high in the sky.

His breath came out in clouds, streaming behind him in the wind as it was carried away. Where had all the time gone?

It had seemed like summer would never end a few months ago, and now it was snatched away. Sam closed his eyes and listened to the world.

The river talked above his heartbeat, strong and steady and shivering along the rocks. Birds called up above him, latecomers as they traveled south.

Behind him the sounds of the castle were muted, a thick wall in between him and the others.

They were out of the frying pan now, and smack dab in the middle of the fire. He opened his eyes, hoping for a moment they would reveal the Chathem army just out of sight.

Instead, he was given the sight of an empty and cold river. Never-ending, barren, desolate. No hope of survival, no plan for saving.

He looked south. A few days' journey that direction and they would be at the port city of Jareth. Bale would be a few more days inland, and then a message delivered.

So how, exactly, were they going to get that message delivered?

He had been on boats before, but was in no way a river-man. A crossing here and there. That was the extent of his experience.

Would it be possible to resupply the castle from the water? Sam squinted, trying to see beneath the surface of the river.

Those who had grown up on the water, or made their livelihoods on it, might be able to make sense of how the water moved around the base of the castle, but to Sam it was impossible.

The water came up to the bank of rock, hit it and swirled around, then continued on to wherever it went. Nothing stopped it, and it kept going.

The bell rang out in the courtyard. Changing of the guard.

Sam sighed and slipped down the steps to the courtyard below. It was his turn—another few hours of standing and waiting, shivering on the battlements and staring at an enemy that wanted to destroy them.

He went to the courtyard outside the barracks, received his bow and allotment of arrows, managing to avoid Mathew.

He followed the others up the steps to the wall, taking his place on the south wall to the west of the gate.

"Any change?" Sam asked, approaching Stave, who he was charged with taking over from.

"Nothing." Stave spit over the edge. "Other than this forsaken cold."

They exchanged words, and Sam bid him a good night. Stave tipped his hat to him and left.

He was a mason, but wasn't as chilly toward him as he used to be. Sam noticed this and noted it for later.

Perhaps Bill was telling them to lay off him, or maybe something else was going on. He wouldn't be surprised if it was a ploy to get him to agree to...

Rebellion. Sam shivered. How could he even consider it?

But they were in desperate times, and men in these kinds of situations did desperate things.

What had driven Bill to it? Was it something in his past, a proclivity to it?

Something moved in the distance. A man appeared at the edge of the Belmarch camp and stopped. The figure moved around, then went back inside.

A few more streamed out of the camp. They, too, had their change of guard. They went into the forest, hidden from the prying eyes of the defenders, and dispersed to wherever they had set their watches.

Sam tried to follow them, hand tightening on his unstrung bow. He thought they might turn to the castle, launch an attack.

But they didn't. A few minutes later, men emerged, probably the relieved, and went into the camp.

Their fire burned where the old Square had been, bright and cheery with happy billows of smoke.

The nerve they had to do it. Sam had spent a few happy nights there, filled with food, laughter, and decent ale that slaked the thirst after a long day of work.

It was a different time, one he had hoped would last forever, but one he knew must end. He had hoped it would be after the completion of the castle. Sam would have stayed, been a resident of the new town to be built within its walls, safely nestled behind the gray stone.

Instead, they were trapped here. He leaned against the hard stone, watching the forest for any sign of movement.

It was quiet and still. The bare trees had gained a dusting of snow, but it had stopped.

The cold was draining his feet of heat, his shoes long ago in need of repair. He would have to see if he could get a few rags to wrap around his feet to keep them warm, but until he did, he had to resort to lifting first one, then the other, after he couldn't bear the chill anymore.

The rest of the watch passed with little to note. Only that dull monotony he had grown so accustomed to.

He hated it. Always had. Better to be dressing lumber than sit doing nothing all day.

It was a relief when the dinner bell rang, and Kerien came to relieve him about a half-hour later.

"Evening," Sam said, slapping his arms to regain some heat.

"Mmm," Kerien grunted.

"Dinner not good?"

"No. You'll see." Kerien's eyes narrowed as he looked to the enemy camp. "Is that...?"

"Best not to think about it too much." Sam's mouth was watering. "They're doing it on purpose."

Kerien groaned. "What I'd give for a bite of that."

The Belmarch had killed a deer and were roasting it on a spit over the fire. Every so often, a flare from the fire would raise up as a dripping caught fire and was consumed.

"I think they want to kill us, but they're willing to take their time."

"Gruel, again. And cold."

Sam frowned but hiked up his bow and took up his arrows. "Good watch."

Kerien stared, and Sam left him.

They were going to wait them out, let them all starve to death. As Sam's cold feet squished the thin layer of snow, he knew he couldn't let that happen.

The problem was, what was he to do about it?

What good would it have done, anyway?

He strode across the cold floor, giving greetings to those who had the heart to look up at him and respond back.

Their bowls and dishes were filled with more of the same. Sam grimaced. He wasn't looking forward to this.

"Good evening, Martha," he said, producing his bowl from beneath his tattered coat. "Mutton stew tonight?"

She narrowed her eyes at him and wagged the spoon in his direction. "None of your jokes tonight, Sam. I don't have the heart to hear it."

"What's wrong?" He didn't mean to offend her.

"It's Mary. I don't know what's wrong with her, but the stubborn girl refuses to work." She reached into the pot with the spoon, wiggled it around a little, then scooped out a clump. It clung to the pot, fighting as if it wanted to stay, but then came off with a slop.

Into his proffered bowl it went. She banged a few times to get it to release. "I see," he said sympathetically. "Anything wrong with her?"

"You know what's wrong with her. Heartbroken." Her normally hard eyes turned soft and glistened in the dim light. He sniffed at his bowl. It smelled like water and wheat. Unsurprisingly, that was what it was.

He thought.

"Her, among others." His first thought was of Belinda. Alone, afraid, with a young son to take care of and no father to help. His heart tweaked, and shame rose inside. "It has come to hard times."

"But we expected hard times, didn't we?" She sighed and leaned over her bowl. "Coming up here. Doing what we did. My poor Davy wanted me to stay away, but I told him that by his side was where I'd pledged to be, and by his side, I'd stay."

"An admirable quality."

"Not everyone agreed with me. They'll be wishing they were here now."

"I doubt that very much." Not all the families had come. Some stayed with family and friends elsewhere, unaccustomed or unwilling to pull up their roots. Not until the castle and walls were complete and a full garrison stationed, at least.

Sam couldn't blame them, and often felt bad for the men who barely saw their families. He wondered what they thought now and looked down the line of tables.

There was Eric, a stonemason with a young wife and no children. His wife had stayed behind with her mother. Sam had overheard her say as much.

And there were others. Eric seemed to be doing fine, other than looking skinnier than he used to be.

"What about you, Sam? Leave a sweetheart behind?" Martha twirled her spoon around. There was no one in line behind him to hold up.

"No one." His meal was getting cold. He knew he should go sit down and eat. It was better lukewarm.

"I'm sorry to hear that." She sounded it too, genuine. He had often wondered how life would have turned out if he had stayed.

Would he be promised out to someone by now? Living in the countryside with babies? His former home was a peaceful place now, by all accounts, the old wars calm and settled, and general camaraderie with neighbors.

Since they had won their freedom, at least, from the assessor. But that had been a long time ago now.

"What will you do after this?" Martha asked, bringing him back from his thoughts.

"I hadn't thought about it." He wondered if there would be an after.

6

STORM IN THE KEEP

The door slammed shut behind him. Blessedly, it stopped the wind from cutting through his cloak. Sam rubbed feeling back into his arms.

The Keep wasn't warm, but it wasn't as cold as outside.

The great hall had been returned to its former status, or rather, what it would be when complete. Tables ran down both sides, rough timbers that had been repurposed from their original intended use within the Keep itself.

Men and women sat at them, eating out of bowls and drinking from cups of wood.

It was the body heat of everyone inside that kept away the worst of the cold. The fireplace was cold and bare.

How he wished it were filled with logs cracking orange and red, sending their smoke into the room and up the chimney. Instead, it was wet and dead.

At the far end Martha was serving food. She had become a de facto leader of the women, keeping them busy and directing their efforts.

Once plump and rounded, she had slimmed down. Her straight, black hair accentuated the change, making her face seem thin and drawn.

What must I look like?

Sam stroked his beard, now three inches long. It had kept out the worst of the cold. His hair hung shabby and long. He hadn't had the time or the desire to cut it.

"What will you do?"

"My family is from down south, in Bevonshire." The cook-fire was out now, banked down to preserve every bit of wood and fuel. She had wrinkles at the corners of her eyes, just beginning to show. "I think I'll go back."

Sam wondered if he should ask about her husband, lost to the sickness that took so many. He had wondered why she had stayed here. But he thought better of it.

"What's it like?" He scooped up his meal. Here was as good as any.

"I'll join you. You were one of the last." She turned her head back to one of the younger girls. "Nancy, watch the food."

They sat down at the table. "It's a peaceful place. More sheep than people." Martha slipped behind the table and sat gracefully.

"It sounds nice."

"Except when you have to shear them. The smell." She wrinkled her nose up. "Worse than rotted food if you don't clean them well enough. Or it rains." She tilted her head off to the side. "Nothing like the smell of damp sheep." A faint smile played over her lips.

Sam looked away, painfully aware that he had been staring at them. "I can't say I've smelled it. Or that I've seen many."

"You haven't seen sheep?" Martha laughed. It was strange—there had been so little laughter around here. "Well, that is unbelievable."

"Is it?"

"What about you? What reminds you of home?"

Home. That was something he wasn't sure what to call. He took a bite of his food. It was bland but edible. It stuck to the roof of his mouth.

"You're avoiding the question."

"Mmm-hmm." He pointed to his mouth, trying to ignore her eyes, filled with a touch of mirth and a dollop of annoyance. "Not trying. Just hungry. The forest. That reminds me of home."

"Is that what drew you to working wood?"

"I hadn't thought about that before. I liked walking through it, cool in the summer when the sun was so harsh in the pen. The way the leaves crunch under my feet and tickle my toes." The memory of it made the hall disappear for a moment.

He was back on the path now, walking beside the brook as it bubbled and worked its way down the hill. The smell of the leaves was thick, the summer raging, but it was cool.

Is that where I want to be?

"I'm not sure what my home will be, or when I'll get there." Her eyes seemed to ache.

Was that for him? Or something else? "Thank you for the meal, for leading the other women." He finished the meager portion left. "I should go. We have a lot of work to do." True enough, for now, but what would he do when they had no supplies, when they had no work to occupy themselves?

It nagged at him, it burrowed into his brain and refused to go away. They would need more food if they were to last. They would need more wood if they were to build.

But they still had plenty of rock. It was just Bill who he needed now. Command him, and he had the masons.

Martha's face fell. "I will see you at dinner."

Sam felt hot all of a sudden, unaware of what he had said. She stood up and rushed off back to the other girls, starting to give directions before she got there.

There was a creeping feeling on his back, but Sam pushed it off to the side. He did have a lot of work to do.

How he would handle it all, he wasn't sure.

***

The world was a groggy haze. Sunlight snuck in at the top of his room, casting a harsh glare upon everything.

Evan groaned. His head was pounding, and he felt sick to his stomach. He opened his eyes, cracked and dry.

Next to his head was a pile of vomit. It smelled horrible, so he turned away. The residue of it cracked at the corners of his mouth.

What time it was, he did not know, nor did he care. He wanted to go back to sleep, but the drink had worn off. He wasn't sure what kind of dreams would haunt him.

They still did, despite the wine. His father standing over him, bringing down his sword in retribution, his eyes burning like fire as it consumed him.

Evan squeezed his eyes shut again, trying to banish the thought. Overseer Rhys hadn't come to see him yet—it must be before noon.

Unless he had given up.

He tried to get out of bed, shoving off the covers. His head swam as he sat up, and he almost fell back again.

What am I doing? Back to my old ways.

He just needed a pack of pigs, and everything would be complete.

The ground was cold, the bare stone sapping the warmth from his feet. He was still in his clothes, not bothering to change apparently. He didn't remember much from last night after the fifth or sixth glass of wine.

Had he really drunk that much?

The goblet was on the table, knocked over. He shuffled over to it, making sure to go slow so that he wouldn't fall over.

The bottle was empty. The one next to it too.

There was a cask in the cellar left. Three or four, he couldn't remember. He didn't pay much attention to the numbers when Rhys droned on.

"Attention to the management of your lands is hardly exciting," his father had said one afternoon when he had drifted off to sleep. *"Those who neglect it are foolish."*

He had been only nine or ten summers old then, but he remembered it like it was yesterday.

His mouth ached for a drink. It felt dry, like cotton, and he wished for something to slake the memory. To wash it all away.

It would be washed away, one way or the other. His father would never take him back now, let alone his uncle. What a disgrace to the family.

The tree whose roots run deep? Not mine, he thought bitterly.

Where was that servant? Evan rang the bell and waited, but no one came. He rang it louder. They were supposed to be right there, waiting in case he needed something.

"Is there no discipline around here?" he growled. "Who's out there?"

There was no response. Head pounding, Evan tugged on his boots and stumbled to the door.

It wasn't quiet like it usually was. Every so often, there was a loud bang.

He wrenched open the door, scowling.

The corridor was empty, not a servant in sight.

"Where are they?" He stepped out into the hallway. "Hello?"

There were shouts, but from outside, and he couldn't make out what they were saying.

Some of his hangover receded, replaced with fear. *What was going on?*

He went back inside, hurrying to strap on his sword. His fingers were thick and slow, and he fumbled with the clasp. Finally, the metal ends clicked together, and it was around his waist.

He went back to the door, then stopped. He didn't want to go out there, to find out what was happening. He wanted a drink.

His eyes shifted to the right, to his study. There would certainly be more there. To his left was the exit, out into the courtyard.

He hadn't been out there in weeks. Every time he tried, he couldn't make it. It was as if there was a hand pushing on his chest, crushing him. Preventing him from going out.

A few steps, a few doors. That was all that he had to do.

Evan shook his head, fell against the door. Instead of taking that path, he went back to his study, fingers trembling as he opened the door.

He got inside and locked it, a great weight off his chest, but a wave of shame to replace it.

He should be out there. He should be with his people. But they weren't his, really—they were his father's.

The great seal of the Hornbloods loomed above him over his desk. He looked away. He couldn't bear it.

What was happening outside? It didn't sound like fighting, not exactly. He had heard that before, but it didn't sound pleasant either.

He could make out the ringing of something—sword on sword, he thought.

All the blood drained from his face. What if they were inside? That they had taken the outer walls?

Only the walls of the Keep would keep them out. Only a thin layer of rock was between his sworn enemy and himself.

And there was nothing he could do to stop it. His hand clutched at his sword, both a comfort and a reminder of what he should be doing.

His nose was running, and he wiped it with his sleeve. Pressure, there was so much pressure. He shrank down.

He felt pinned against the door. That hand, there it was again. His breath was short, his chest on fire.

Sweat was running down his forehead, despite the cold of the room. Clammy hands pulled at his collar.

His head still ached. He wished he was anywhere other than here. Agony filled his body, his mind, his soul.

Evan Hornblood collapsed to the floor, his sword ringing against the stone. He should draw it, charge outside, and face the Belmarch head-on.

He could go out in a blaze of glory, one man against a thousand, sword flashing in the sun like a blade of fire.

But he was here, cowering on the ground.

Yand wouldn't have said anything. He would have picked him up, dusted him off, and sent him to the training yards.

He would have beat him in combat training, not with the whip. Even now, he remembered those lessons—the forms, the exercises.

But here he was. Evan moaned and caught a glimpse of the tree again.

It was too large, too overpowering. Blast that carpenter who made it. He should have chucked it into the fire. His own pride had done him in.

He pulled himself to the bar and took out a bottle.

It was empty.

The next was empty too. Bottles flew as he flung them away, crashing and cracking, some shattering into a million pieces.

There wasn't a single drop of wine left.

Evan slunk to his knees. He was going to die in this room. Alone, and like a coward.

There were voices outside his room, rough voices shouting something he couldn't make out.

They are here!

Evan pulled himself to his desk and crawled under it. The door rattled and shook.

There, hiding beneath his desk, Evan felt the worst he had ever felt in his life.

Something cracked inside him. He wasn't going to die like this.

Pushing aside the pain, the shame, the cowardice, he rose to his feet and drew his sword.

"Come and take me if you can," he shouted, then strode to the door and unlocked it.

7

HOPE LESS

Evan braced himself, eyes bloodshot and heart pounding, as the invaders slammed open the door.

He gave a war cry and raised his sword.

Overseer Rhys raised his hands in defense. "Sire!"

Evan stopped himself before the blow landed, breathing hard. "Rhys, what... what's going on?"

"Someone heard sounds from your room. I had to come check." Still shaken, the Overseer rose from where he had crumpled down to avoid death.

"I called for the servants. I—where were they?"

"Apologies, my lord, I had them in the storeroom. The others were busy with practice."

He ran a hand through his hair, now giddy. "We aren't under attack?"

"No, your highness." Evan turned, looking down at the sword in his hand and the remains of the bottles around his room.

There was a strange feeling inside him. The longing for the wine, that escape, was still there.

But there was something bigger than it, something that overcame it. He laughed suddenly, and turned.

The servants behind Rhys looked at each other in concern. Evan clapped the Overseer on the back. "Apologies for the smell. It seems I got carried away. Give me some time to wash up and we can discuss matters."

Surprise was an understatement for the look that flashed across Rhys' face, but he covered it up quickly. "Certainly, we still need some time to finish the inventory. I will come by as soon as we are done."

The overpowering feeling of relief was still there when they left, and Evan couldn't stand still. He paced around his room, alternating between laughing and frowning.

He had been a coward, there was no use in lying to himself. He had taken the easy way out.

That was the Evan of yesterday, though. Now, he was a different man. The simple act of defiance, being prepared to die with a sword rather than cowering beneath a desk, was heady and filled him with giddiness.

For the first time in a long time, he had hope that things might change. And, as he looked up at his looming family crest, a glimmer of hope that he might be worthy of the name Hornblood.

***

A soft knock at the door reached him at his desk. "Come."

Overseer Rhys walked in, a bundle of scraps of paper and records under his arm. "Good afternoon, your highness."

"Come, come, sit down." Evan motioned to the open chair. Even though his head still ached from the hangover, the cold bath and clean clothes had done wonders for it. His bed was being washed now, a luxury he knew the others might not have.

The Overseer glanced at his hair, combed for the first time in weeks, and over his clothes, but he sat without comment.

"I haven't been the best Duke," Evan said, "and we might as well address that now."

"Your highness," the Overseer protested, but Evan cut him off.

"We'll move past it, no need for flowery words to try and cover it up. Once we're done here, I need to go inspect the guardhouse and the walls, see what state they're in. Father always said seeing the thing was far more important than hearing about it." Rhys had always included a report with his meetings.

His words caused a strange tightness around the Overseer's eyes and lips. "What is it? I'm certain you've done what you can, and I have no reservations about what you've told me."

"That isn't it." He took his time to answer. The Overseer was choosing his words carefully, and Evan leaned in when he finally said them. "It might be best to be out of sight. The men are... restless."

His heart dropped, and his voice caught in his throat. "You don't mean...?"

The Overseer nodded. "You're safer inside."

"I don't believe it."

"It's rumors, your highness, but these rumors tend to lead to... nasty results."

Evan shook his head. Then, anger rose up inside him. "They would dare overthrow their lawful ruler? I'll have their heads on pikes."

"Talk like that might not have the most soothing effect." The Overseer's face looked drawn and tight. "The rule of law is already on the edge of a knife. One push might be all it takes."

"Surely you exaggerate?" More than a hint of fear entered his voice. His father was right to send him here, to prove that he would fail.

Or had he sent him to redeem himself, to prove that he could handle a situation like this?

Either way, this ill news was too much to bear. The thirst came back, that precious liquid that would send him into oblivion. He would take a peasant's homebrew if he could get it.

"Perhaps I've misjudged the situation." The Overseer didn't look like he had any doubt of it, though. *Blasted politician.* "But a few more days of caution might be called for. You can rest and recover from your..." He paused, then found the word he was looking for. "Ordeal."

And that was that. The topic covered, the Overseer brought out his inventory and records and proceeded to drone through them.

Evan paid more attention this time, but he couldn't help but think about it, always clouding his thoughts like a thunderhead in summer a few miles off.

A looming threat, that might dissipate and blow to dust, or one that could take a sharp turn and be on you in an instant. One would be easy to bear, the other required good shelter.

So, what would he do if it were true?

***

The guards sweated and groaned as they trained, the tradesmen even more so.

Sam trudged by them, glad that his squad was not until after dinner.

"Sam, wait up." Mathew joined him, matching him stride for stride. He couldn't help but feel a hint of annoyance, and it must have shown on his face.

"Have you reconsidered?"

"There isn't anything to consider. Didn't you hear Overseer Rhys?" He seemed warm against the bitter cold. Sam remembered that feeling, being hot despite the cold.

He wondered if they should be doing it. Training was important, but it was taking energy. That, in turn, led them to hunger faster.

It would be a drain on their food. The training would need to be focused, and only what they needed, nothing more, to avoid waste.

Even now, he observed two men sparring and doing a terrible job of it. They circled each other, bashing one another with their swords. It would have been fine in a normal army, but here it was wasteful and unneeded. Every excess movement was a waste, from how they swung too much and lunged too far.

"I see you'd like a turn?"

Mathew stared at him, and Sam broke his gaze. *If he said anything...*

"Just watching." Mathew's face fell. "You should get back to training."

"There isn't much else to do, other than watch."

Little did he know. That was a blessing. "I must go." He bid Mathew farewell and strode off, letting him fall behind.

Bill was there, and Sam felt his eyes on his back.

Sam hurried into the workshop, eager to pick up his tools again. His work helped ease his mind, and the time passed quickly.

Dinner came faster than he realized, the peals of the bell ringing out. Everyone looked up as it started and relaxed when it was the simple call to dinner.

They put away tools and streamed out, but someone caught hold of his arm as he went.

It was Bill, motioning for him to keep quiet. Sam furrowed his brow, but he only nodded his head and slipped inside the workshop.

"I forgot something, you all go on ahead," Sam said, waving the others away. When they had gone, confused looks on their faces, he went back in.

Bill was at his workbench, touching his tools. "Hands off," Sam said, his voice gruff and lower than normal. His body had tensed up at the sight.

Bill stopped, then raised his hands with a smirk. "I mean no harm. Nor insult either."

After taking a deep breath, Sam remembered his manners. He shouldn't have done that. "What is it you want to talk about?"

"I think you know."

"I grow tired of these men."

"I presume you expect me to have changed my mind?"

"You know the rumors just as well as I do."

Sam folded his hands across his chest and leaned back against the wooden support of the workshop. A faint hint of smoke was in the air. He wondered if it was from the meal or if it was from the Belmarch camp.

Sometimes it seemed like they did it to torment them, creating huge bonfires that you could almost imagine feeling from the top of the wall.

It was torture, but didn't drive the men to do what the Duke was doing.

"I haven't heard the latest. Enlighten me."

Bill ran a finger along a board, picking up some sawdust. He crushed it between his finger and thumb, rubbing it around. "Life has become... too much to bear for the Duke. He's draining the wine faster than if it had holes in the cask."

It was the same rumor he had heard. Late nights, sleeping through the day. "That doesn't give anyone the right to kill him."

"Kill?" Bill's eyes opened in feigned surprise, and he held up his hands. "Who said anything about killing?"

Sam narrowed his eyes by reflex.

"I never said I wanted to kill the Duke. He needs to be set aside though. He isn't fit to lead."

Sam almost defended the Duke but wasn't sure where to start.

"Ah, I see it in your eyes. You agree but don't want to admit it."

"Why haven't you done it by yourself?"

"I've thought about it, but you and I know the rest of the men aren't in my grip the way the masons are. And I couldn't convince all of them on my own, even if I wanted to."

"You want someone else to do your dirty work, so that your hands stay clean."

"Not necessarily, although I have thought of it." Bill shrugged. "I want to get out of here alive, Sam. Both you and I know it won't happen unless we have someone who can lead and inspire the men."

He was stroking his ego to try and get him to do what he wanted. Sam saw through it, but his voice seemed so sincere. "You've mastered lying."

"We need to get help, and no one else seems to want to take charge," Bill said. "If we do that first, if we can work together to find a way to get aid, would that satisfy you?"

"No, it wouldn't. He's the Duke, the future ruler of this castle."

"He's a drunken little boy who is going to get all of us killed," Bill hissed. "What good will he do ruling over a grave?"

"Then you go to him. You convince him to abdicate and leave the power to you." Bill started, and Sam pressed the attack. "You never thought of that, have you? Always quick to anger and never to the simple solution."

"He won't do it. I know men. They don't give up power willingly."

"You don't know that. The Duke may not want to be here. He may be more than glad to get out of the way for you to lead."

"You're trying to distract me, to keep me confused." Bill shook his head. "I won't have it, not this time."

"No one is coming to save us. Face the truth, Bill."

"Since when did Sam Freeman become so hopeless?" The wind lifted the flap of the workshop and blew sawdust up, scattering chips and curls of wood.

Had he given up hope? He caught a glimpse of the spear, its broken handle shattered still, and wondered.

It seemed to him that there was no choice. They were too few and too ill-trained to try and counterattack.

Unless...

"You haven't answered my question. Will you reconsider if we can get help?"

"No." Bill started to walk out. "What did you have in mind?"

Bill shook his head. "We'll talk another time."

The flap swung back and forth when he left, until it finally came to a stop. Sam pulled his coat tighter. The worst of winter hadn't even come yet.

He closed his eyes and leaned against his workbench. A million thoughts raced through his mind, all competing for attention.

Bill was right about one thing. If they didn't get someone to lead them soon, they might not survive another night.

Every time he tried to avoid it, he kept coming back to the same conclusion.

There was only one man with fighting experience in the castle. One man who had led before and could lead again.

He had to do something.

There, in the dark of the workshop he used to create, Sam decided.

8

Handed Down from One to Another

Evan paced his room. The walls felt like they were closing in on him. It had been so long since he had seen the sun that he wasn't sure what it looked like anymore.

Even though the chill of winter was in the air, leaking through the stone and cracks in the walls, he still thought it was stuffy inside.

Ever present, his desire for drink ate at him. Less than a hundred feet below him, the remaining three casks of wine were stored below in the cellar.

His mouth watered at the thought, the distraction that would take him away from this room, away from his troubles.

A candle flickered by his bedside, giving off the smell of tallow in its small flame. It seemed like it would go out at any moment, the candle down to a stub. He had asked for a new one, but the Overseer had refused.

He refused him! He was no Duke in this place, not anymore.

The shadow of his father haunted him, stroked behind him, ever out of sight. He thought he could see him sometimes, at the corner of his eye, but when he turned his head, nothing was there.

The days had become a blur. One day stretched into the next. Only the small amount of light coming through his study window let him know that time was moving on. For all he knew, they weren't progressing through time at all.

His stomach rumbled. It must be getting close to dinner, but he balked at the thought of eating. The meat was all gone, eaten days ago, and they were down to the dredges of vegetables and grains stored in the cellar.

A knock sounded on his door. He bade them enter.

A servant entered and set down his plate. Evan felt his mouth water even as he saw what was on it. A bland porridge of water-soaked oats and wheat. Uncooked, hard, barely softened by the water they kept it in overnight. The servant departed, and he sat down to eat.

He longed for the days of his youth now, the great hunting parties that brought back fresh venison and game to a table loaded with food of every kind. The kitchens of the Arch Duke were always staffed by the best cooks, who might even be able to make this palatable, given enough time.

But he was too hungry to reject it and ate. There was a hint of something, and he dug around in the bowl. It looked like, among the mush, there were spots of brown. He looked closer and tasted one. Mushroom. It gave the meal a bit of earthy flavor, welcome after such a bland time. *Where had they found them?*

It brought him back to the days of his youth, to the harvest festivals in the Hornwood. His mouth watered with the thought of those mushrooms—some as big as a man's head—that popped up in the dark places of the forest where men feared to tread, then baked like pies in the ovens of the palace.

Even then, he had felt the sting of loneliness, watching the other boys and girls at play on the palace grounds. He remembered slipping out one night to try and join them, thinking he was clever in slipping his guard.

They had known it was him, even in the dark. None of the other children would play with him. They called him "Your Grace" and bowed and scraped, then fled as soon as they could.

What would it have been like to have a normal childhood, to laugh and play and not have a care in the world? They didn't have to carry the weight of a dukedom on their shoulders. They didn't know what it was like to bear the future of his people on his back.

It was crushing. Even now, he itched for a good glass of icy ale, a thick, foamy head on it that clung to his lips and tickled his nose. He sighed, imagining the thick, hoppy smell of his favorite brew from down in the valley.

What am I thinking? He knew he was restless, cooped up like a dog in a kennel. He wanted to be outside, to see the sunlight again, and considered the Overseer's words.

What if it wasn't the men who wanted to overthrow him, but Rhys himself? What better way to seize power than to feed him a stream of lies designed to keep him afraid?

He longed for Yand and his counsel, once more feeling his absence keenly. What would he have said? What would he have advised?

Wallowing in self-pity in his room would not have been his words, let alone his counsel. Evan pushed the empty plate away, still hungry.

What would father do? The man seemed as hard as iron but would bend if he needed to. Had he ever faced a situation like this? Evan doubted it.

He saw again the image of himself on horseback, leading a charge out of the gate and smashing the enemy ranks to pieces. His sword flashed in the glorious sunlight, red with the blood of the invaders.

He gnawed on his lip and wondered, thinking of a way to get out of this situation. He thought until the sun was gone and his room was as dim as a cave.

Even when everything was black, he kept thinking. Long into the night, until his eyelids were too heavy to keep open anymore.

He still didn't know what to do.

***

"I'll do it."

Mathew jumped, surprised at the sound of his voice, then turned. "What will you do?"

Sam grimaced. "I'll train the men," he said through gritted teeth. The only other option would be to have them die or spoiled by poor instruction.

"That's great news." A smile spread across Mathew's face.

"There's a catch." Sam held up a finger. "You'll have to convince the Overseer yourself. I'm not going to go groveling to him about it."

"I wouldn't dream of it." Mathew looked around. "Here, we're starting earlier tomorrow. What can you teach us?"

"What are you doing?"

Mathew was rummaging around the barracks now, looking in chests and the solitary cupboard that sat in the corner.

"I'm looking for—here it is."

He turned and held out a stick, pulled from behind the cupboard.

"What are you going to do with a practice sword?" Sam felt his eyebrows arch on their own accord.

"Not just any practice sword. This was Captain Yand's practice sword." Mathew held it out. "You should take it. I'll find a way to convince the Overseer that it's the right decision."

It lay there, smoothed from years of use, shining in the dingy barracks. Someone had polished it recently, but it couldn't hide the dents and scratches of what must have been a thousand sparring sessions.

He remembered it well, how Yand had wielded it like an expert.

"It should not come to me."

"You need to take it." Mathew thrust it at him again. "No one else deserves it."

"I don't deserve it."

"We know what you did. Some of us saw what you did on the walls. You took down that giant."

"It is not for me." Sam pushed it away.

"You gave us hope." Mathew's eyes were glistening, and his words moved Sam.

What would it mean? To take up the sword of a dead man? Would he fall under its owner's fate? Would he too be destined to die in this place? A whisper from the door broke him out of the questions.

"I don't deserve this." Sam put his hand around the hilt and closed it on the cool wood. Even this had taken winter upon it. "But I will take it. I will do my best."

There is no going back now.

"Thank you." Mathew turned. "I was afraid it would fall upon me."

A weight had descended on Sam, pressing on his shoulders. *Was this what Mathew felt?*

He was too young. They all were, even the old like Ned.

"Before nightfall, we will assemble in the yard." They had taken to calling it that—the section of the courtyard reserved for practice that the children played on when it was vacant.

It was hard-packed earth now, stamped by the feet of many men over many days. Sam considered the training sword and felt a twinge of annoyance and a hint of... what was it?

Hatred.

Duke Hornblood should be taking this sword. Duke Hornblood should be out here every day.

He knew what Bill felt, but he knew it wasn't right. He was the rightful ruler of the castle, not Sam.

Why then did he refuse to rule? It made him afraid that he was starting to see the sense in what Bill had to say.

"I will meet you then." Sam left him.

The wind grabbed at his cloak, and Sam had to hold onto it as he left the barracks. His teeth started chattering a second later. The sky was gray. It would be colder when the sun went down. *A perfect time to attack.*

If the conditions were right. So far, they didn't seem to be. Or the Belmarch were content to let them starve. Every day, he expected another attack. Every day, it was the same. The watchers on the walls would grow complacent. They would expect each night to be quiet.

Were they lulling us into complacency, just to have them strike? It was so confusing. Webs within webs of plans, and every one could be a false assumption that made your enemy stronger than he really was.

It was going to take all he could give to do this job. Sam shook his head and tromped across the fine layer of snow. More would be coming soon.

He wasn't sure he had it in him. He longed for the cool forest in summer, to be away from this place. Each time he thought of it, his heart sank a little.

Belinda was up ahead, her young boy in her arms, at the grave of her dead husband. His heart ached to see it. The wind tore at her hair, whipping it back and forth. A faint cry came with it, the boy.

He was cold, just like Sam.

Sam gnawed on his lip, looking at the door to the Keep. It would be warmer in there. He almost went to it when his feet seemed to change direction mid-stride. Her body was shivering. Sam took off his cloak. Now bare, his skin felt the full weight of the cold. He didn't care.

"You should take this." Sam offered it to her, a hand outstretched between them. She had sensed him coming or heard him, but stared hard at the grave marker.

"No."

"You can't be out here with this cold and that coat." There were huge gaps where the wind tore through her coat. It was threadbare.

"You won't have one."

"It was getting too warm out here, anyway." His teeth chattered as he said it. *How cold is it going to get this winter? Worse than last year?*

Last year had been filled with burning fires and cheery huts that beat back the cold at the end of the day. And warm food.

This winter, he wasn't so sure.

"Leave us."

"At least take it for the boy." She moved at that. Then, she turned her head. A hand snatched the coat away, and a few turns and twists later, the boy was wrapped in it.

Her eyes were clear as she looked at him, something other than hatred in them, he hoped.

"I will leave you to your mourning." Sam touched his head in respect, gave a quick glance to Archie's grave, and turned.

He strode away, not wanting to show how cold he was. He felt like crouching down, conserving as much heat as he could. Instead, he kept his back straight, unwilling to show a hint of weakness.

He left her, a widow on a hill mourning her husband, and wondered what would become of her.

9

One to Send Forth

Sam stood over his bed. It was a new day, colder than the one before, and the snow was no longer a light dusting on the ground.

It had started the night before. He saw it through the windows, drifting down in large clumps. Every so often, one would come in and fall on the floor, then melt. How long until they had no heat at all?

"We aren't prepared for this," Ned said. "My bones can feel it. They ache, Sam."

Sam nodded. He didn't feel good either. The cold had set into him, settling down deep into his bones. Sometimes, he wondered if it would ever leave.

"The worst is yet to come, I imagine."

"We aren't going to survive the winter. I heard the ladies talking about how much food was left."

The others had gone off to their respective duties for the day. They were alone now, except for a young boy playing in the corner.

More weight. "There won't be enough to last, will there?"

"Not through winter, or spring."

"We're going to starve to death then." Sam straightened, then turned. "What can we do about it?" There was some irritation in his voice, and he saw it reflected in Ned's look.

"Nothing." Even in here, out of the worst of the wind and the cold, Ned shivered. Most of their winter wear had been burned up in the initial attack.

They needed fire. They needed warmth. *But what can I do about it?*

"I can't make food appear out of midair. I can't fill bellies with nothing but air." Sam felt his face pull into a scowl, and he tried to relax it.

"I didn't say you had to."

"Then why come to me about it?"

"Sometimes an old man needs a friend to talk to." Sadness filled his eyes, the corners wrinkled, and his eyebrows thick.

Shame struck Sam then. What had Ned done to deserve his condemnation, to deserve hard words?

He had been faithful, fought well, and always treated him with kindness and respect.

"I'm sorry, it's just..."

"We all have our burdens to bear. I wish yours was lighter."

"It feels like a mountain," Sam confessed. "Like a weight crushing me, pushing me down. There are..." He sought the right words.

"Rumors?"

Sam nodded.

"I've heard them too. It's hard not to." Ned sat down on the lumpy cloth that served as his bed, knees creaking and joints popping, and settled with a sigh. "They keep pestering me to join in that foolishness."

"What are we going to do about it?"

"Stay out of it, that's what." Ned leveled a hard gaze at him. "That's what I intend to do, and I suggest you do the same."

"But what if... it happens? Won't we be labeled as traitors and executed?"

"I assume so, unless we can plead our case." Ned scratched his beard, wispy and scraggly. "Like you said, though, we won't last long enough to see it."

"It doesn't seem right, him sitting there." Sam spoke softly. "Locked away behind that door while we suffer. It wouldn't be right to kill him, though."

"Imagine going through what he is. A life of ease and luxury taken away, sent to oversee a fortress being built under the noses of our worst enemies."

"Not a desirable position to be in." The scent of breakfast lingered in the air, a faint hint of the tasteless gruel that had become too normal.

The fireplace lay empty and bare, barely any ashes in it at all. Rogue snowflakes settled into the hearth, then melted.

"I wouldn't want to take his place." Ned moved, his body groaning in protest. "The others are coming in soon. Anything else to discuss?"

"Many more. How is Trent?" He hadn't seen him today. Even though Sam wasn't that busy, the hours seemed to slip by.

"He's a man."

"Not quite." He was young. Too young to be in a situation like this, but then Ned was too old to be in a situation like this.

No one should be in this castle at all. They should be out in the village, laughing and creating. Not waiting for their death.

"You don't give him enough credit. How was it that he held the walls?"

"Through his own skill." Sam remembered seeing him hold his own. Pride had blossomed in his chest at that, but also a great sadness that one so young could shed blood so easily.

And it reflected the thing inside him—so eager for violence, too ready to kill.

"And he's been invaluable to us since. He puts in the longest hours on the wall out of anyone, and more practice with the bow."

"You've been teaching him?"

Ned glanced at him from the corner of his eye. "Some."

"I haven't worked with him in weeks now. I should."

"Yes, you should. Teach him, Sam." Ned turned to him, imploring.

Sam shook his head slowly. "I don't think he wants me to."

"Nonsense."

"I haven't talked to him much since that day on the tower." Sam told the story quickly, rushing at the memory of the look of disappointment.

"I don't think he thinks you're a coward, not after the attack." Ned stretched his hands. How many things had those hands done, wrinkled and scarred? "You proved that to everyone, taking on that giant."

"And almost dying." He rubbed his arms, still sore from the beating that man gave him.

"Lesser men would have died earlier, and brave men would have cowered. They did." Men were starting to come back now, trickling in and talking among themselves. "We can talk about it more later."

One of the men yawned. Like Ned, they were coming off the night watch. "I'll leave you to rest. Get some sleep." Sam stood, but Ned caught his arm.

"Talk to him. Today, if you can."

"I've got a lot to do." Sam tightened his coat in preparation for the cold. He could feel Ned's gaze on him as he walked away.

Snow was drifting down, adding to the few inches of white that already carpeted the castle. Thankfully, there was no wind, and Sam stepped outside with reluctance.

The Keep didn't offer a warm bastion against the cold, but it did offer some protection. Out in the yard, he could feel it.

It started at his feet, worse at his exposed hands and head. The ground pulled the heat out of his feet and seemed to drain it from the rest of his body.

He followed footsteps that were being covered up. Men walked along the castle walls, pacing along the battlements with a keen eye to the south.

Sam knew they wouldn't attack now. There was too much snow. Even if the Belmarchers could get across the plain in front of the walls, they would have a tough time scaling the walls, ladders or not.

No, they would dig in and wait them out. Sam wondered if they could launch a counterattack, take them by surprise.

He ran through the number of fighters they had within the walls, then the number of fighters that were camped outside.

It would be suicide, and the attackers wouldn't last long. He was more confident about the men now, but he still wasn't sure they could do anything other than keep the attackers away.

The tracks split—some to the forge, some to the masons, some to the carpenter's workshop. Sam chose to follow the ones to the mason's area, the most used out of all of them.

It was going to be a hard time, and he knew it, but Sam had to do this. Tired, hungry, and afraid of the confrontation that awaited him, Sam walked through the rough stone walls of the new mason's workshop.

Hammers were striking chisels, the masons chipping away at the worst of the stone. Bill was in the corner, lounging in a chair. From where he had gotten it, Sam didn't know.

The masons went silent as Sam stood there, the air thick with the dust of the stone. Gray chips littered the floor like sawdust, and they crunched underfoot.

"Sam Freeman, come to see me in my natural habitat?" Bill stood up and grinned, completely at ease. He was surrounded by ten or fifteen of his masons, so it wasn't surprising.

"If you can spare it." There wasn't the air of hostility Sam was expecting, or would have encountered just a few months ago. Walking in unannounced then would have been... foolish.

But now, there was a hint of respect, even among the masons Bill had worked so hard to turn against him.

It was surprising and, Sam wondered, refreshing. Almost heady.

That scared him the most. "May we talk in private?"

Bill nodded to the mason by his side and motioned to follow as he stood. "Keep up the work, boys."

Sam crunched across the room, stepping around the rock pedestals they were using as workbenches. The hammers resumed, and chips continued to fall once again.

They were cutting off the worst of the jutting sections of rock, the sharp points that would interfere with a good grip. Layers of rough rock came in one end of the workshop, and the smoothed, prepared rock went out the other.

Bill had taken his time thinking through the layout, for Sam was certain it came under his direction. That, or he took good advice.

Sam noted that and entered into a small shack outside and around the corner. It was dark inside, tucked up against the wall that made up one side of it, with a small window that overlooked the yard and the snow that hushed the world.

"I see you've come around to my idea."

Sam took a deep breath, preparing for what was to come. "No." Bill frowned, but didn't look too surprised. "But I've thought of something else."

"And what, pray tell, is that?"

"The crane." Bill looked at him blankly.

"Am I supposed to guess? I don't have time or patience for games," Bill said.

"The Golden River will take a message for us. Or, rather, a messenger."

It had been in his mind for a while now, since before the attack. The Belmarch had set up too good a defense to get anyone out the now-ruined gates. And, if they did, Sam wasn't sure they wouldn't end up like the last messenger.

If they did, then that was another life wasted.

"I'm listening." Bill sat on the stone bench that seemed to function as his desk. Sam joined him on the opposite side. It was cold, and sucked the heat from him.

"We can move a crane, take it from the tower since we aren't going to finish it anyway, and put it on the wall that abuts the river. I think we have enough room, if we can position it right, to swing a boat out over the river."

"Once we do that, we add a person, send them down and around the Belmarch, and get help."

"Interesting. Why come to me about this?" Bill rubbed his fingers together, making Sam aware of how cold his hands were.

"Two reasons. I need your help to set the crane in the wall. Stone will need to come out, and I'm not sure we can make it unless we take out a merlon."

"And the second?"

"I need you to convince the Overseer to let us do it. He isn't going to listen to me."

"Who will go on this boat?" Bill's brows furrowed. "We don't have a boat."

"We can take care of that." Sam hid his fear that they might not have enough wood left to make it. "By the time we get it ready, we'll have a functional boat."

"Have you ever built a boat?" Before Sam could answer, Bill went on. "Never mind. Let's take a walk. I want to see it."

They left, walking across the fresh snow that compressed beneath their feet. "And the messenger?" Bill asked when they were far enough to be out of earshot. "Who did you have in mind?"

"I didn't. It would have to be someone who could convince the King to come."

"Perhaps the Duke himself?" Bill mused, almost to himself. "I'll have to think on that. There are some good candidates." Sam stared at him out of the corner of his eye. *What is he planning? And have I become an unwilling participant in it?*

There was no doubt that with the masons behind him, Bill was the most dangerous man in the castle, but the Overseer still had control of the guard, and the weapons.

"This is the closest point," Sam said, stopping at the location he had in mind. The waters of the Golden River flowed beneath them, rushing by. It was fast, which would take a boat past the enemy quickly. "I haven't seen any of their sentries focused on the river either." Sam had asked to be put on this wall during his watches.

Bill leaned out over the edge, judging the distance, and then examined the wall. "I think we could do it. The crane will fit, for sure, but I think you're right."

A trick of relief flowed through Sam. It was reassuring to hear after thinking about it so long and hard.

"Take out a few here, and we can demolish this," Bill put his hand on the merlon. "Maybe the one next to it to get some space to swing the crane over."

"And the boat," Sam reminded him.

"The boat too. How long is it?"

"Not sure yet." That was something Ned was going to have to lead. Sam had no idea how to build anything that floated.

"I could see this working." Bill stared downriver. "We could get help." The snow obscured their visibility, and they couldn't even see the other bank. "But I have a condition."

The glint in his eye made Sam reconsider what he'd just asked. "What is it?" he asked, wary of the response.

"I get to choose who leaves."

10

An Exchange

Sam stood in the falling snow on the wall, examining Bill. The wiry man was hiding his intentions well. Sam couldn't read him.

He thought about the proposal. "Is that the only condition?"

"That's it. I'll help you build your crane, and work it too, if you need it."

Sam had expected something else, a promise extracted or a favor that would be hard to swallow. He couldn't help thinking there was some ulterior motive driving Bill's thought process.

But, for the life of him, he couldn't figure it out. It was getting colder now, and the light of day was growing stronger. There might be an end to the snow soon.

His thoughts wandered to the Belmarch lands. Since they were to the north, they had to be used to the cold—if not better suited to it. Had their attackers come prepared for the bitter winter ahead?

Maybe there was another reason they had stopped attacking.

He breathed deep of the fresh, crisp air, cleansed of anything by the snow. He had never smelled anything cleaner.

"I hope I don't regret this." Sam held out his hand, and Bill took it. His grip was iron, and they sealed the pact.

"How soon are you planning this?"

"Give me some time. I've got a boat to build."

Bill nodded. "Don't take too long. I'll go see Rhys and work on him. Drop a few hints."

"Make it sound like it was your idea, and I know he'll say yes."

"You make me more powerful than I really am." Bill spread his arms out and gave a small shrug. "I'm just a humble mason."

Sam snorted. "You're nothing of the sort." Bill grinned and bid him goodbye, sauntering to the Keep.

Sam looked out over the river, trying to pierce the snowfall. That direction lay their salvation.

He hoped they would get to it in time.

***

The workshop was freezing when Sam entered. He blew air into his cupped hands, which looked an alarming pale color. Ned, Trent, and Kerien were there working.

Or trying to. It was cold, and all of them were shivering. If only they had material to make coats.

But where would that come from? The nonexistent animals? The river reeds below?

The thought struck him like a lightning bolt. Maybe they could use the crane for more than just a message.

They might be able to use it as a way to sneak out of the castle during the night, collect much-needed supplies.

His fingers tingled—not just from warming up, but from the excitement running through his body.

"What is it?" Ned stopped, his saw poised to cut through a board. "You look like the siege has been lifted."

"No," Sam said, taking a deep breath to get control of his body. "We need to build a boat. Ned, I'm going to need your help."

The carpenters looked at each other, then back at him as if he had sprouted wings and was floating in midair.

"A boat?" Ned said finally.

"What do we need a boat for?" Kerien asked.

"I've got a plan." Sam ran through his idea quickly, leaving out the promised favor to Bill.

In the worst case, he would pick the Duke, which might be the best option. Best case would be another mason, one familiar with the paths back to the capital.

One thing kept nagging him, though. Who would believe them? And, even if they were believed, what kind of aid could they possibly send?

They must know something was wrong by now. The shipment of supplies and men was supposed to arrive before winter set in.

Unless they had left too late, or were captured or killed along the way. Then, they wouldn't expect them back until later.

However Sam looked at it, their chances were not good.

"It could work," Trent said. The boy was harder than he had been, and looked stronger, but thinner.

"It's been a while since I've even worked on boats." Ned rubbed his bushy eyebrows and stroked his beard. "I don't know..."

"We don't have much choice, do we?" Sam asked.

"It's not like we're doing anything better anyway. Stupid Belmarchers haven't attacked in weeks." Sam was surprised to hear a measure of support from Kerien. "Besides, I learned boat building during my apprenticeship."

They turned to him. Kerien shrugged. "I never thought to bring it up before. It didn't seem important."

"That... is a good surprise," Sam said. "That means we have two boat builders."

Ned shook his head. "One and a half, at best."

"So, what do we need to do then?"

"Look through the stock," Kerien said, turning to the wood stacked in the corner, blessedly safe from the snow.

"Agreed." Ned joined him.

***

A few hours later, they had combed through everything and segregated the wood that they would use for the boat.

Ned stood over it, arms crossed, with a frown on his face. "It isn't enough."

It looked like a healthy pile to Sam.

"Why not?" Trent asked.

"We'll use most of it making the curves. There isn't enough bent stock." Sam groaned. They had sorted out the best, straightest stock to haul into the castle, and some of the other wood had been burned long ago for warmth.

"So we're back to square one." Sam sat back, leaning against his workbench. "This is going to be a problem."

He knew this point would come without a forest of trees to draw on. Even if they could suddenly go out and fell a few more, it would be months before they were ready and dry enough to use.

"We could join some together," Trent said.

Ned shook his head. "It would be leaky as it is. We don't have the pitch to seal the joints we're going to have to put in, let alone adding more."

"I've heard and seen it happen." Kerien's face went grim. "The one time we did it was bad—it sank the boat next to the dock. Luckily, the water was shallow."

"Was anyone hurt?" Trent asked, eyes wide.

"No, it was overnight, so no one was in it."

"It took that long?" Sam leaned back, thinking. "If we can't make it watertight, what are we going to do?"

"Give whoever is riding in it a bucket." Ned took the biggest piece they had. "We'll get started, if you can handle the rest of the work."

By the rest of the work, he really meant the arrow-making. They had enough bows to comfortably outfit almost all the men. Enough to give the Belmarchers pause if they tried a frontal assault again.

Even now, Sam thought they were lulling them into a sense of complacency. The sentries could only hold out so long before they started paying less attention.

He had seen it—men staring off into the distance on the wall as he walked by, or looking in the courtyard to watch the young ones play. If that was their strategy, the Belmarchers were winning.

But winter had come, and with it ice and snow, horrible conditions to try and scale a wall or break open a gate. Though the ground might be hard because it was frozen, it was also slippery.

That gave him another idea, and Sam tucked it away in his memory for later use.

"Can you make do for now, until we find another way?" Sam asked.

Kerien and Ned talked it over, then agreed. "Yes, we'll start with this."

Another problem to fix, in the now ever-growing line of them. It seemed like every time he solved one, another popped up.

Somewhere in the back of his mind, Sam was curious about the pile of planks. They were straight, not that wide, and thin. There were a few offcuts that were chunkier, but nothing that resembled a boat.

How were they going to get all those straight lines into a curved boat?

He was a little afraid of the answer, so he kept the question to himself. This was not his expertise. Let them work unhindered. I have work to do.

He couldn't remember the last time he had felt ready to work, but he still forced himself to return to his workbench and let the others go.

He turned to making arrows, splitting them off the edge of one of the smaller boards.

It was still green, the rough bark on two edges. The curve of the grain traveled up the edge, but he wasn't sure if it twisted.

A few cuts from his plane removed the dirty endgrain. It was all sapwood, oak. A faint trace of pungent odor from the fresh cut end refreshed him.

Kerien and Ned were talking over the boat construction, picking over the pieces and arranging them in a suitable manner.

It went on the rest of the day, but Sam couldn't get into his work. He was distracted and kept making errors. Each time, he would slow down and refocus, only to be distracted again.

Lunch came and went, if you could call a meager portion of whatever was in the pot a meal, and the afternoon light quickly faded as the evening came over them.

"The days are getting short," Ned said, squinting at his handiwork. He was shaving the biggest piece down with a chisel. "Less time for work."

Sam frowned, seeing how dark it was getting. Candles, or even the fire, would have kept them going in the darkness. It would have provided light and warmth.

But they didn't have enough candles to spare, and even less wood to burn.

"We'll work for another half hour."

"When are we supposed to finish this?" Kerien asked.

"As soon as possible. Yesterday, if we could."

"Then someone should have thought of that sooner." Kerien's face darkened, the corners of his mouth pulled down. "Why can't anyone think of what we need ahead of time?" With each word, the volume of his voice grew, until it seemed he was shouting.

"Watch your tongue," Sam warned.

"No. I won't." Kerien threw down the chunk of wood he was holding. It clattered on his workbench, then fell to the floor without a sound.

Anger flashed up inside Sam, fueled by the conditions and the pressure. He held it back, though, even though he was tired of Kerien acting out like a child.

Instead of saying something else, Sam took a deep breath. Tension filled the air, and Trent was staring at him with wide eyes. No one said anything for a while.

Kerien looked like he wanted to fight, tense and ready. He rocked forward onto the balls of his feet.

Sam could have fought him then, but there was no point. He would have won, but then he would have given Kerien what he asked for. Practicality begging for it.

"Go somewhere else tonight," Sam finally said, keeping his voice down.

"I know it's a hard time right now," Ned said, stepping forward and partially blocking the way between them. "We look outside and see the bleak winter and the enemy surrounding us."

"How will we survive if we can't work together? How will we get out of this and live to see another day?" Sam wasn't sure he wanted to be around Kerien right now. He wasn't sure Kerien would survive long enough to see the Belmarch attack again.

"Yes, we must work together," Sam said woodenly. The words came out, but they were forced.

Kerien turned and left the workshop, rushing out into the gloom of the night. Sam was glad, even though his entire body was quivering with anger.

"It's been hard on him too," Ned whispered, walking up to him. "He hasn't had anyone to turn to."

"Turn to?" Sam stared at him.

There was sorrow beneath Ned's bushy eyebrows. "He and Archie were closer than you knew. They were like brothers."

The anger dissipated, cut through to the bone with those words. Sam stared at him. "I... didn't think about that."

Ned smiled a gaunt smile. "He doesn't show it much, but it's always a constant reminder whenever he's around the workshop. Archie helped him as an apprentice."

"They apprenticed together?"

"No, Kerien was apprenticed at the same master that Archie was working for years ago. He showed him a spot of kindness in a sea of trouble and pain."

"Pain?"

"He had a hard master. He beat Kerien whenever he made a mistake, or went too slow, or even went too fast."

"How do you know this?"

Ned shrugged. "People talk to me. Or around me. Not the same as around you. He looks up to you."

Sam hadn't even stopped to consider it. Ned patted him on the shoulder and followed.

Maybe he had been too hard on Kerien, hadn't spoken enough soft words.

It was too late for that now, and Sam felt the emptiness of it deep in his stomach.

11

CONVERSATION IN THE COLD

Trent lingered in the workshop and fidgeted with a few arrows.

Sam felt mixed up and horrible for what Ned had revealed to him. To have been so blind, to have not seen why Kerien was so angry.

The workshop was where they had spent most of their time together. True, that was the workshop outside the gates, but even here, Archie had left his mark.

Archie's workbench was cold and lifeless. A spiderweb shivered in the breeze beneath it, and dust and sawdust coated the tools there.

Sam thought they were untouched, but when he looked closer, he realized that they were lined up in a neat row, uncharacteristically. Archie never kept his tools neat like that.

But Kerien did.

Was that part of his mourning process, and the reason he couldn't let go?

Near the door, Trent cleared his throat. It broke Sam's thoughts, and he turned.

What am I supposed to say? "How are you?" Sam said, settling for the least cringe-inducing thing he could think of.

"They're treating me better. Bill, and the others, I mean."

"I knew what you meant." He was so young in Sam's eyes. Just a boy.

"I have you to thank for that." Trent's eyes dropped to the ground. "I know I haven't been the most grateful apprentice, and I want to change that."

It surprised him. Gone was the strange look, one of almost hate, that Trent once bore for him. He hadn't noticed it before, but once he said that, it was obvious.

"I haven't been the best master either. For that, I am sorry."

"You taught me to fight, and that kept me alive."

"It did more than keep you alive." Sam moved closer, the light almost completely gone. He wished there was a candle he could light, a place where they could go to see each other.

But then, he wasn't sure Trent would be able to talk to him if there was.

I have been a poor master and an even worse teacher. Sam hadn't really talked to him since the last attack, the one that took Archie's life. That was days ago, weeks even. He hadn't taught him anything, hadn't trained him.

Sam had been so caught up in everything around him, he had almost forgotten Trent even needed him.

"I think I took it for granted that you were learning so fast," Sam said. "You've made more progress in these last few months than any I've seen."

Trent, even in the darkness, seemed to swell. "I have a confession to make." Trent seemed to be waiting for something, for Sam expected him to say something.

Instead, he heard Trent squirming in the dark. It gave Sam time to prepare himself, thinking of the worst. Had Trent found out his secret past? That was absurd, considering who he was. Then, what was it?

Perhaps Trent had talked to Bill, was going to join him in his deadly plans. What if Bill had convinced him to be the one to do it, to kill the Duke?

"I—I thought you were a coward," Trent said at last.

Sam cocked his head, waiting for more. When none came, he couldn't help but laugh. "That's it?"

"I'm sorry for it. You aren't."

"Trent, I knew you thought that about me. Let's go outside." It was too dark to talk at all in the workshop, and Sam pushed open the flap, letting starlight flood through.

Night was in full regalia now, stars shining and twinkling up above in a clear, cold sky. The wind was dead as they left the workshop behind.

"You knew? The whole time? Why didn't you say anything?"

Sam shrugged. "If I would have said something, would it have changed your mind?"

"Yes, it would have," Trent said, pulling his arms around himself in a hug against the cold.

"Only action got you to change your mind about me, and that action was spurned by another."

"What other?"

"You." The smell of woodsmoke drifted through the air. Trent looked confused. "When I saw you fighting on the walls, it made me think back to what I had sworn long ago and consider it again."

"I had sworn never to do violence again on my enemies." Sam shook his head, feeling his forehead tighten. "But I never considered that there would be others who would fight in my stead, especially one as young as you." Trent listened keenly.

"I realized that it would be a cowardly thing indeed to abandon my friends, those I love, and not fight when I have the skill and ability. I couldn't let you fight alone, while I refused to do anything."

Sam looked up at the sky. The Deer and the Boar were low on the horizon, followed by the Hunter. Winter had truly begun, and the Raven was halfway visible above them.

Four months. Four more months of this, at least. Maybe longer.

"That's what drove me to fight, and I've been thinking about it ever since." Sam shivered in the night air.

"I miss our nights of training," Trent said. They crunched through the snow, the top layer cracking from where it had melted and refrozen. "They saved me too. I couldn't have fought without you teaching me. Will you teach me again?"

Sam smiled. There was something warming about the thought, that he hadn't messed everything up like he had feared. A wave of relief washed through him.

He hadn't expected it. Sam hadn't expected the glimmer in Trent's eyes either, reflecting the starlight so subtly.

The Keep grew before them. They would be there in a few more steps. Sam didn't have much time alone with him, and it was too cold to linger.

"I'd be honored to teach you more," Sam said. "After dinner, we'll train." He was going to do better. Sam couldn't change the past, but he could do something about the future.

"I'm not looking forward to dinner," Trent said after he nodded. His teeth chattered in the cold.

"To be honest, neither am I." Sam knew he should have been happy they had food, but the same over and over again. It wasn't going to get better anytime soon, either.

Yet another reason to get that messenger to the capital. Bill's favor hung over him, then he thought about something he hadn't before.

What if Bill chose me to go?

He tried to push it to the side, but the thought lodged a sliver of dread within him, not over the act of leaving itself, but of leaving everyone else alone with Bill. No matter what he said, Sam still wasn't sure about him or his intentions.

"Let's go inside," Sam said. He pushed open the creaking doors and stepped out of the wind behind Trent. The bell sounded, beckoning them to dinner.

Compared to outside, the wave of warm air that greeted him felt glorious. He let it wash over his face, bringing some life back into his cheeks. They burned as the blood came back to them.

Everyone else was eating. There was little conversation, but enough to make a hum in the air.

The days of laughter were gone, and Sam felt it all the more keenly now. Would laughter ever grace the halls again? He wasn't sure.

He wasn't even sure the great fireplace would ever see fire again.

Seeing them there, he was reminded of just how hopeless their plight was. Even if they were to survive the winter alive, without dying of starvation, the Belmarch army would surely arrive come spring.

And they would not hold back from attacking, of that Sam was certain. They would break through the wall or the gate, and they would slaughter them one by one.

Unless they had help, they would certainly die. And they could not work in the night, not without squandering their resources.

It was beyond frustrating. He needed more men working, he needed more supplies. And where was the Duke? Still holed up in his quarters, enjoying the best of what they had left. He even had a fire going, probably.

Belinda was sitting with her child, feeding him the evening gruel. He was eating it, but didn't seem to be enjoying it. Sam followed Trent up to get his food, which was dispensed without a word by a sorry-faced woman. She seemed depressed.

He wanted to say something kind, but all he could muster was "Thank you."

Her eyes flashed up to his for a second, then fell back. She sat back in her seat for her own meal, spooning it up in a big glob.

Sam joined the other carpenters, eating by the light of the moon and stars. It was difficult, and unappetizing, food to eat. The third bell rang, and the men finished their meal. Those destined for the first night watch went to the side of the hall filled with beds to sleep in, while the others went back into the cold.

The practice weapons were handed out, the men complaining bitterly of the cold. Sam wanted to join them but knew that things were about to change.

There was an energy in him when he reached into his cloak and pulled out Yand's old weapon. It had been next to his body the whole time, he slipped it there after dinner, and it was warm.

It traveled up his arm and into his soul. A part of him loved the thrill, loved the anticipation.

And yet, there was that other part that loved something else. The part of him that scared him, that he detested. The dark part of him that smiled when bone crunched and flesh tore.

He tried to bury that part of him as he took up his place next to the guards. Even in the dark of night, the questioning glances showed up on the faces of the others, and whispers ran through the crowd.

"From here on out, we're going to change how things are done." Sam's voice rang out above the whispers, silencing them. "We're going to focus on the basic moves you'll need to survive and nothing else. We don't have the time to do otherwise."

"We survived this far, haven't we?" someone asked, voice lost in the crowd. Sam had anticipated this.

"You did well during the last attack. You stood your ground like true men of Chathem." He paused and looked around. "But I suspect the next time we're attacked, it won't be a simple raiding party twice our number, but an army thirty times our number. Can you fight them off then?"

Gasps and whispers erupted at his exclamation. The men started talking. Sam held up his hands, trying to get control back. "Listen."

Mathew joined him, along with the other guards, echoing his command.

The talking died down. "You can listen to lies if you'd like, but I've chosen to tell you the truth. Is there any other man with experience in battle who will step forward? He is more than welcome to take my place."

Sam waited, watching his breath freeze into puffs of air in the faint moonlight. When he turned his head, the snow on the ground caught it, shimmering.

He waited some more. No one came forward. More than half of him wanted someone to do it, to take it away.

He would gladly give it up, return to the life of creation instead of destruction. He didn't know for sure that he was the only one that felt that way, only suspected it from seeing them fight.

Even the guards had done a middling job of fighting, at best.

But he waited in vain. A few men coughed, more shuffled and stamped their feet in the cold, trying to stay warm.

He waited some more, until the silence was uncomfortable. No one was going to do it. Even Bill was standing, looking anywhere but at Sam.

That gave him some hope. If Bill truly wanted to enact an uprising, taking control of the fighting training would have been a good place to start.

"No one? None of you will meet my challenge?" Sam said, voice raised. He lowered it, still loud enough so that they could hear, but have to strain to do so.

"Fine. Let us begin."

12

BACK TO THE BASICS

After less than an hour of training, almost all the men in the yard were sweating. Considering how cold it was outside, Sam was satisfied.

"That's enough," he said.

"That's it?" Mathew asked. "We train more than this normally."

Sam had run them through strength training, striking, and defense. They'd even got a few rounds of sparring in.

"It's enough. We don't have the food to recover our strength if we push too hard."

"I hadn't thought of that." Mathew turned and nodded to the other guards.

Sam stretched his muscles, which were yelling at him. It was a good feeling, all the way down to his legs and calves. He knew that tomorrow they would be sore, but for now, it wasn't too bad.

His old wounds, mostly healed, flared up in pain again. He had pushed too hard tonight.

The guards dismissed the group, each squad leader taking aside his respective squad to give them the night's orders. Sam joined his squad and felt awkward as Verith went through the watch assignments, then dismissed them.

Sam kept an eye on Trent, who had done well during the training. He was picking up the sword fast—faster than anyone Sam had seen in a long time. Trent had even put a few others to shame in the sparring sessions.

Sam watched for signs of hostility or darker behavior he suspected might be lurking against Trent, but he saw none. A joke was passed, and the group laughed quickly before dispersing. Trent stood shoulder to shoulder with them, steam rising off his shoulders like the rest.

"You did well tonight," Sam said, approaching him. "But I'm afraid you can't do any more tonight. We have the second watch, so you'll need to rest before."

"I understand. There's always tomorrow."

"Tomorrow it is. Meet me after training, and we'll go through a few forms I think you're ready for."

They were at the Keep now, and slipped inside its cool halls. Men were slipping into their beds, nothing else to do without light.

"Goodnight, Trent."

"Goodnight."

Sam unfolded his nightclothes—just another set of clothes that was wearing thin, and slipped under his thin blanket.

He didn't sleep well and was soon awakened for his watch. Sam stumbled out of bed, shivering in the cold, and put on as many of his clothes as he could.

He headed to the guardhouse, meeting the others. He took the bow and arrows issued to him and took up position on the south wall as directed.

Sam knew he could have changed locations, but he wanted to watch the Belmarch and their camp.

The night was clear and calm, any hint of cloud cover gone. The moon hung in a shallow crescent just behind him, the tip of it touching the top of the unfinished Keep.

The Belmarch had sentries patrolling. They weren't relaxing, he even spotted a few near the forest edge.

They're prepared for us to do something.

They didn't go anywhere near the river, as far as he could tell. The bare branches stretched into the night sky like bony fingers reaching up from a grave.

That dread crept into him again as he considered his fate. He could join Archie tonight if the Belmarch attacked. Whether by arrow or blade, they could end his life.

And what kind of life would end? A miserable existence in a half-finished castle? The pain of hunger in his belly he had known before, and he knew would only grow deeper.

Sam closed his eyes for a moment. He had wanted peace, quiet in his life after a less-than-peaceful childhood.

Then why did you come here? It slipped into his mind, making him snap open his eyes. He had come here to build, to create, to make.

Not to fight.

The thing inside him stirred. It had been asleep for too long and wanted to wake up. Sam, deep down inside, needed to tear and rend flesh, make others feel pain, the pain that he had felt.

No. Sam tightened his freezing fingers on the unstrung bow. *I have done enough killing.*

Then why did you come here, almost to the heart of enemy country? A bloodthirsty, savage enemy.

Sam knew why he did it. It wasn't just to build. He had always known there was a chance of conflict, and there in the cold of the night, he had to confront himself about it.

All the while the enemy was safe in warm huts, a comfortable camp. This was the life he had always resisted, but one he knew he would return to.

"How long do I need to do this?" Sam's voice was quiet in the darkness, a whisper. "How long am I going to keep living this life?"

The thing within him coiled tighter, stirring from sleep.

A snowflake landed on his head, then another. The sky that had been clear an hour or so ago was now filled with clouds and snow. The bitter cold had receded with its arrival, but hadn't gone away.

Sam felt a snowflake land on his cheek and melt away to nothing. *That is my life.* A moment, formed like ice, then gone. Nothing left except a trail of water, which would soon disappear.

———◄O►———

Evan was more than restless now. He paced his room, chewing on the end of his thumb. He had ordered Rhys to keep the wine away from him and was regretting every second of it.

He was caged like an animal, trapped in a prison of cold and damp. They wouldn't let him have a fire anymore, even though it was winter and cold. Rhys had barely given him a candle, despite his protests.

Claimed there were too few left to waste. He didn't know what that fool was saying, light was no waste for the Duke of Hornblood.

His last ration of candle was down to the nub, just like his thumb would be if he didn't stop chewing it.

There was nothing to do but wait for Rhys. His eyes wandered to the bookshelf. Evan had always considered it superfluous—ornamentation to make him look better. He didn't consider reading any of the books it contained.

And it had a few, a small fortune in its own. Nowhere else in the castle had them. It was his library, given by the generosity of his family.

He went over to it, stuck a finger on the spine of one. It came away filthy.

Evan pulled out a book and blew the dust from the top.

Never much of a reader, he didn't see the use in books. He pulled one out and read the title: *History of Chathem.*

He dropped it on his desk, staring up again at the enormous crest above it. Having it there was a burden and a reminder, and he was sorry it witnessed his breakdown.

If Yand were here, what would he counsel?

Evan knew Yand wouldn't tell him to sit there and do nothing, but Yand hadn't been well-versed in politics and suspected Yand wouldn't have much to say on the matter except to use force.

But Evan had no forces loyal to him at the moment, according to what Rhys said and implied, other than through him to the guard. Less than a dozen men now, after the attack.

His fist clenched into a ball and he struck the desk. *Blast that resupply, where was it?*

It was supposed to be here months ago, and included the rest of his luggage. His father hadn't let him take more with him, promising that he would send it soon.

In truth, he knew that it was the other supplies they needed more. The food and tools and weapons that were planned to fortify it. More men, more workers, what little they had been able to recruit to go north. Few men had wanted to make that trip, even if they would be able to take their families.

And now he too knew the reason. It was too dangerous, that was what the advisers had said, that they were doing their best. Their best wasn't good enough. If it had been, Evan would have marched to Hornblood with a hundred men-at-arms ready to garrison it and a hundred craftsman to make it whole.

Instead, he was sitting in a moldering, festering ruin with no way to get out and no hope of escape.

"Improve yourself first, then you can work on others." That was what Yand had said on more than one occasion when he had been caught out or returned home drunk.

So how am I supposed to do that in here? Evan paced around again, taking yet another lap around his room. The walls were suffocating.

He had to do something. Dinner was still hours away.

He made up his mind. Yand had taught him to fight—he would practice. Evan pushed the table and chairs back against the wall, giving himself enough room to move freely. He practiced his breathing, then moved into his forms.

The sword came out of the scabbard with a whisper of steel, and a slight ring that echoed through the room. The hilt felt cold in his hands, but the sword was balanced well. It was a joy to swing, and doing it brought back memories of days in the practice yard, covered in dust and sweat and bruises, but that were the best times of his life.

He felt alive then, like he did when he was sneaking into an inn as a commoner and drinking their bravest souls under the table.

Lunges first, then parries. Evan went through all the basic forms. He was rusty, not having practiced since Yand had forced him to on their arrival. He kept making mistakes and had to go back through them all again.

"Focus on the forms," Yand's voice echoed in his memory. *"Don't try to be fancy."*

So he focused on the forms. He ran through them until he had them smooth again, then ran through them again. He went through the forms, forgetting everything else in the world, pouring his thoughts and desires into his muscles.

Before he knew it there was a knock on his door. He was covered in sweat, and his arms were shaking from holding his sword for so long. Evan caught his breath, then let the servant in with dinner. He wolfed it down, then returned to his practice.

The candle flickered and went out, but he kept going. In the darkness he was able to concentrate more, feel the forms as they flowed through him.

His arms started shaking, then his legs, but there was no desire to drink anything. It had been banished by pain and effort that flowed through him.

Finally, it was too much for him to bear. The sword clattered out of his grip and onto the stone floor.

He stood, panting, and then leaned over his desk to catch his breath. What would Yand think of him now? He wasn't sure, but he knew it wouldn't be bad.

He couldn't see in the dark more than faint outlines in the small amount of moonlight that came in the window near the ceiling, but he knew that crest was up there.

For the first time in a while, maybe ever, he stood under it and felt that maybe, just maybe, it wasn't so imposing than he first thought.

13

Evan woke late the next morning. His body was screaming at him with soreness and his arms were so stiff he could hardly move them. Sunlight poured in his window, and bathed him in a warm glow as he tried to bend his elbows. Pain shot up his arms, and he groaned. Knocking on his door made him sit up, and made his body throb with soreness.

"Come in," he said, managing to raise his voice enough to be heard. It was the one part of him that didn't seem to be aching.

Overseer Rhys cracked the door and peeked inside. His face smoothed as soon as he saw Evan, hiding something.

"Good morning, Highness."

"Is it still morning?"

"Yes. I've come to go over the figures with you. You weren't in your office, so I thought..."

"I'm not drunk, if that's what you're asking," Evan said, trying to slide his legs to the edge of the bed. He groaned again.

"The thought never entered my mind." Rhys furrowed his eyebrows and set down his bundle of records. "Do you need help? I can call the servants."

Evan almost went white with shame. What would everyone think if they had to drag him out of bed like this? "No," he snapped. "I can manage," he said, in a kinder tone.

"Very well." Rhys cocked his head as Evan tried to struggle to his feet, falling back. *How did my toes get this sore?*

Rhys grabbed one of his parchments. "Perhaps it would be better to go over this here?" he asked with an arched brow.

Evan dreaded the short walk to his office. It was next door, but it might as well have been in the capital.

"Why don't you start here, and we'll see how it goes." Evan was bending some life back into his body, one finger at a time. Yand always recommended moving after a hard training session, and Evan went through his limbering form.

"Starting with the inventory," Rhys said, pausing for him to nod. When he did Rhys continued. "As for food stores, we are—"

"Before that," Evan said, cutting him off. There was something bothering him even more than the food. "Tell me about the... conditions out there."

Rhys rolled up his parchment and set it back on the table. He had sat down while Evan was trying to bring his body to life, which had been somewhat successful. At least now it didn't hurt like he was being cooked.

After a short pause, Rhys folded his hands. "I wish I could report better news, but not much has changed."

Not much. Evan was hoping it had died down, or that everything was a big joke and that he could go outside again. The sliver of light from his windows wasn't' enough of the world for him.

"How has it changed?"

Rhys shifted in his seat, but his face remained expressionless. The man was a true politician and seemed to be able to hide what he was thinking with ease.

Evan didn't like that. Not one bit.

"I'm working to ease the situation. Unfortunately, as you'll soon discover, there isn't much in the way of goods to do it."

"What do we do, then?"

"I'm not sure, Your Highness."

Evan closed his eyes, trying to process everything. His father would know what to do in a situation like this. Oh how he wished he had a man, or beast, to send to him now.

"And I can't go outside to help at all?" Evan asked.

"I'm not sure what good it will do."

"It will show my face—remind them who walks the Keep and who will inherit this place."

"Would that be better, or worse, for the situation?" Rhys was calm. *Expecting an outburst?*

Evan didn't blame him if he was. Even now, his anger was rising. But who was to blame? Rhys? Yand? His father? Or was it his own actions—his own stupidity—that had led him to this road he now had to travel alone?

"I'm not cut out for these games, Rhys. It doesn't suit me."

"I will try my best to help you." He reached out and patted Evan's hand, what appeared to be a sincere look of pain and pity on his face. "But I've never been in this kind of situation either, I'm afraid."

Despite his soreness, Evan straightened his back, pulling himself up. "I'll try to do my best then, if I can do anything at all." He licked his dry, parched lips. "Let's get on with the inventory then."

Rhys nodded and took out his records. "We're down to three months' worth of dry goods. All of the fresh vegetables are gone, as well as the meats."

That explains the lack of variety in the meals.

"Do we have any way of getting more food?" Evan buried his head in his hands.

"The birds have all migrated south for the winter. I would have told you we could catch a few, but that won't be true in this weather. We have nothing planted within the walls of the castle."

"So our only hope is to get resupplied by someone else. Like my father."

"Or the King, if I can get a message to him," Rhys said.

"Or the King," Evan repeated. Great, just have to get a message to him through this attacking army that killed our last messenger. "What about the river?"

"I don't know what you mean."

"Could they resupply us by the river?" Evan asked.

Rhys wrinkled his brow. "I suppose so, except they would have to go by the gate."

"Then that's out too." Evan sighed and leaned back on his hands. It burned his shoulders, but felt good to get some relief off his lower back, it was killing him.

A *source of life and an easy way to travel.* Evan had expected to use it more than it had been.

"Do we risk another messenger through the woods, then? Or try to break out before the Belmarch can fortify their position?" Evan wondered aloud, not expecting much of an answer. Rhys was a politician, not a tactician.

"My reports say the Belmarch keep up their sentries in the forest and have enough men to stay on watch all night," Rhys grimaced. "Who would be the one to send if we could?"

"So we sit here and wait. Hope that my father finds out on his own." Evan's body burned, but not as much as his inability to do anything. Evan clenched his fist. "Move on, I can't stand it."

A look flitted across the Overseer's face, but he nodded and continued. His reports were as disengaging as always, but Evan paid attention this time, as much as he wished he didn't have to.

As soon as Rhys left, Evan would be alone again, so he relished their time they spent together. He had never had friends like others did, even his cousins always had some sort of ulterior motive. Evan wasn't deluded into thinking Rhys liked him for who he was, or that he liked him at all, but as an adviser he had some level of freedom to speak his mind.

Then he was done and rising. Evan tried to get up too, groaning with soreness.

"Please, stay, Your Highness." Rhys motioned him back, then bowed and left.

Evan stretched more, getting some feeling back in his body and massaging some of his muscles to movement again. Now it wasn't a complete burning pain, but a dull constant pain spiked whenever he moved.

He looked to his sword, but couldn't bear the thought of trying another workout. He walked instead, slowly shuffling around his room, then out the door to his study, sword in hand.

The room was as he left it, with plenty of room to word. Drawing the sword was painful, and Evan could barely get through the first form.

He had to stop, and sink into a chair, panting. At least the sun was up.

The room was bathed in a warm glow, the cool stone on his feet felt good. He marveled at how even his toes felt sore and stiff, and stretched them out.

His one candle in the corner, graciously granted by the Overseer's inventory.

It felt good to get off his feet, and he closed his eyes to just listen.

The castle was talking. Somewhere above him wood creaked, a low whistle of wind next to it. Far off in the distance he thought he heard people talking.

It made him long to go out all the more. How could he lead them from in here? And how could he stop a rebellion with no way to reason with his subjects.

He opened his eyes, looking around the room for something, anything that might help him. Furniture, the bar cabinet, his eyes rested on the bookshelf.

Tickles of his former tutors ran through his mind then. One of his first, Archelwaid, had told him books were distilled knowledge, transmuted from age to age.

Could they help him? He doubted it, but there were stranger things that had happened. However, to get there he had to get up first.

He wasn't looking forward to it, but Evan built his resolve, and then finally stood.

Body protesting, he went across the room and stood next to the books, taking in long breaths.

Other memories flooded back to him. Long, boring days listening to old tutors drone on and on, never varying their tone. Hot, warm rooms that made him fall asleep within minutes of the lesson, and sharp raps on the knuckles to wake him up.

It made Evan feel stuffy just to remember, and he hot around his collar. Luckily, it was cold, and that helped to stave off the worst of the thoughts. There was no crackling fire in the hearth, or huge beams of sun to heat this room.

He picked up the one he had taken the other day. It's spine was leather, and aged by time. How long had this book been in his collection, forgotten and lost to time?

Evan turned it over, feeling the embossed letters on the front, and slipped his finger between two pages.

What would Yand think of him, working himself to injury and reading books? Evan smiled, knowing the shocked reaction that would have been visible to only a few that knew the man really well.

Never a scholar himself, Yand knew quite a bit more than he let on. Evan only caught it from others, who had been surprised by Yand's references to popular stories and history, most of it military related.

"Never discount what you can learn from the past. It may save your life one day," Yand had said. Evan grimaced, hard to think of it.

It cracked as he opened it up, all along the spine. He winced, and examined it, but nothing seemed out of place.

Hobbling over to his desk, he took it with him and held it up to his little light coming in the window.

The letters were small, but neatly typed. The first letter was larger and ornamented. Whoever had written this book had taken his time, for vines traveled up the "s" on the first page.

"So follows the history of Chathem from founding to the year of the sun, 9th summer."

He fought the urge to put it down, feeling all his former hatred of letters and words come back in force.

Whoever invented the art could have made things easier. Evan yawned, and settled back in his chair.

He set the book down and tried his arms again, but they were too sore to move.

With nothing else to do, he read. Slowly, at first, with frequent stops, but something about the words caught him, fascinating him.

Soon, he was swept into the history of his people.

14

THE ONE TO LEAVE

The next night was easier for Sam and proved to be more successful. He saw improvement, even in the small amount of work that had come from the workers.

The guardsman, no strangers to fighting and training to fight, had improved as well. Sam stood in the cold, seeing his frosty breath fill the night sky and taken away under the light of the moon.

"I see we were right to trust you," the Overseer said.

Surprised, Sam turned. He couldn't make out the expression in the man's face in the dark, other than he was looking at him.

"Overseer," Sam said, bowing slightly. "I didn't expect to see you out this late."

"I wanted to come and see how everything was going." Overseer Rhys stepped next to him, watching the last session of sparring. Men grunted and struck at each other, practicing the techniques and forms Sam had taught them.

He's out here to observe me. Bill had done everything he said he would so far, and from all that Sam could tell was instrumental in getting his permission to train the men.

"It's a nice night, isn't it?" The Overseer was bundled in clothing, a thick winter coat covering his shoulders and dwindling form. "And how does the training go?" He turned to face Sam.

"Well."

"That's all?"

Sam shrugged. "The men are listening and practicing what I tell them. If it were that way with so many others, the world would be a better place."

The Overseer let out a short, bitter laugh. "Perhaps it is on the other side too."

Sam looked to the walls and the Belmarch that lay encamped on the other side of them. "I don't get the feeling that's the case."

"Oh? Go on."

"We haven't seen much action from them."

"I've had reports the enemy still sets up sentries, sends out regular patrols within sight of the walls," the Overseer said.

"All true, but that is a simple matter to attend to, and any leaderless army could do it." Sam shook his head. "They're waiting for something—or some time. I wish I knew what it was."

"Well, in the meantime, you have some work to do." The sparring was wrapping up, and each of the squad leaders was calling an end to the session. "We'll need them well-trained in the event of another breach."

"There was something I wanted to talk to you about that," Sam said, then hesitated.

"Go on," the Overseer said.

"When Yand was here—still alive, I mean." His body had been laid to rest in the makeshift cemetery. "We discussed additional defenses for the castle."

"I remember."

"I think now would be a good time to start. I've noticed the masons don't have much to do and think it would be a better use of their time."

It was a mystery Sam was still trying to unravel. Where was all the effort going? His plans would have taken it all, and then some.

"Yes, I've discussed that with Bill," the Overseer said. Sam shivered as he cooled down, the heat from training wearing off. "I think it would do with some changes, but overall, I'm satisfied."

Everyone was trickling out of the courtyard, putting up their training weapons and returning to the shelter of the Keep. The makeshift shacks now lay abandoned and dark, unusable in the cold.

"I'm glad to hear that," Sam said, thinking carefully about his next words.

"I can see you're thinking about what the drawback is—the price you need to pay." The Overseer stuffed his hands into deep pockets.

"There are some conditions to it. Bill has told me of your plans with the river. That's something I hadn't thought of, and I think it might work."

Sam was glad Bill had some success with the Overseer.

"Come inside, to my room. It's too cold to talk out here," the Overseer said. He turned and walked to the Keep without waiting for Sam to follow.

Sam had to walk fast to catch up but did before they got there. Passing through the door brought a measure of relief from the cold and quieted his shivering muscles.

They didn't say anything else until they were back in the Overseer's office.

After taking a seat at his desk, the Overseer motioned for Sam to join him.

Sam sat, letting his muscles ease into relaxation. His leg throbbing quietly.

The Overseer pressed his fingers together and considered him. A candle gave them light and a tiny measure of warmth, but not much.

"I will be the one to leave."

Sam looked at him, not understanding. "Leave?"

"When you get this boat built, I will be the one to take it for help," the Overseer said.

It took a few moments for the words to sink in. "What do you mean you'll take it? You can't take it."

"I will. I've piloted boats on the water in my youth, and I have the connections. There isn't anyone better to go."

"Who put you up to this? Was it Bill?"

"Bill and I have an understanding." The Overseer's lips tightened.

Sam's heart was racing, wondering why this was happening. *What is Bill planning?*

"What makes you want to go?" he finally asked.

A rueful smile played across the Overseer's lips. "Other than being the one to survive?" he asked. "I don't hide that thought crossed my mind as well, and it is a little perk, assuming its safe to leave in the first place. No, that wasn't it. I want to go because I'm not sure they would listen to anyone else, except perhaps the Duke."

"So, you'll leave him." It wasn't a question, but there was an unspoken one behind it.

"Duke Hornblood has... changed. I know it might leave a precarious position, but what other choice do I have?" The Overseer shrugged and held up his hands. "Who else knows the way to the capital, let alone who can get into the court to bear witness to what happened here?"

Sam knew he couldn't do it and frowned. The long list of people in the castle ran through his mind, but not a single one other than the Duke seemed able to perform that act.

"Then why not send the Duke?" Sam asked.

"It's still a risk. We don't know how well the Belmarch are watching the river, and assuming they are, we all know what will happen to the man in the boat." The Overseer arched his brow. "Assuming it can float, that is."

"It will function as designed," Sam said. He had total confidence in Kerien and Ned, except for that small nagging doubt that lived in the back of his mind. "You said you've done some piloting—what does that mean?"

"It means I know a little something about boats," the Overseer said, smiling. "Don't worry, I can remember it too. I grew up on the river, more than a few miles downriver perhaps, but I'll know my way around when I get there."

"It doesn't seem to be the smartest option," Sam said. "You've been put in charge here."

"Of building a castle fortress. How am I to do that without supplies?" *He has a point.* "With the Duke here, my authority is already lessened. He will pick up the mantle and keep things going."

"How, exactly, will he do that?"

"That's where I need your help. The Duke is young and needs some guidance."

"Guidance? I'm no adviser."

"No, but you do command the respect of everyone in the castle with the way you handled the last attack." The Overseer's eyes glinted in the candlelight. His office smelled of paper and animal skins.

"I can't do it."

"You haven't even heard my proposition yet," the Overseer said.

"I don't need to. I'm not able to be a royal adviser. I can't even really be an adviser on carpentry," Sam said. Each word felt pulled out his body with force, and he felt lightheaded. *What happened to the Overseer Rhys that hated me, that wanted to see me fail and blamed me for everything?*

He couldn't do it. Sam wasn't a general, wasn't even a captain. Now he expected him to be a Duke?

"Perhaps this isn't the best time to discuss it," the Overseer said, his tone softening. "But I will be leaving eventually, so you would do well to think about what life in the castle will look like when that happens."

It didn't feel real. It felt like Sam was in a dream. Like he was enveloped by water. Even the Overseer's voice seemed to be distorted.

He hadn't considered this outcome, not one bit. Sam had wondered if Bill would try and convince the Overseer to send the Duke himself, take care of two in one go. He would be out of the way and one of the best chances to get them help, had he survived the trip downriver.

Never once had he thought the Overseer might want to go, or that it was even an option.

But here it was, staring him in the face.

Sam licked his lips, his mouth suddenly dry. "This is…une xpected is all." he was going to talk to Bill about this one. "We aren't even ready with the boat, let alone the stonework to remove for the crane."

"I can assure you the masons will be ready long before you are." There was the veiled insult. The Overseer kept a blank face as he said it.

"I'm glad of that."

"One less man within the walls means one less mouth to feed," the Overseer said.

It made Sam think about the women and children that were still here, trapped within the walls of the castle. Who was going to get them about? Would word spread about the boat, make it seem like they would be making an escape without them?

Sam's plan suddenly wasn't as good as he originally thought. He grimaced, thinking of Belinda and her child. He imagined lowering them down to get them away, but then something awful happening to the boat and it sinking, taking them down to a watery grave.

He realized then how much of a risk the Overseer was taking, and how much trust he had put within the carpenters of Hornblood Castle. Far more than Sam gave him credit for.

He looked at him in a different light. Gone was the plump of the rich man that had overseen them, gone was the life of ease. He had aged more than Sam had realized, great sunken bags beneath his cheeks accentuated by the candlelight.

The Overseer was a slim man now. *How much was he eating?* Not much more than anyone else, maybe even less.

But there was a strength beneath those eyes, resolve that hadn't been there when they had just been building the castle and not trapped inside. Where had it come from?

Sam swallowed and cleared his throat. "Before I go, we need to discuss something. The defenses."

"Go on," the Overseer said, watching him closely. *What kind of reaction is he expecting?*

"You mentioned changes. What did you want to change?"

The Overseer leaned back and flitted his hand. "Nothing much, a change here and there to make things a little easier on the masons to build."

Sam knew it was too good to be true. Changes to that plan would have neutered its effectiveness. He had seen it happen too. Still, he smiled and tried to be polite. "Can you be more specific?"

"No. Not at this time. If you'd like to know what you'll have to talk to Bill. He knows what he wants." *As I suspected.*

"I understand," Sam said. There was nothing left to discuss, so he stood. "I must be going now, Overseer. It was a pleasure."

"No need to lie Sam. I know this isn't pleasant for anyone, you least of all." He looked off in the distance. "For anyone here."

Sam wondered what the real reason the Overseer wanted to leave was. The attacks had come under his jurisdiction, even though the Duke was here it didn't matter for some reason. The specific reason Sam didn't know, but he knew that it fell to the Overseer to make the castle defensible.

He had failed in that respect, and might be trying to salvage the situation.

Whatever the case, Sam didn't want to spend another minute in the Overseer's office. The scent was getting to him, and it felt stuffy after being outside in the cold so long and so much.

He bid the man goodnight and left. As the door shut with a click behind him Sam knew what he needed to do.

He needed to pay a visit to Bill.

15

Sam wondered when the best time to talk to Bill would be. It was too late that night and too cold outside.The next morning he didn't get a chance, or he didn't feel like it, and even though he saw him at lunch he said nothing to him, only nodded politely and continued on his way.

Bill had changed some, and Sam didn't know if that was a good thing or a bad thing. He didn't think the man had much animosity towards him anymore, but his scheming was even more pronounced now.

"I'm afraid to ask him," Sam said, after he caught Ned alone in the workshop, before the others came back, after he had explained the situation. At least, what he felt comfortable sharing.

"What is the worst that could happen?"

"He wanted too little last time." Sam examined their progressed, feeling the curve in the little bow that was starting to take shape. "I've known Bill long enough to know he asks for more than that." He shook his head. "What is he trying to get out of me?"

"The better question is what is he trying to get for himself?" Ned carved another curl from the wood.

Sam thought about that long and hard, even as the others came in. He made motion for Ned to keep their discussion quiet, which he acknowledged with a nod.

As they ran out of material, they were running out of things to work on. The castle had a good bundle of arrows now, considering they hadn't used any since the last attack they were well stocked.

The iron had run out so they were down to flints and bits of stone that the masons provided, attached by long, thin slivers of bark.

He hadn't been to see Dale in some time, so Sam resolved to go see him. He knew Bill the best of anyone.

Stretching his hands against the cold wasn't helping anymore. The flaps of the workshop did a horrible job of keeping out the wind, no matter how tightly they tied them down, and sucked all heat out of them.

Sam worried about where they would go. There was no warm spot left in the castle, winter had come in full force. Even the snow that was now ankle high offered little relief against it, no matter how high it packed up against the walls of the Keep.

An hour before sunset, came all too early, Sam put up his tools and left the others to their work, checking on the progress. He gave Trent some encouragement, who was helping to prepare the wood for Ned and Kerien, who gave him a small smile in return.

Late-night training sessions wouldn't be possible in a few more days. The wind howled across the courtyard, buffeting him.

His ears stung from little bits of snow that rushed into his face and around his head, and they went into his eyes and made them sting and water. The rivers were kicked up and made a terrible noise. he knew from the last few days they would be raging and foam covered if he went up to see it.

Another thing in the long line of ways to kill their chances. Now they would have to wait for a calm day once the boat was finished to set their expedition to sail.

He was shivering uncontrollability when he stepped into the smithy, which was dark and cold uncharacteristically.

No one was there.

Where could he be? Sam sat near the dark forge, staring at the tooling. Everything was well kept and in its place. Besides a small cobweb here or there it was as if it was waiting in the morning for the forge fires to be lit.

He glanced to the corner. There was some fuel left, a heap of charcoal in its assigned spot. Sam suspected Dale would have another stash, a secret stash, hidden away.

The smell was different. Wrong, somehow. It should be filled with the smell of smoke and burning hot metal, but it was filled with the tasteless bite of winter instead.

"Didn't expect to see you here," Dale said. He came in and stomped his feet. "No one comes around."

"How much fuel do you have left?" Sam asked.

"A few days, maybe a week, if I keep the fire going." He sat down next to Sam, pulling up a stool. It wobbled. "I've been meaning to ask you to fix that. Hadn't had much time to sit on it though."

"All it seems you have is time," Sam said.

"Ha," Dale said. "I haven't seen you much, just at training. I see you're leading it now." He looked at him through the corner of his eye.

"They asked me to." Sam shrugged.

"That's not the Sam Freeman I knew." It was warmer in the smithy than outside, shielded from the wind, but only just. Still, Sam wanted to talk alone, to figure things out together.

"A lot has changed. I realized there are people here I care about, that need a chance."

Dale nodded. "We could all use some of that. There is a fragileness in the air, Sam. I know you feel it too."

He did and didn't want to think about it. "I need your opinion on Bill."

"I wouldn't trust him with a hammer or tongs. You avoided the question."

"You didn't ask a question."

"Fine. Can you feel it too?"

Sam paused. "I feel it. Anarchy, rebellion, that's what I feel. All at the wrong time." He shook his head. "We shouldn't be fighting among ourselves."

"Not everyone sees it that way."

"Then how do they see it?"

It was Dale's turn to pause. "Some see it as casting off the old, so that we have a chance to survive. I've even heard talk of surrender to the Belmarch from some of the younger ones."

"Surrender? Would they accept it."

"They'd accept it all right, then come in a kill us anyway and take the women back to Belmarch as slaves and playthings." Sam bristled at the thought of it, at Belinda being abused.

And Martha.

It touched something strange within him to think about. *Why did I think of her?*

"They'd be fools to do it, but desperate men are foolish creatures."

"And that's what I've come to talk to you about." Sam filled him in. "I know we need the masons to put up any real defenses. Stone is the only thing we have plenty of, but how do I trust a man not worthy of it?"

"You can't, can you." Dale leaned back on his stool, resting his back against a bench. "I'm not sure you have much of a choice though. You think these defenses would work?"

"I do."

"And you're willing to risk all our lives on them?" Dale's eyes bored in to his.

"I don't think I'd be doing that. We have the walls, we have the gate. I just don't think they'll stand."

"What if they don't come in that way, that they break through somewhere else?"

"I've thought about that," Sam said. "Every time I keep coming back to that weak spot. It's too good to pass up. The walls are too thick and they know it."

"How do you know?"

"Because if they thought they could break into the walls they would be bombarding us every day with that catapult."

"But they aren't."

Sam nodded. The sky was changing color already, the sunset already coming on. "They haven't yet, and I don't think they will unless someone else is in charge." It made sense to him, but this was the first time he had voiced it out loud. "They are going to starve us, Dale. And I think they'll succeed."

They were silent as the wind ran through the workshop roof, howling and screaming as it went. No children played outside now. the stool creaked as Dale shifted his eight.

"What did you come to me for?"

"I need to know what you think Bill is after."

"After?" Dale's eyes widened a hair, and he scratched his beard. "Seems to me that Bill is after what most men are after. Power."

"That's what I thought too, but then why wouldn't he take it earlier? Why would he ask me to lead a revolt?"

"In hopes that you fail, or better yet, that you succeed. He's probably thought about both outcomes and how he might use either to his advantage," Dale said. "Be careful of him, he's smarter than he lets on."

"I know, and I've felt some of it already." Sam thought back to the Overseer and conversations he had with him. "Have you... sensed any change within Bill?"

Dale frowned. "Changed? No, I think he's still the same man he always was. Why do you ask?"

"Hes' talking to me, for one thing," Sam said. "Something he said to me, a conversation we had. I don't know, maybe I'm giving him too much credit."

"You might be. But, then again, you might be right. A lot has changed. Almost everything. You can expect men to stay the same after that, even if they seem like they are. You're a good example."

"I don't see it that way."

"And you don't have to, but you know it to be true anyway." The sky was orange now, big clouds racing across the sky. Hints of red were starting to show. "Either way, you have to decide if this course of action is something you believe in enough to take the risk."

Risk. He wondered what kind of risk it would be. To be in the service of a man he hardly trusted, but had something inside that made him hope for the best.

And it could all be for naught. He could put himself in Bill's hands only to be wrenched and betrayed, cast aside like some little used piece of cloth, or moldy food.

"I don't know what to do."

"You'll have to figure that out soon." Dale nodded and looked out the door. Bill was walking across the courtyard, flanked by masons. It was like he was a king holding court, the way they simpered and deferred to him.

Sam burned with anger, and more than a hint of jealousy. Perhaps he had run from his old life for more reasons than he was convincing himself of. There was a yearning desire inside him to be loved and respected.

But he expected that Bill has the Sam desire, as did all of them. The thought gave him pause, made him consider the choice before him n another light.

"Thank you. You've given me something to think about," Sam said, standing and taking Dale's hand. He knew his hands were cold, he never expected Dale's to be. Not after working in the smithy for so long, the man was always warm.

"Whatever you do, make sure you know it's the right thing." Dale's eyes burned into his, a deep fire raging within him. His hand throbbed with strength. Sam was sure he could crush his hand in an instant.

For all the times he had seen Dale work, he had never seen him angry. And, to think of it, he had never seen him fight.

Right then, though, he was glad Dale was on his side.

"Can I count on your friendship and support?"

"I might want to call it a favor," Dale said, his eyes twinkling and creases of happiness appearing around his eyes. It was the first time Sam had seen him happy in a while.

It was the first time he had seen anyone happy in a while. Imagine that.

He longed for the old days, the simple days of sweat and toil, a hard, hot, long day that had a feast at the end of it and a great, big bonfire where the workers and their families could gather and talk and laugh and sing.

There was none of that here. Even if they were warm enough, they were too hungry. Even if they were fed, they would despair. He saw it every time he went into the keep.

They might lose more of them to hopelessness than anything else.

"I'll take what I can get. You won't have much use of a favor from me if I'm dead." *Not that I want to die.*

"Then you best keep yourself alive." Dale rubbed his hands together. "Back out into the cold again."

Sam nodded. "Back out once more." He started first, leaving the cold smithy to sit undisturbed.

"Where are you going?" Dale asked.

Sam looked over his shoulder, face set in a grim mask. "To make my decision."

16

History of Chathem

Evan read the book. In it he discovered things he had never known and remembered hard lessons his tutors had tried to teach him long ago.

It took him back to days by the river, an exercise his father frowned upon, listening to Master Raupth drone on about the early history of the Chathem tribe.

He had soaked in the sunshine those days, and retained little of his lessons, but those lessons started to come back to him now.

It took a different light, when he was finally able to put away the hard words and work through the letters. As he went, he discovered more.

The story of Adol and the Snake, how he had tricked the pour beast into blessing his future line, thus beginning the tribe of Chathem.

The guile, the cunning it took to convince the snake to come out of his hole, the bravery to grab it by the throat despite the fangs dripping venom, Evan wondered why he had never heard these stories before.

But, as he thought about it, he realized he may have. Evan, as bad as he was with studies and books, had tried to avoid them as a child.

Now, he realized that within the pages of these tomes he could find something else. Something of his descendants, those who had gone before him.

He flipped through the pages, learning and absorbing more and more. The crease of the spine, the smell of the leather and animal skin, it took him to another world.

Shimmering on the page, the deep black ink invited him in in stark contrast to the dull gray of the stone that surrounded him. At each new story there was a small illustration around the first letter, drawn with great care and related to the history that followed.

He started to look forward to these new pages, even the long chronologies that punctuated some of the book that bored him.

A knock on his door announced the arrival of lunch. Evan looked up, surprised that it was already that late in the day.

He set the book down and stood, glad that some of his soreness had abated. He used the opportunity to walk around and stretch out his muscles some more as the servant set his food on the table.

He was a young man, dark eyed and dark hair. Evan had seen him before, recognized the face, but realized he didn't even know his name.

"Good afternoon, Your Highness," the man said, bowing to leave.

"Wait, what is your name?" Evan tried to suppress the feeling of annoyance as a flicker of fear went across the man's face.

"It does not matter, Your Highness." He wouldn't look Evan in the eye, but he couldn't blame him for that.

"Nonsense, I asked you a question and I demand an answer." He was used to having better conversation, and thought as he said it he might have been missing the sound of another human's voice.

It was tiring to listen to Rhys for an hour or two and then spend the rest of your day in solitude.

"Barger, Your Highness," he said, mumbling it quietly.

"Barger?" The man's lips tightened. "A...solid name, for a solid man. How long have you been a s-" Evan hastily changed his question, "with us?"

"A year, your highness."

A year? There was no way that was true. Evan though back, realizing with a sickening feeling that the man was telling the truth. He had come with him in the spring, and had served him the summer before that. Evan remembered him being at the harvest festival.

His cheeks reddened, also remembering the amount of wine he had consumed that night.

"Yes, good to have you too." Evan smiled, the smile he used when he didn't feel like it but was told to anyway. Silence stretched between them.

"Shall I leave you to dine, your highness?" Barger asked.

"Oh, yes." The man turned and opened the door. "Thank you," Evan said as he walked out, trying to overcome his previous ineptitude.

The man stopped mid-stride, then continued on, shutting the door without even a click.

That made him remember even more. Barger was his silent servant, always sneaking up on him. You could never hear him coming.

Evan took another lap around his room, glancing at the tray. Served on the best dishes the castle had to offer, it was still going to be a tasteless gruel of mashed up wheat.

He took off the metal cover, fearing he was right. Evan sighed and sat down to eat.

It was as he feared, and each bite had to be chewed what seemed like forever before he could finally choke it down.

But he needed the sustenance after yesterday. After he finished he pushed away the dishes in disgust and found he felt better.

Wine would make the bland taste out of my mouth. Evan glanced to the cupboard. All he had to do was summon his servant and Rhys and send them to get the second to last cask. It would be a relief.

And it would bring oblivion.

Evan stared at it until he couldn't look at it anymore. He ripped himself away from it and practically lunged at his sword, drawing it in a flash.

The sword rang out, caught by the edge of the scabbard. He immediately went into his first form, letting it flow through him.

He thought about little as he did, a momentary question of how many times he had done this floating to the top of his consciousness, then swept away into the forms.

His body was looser than when he started. It still was sore, but not as severe. Evan continued on, working on the next forms in series.

Each one was more advanced than the last, adding more motions and techniques with every step. Eventually he finished them all.

Sweating, he stopped to catch his breath. Panting, he realized that if he kept going he would end up worse off tomorrow. Reluctantly, he sheathed his sword and took it off, setting it carefully over the edge of the table.

He went back to the book. Later, he wasn't sure if it was a few hours or a few minutes, Barger knocked again and came in to take his plates.

Evan said nothing to him except "Thank you" as he left. Barger bowed with politeness, but said nothing in return.

Evan was surprised he spoke the first time. He returned to his studies, poring over the book.

There were more interesting stories the more he read.

Belthaz and his double hammers, making the enemies flee before him in battle. Shiraf the Thief who managed to bring an army to its knees planting treasures within it.

But it was Miral that captured his imagination and attention. There, in the dark light of the room, he stumbled upon a story he had never heard of.

A son of Yuoled the Bold, Miral had been a disappointment to his father in his youth, so much so that he was passed over to inherit the kingdom of Chathem in favor of his uncle.

Before his father's death, Miral tried to entreat with him to earn back his inheritance. Yuoled refused, and within a few hours had breathed his last.

Before the coronation of his uncle, they were attacked by Belmarch armies from the north. Each page revealed more and more desperation the kingdom faced as a power vacuum emerged.

The coronation was put on hold, the nobles tried to raise their armies. Each one fought against another, vying for the kingship.

All the while the Belmarch army marched south, burning and looting as they went. Lacastia fell, then Mayfield. His uncle tried to unite then under one banner, but only succeeded in taking half the kingdom's forces to Antilia and a final defense.

All the while Miral was helpless in the capitol, then Goldever. He had taken to drink, and was ridiculed by all.

But the news of his uncles death at Antilia roused him from his stupor. Miral swore off all drink and shaved his head in mourning. There was no clear successor, and he was not sure the nobles would accept him.

They didn't, at first. Miral enlisted the aid of his mother, the Queen Soleth, and began to turn them one by one to his cause.

The Belmarch, not desiring anything other than complete domination and the resources of Chathem, pushed forward into the very heart of Chathem.

Miral was told of a weakness, their supplies and baggage train that trailed all the way north to Belmarch. He took his much smaller army and headed north, proclaiming his intent to fight on the field of battle and earn his father's crown.

The light faded as he read, and he had to pause to light a candle. The small flame danced and tricked its way around the wick, filling the room with the aroma of smoke.

Soreness had set back into his muscles, and he worked them loose again before he returned to his book. Dinner came while he did, and he wolfed it down and returned to the book, marveling at how much he looked forward to it.

Miral traveled north, but not to meet them in battle. He turned east, and using old roads and trails unknown to the Belmarch, circled around them with forced marches.

All the while he kept his head bald and trained harder than he ever had. Master swordsmen taught him everything they knew, and he quickly became a deadly fighter.

When they reached the back lines of the Belmarch they stood unopposed. Miral freed prisoners and took weapons and arms, and cut off their supplies.

The Belmarch were not dissuaded, and kept their troops fed from the ravaging of the lands. But, winter was nearly upon them, and the Belmarch didn't plan for a cold weather encounter.

Miral had, and he had grown his ranks with prisoners and converts alike. He made promises to the nobles, and increased his strength. Dukedoms were established, and with a thrill Evan realized that a minor noble was granted the Hornblood line in that very story.

He continued reading. Miral trapped the Belmarch in the low country, defeating them in a climatic battle that clinched his title to the throne and established his right to rule. The few Belmarch that survived fled north, around his army, and barely any survived. He established peace in his time and became a great rule, enacting justice fairly and impartially and growing his kingdom. Lands to the east and west joined, establishing the boundaries up to the Golden River.

Evan sat back, the end of the tail finished, and basked in the glow of the candlelight. By all accounts Miral was a failure that had risen above his previous failures to become something better.

The candle flickered. It was late now, and his eyes were heavy. His body would recover with rest, but his mind was on fire and alight with what he had read.

It could be possible.

He went back through the chapter, making sure he hadn't read it wrong. He didn't.

Why had no one told me this before? Did they even know? The books on his bookshelf were little used, but varied. What else lay within their covers?

Evan wanted to read more. It was a strange sensation, and one he had never expected to feel. he got up and paced around the room, both to stretch his legs and clear his mind.

Thoughts ran through him, flying past one another at an astounding speed. He thought about what he could do from these rooms, how he might have lost a chance before but might have another one.

But was it too late? Evan chewed on his lip and stretched his arms. they too were still sore, even more so than his legs.

He couldn't sort it all out though, and his candle was getting too low. It smelled less like smoke and more like tallow, and Evan took it with him to his bedroom.

There was no one in the hall, and his footsteps echoed. The door creaked as it opened and shut behind him.

Evan dressed for bed, staring hard at himself in the water of his washbasin. He looked different than he had, and wasn't sure why.

From somewhere far outside his room he heard an owl hoot. A good omen, this far into winter. It meant that good weather would come, and that the winter would be short.

Evan watched a smile grow on his face. Things might be the same tomorrow, or they might be different. Evan suspected they would be different.

17

BITING COLD

Sam stood in the freezing cold, barely able to handle it. His entire body was shaking with shivers.

There was nothing happening, and he wished he could be inside, away from the cold blowing win that cut right through him to the heart. The sun was obscured by a thick layer of gray clouds.

He checked the southern horizon, not seeing any movement, and looked back into the castle and the courtyard.

No one was out. Everyone not on watch on the walls was tucked inside, away from the wind and blowing snow. They had made a path through the drifts, from the keep to the stairs coated in ice up to the battlements.

The Keep looked pitiful. It was squat and coated in snow, icicles hanging from beams and roofs. It should have had tall towers and another floor.

Sam lamented this. Had they been able to continue their work the next floor would have been on by now, and the southwest tower would have been driven into the sky.

He imagined knocking home the final beam, standing astride it and looking into the wilderness beyond. He would have been able to see into Belmarch clearly, and far upriver.

Instead, it was a shell of its former self. And he was no closer to finishing it. He supposed he should be grateful, that he was still alive when others had perished, but strangely enough he wasn't.

Hie was deeply unsatisfied. So much so he couldn't look at it anymore and turned back to the village below.

Sam gripped his bow tight, hoping to squeeze some amount of warmth from it. They were doing hour long watches now, it was too cold for anything longer.

He didn't know what time of year it was, but he knew they had reached the coldest and bitterest part of winter. Hardly any sun light up the days now, and when it was clouds covered over most their light.

It started to snow a few moments later. a rough, biting snow that stung his cheeks and made his eyes water.

A man came up to relieve him. He couldn't tell who it was, his face was covered in threadbare cloth.

Sam turned over his bow and arrows, hands thick with cold, and went back into the warmth of the guardhouse.

They had half the number of sentries on the wall then usual, partly because of the cold and partly because there was no way an attack would have been successful in those conditions.

Inside, men were shivering and huddled together to keep warm. Sam joined them, pressing into the mass.

"Bitter cold out there," he said. The door swung open and shut, letting in a blast that set him shivering.

"It won't let up," Mathew said. His ears were an unnatural red color. He rubbed his shoulders and joined the rest of them.

There was little conversation as the newcomers tried to get warm again. Sam longed for a thick, fur coat to wrap himself in. They had scarcely any more clothes to protect themselves from the cold, and it was starting to take its toll.

A man had died out there, young and in his prime. His name had been Nathula, and he was a mason. Bill had stumbled upon him when he went to his watch, frozen up on the wall.

He had been blue and stuck to the rock. It had taken hours to thaw him out enough to get his clothes off, and they put him outside in the shelter of the Keep. The ground was too hard to try and dig up, but his body would stay preserved.

It was one more life lost, one more death. The specter of it hung over the survivors, and that had made them shift to shorter watches. It had been Mathew's idea, and a good one.

"One of the worst winter's I've seen," a man said, from back in the group. "We've been cursed. We'll never make it through the winter."

"We've made it this far," Sam said, finally getting a hold of his chattering teeth enough to speak. "We'll make it."

But he wasn't sure. It was bitter cold, much worse than last year. He hoped his words didn't sound hollow, but couldn't be sure.

In no time at all their respite was up, and the next group of sentries pushed out into the cold to take their turn. The group shifted around and pressed together, and Sam found himself closer to the center.

A few minutes later the relieved sentries came in, stamping and puffing, and joined them. It went on like this all through their watch, until the light was gone and th next squad had their turn.

Sam joined the others in turning over the equipment, and wondered how far Ned and Kerien had gotten. If they didn't finish soon they wouldn't have a chance of getting that boat launched.

The winter storms had driven the rivers into a frenzy. How they were going to a get a boat to float on it, he didn't know, but they couldn't wait for better weather. Every day brought them one step closer to starving.

They fought across the courtyard through the driving snow, and into the Keep in a mass. Dinner was served, a cold mush of unidentified grains, that barely filled their stomachs.

Martha was there, scooping out their portions. Sam's heart skipped a beat when she looked at him and then quickly looked away.

Sam greeted her when it was his turn, and held out his bowl.

"Thank you," he murmured, shivers still racking his body. Her hands were cold as he took the bowl from her.

"How bad is it out there?" Worry creased the corners of her eyes.

"Bad," he said, shoving the mush around his bowl with a spoon. How long he could stand it, he didn't know. They tried their best, but the cooks had nothing to work with. Just stores of grain. "I'm afraid the ice might take someone over the side."

How long would any of them last, with things how they were now? Martha seemed to sense his discomfort.

"You don't bear the weight of the world on your shoulders," she said softly, tenderly.

Sam looked away from her. He couldn't take the look in her eyes. It was... too much to bear.

"I have enough of it to last me a lifetime." He lingered in line, as the last man there was no one behind him.

All of a sudden he was starting to get warm. His mind had wandered, thinking of if Martha was available to eat with him. It seemed absurd, against the backdrop of everything else that was going on.

"Don't be too hard on yourself," Martha said. She turned back. "Girls, go eat."

"Have you ... eaten?" Sam asked. He didn't know why his mouth felt like cotton all of a sudden, or why his palms went sweaty.

When was the last time he had thought about a woman this way? It had been months, years perhaps. Not that he didn't mind admiring some of the better-looking women around, but they were all taken and married.

Belinda. His mind raced to her without thinking. Not all of them were taken now. Far too many widows had been made already, and he hoped there would be none more.

But he knew that was a vain hope.

Martha was staring at him. "I haven't eaten yet." There was a long pause, and Sam shuffled.

If his food was warm, it would have grown cold. He didn't know what to do. He wanted to talk more to Martha but couldn't invite himself to invite her to eat with him.

No matter how hard he tried, and how he opened his mouth, the words didn't seem to leave his lips. It was like they were stuck at the back of his mouth, clogged and caught in his throat.

"If you don't shut your mouth, you'll look like a fish," Martha said, her lips flattening.

Sam's eyes opened wide. "W-What?" he stammered.

The other girls were being dished up. Martha plopped a portion into bowls and passed them out. When the group had come through, he found himself alone with her.

His eyes cast around the room. He found there were many staring at him, and he balked.

"Are you going to eat, Mr. Freeman?" Martha asked, folding her arms with a spoon. Her eyes twinkled with mirth.

"I'm not a—" Sam stopped, realizing she was joking. "Oh." Finally, he rushed the words out, trying not to think of them. "Would you care to sit with me?"

Martha lowered her head and looked out from under her eyelashes at him. "I'd be delighted."

His stomach turned somersaults, despite how empty it was. Even though it wouldn't be filled, he felt a small thrill of giddiness.

They walked to an open spot on a rickety bench, and Sam let her sit down before he took his seat. It was cold in the great hall, but having her next to him felt good. It was as if she warmed the air around herself.

They ate in silence for a while, a strange feeling lingering in the air. He noticed her long, brown hair was unkempt but had a luster of beauty. She had been plump, but like so many others, had lost weight.

Now she looked too thin, and it pained him to see the loss of life in her cheeks. That was one thing he remembered from before the siege. She'd had such rosy cheeks when she was happy.

"Have you been working on anything?" she asked.

"Yes. No, I mean." Why was he all twisted up in knots? He hadn't been like this since he was a child. "I have the others working on a boat."

"A boat?" She turned to him, surprised. "Why on the green earth are you building that?"

"I hope to use it to get help," he mumbled, all of a sudden feeling very foolish. It seemed like the better plan was to wait, but when he explained it to her, she nodded.

"That's a sensible plan, a right fine one. Do put what I said before out of your mind."

"I wish I could do more." Sam stirred the little remaining gruel around in his bowl. He thought he might be able to use it to hold up the castle if he waited long enough; it was so thick. "I can't sleep much at night."

"The cold bothers me too," Martha said.

"No, it isn't that. Not just that, at least." He looked up through the small opening that served as a window at the top of the ceiling. It let in the cold, but it let in light too.

"What is it?" Martha's voice was soft and warm, barely a whisper.

"What am I supposed to do for Belinda and her child? It tears me up inside to see them ... like they are."

"Do you not feel like you're doing enough?"

"No." He shook his head. There wasn't much other conversation, barely a hushed whisper here and there. His voice was lost in the cavernous room. "She deserves better than what she has." He turned to her, earnestly looking in her eyes. "So do you. All of you."

"We did know what we were getting into."

"But she didn't deserve to lose her husband." As soon as he said it, he knew it was a mistake. "I-I didn't mean..."

"No, it's fine." She wiped her eye with her hand. All of Sam's hope drained away from him then, seeing her in such a state of sadness. There was a clatter from the makeshift kitchen. "I have to go now, can't let the girls get away with not doing their fair share."

Martha stood and lifted her chin. Sam knew he should say something to her to make it right but didn't know what it would be.

Once again, he had made a mistake that he couldn't recover from. Another, in a long line and a long list. She marched away, head held high.

It must still be fresh for her, a wound that hadn't healed. Her husband had been dead for some months now, but he had just wanted to talk to her about Belinda. He never meant for it to come to this.

He watched her go, helpless

18

BOTTLES

The next day was easier for Evan. His body was less sore, and he had started to recover. He only groaned a few times getting out of bed. Most days he was woken by breakfast, or they waited until he was awake to bring him his food. That morning he was up long before breakfast, and had enough time to stretch and massage his muscles.

Cold and damp had set into his room, and he shivered as he ate the tasteless meal. Rhys had advised him not to use too much of the candle at once, so he ate in the dark, barely able to see.

When he was finished Evan pushed his meal away. He thought about going through the door that went directly into his office, but then looked at the door to the corridor.

Indignation rose inside him, and anger. He should be able to go out there, to walk among his people without fear. They were his subjects.

But, then again, are they? His father had always said he needed to earn his place, earn the respect of his people. It was one of the most infuriating comments that Evan had to endure, but then again he wondered if there wasn't some wisdom to those words.

"Finished, Your Highness?" Barger was at his elbow, and Evan jumped a little.

"I didn't see you there. Yes, I'm done." The door was open, but he didn't remember hearing it.

"Apologies, I didn't mean to frighten you, Your Highness." Barger took the dishes away with a grace and efficiency Evan couldn't help but admire. The man was quiet, almost too quiet.

"Have you eaten already?" Evan asked.

"Yes, Your Highness." Barger walked to the door, and turned. "Is that all?"

"Yes, that is all." Barger gave a small bow, then left. The door creaked shut, but barely clicked.

Evan dressed, then went into his study. he spent the first part of the morning running through his form work, until he had a light sweat running and dispelled some of the cold.

After that he refreshed himself with water, almost ice cold from sitting out all night, but it felt good on his throat. It consolidated in a lump in his stomach, a strange sensation.

He was glad they had dug the well last summer. From what Rhys had said they weren't going to do it, but it was more convenient for the workers to be able to use the water for their mortar rather than lugging ti up from the river. Of that, Evan wasn't sure, but he was glad that they weren't running out of water like they were everything else.

He still had some time before lunch, so after a few laps around his study, it was light enough to read.

Before he returned to his histories he perused the bookshelf once again. It had twenty, maybe thirty books on it, a small fortune. Evan had wanted to leave them behind, lighten the load of his luggage, but his mother had insisted.

Thinking of her brought a pang of sadness. He wished he could see her now, talk to her. His mother always had good counsel.

And she would know what to do in this kind of situation. She had spent her whole life in the land of courtiers and counsels, a daughter of the neighboring Dukedom of Haverville.

Evan tapped the spine of a book, then pulled it out. She had selected these for him, perhaps there was something within their pages that she was trying to tell him.

On a whim he swept up three or four random books and took them to his desk.

He laid them out in a square, the histories off to the side. There was a brown one, a light blue, and two darker brown books. He picked the one with the most cracks on its cover and opened it.

Its pages were yellowed with time. They gave off a strange smell, one he couldn't describe, and he had to be careful of them because they felt so fragile. Each time he picked up a leaf he held his breath, then turned it.

His eyes narrowed as he read the title. Boat Building? *What reason would I ever have to build a boat?*

There it was though, in black in that was faded around the edges. *Boat-building on the Venti; Historical Accounts of the Drydocks.*

Evan put aside his trepidation for a moment and dove into the reading. It might not be as boring as he thought.

But, that turned out to be a fear realized. It was so boring he found himself nodding off within a few paragraphs of the detailed account of shipbuilding drydocks and the years they were established.

He shook his head and shut the book. Why would anyone even consider writing this book, let alone reading it? It was a waste of paper and ink, as far as he was concerned.

He set it off to the side, then leafed through the other books, getting up to get the rest of them off the bookshelf.

A few minutes later he had them separated into two different stacks, one stack had a glimmer of something that might be interesting. Books on war tactics, fighting, and history.

The other stack he wasn't sure what he was going to do with. They had books on industry, mathematics, and architecture. Each one almost put him to sleep within seconds of reading through them. the one on architecture made his eyes glaze over just at the title alone.

Barger brought in his lunch then, after knocking. This time he heard it.

Evan looked at the space on his desk taken up by books, and the table covered with his sword and belt set there after his form work.

Barger also looked from one to the other, holding the tray carrying his food. There was nowhere to set it down.

He watched the servant in his conundrum, then Evan was finally compelled to stand and do something about it.

He picked up his sword, setting it on his desk among the books. The crest of the Hornbloods loomed up above him.

"Anything else, Your Highness?" Barger asked. He glanced tot he books as he stood straight.

"Can you read?" Evan asked.

"A little. Not much."

"Be glad of that. I've been looking through them all morning and might need to take a nap now." Evan smiled, hoping to see something of a rise from his servant.

But, he hoped in vain. Barger's expression never changed, and he didn't say anything.

Evan's smile faded. The hatred he heard about had spread even to his own servants.

But as he thought about how he had treated them, how he didn't even acknowledge their existence, he started to realize why.

"Would you fill up the bottles and bring them back." Barger stared at him. "Please?" Evan said through grounding teeth.

I shouldn't have to beg for what is mine.

"I was...advised against it, Your Highness."

Evan's face flushed. His anger grew. "By whom?"

Barger shifted from foot to foot, and then looked down at the ground.

"Fine, don't tell me. I already know who. You will brig me the wine, however. I still hold some sway in this castle." A simple letter would take care of all of this, if he could only get it delivered.

How had his mother handled their servants? He tried to think back, to remember the interactions between them. He had heard she held a particularly strong sway over them from others, but hadn't the foggiest clue why. Nor did he care enough to find out.

He supposed she treated the same as everyone else, with a light touch and a large amount of care. Always coming in behind his father, as strong as iron, to clear things up and smooth over hurt feelings.

"As you wish, your highness. How many should I fill?"

"Three." That would be enough to last him through the night. His throat was parched anyway, the reminder of it making him thirsty. "Make it four."

Barger crossed the room again, after a quick bow, swept up four bottles in his hand, and was gone a few seconds later.

Evan cursed himself inside, and paced around the room. His anger subsided, and he realized that he made a mistake.

It was easier to avoid the drink if he didn't have any around him. Evan chewed on his lip. *What would it be like to have more than he needed within arm's reach?*

He wished Barger had told him no more forcefully, that Rhys had taken it and gotten rid of the wine. He wished he had the strength to put it away.

He wasn't sure he could resist it, but he wanted it. To loosen his body and mind, to escape the thoughts that ran through his mind.

To ease the pressure that fell upon his shoulders.

Once again he wondered what it was like to be a commoner, to not have the burden he carried. There were no late-night conversations with Yand to be had now.

Evan had to face it. He was on his own now. No father, no mother, no advisers to guide him on his way through the twisted wood of life.

He heard Barger coming this time, the tinkling of bottles proceeded him. Evan paced, waiting for the inevitable, the danger he had asked for brought into this room.

Without a word, Barger entered and knelt by the small cabinet that held his bottles and goblets.

One. Two. Three. Four. Each bottle set down quietly, all in a neat row. Four, just as he had asked.

Evan stared at them. They were filled with dark, red wine, still moving as they settled into place. His body screamed at him to take it in, to drink it.

His mind screamed at him to order Barger to take them away, pour them out, destroy them. His mouth dried up, and he took a shaking breath.

Barger was staring at him, expectantly. Evan's eyes flicked from him to the wine and back again, and smiled nervously.

What did he have to prove to his own servants? Evan pulled back his shoulders and stuck out his chin, then walked over to the cabinet and poured himself a goblet of wine.

It splashed with a tinkling, happy laugh into the goblet, inviting him to drink it in a long pull.

He saw his reflection in the surface of the wine, dark as night. Eyes that were hollow and drawn. *Is that was I look like now?*

It wasn't good to drink alone, that lesson he remembered from long ago. Those that did so had a problem.

But there was no one to drink with, except Barger. Rhys wouldn't be in for another hour, and the glass was poured.

"Would you care for some?" Evan thrust the goblet to Barger.

Shock was an understatement for the expression that came across the servants face.

"It wouldn't be proper, Your Highness."

"I've drunk with commoners many a time before. Besides, I have no need of any, and you look like you could use some fortification." Barger touched his cheek, which was thin from lack of food. "Come, joint me at my table. You don't have anything better to do, do you?"

Evan sat down, and pulled out a chair for Barger to sit in. "I-"

"Don't make me give you an order. It wouldn't feel right."

Barger, who looked like a hapless deer caught in a trap, took a seat and the offered goblet. His mother might have her way of keeping her servants happy, perhaps he could come up with his own way.

"You look uncomfortable, why not sit back?" Evan asked.

Barger looked like he tried to relax, putting a stiff back up against the chair. the smell of wine drifted out of his goblet. Evan wanted to take a sip so badly, but hid it with a smile.

"Go on, I'll have mine later." Evan watched as Barger lifted the goblet to his mouth, sniffed it, licked his lips, and finally took a sip.

Evan felt somewhat of a thrill, as something forbidden always tastes sweet. But, just as the feeling never lasts, it turned bittersweet as he noticed the expression on Barger's face. He liked the wine, perhaps too much.

Like a rush of water, Evan's own desire to drink welled up inside. He gripped the edge of his chair, but he wasn't sure he could hold back from the temptation.

Evan looked over to the wine, mouth watering.

19

Dreams and Fire

Evan stared at the wine, feeling the crushing weight of wanting. *This was a mistake, yet again.* Barger was being polite, taking small sips of wine, but Evan could tell he wanted to drain the glass in one go. He didn't blame him, either.

"How was it you came into my service?" Evan asked.

Barger paused drinking, and set down the goblet. Streaks of wine ran down the rim back into the goblet. The smell was so overwhelming that Evan couldn't take it. He listened to try and keep himself preoccupied.

"I've been serving the Hornbloods since I was a child. My father and mother served the Duke. Naturally, it fell to me to continue the family business." Some of his stiffness had gone. The wine was fortifying him.

"And you came with us on the journey north?"

"Naturally."

Evan didn't remember Barger coming with them, but there had been a long train of people and carts that accompanied him—supplies for the castle, for the most part. Men were part of that, supplied for labor and garrison.

"I would have preferred to stay in Hornblood Hall, but..." Barger dropped his gaze as he trailed off.

"I understand. I didn't want to leave, either." Evan's fingers itched to hold the goblet, to feel the coolness. He felt the pommel of his sword instead. "Did your father force you to go?"

"No. Not my father."

"I see we have something in common, then. Did you leave behind a sweetheart or a wife?"

Barger shook his head, each movement precise and only as large as it needed to be. The man seemed to be restrained in everything. "No wife. There was... a girl."

"Ah." Evan winked at him and tapped the side of his nose. "Say no more, as long as she wasn't too much money."

Barger turned white, then the color rushed to his cheeks as he realized what Evan meant.

"I-I must be going. I have a lot to do." He stood up, nearly knocking over the chair behind him.

"I meant no insult by it."

"No, it isn't that. I'm sorry, I shouldn't have stepped out of my duties."

"At least finish your wine."

"Excuse me, Your Highness." Barger was strait as an arrow again, back stiff as a tree trunk. "I must attend to my duties."

"Very well." Evan waved a hand, and like that, Barger was gone, leaving him in silence. Alone.

It was all he was ever going to be.

Evan stood and walked over to the goblet. It was mostly gone, a few small drops at the bottom. It would be so easy.

But he knew he shouldn't. He knew what would come of it. The pounding head, the feeling in the morning after.

He swept the sword out of its scabbard and into the first form. He fed everything into that form, his desire, his frustration, his longing.

When he was finished, he moved into the next form. Then the next. Then the next.

By the time he had finished them all, he was feeling better, although he was covered in sweat and breathing heavily.

Enough time had passed that he felt little need to take the wine now.

Instead of continuing his practice, focusing on adjusting each technique until it flowed well and right into the next one, he slid his sword back into its scabbard with a click.

It was darker now, and it looked like it was snowing heavily, so he lit a candle and went back to his desk and the books piled on it.

He flipped through a book on military tactics. It was dry, running through battles in an ordered and academic way. All the fun had been sucked out of it, but he kept reading.

He had to go over some of the sentences a few times, they were so difficult to understand, but he started to get the hang of it. He even started enjoying the reading, when it wasn't too boring.

His heart skipped a beat when he came to a chapter on sieges. He devoured the whole chapter in one go, not stopping to reread anything.

It set out the reasons for sieging, and tactics to do so, then went to the defending side on how to break them. Preparation seemed to be the biggest factor of success, according to the author.

"Set up large stores of food, fuel, and timber. Segregate each by type, and keep it free from damp and pest. Rationing is vital to the preservation and success of a siege."

So far, everything he had read seemed straightforward, but none of it was particularly helpful.

His heart was beating fast when he came to the end of the chapter. He read it again, to be sure. When he was done, he set the book down and tried to think about how he could use what he'd read.

They couldn't break out—not with fewer defenders in the castle than attackers outside—without suffering major casualties.

Rhys would be here soon to update him on the inventory. Evan sat up in his chair, remembering the report from yesterday. They were running out of everything. They weren't ready for a siege, but one had come anyway.

And now he realized the Belmarch intended to wait them out, not waste lives on attacking when they could expect the Chathem defenders to give up or starve to the point they would offer no resistance.

And then they would kill them. One by one or all at once through starvation.

The weight on Evan's shoulders grew.

Bill caught him in the entryway. "Hold on, Sam."

Sam stopped, his hand on the door. It, too, was cold. Not as cold as the stone that surrounded it or the icy air outside.

Small swirls of it blew back in from under and around the door. It set his teeth to chattering. How he longed for a thick winter coat then, like a bear or a sheep hide wrapped around him.

"Bill. I've been meaning to talk to you." Sam looked for an escape, but couldn't see one. No one that was easy, at least. He was going to try one anyway. "I was just going to the workshop to see how things were going."

"I'll come with you, then. Nothing like seeing a boat being built, eh?" Bill slapped him on the back. "Lead the way."

"Certainly." Sam hunkered down and pushed open the door. The wind howled in, nearly covering him with a big puff of snow that stung his eyes and got in his mouth.

It was bitter cold outside, and Sam pushed forward through the deep drift at the door.

How to ask it? He needed Bill's help. Or, rather, he needed the masons to help build what he envisioned, and they wouldn't do anything without Bill saying so first. Either way, the man following him through feet deep snow was important to him and the potential survival of the castle.

They pushed into the workshop, and Sam took deep breaths of the slightly warmer air. How he wished there was a fire crackling in the hearth again, casting a merry warmth to steal away this cold.

The frame of the boat was nearly finished now, and Trent was on top fitting a lap joint. It wasn't the best looking boat Sam had ever seen, but it was going to work.

He hoped.

"That's it?" Bill asked.

"Now give us some respect," Ned said, turning to them. "Unless you want to find yourself helping."

"We've run into a few...complications," Sam said. There was no use hiding the fact now, Bill could plainly see that there wasn't enough wood to finish the hull. "And as much as I'd like to move the crane over to the wall, we might need it for something else."

"And that would be?" Bill asked.

"The southwest tower. We need to scavenge the beams in it," Trent said.

Sam sighed. he was hoping to have phrased it a little better. "He's right. I've gone over it many times. We just don't have what we need."

"But the Keep does," Bill said. Sam nodded. "Since we've started down this path, I don't see any other way. We can help."

Bill walked around the boat as Sam worked his fingers to keep the cold out of the joints. He was hungry, like everyone else.

"Shall we go up there to see?"

Sam would have preferred not to. Not in this wind.

They stood at the top of the unfinished tower. As he suspected, the wind was brutally cold up here and blew right through him. Sam couldn't stop shivering and held himself tight.

Bill had a thicker coat on. Like everything else related to Bill, Sam had no idea where he got it from.

"A few courses would do it. Shame to see all the hard work undone."

"If there was another way..." Sam wished it had never come to this, that they were able to build in peace.

"No chance of sneaking out late at night, harvesting a few trees, and bringing them back in?" Bill asked.

"Let's get out of this wind," Sam said, retreating back down the unfinished stairs. He sighed as he got beneath the protection of the walls. Snow drifted down the stairs. Up here the warm air escaped up the opening from the castle below. Bill followed, not as affected by the cold stone beneath his feet. His shoes looked thick and not as worn as everyone else.

"It is a cold winter," Bill said, tightening up his collar. "Shame about Nathula."

"You knew him well?"

"Well enough. The Overseer is going Sam." They were withing the protection of the tower now, the cold and snow of outside blunted.

Sam turned to face Bill. "I was afraid you were behind that." Bill shrugged. "Why?"

"He wanted to go. He gives us the best chance of salvation, should he survive."

"And the Duke loses a key ally."

"I wouldn't put it that way. Now that you mention it, though..." Bill looked up at the ceiling.

"You can't do it," Sam said.

"I'll do what I need to stay alive." Bill's face hardened, his eyes snapping to Sam's. "Do you have the resolve to do the same?"

"What good would I be if my life is all I considered? I've been that man before."

"So you want to be known as the savior, then—the man who sacrificed himself? Such a self-righteous man," Bill mocked.

Sam's face felt too tight, like a hide stretched on the tanning rack. "I can see coming to ask you to help wasn't the right decision."

The nook they had taken refuge in was dark and tucked int eh corner of the tower, the door to the rest of the Keep just on the wall behind them.

No one came up here, no one ventured this far. In his rage Sam thought about killing Bill, and leaving his body in the corner.

The flashing thought frightened him at how easy the thought came. he took a deep breath, trying to control the rage and anger and helplessness that fought inside him.

Bill had taken a step back, and was crouched into a ready stance, a few movements away from a fighting position.

It was silly. *How am I a threat to Bill.* Then Sam looked down. His fists were balled up, and he looked like he was about to attack.

"I mean no offense," Sam said, relaxing himself. He was reminded of the fact that Bill was afraid of him, something he wasn't sure was true up until that very moment.

"None take," Bill said, relaxing into a more natural and carefree posture. But Sam could tell there was something about him that was ready, coiled like a snake ready to spring.

This wasn't going to get him where he needed to go with Bill, and certainly wouldn't get him goodwill. The thought of him asking about the plans for revolt was too much for Sam to think of.

"Instead of fighting, I'd propose we work together. I have some plans for expanding the denseness of the castle that we can work on even now."

"I heard of your plans," Bill said. "I wasn't impressed by them."

Sam smiled. "You don't have to be. They just have to work."

20

TEMPTATIONS

"What you're asking for is too much. No way am I going to ask my masons to go out into the cold and build a bunch of walls we aren't going to use."

Thy had moved to a cellar room in the castle, previously filled with food. It had a few stacks of grain left, and not much else, but it was warm and out of the way.

Bill, however, had failed to move.

"I'm telling you it's going to work. The gate is the weak point, and always has been. The Belmarch aren't stupid, they know that too." Sam sat on a makeshift stool, a small barrel.

Bill sat opposed, on an overturned crate. "They haven't tried the gate before, other than the ram."

"That doesn't mean they aren't going to try it again." Sam rubbed his head. He was starting to get a dull throb behind his eyes. It wasn't pleasant, combined with his hunger.

"They've gone for the walls every other time though, why would they suddenly get through our gate, and how would they do it?"

"How many sieges have you gone through?" Sam snapped. Bill's eyes narrowed. Sam took a deep breath and smoothed out his voice. "The gate is a few inches of wood. The walls are a few feet of rock. Which one is going to be easier to get through?"

"Up and over both of them."

"It hasn't worked yet. They know we can repulse them."

"Not if we're all half-dead and starved."

He had a point, but one Sam wasn't going to cede. "For all we know they don't have the supplies to keep this siege up. They might try to get through the next time the weather is good enough to allow them to attack," Sam said.

Bill snorted. "They'd be fools to attack before spring."

"Unless they took us by surprise."

"In that case your walls won't help us."

"It's a trap, Bill. Even you can see that."

"And what if this trap springs, and doesn't work. What then? We've invited them within the walls and we're all dead."

It was frustrating trying to reason with him. They had been going at it back and forth for what seemed like hours. Each point was argued over, each time Sam tried to show him the error of his thinking.

It just felt like he was going around in circles, but he couldn't appeal to the Overseer. Bill had too much sway over him, and the Overseer had made it clear this was between them.

Nor could he talk to the Duke and try and convince him either. Sam was afraid doing so would set off the spark that lit the wildfire of revolt.

So, here he was, sitting in a damp cellar in the dark, breathing in moldy air that tasted rotten. He even though he heard the squeak of rats, and saw things out of the corner of his eye, but could never see it when he went to look.

Was he destined to go around these same points with Bill forever?

"This isn't working," Sam said, crossing his arms. Up until now he had tried to keep his posture relaxed and open. "What do you propose instead? Should we let them take us without doing anything?"

"No. We fight them."

"And when we can't fight them anymore, when we can't hold them aback any longer, what do we do then?"

Bill paused. "We fall back to the Keep and keep fighting them."

"With no source of water?" The well was in the courtyard, well outside the walls of the Keep.

"Then we have to have help. Someone is going to have to sweep the Belmarch away from us, and keep us alive."

Sam wondered about that, if it was even possible. The King had to have known that something was wrong by now. "They know we're in trouble," Sam said, in barely a whisper. "You and I both know that."

Bill considered him, looking at him with that studying look that told Sam there was something deeper going on behind them. Bill knew.

"I've thought about it on watch. In the cold, when I couldn't feel my fingers." Sam saw Bill flex his own hand at his words. "Why would they leave us, why would they abandon us here?"

"They haven't abandoned us," Bill said, but his voice wasn't confident.

"The Belmarch aren't the most pressing matter in Chathem. You know the rumors as well as I."

"The eastern raiders have never been a threat to Chathem," Bill said.

"And yet, here we are with no supplies and no reinforcements." Sam felt a chill run up his spine at his own words, words he had kept deep inside, never wishing to speak them.

But here they were, pouring out of him like water.

"We are well and truly alone. I can't count on anyone going for help to be successful."

Bill sat, his shoulders slumped. Sam knew in that moment that Bill was counting on rescue. He believed in the power of the king, but didn't know the reality of their situation.

Chathem didn't have a strong monarchy. It was barely a collection of states held together, and the current King wasn't strong enough to do anything but keep them together.

No, Sam suspected the Duke of Hornblood was the real driver of the castle construction, and its primary benefactor. At the extreme northern end of Chathem, the Dukedom of the Hornbloods bore the brunt of the Belmarch invasions for generations.

But, it appeared they had given all they could, and their support was dried up. Or, he suspected, they had lost their favor at court, and their source of treasure to keep the construction going.

"Think about it. The lack of resources, less and less workers coming in when we needed more and more," Sam said. The musty, rotten smell was overpowering, and it was making his headache worse. "No one is coming to save us Bill. Were' going to have to do this on our own."

Bill hesitated, then spoke. "You don't know that for sure. Bedsides, even if you were right then we wouldn't stand a chance at all."

"We could buy time."

"There would be no hope for us."

"I've thought about that," Sam said. "I've seen wild things happen, things I never expected. Things that turned the tide of battle from certain defeat to victory." The red eagle taken down by a single arrow. "We could plan for the worst and give us the best chance we would have."

"You might be right, but I don't think so."

Sam stood up and stretched his legs. He was getting tired and needed to sleep before his watch. As warm as it was down here, he was considering bringing his rotten and flea ridden blanket down here to do it. "I don't have time to try and convince you. Maybe when we've sent the Overseer on his journey downriver you will see the benefit to my plan."

"Your plan will take too long to build."

Sam shrugged. "You're making excuses, not good arguments. Why don't we call it a night and think it over." Sam walked to the door and opened it, but paused as he walked out.

Bill was still sitting in the dark, the single candle he had produced burning in the corner. It struggled to stay alive, the flame dancing on the edge of the wick. Its rays went less than halfway across the room before dying out.

"I'll ask again, have you ever survived a siege before?" Sam asked.

Bill turned his head but said nothing.

"Good night, Bill."

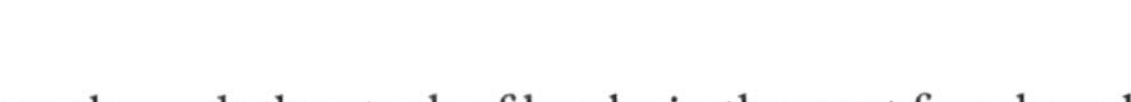

Evan tore through the stack of books in the next few days, his workouts getting longer and his muscles adapting to them.

It felt good to get his movements back, to feel real improvement once more. The first form was more fluid, and easier to perform than it had been, and the others were improving with every practice session.

The days turned into a blur, not knowing when the sun came up and the sun went down, he read when he could see and he lit the candle when he couldn't. The sky was so overcast so often he wasn't sure if it was night sometimes, or just a lack of sun.

He longed to see it again, and feel it's burning rays upon his face. The feeling was even more intense than other winters, and it was because he was stuck indoors.

His only interruptions were mealtimes and visits from the Overseer. Evan hated those the most.

It only cemented the feeling he had that he had no control of the situation. The only joy he took in it was the look on Rhys face the first time he had come in to see him reading.

"Surprised?" Evan had asked him. The man's eyebrows had almost reached his receding hairline before he had gotten control of them.

"Pleasantly," Rhys had said.

Even now the memory helped to dull the feeling of hopelessness, and the draw of the wine.

That had been the hardest thing to handle. Every morning Evan woke up and thought about asking Barger or Rhys to take it away, but every night he came to the end of the day not able to say it.

He sat in his chair one night looking at it. Four bottles, neatly arranged. Untouched since Barger had drunk one glass.

The candlelight flickered in the reflection on the glass. How much money was poured into those vessels alone? More than any one of the workers in the castle would see in their lifetimes.

He could just make out the faint line of the wine inside. Dark, almost as black as the night sky in the green glass. He looked away, his eyes hurting from staring so hard.

Evan put a hand on his head. How many nights had he wasted in that smooth liquid? How many years had he abused it?

No, I never abused it. It was just a drink, a taste to ease the pain.

The pain of failure, the pain of being alone. Even now he wished for Yand, the closest thing to a friend he had ever had. He was a hard mentor, but fair in what mattered.

They never shared a friend's discussion, but there was a familiarly that Evan longed for now.

It would all be so easy. Just a few sips. It had been so long since he had taken a drink. He swallowed the saliva that had built up in his mouth.

The warm, sweet notes of the grape, the bitter aftertaste as it went down. That lingering sensation that took on so many different kinds of flavors. Oak, butter, nuts.

The wine he had brought with him had been some of the best Hornblood had to offer, the local vintage made from the hardy grapes that grew in the glades of the forest. Starved of light from the canopy of the trees, the grapes were small and puny looking, but packed with flavor that only made it better when it was fermented.

Evan licked his lips, imagining the wine washing over them and into his waiting mouth. He put a finger to them, rubbed therm.

They were cracked and dry. *A hint of wine would do them good.*

He snatched his finger away. *No, I can't.* The room felt hot, and his head spun with the longing. Why *did* it have to be this hard?

Why I do I resist it? It isn't wrong. Another voice spoke up inside him, warning him of what had happened so many times before.

The ditches he had woken up in, the pigsties he found himself covered in. Mud and filth piled up on his body, his head and body rebelling against sunlight and noise.

The shame he felt the next day after what he heard from his drinking companions, and the sidelong glances they sent him with smirks lingering on their lips, just out of reach. The whispers behind his back.

Evan bit his lip, then turned his chair around, out of sight from the cabinet and the looming bottles. It wasn't the first time this had happened, he struggled through this every night only to be haunted in his dreams by it.

It's just a liquid. Even now, looking away, he could see it. He saw it tumbling out of the bottle, filling up the goblet, shining in the candlelight.

He felt himself being pulled from his chair, as if his body had a mind of its own, but he knew it was his own action that was doing it.

Evan had such a horrible feeling overpower him. He couldn't stop it.

With shaking hands, he took a bottle and a goblet, and poured a glass of wine.

21

Evan closed his eyes when the wine his lips. Even before then the smell of the wine was overpowering and heady.

The taste, however, wasn't what he imagined it would be. It wasn't as sweet as he remembered, or as filling. The mouthful went down his throat and all the way to his stomach, settling there as a cold lump for a second or two.

He had expected something to happen, something bad. When it never materialized, he took another drink, then turned back to go to his seat.

Evan froze mid-step. For a second, he thought his father was on his chair, sitting and watching him sternly, but he was mistaken.

No one was there.

But above his seat the crest of the Hornbloods looked down on him. The Tree of Everling spread out its branches, shaking them as if they were fists at him.

He was transported across time and space to his first Midnight Watch. The candles flickered in their lanterns, the long train processing through the woods.

They were bare and desolate. He remembered being carried of their branches, that they might reach out and pluck him from his mother's grip.

Evan moved closer, clasping his mother's hand even tighter.

"Still, Evan," she said, in a soothing voice, with a hint of sternness. He peered up at here, seeing her head illuminated against the backdrop of the thick, black night sky. "It will be over soon."

The Tree still had its leaves, even now in the dead of winter with a frosting of snow. It crunched as they gathered around the base of it, the headstones scattered among the gnarly old roots.

It smelled of winter, and felt it. The icy wind stung his little eyes and burrowed behind his coat and down his neck. Someone was saying something, but he couldn't hear very well.

He caught parts of the speech, from his grandfather perched at the tallest root of the tree. The rest of the family was scattered out around the tree, the women and children on one side and his father and the men on the other.

He had been promised that one day he would join his father's side, both in life and in death.

As his grandfather spoke the first leaf of the tree came down, shaken free finally by the winter winds.

It fell in front of Evan, as black as night. Before his mother could stop him, he stooped down and touched it.

"No!"

It was too late. Evan had the rough stem in his hand, the leaf almost as big as his head held up before him.

"Cursed," his aunt Delores hissed. "You have seen it all, he is cursed!"

"Put it down, Evan," his father said in his stern, cold voice. Evan dropped it, and the leaf fell once more into the snow.

Tears stung at his eyes, and he could stop the hot liquid from coming. His whole family was talking now, breaking the ritual silence that had pervaded before.

"We continue with the ritual, everyone return to their places," his grandfather had said. The voices died down and everyone returned to their original spots, but Evan clutched at his mother's leg.

She didn't say anything to comfort him, only held his head. Grandfather waited until the tree had shed all its' leaves and then picked up the biggest one and offered it into the fire burning in the stone pit near the trunk.

"We offer our thanks and praise. We ask you, the ancestors of the wood, to bring us peace and prosper us. Bring our enemies to their knees and our friends to our table." Grandfather held his hands up as the smoke drifted up through the wood, swirling around them with the aroma Evan couldn't describe, but would never forget.

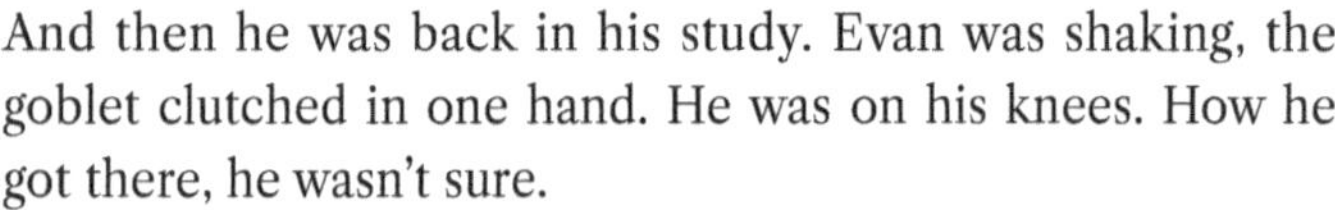

And then he was back in his study. Evan was shaking, the goblet clutched in one hand. He was on his knees. How he got there, he wasn't sure.

"Cursed." He remembered the words, floated back through his mind from his childhood. He had done that which was reserved for his grandfather, the patriarch of the family.

He had brought dishonor upon his line, and cursed it forever.

He was the reason they were under attack. Had it not been for his coming the castle would have been built in time and fully manned, ready to propel the attackers and send the Belmarch back into their land where they belonged.

A low moan escaped his lips. Evan squeezed his eyes shut and brought the goblet back to his lips.

His trembling hand splashed wine up onto his face, little drips of it that ran down his nose and eyes.

"Cursed," he said again, after he had taken a deep draw. More and more he wanted to drink the whole cup, and then the rest of the bottle, but something inside him held him back.

Was it the look in his fathers' eye? The feel of his mother's touch? Something had changed that day.

But why had his father and mother not cast him off at that moment? he deserved to be cut off from the family, to be thrown to the wolves and be devoured. That was the punishment for his crime, and it had been enacted before.

Evan held the goblet to his lips and drained it. Wine spilled on his shirt, but he didn't care. The smell of it pervaded his senses, pushed away that memory of the Everling smoke out of his mind.

He had gone back, year after year, and never touched a leaf again, but the damage had already been done. It was finished.

He was cursed.

He was destined to ruin. A prophecy and a warning come to fruition in the cold, damp room he now occupied.

What could he do? The goblet was empty now, and he let it slip from his fingers with a clatter. It rolled away from him, and Evan fell to the floor.

He imagined a life that would have been had he not done it. He would have the love of his mother still, and the succession secure. There would have been friends, waiting for him after a long campaign, or joining him in it.

And that was all gone now, never to be. He would drink his cup of suffering, and drink it to the fullest, to die in this place a lonely, broken man.

"Your Highness," Barger said, a note of panic in his voice. Hands were on his back, pulling him to his side.

"Leave me be," Evan groaned. Barger's wide-open eyes were filled with concern. "I'm not worth helping."

His eyes flashed to the cup and the wind spilled upon Evan's clothes. "I'll help you to your bed."

The wine had gone to his head now, bringing in a buzz that made his muscles loose and hampered his inhibitions.

Barger shouldn't bee here, shouldn't see him like this. Evan struggled to his feet, and pushed him away.

"Go. I don't want you here." Evan looked around wildly. Was his father here?

"You aren't in a good state," Barger said. Evan saw a bottle near the goblet, a tiny drop at the mouth.

It was empty. *How much have I had to drink?* Evan didn't remember having that much. Somewhere in the last hour though, he recalled pouring more than one glass. *Was that after the memory?*

From the swimming in his head, he thought it might. The room was wobbling, and the walked to the closest chair at the table pushed up against the wall.

Barger was there at his elbow, guiding him to sit. He collapsed into the chair, the hard back pushing into his spine.

"What do you say?" Evan asked, as Barger went to clean up the mess. The servant was on his hands and knees, scrubbing with a rag he had produced from somewhere.

"Pardon, Your Highness?"

Evan waved a hand toward the door. " I know what they think. That I can't do anything right, that I'm useless. That they're better off without me. What do you think?"

Barger considered his words carefully. "It wouldn't be right-"

"Blast it all, answer the question!"

"If Your Highness insists." Barger bowed, infuriating Evan even more. The haze of drunkenness drifted through his vision, but his anger and hatred kept the worst of it at bay.

"I don't think you are useless. These last few days something has changed in you. In all my years I have never seen you read, or train as hard as you have, or even talk to me like you have these last few days." Barger didn't look pleased and kept his eyes on the ground.

Evan didn't know what to think. Barger had spoken what he thought, but Evan had asked for it. Had he really gone all these years without speaking to him?

he knew it was true, even if he didn't want to believe it. Evan licked his lips. "I'm cursed, you know. That's why this has happened." He gestured around him with his arms. "You have me to blame for all your troubles." Had he not taken that leaf, had he just left it on the ground like he was supposed to...

What would his life look like then?

"I've known the bottom of a cup. There isn't any good in it," Barger said. He was still cleaning, hands on the floor, eyes downcast. The wine had fully taken Evan's mind now. He thought he heard a note of sorrow in that voice, but it couldn't be true. Barger had always intoned his words in a cool, calm way with no emotions. "You don't want to go down that path."

Evan stared at him. He was hardly older than Evan was, or so he first thought. But there were creases as the corner of the man's eyes, something he hadn't seen before.

Why was he talking to the servant? Why was he speaking this way?

"I'd like to be left alone," Evan said. "Finish that and get out." he would have another taste, another sip. It would help ease his suffering, help him to feel better.

"As you wish, your highness." Something flashed across Barger's face, and was gone a moment later. Evan blinked, but Barger was still there, still as calm as always.

The man finished his cleaning, then stood. He walked to the door.

As he did Evan watched him go. His eyes traveled momentarily to the floor, and the book caught his attention.

The *History* had fallen somehow, either knocked down by Evan or Barger as he helped him. It was open to the chapter on Miral, the illustration of the former King staring at him.

Behind him, a tree that looked like the Tree of Everling spread out its branches, blood red leaves upon them. It seemed to be embracing the man.

From a failure, all the way to one of the greatest Kings. Evan put his hand over his eyes, trying to blot out the eyes that stared at him.

Mocking him.

Telling him he was a failure. That he would never amount to anything. That his father was right.

That his family curse was real. He was the last and only Hornblood to reside in this castle. The only Hornblood to keep watch, and fail in the act of it.

All hope drained from him then, like wine in the cup he had drawn from.

Emotion racked his body, and Evan couldn't help but let out a sob. He had tried so hard and had come up short.

Above him, his family crest mocked him. He turned to it, tried to tear it from the wall, but he was too drunk.

Evan couldn't get his hands around it, and slipped to the floor.

His head hit the book, dazing him. Evan pulled himself up from the ground.

The page had turned. It was the moment Miral had snuck from the camp, the pivotal moment when he was at his weakest.

The artist had drawn fear in his eyes, a cloak pulled up to hide his identity. But there was something else too, a sunrise.

It spilled out in red and yellow. Evan remembered how the story ended, how he had come back from nothing, an outcast, the hunted, and had prevailed.

Barger hadn't left. He was standing over him, a look of worry on his face.

Maybe there is hope for me, after all. There would be a tomorrow. As long as he didn't give up hope, there would be another day.

"Barger," Evan said, holding his throbbing head. "Take the wine."

22

A Boat

"It is done."

Sam knelt by the boat, unseaworthy by his estimation. "And she'll hold?" he asked. "I'd bet my life on it," Kerien said.

Ned gave him a look. "She'll be fine, for as long as we need her to be. We didn't have everything we needed..." They had stuffed her joints with sawdust and wood shavings. Ned had wanted to use rope and fiber mixed with tar, but they had little rope to spare and no tar to speak of, so they made do instead.

"But you've done a fine job with her." Sam tried to look through the gaps, see daylight behind them, but couldn't. "It just looks...""You don't mean it looks ugly..." Kerien said, his face darkening." Shorter than I expected," Sam said, trying to smooth over any insult he might have unintentionally given.

The workshop was cold, like everything else, and now almost empty. Stacks of wood should have been piled up on one side, but there were only a few sticks. Everything had gone into this boat, including the beam they had removed from the Keep that now functioned as the main brace.

The rest had been consumed in fire two nights ago, the coldest yet. Sam was glad for it too, because had they not more than one wouldn't have survived the night.

He shivered thinking of it now. The workshop didn't smell the same as it used to. He didn't know if it was the cold that made it different or the lack of wood and dust, but he didn't like it.

"We could launch it tonight?" Sam asked, looking up from his inspection. Trent was with them too, everyone but Archie. The thought of him made him think of Belinda. *Poor child.*

"If we had to, yes." Ned put up a gnarled hand to her prow. "She took everything I knew, and then some, to get her together. Make sure you take care of her.

"We'll do it soon. The sooner the better." Sam frowned. He would have to get Bill and his masons to finish their work. "We'll take down the crane and see how far we can get."

Bill had wanted to do his work a long time ago, but Sam had insisted he not do it. There was too much risk in it.

The Belmarch might see them working on it and get interested, find out a way to watch the river and even get close enough to foil their plan. Sam wasn't sure how they could get away with it, but didn't want to take the risk. In the end Bill had agreed, but only after much arguing and bickering.

The man was like a stone wall himself. Hard to get through unless you could break him down.

So, instead of taking out the merlons, he only prepared for it, having a mason take out some of the wall stones where the crane would sit and remove some of the backing rocks. The rest of it would have to be taking out in the same night as everything else.

The only thing they had that winter was helping on was how long night was lasting. The days were already growing longer now, but the long nights were still here.

he wasn't looking forward to the night, but the moon was going to be full soon. It might help with light, at the very least.

"Let's get her out of here and up the hill," Sam said. "Should be easy enough to carry."

Ned and Kerien looked at each other.

"What?" Sam asked.

"I'm not so sure about that..." Kerien said.

"We used a lot of wood. Dense wood," Ned added.

"We have four. Let's try and see. Trent, get on that side, you two on this one." They repositioned, each man taking a corner. It was hard to grip the round bottom, and Sam struggled to find something to hold onto.

Finally, he used his opened hand to get some grip, the other positioned over the lip of the boat.

"Everyone ready?" hearing affirmative replies Sam gave the order.

He pulled the boat, but it didn't move. Sam strained harder, but still nothing.

"Is everyone pulling?"

"Yes. It's heavier than it looks," Ned said. The others grunted too.

"Let me reposition." Sam changed his stance, trying to wrap his arms around the front of it. They had put it on blocks during the building, which gave him enough room to crouch down.

With better grip they tried again, but failed. For a while they tried to lift it up, to no avail.

"All we're doing is wearing ourselves out," Trent said, after what seemed like the tenth try.

He was right, and Sam knew it. They couldn't keep wasting their strength like this, especially with how hungry they were.

Sam's stomach always felt empty now, the rations getting tighter and tighter. He stepped back to get a better look.

It was in the middle of the workshop, the workbenches pushed to the sides to accommodate it. It was about twice as long as he was tall, and a quarter that side to side.

They should be able to lift it. It wasn't that big.

When he cast his gaze over the others though, he had an inkling of why.

None of them had an ounce of fat on their bodies. They were gaunt faced, cheeks thin, with sunken eyes.

It wasn't that the boat that was the problem. It was the reasons why they had stopped training days ago, why there were fewer sentries on the walls than they really should have.

They were starving to death.

Sam closed his eyes, trying to blot out the image. *When had this happened?*

he knew it was going to be this way, had feared it ever since they had been trapped inside these walls.

Deep down he had known all along, but it was this thing that had made it real to him.

"I-" Sam found himself at a loss for words.

"We'll get more help," Trent said. "With enough of us we can move it."

Why hadn't he thought of that? He recovered from the momentary shock and sadness that washed over him, and then nodded.

"That's a good idea, Trent." About double their number should do the trick, if they all hadn't lost as much strength as the carpenters.

He had to feel something, ground himself back in the real world. Sam reached out and held the prow of the boat. *This was the beam we took from the Keep.*

The wood was cold, but solid. His hand was perpetually frozen. Some men had lost feeling in theirs, and their feet and toes, but the rough wood was there under his fingertips, reminding him of the world.

A cold gust of wind blew through the workshop, cutting through him. If they had a fire going, it would have put it out. Fire—and a good side of mutton. Sam would have done anything for it at that moment.

"Who are we going to ask?" Ned asked.

"Bill will let us use the masons. They've lost..." He coughed and tried again. "They're the strongest out of all of us, except the smiths."

But they too had lost their strength too. Perhaps not all, but enough.

"What about the guardsmen? I don't feel right asking Bill," Ned said.

"I don't either, but I'm not sure they'd help us."

"Let me talk to them first," Trent said. Sam turned to him, surprised. "I have a favor that I can use."

"A favor?" Sam asked, knitting his eyebrows together. *Since when has Trent done anything to get a favor in return?*

"Yes. I'd rather not talk about why."

"Then you ask," Sam said.

"Are we just going to wait here?" Kerien asked after Trent had left.

"Got anything better to do?" Ned asked. He had sat down on his stool, tucked away in the corner and out of the stray gusts that ran through the workshop.

"We could wait inside," Kerien said, rubbing his arms. Today wasn't as cold as it had been the past few days, but snow still covered the ground a few inches thick.

"Give him a few minutes. If he isn't back soon, we'll head back to the Keep. I'm sure he'll find us." Sam turned to Ned. "Do you know anything about this favor?"

"First I've heard about it."

"It's strange."

"I don't think so," Kerien said, also sitting down beside Ned to share some body heat. "He's been standing extra watches at night. Says he has to figure something out."

"Extra watches?" That would explain why Sam hadn't seen him in the workshop as much. Come to think of it, he was on the southern wall a lot more than normal. Why that hadn't stood out to him, he wasn't sure.

"Mostly the guardsman near the gatehouse," Kerien said, rubbing his hands together.

Sam joined them. Together they pressed their backs up against each other. It felt good to be a little warm again in one part of his body.

He had forgotten what that felt like.

"What is he looking for?" Sam asked.

Kerien shrugged. "He hasn't told me, but it is something to do with the Belmarch camp. He's always staring off at it. That, and the forest."

Sam wondered as they drifted into silence. A few moments later crunches on snow drifted into the workshop, the sound of more than a few pairs of feet.

Trent ducked in, followed by Mathew and a few other guardsmen. Others also trailed in, six more in all.

"This is it?" Mathew asked. "Shouldn't be too hard to move if we all work together."

They all took positions around the boat, ten pairs of hands beneath it. After everyone was ready Sam gave the signal.

After a brief moment of doubt, the boat lifted up off its resting blocks. Sam instructed them where to go, and they pushed out into the sunny courtyard through the workshop flaps.

The warm sun felt good on his face, and Sam almost stopped to soak it in, but was quickly brought back to humility by the sharp gusts of wind that stole that warmth away.

They pushed through the snow and up the hill, stopping twice to set it down and catch their breath. There was less than a hundred feet from the workshop to the place where they would build the crane.

The snow slowed them down. It had drifted up against the wall a few feet high, pushed there by the constant wind that even now knocked snow into his face.

Sam squinted against the swirls and pushed on. They made it and dropped the boat down.

"Thank you," Sam said, turning back to the new arrivals. Everyone was breathing hard but wore smiles on their faces.

"We owe Trent," Mathew said, clapping the young man on the back. "He deserves more than we could give him." The others agreed, but the wind was too bad, and drove them out of the sun and back into the protective walls of the Keep.

Sam hung back as the group walked through the yard. He was still surprised and marveled at Trent, surrounded by the others.

Ned joined him, walking slowly. The wind had died down somewhat, but the sun had been covered by a thin layer of clouds.

"Something's changed in him, Ned."

"Are you sure it's in him?" Drifts of snow brushed across the ground.

"No. Not anymore. I don't want him to have to grow up, to be a man that faces this hardship and suffering."

Ned didn't say anything. He just walked alongside him. The others slipped into the Keep.

"I don't know if this will work. I don't know if we'll survive."

"Can't say anything different," Ned said, looking up into the sky. "This is my last winter, Sam. I can feel it in my bones."

"No. You can't say that."

"I'm old, Sam. I've lived my life. I've had my time." Ned nodded toward the others. "This is his time."

Sam felt hollow.

"Don't mourn for me when I'm gone."

Sam's voice caught in his throat. "I'm not sure we won't be going together."

Ned turned to him, a fierce fire in his eyes. "You'll survive, and you'll protect all the others. Promise me that—humor an old man."

Sam couldn't. He couldn't say the words.

23

Leaving

When Barger walked out Evan felt a weight lift off his shoulders. The bottles went with him, to be dispensed and poured out if need be. Evan wasn't sure what was going to happen to them, and some part of him cared.

Some part of him mourned for it, but the greater portion of him was different. He had changed. Nothing had changed him for him, as many times he had wished for something to make him different.

It was the same way with Yand, when his father had ordered him to serve as a bodyguard and trainer. Evan had hoped that Yand would make him better, change him from who he was.

Evan pondered this in his study as the sun went down and the light failed. A knock on his door roused him.

Head still affected from the wine, Evan bade whoever it was to enter and rose to his feet. He closed the *History of Chathem* softly, with reverent affection for the pages.

He was surprised to see Rhys enter. "Good evening, Your Highness," Rhys said.

"I wasn't expecting you," Evan said. They had already had their meeting earlier in the day. "I don't assume anything has changed in the inventory?"

"I'm not here for our normal discussion." Evan bade him come and sit at the table, still pushed out of the way from his training session, but with room enough from them both to take a seat.

Rhys had dark circles under his eyes and moved like a man with little rest. "I have something to tell you," he said after they were seated across from one another. "I'm going soon, tonight if we can manage it."

"Going?" Evan furrowed his brow. "Going where?"

"Away. Down the river."

"On the river? However will you get there?" Evan imagined the once large figure sneaking out of the gate in the middle of the night. "And what boat will you take?"

"The carpenters have been working on a boat for the last few weeks," Rhys said, hands folded in his lap. "It's in the courtyard now, next to the wall. We're going to lift it up and over the wall to the river."

A boat? Here in the castle? Evan couldn't believe his ears, and stared at Rhys without blinking. "What is going on?"

"I should have told you earlier," Rhys said. "I apologize. We've been putting this plan in place for a while, and I wasn't sure until tonight if they would be able to do it." Rhys shook his head, a small smile playing at the corner of his lips. "They seem to hate each other, but suit each other so well."

Rhys filled him in. At the end of it Evan sat, somewhat in shock.

"And so, you intent to be the one to go."

"That's right. Who else would we send?" Rhys sighed, face changing into the old man he was for a second. He regained his composure quickly.

Thoughts were racing through Evan. Feelings and emotions mixed in. Leave the castle, and actually survive. It could be him.

Would it be the best thing for everyone? No one else would have the authority he had, even Overseer Rhys.

"Why you?" Evan's mouth was dry, and his hands shook.

"You are needed here." Evan knew what the answer was going to be, but didn't want to hear it. He looked away.

"No one needs me," he said bitterly. "You said it yourself. I'm one step away from being killed."

"Perhaps that has changed."

"I don't see how it could have."

"Your actions, and inactions, spread faster through the castle. Faster than you think," Rhys said.

Evan had a lump in his throat. "I know I've been a poor Duke, and an even worse leader. I should have done things differently." Evan looked into Rhys' eyes. "What can I do to make things better without you here to help me?"

Rhys considered his words, meeting his gaze. Evan was afraid he wouldn't say anything at all, but he did finally speak. "When you came here, I wasn't sure what to think of you. A spoiled young man, unsure of his place in the world, without a care for those beneath him. Is that the same man that sits here before me?"

"Yes, I'm afraid it is."

Rhys smiled. "Which tells me you have changed. I know you think you need me here, but I am better used on the task that is set before me. When I get to the capitol I will find a way to bring help, don't doubt that for a second."

The gloom of the night, banished by a candle Rhys had lit when he came in, pervaded the conversation and the atmosphere. Evan had a hard time looking pas it, and the quiet of the night. The stillness seemed to flow from the stones themselves.

He was probably right. Evan wasn't much use to the court to begin with, and was an embarrassment to his father when he was there. He had few acquaintances, and even fewer friends there. Even throwing his family name around might not help, even with the threat of a Belmarch invasion.

Rhys was the right choice, and he knew it. A lower-level messenger wouldn't have the pull to get them help right away, and they needed it to survive the winter.

"Tell me what I have to do, before you leave. Teach me what I need to know." Evan stared into Rhys' eyes, trying to take his knowledge and wisdom into himself.

"There is little for me to teach you that Yand hasn't already taught. What I can tell you is that it might be time to take your place among your people again, as a humble and rightful ruler."

Like Miral of old, disgraced and weak, rising up to become the best of what the Hornbloods had to offer. Evan saw a glimmer of hope in that future, one that could happen for him.

"I'm not sure I can accomplish it, but I will try."

24

Preparation Unfolds

Sam stood on the battlements in the late afternoon sun. The wind had died down, giving a blessedly peaceful quality to the day. The warmth of the sun infused his body with life, dispelling the cold from the side of his body the sun faced.

The air was crisp and clean, tasting cold and sweet after the dank air of the Keep. He took a long look around at the barren trees. They blocked the view, so many sticks piled up on each other, but gave hints of what lay beyond.

The mason's hammers rang out. They were working on the merlons as quietly as they could, removing the bottom layer of mortar from the stone. When night came, they would remove the rocks one by one with cloth wrapped hands, but for now they only prepared.

Ned had recommended only a few men up on the tower to disassemble the crane, and Sam was glad they had followed his sage advice. Even now, with the three other carpenters working on it, Sam winced, hoping they didn't alert the Belmarch to the plan.

The sun was already almost at the horizon, given a few more minutes it would be. Bill stood beside him, supervising the work.

"Do you think they will notice?" Bill asked.

Sam looked over to the white smoke that rose into the air above their camp. They had plenty of fuel for cooking and warmth, surrounded by the timber forests that were theirs by right.

Sam hated to think of it, but remembered watching them fell large oaks and drag them back to their camp. They chopped it up, not for building, but for another purpose.

To burn.

Destroy, maim, kill. That was what the Belmarch were here for, and they were good at it. Even the forests and the land couldn't stand up to them.

He mourned for the loss of the trees. They would have made good beams and timbers. Solid after generations of growing, he would have shaped them to fit into the careful constructed holes in the stone wall so that it could continue, building towers that reached up to touch the sky.

But that was all gone, for now.

One day, it may happen again. It was a glimmer of hope, and one he held onto with a fierce passion and desire.

"We must do it whether they notice or not," Sam said at last, after he had broken free of those painful memories. He still feared they would never survive.

This was not a sound plan, but the only one he could think of with any real shot of success. Like an archer in the woods, starving and depending only on their skill to survive, they had one shot to take at this.

"A lot of hope rides on this one act then," Bill said. Sam nodded, grimacing.

The three figures on the half-finished watchtower slipped down, beneath the sight lines of the enemies. *They must be done.*

Like the masons, the carpenters were waiting until the night had fallen in earnest to enact their plan. They needed the cover of darkness and surprise to give them as much of as advantage as they could.

And as much of a head start for the Overseer to get as far away downriver as they could.

There was no going back now. They would have one shot at this, he feared, before the food would run out and the starvation would take them.

"The river isn't calm," Bill said. He was right. It was swollen, and turbulent. Not the most that Sam had seen this winter, but not nearly as peaceful as eh would have liked it to be.

"The Overseer is a boatman. Or so you said."

"So I did, and so I believe."

"Do you still really intend to carry through with it?" Sam asked, turning as the masons went back inside, as much done with the wall as they could until the appointed hour.

"Do you see any other option to make it out of here alive?"

"Yes, we get reinforcements and rescue from the very man you hate. There would be nothing given to a rebellion that killed his very son."

"And he would have to know about it, and know how it happened, for that to happen. If, however, the son died heroically in battle, leading his makeshift band of fighters..." Bill shrugged.

"Don't do it Bill," Sam implored. "You know that it isn't right."

"He isn't going to change, Sam. You know that must as well as I do."

Sam looked back at the Belmarch camp, sickened by the sight of Bill. "I know that men have done wrong for generations."

"Don't get preachy with me."

Sam turned back, eyes flashing. "And I know men have changed. Even though all the world thinks they won't."

Bill held up his hands. "I can see you're angry. Save it for tonight, save it for them." He pointed to the Belmarch.

The sunset had started, casting colors of red, gold, and orange upon the puffy, swollen clouds in the west. The bottom of the sun had touched the tops of the trees, and was nearly to the horizon.

Part of him was right. Sam should save his strength for tonight. He looked down at his emaciated body and spindly arms. The vitality of life he had known when he first arrived had vanish, taken like a mist before the sun.

"We'll talk about this later," Sam said, smothering his rage and anger, not just at Bill, but at everything. He had to put the thing back to sleep, keep it from hurting anyone else.

"I'll go get the others," Bill said, giving him a funny look and then disappearing down the steps.

Sam looked one last time over the Golden River, reflecting the glory of the sunset. A star shone in the north, a reminder of the worlds that lay far away from their reach.

He took a deep, ragged breath, and gathered his strength. They would have only one night. They would have only one chance.

Sam turned back to the castle, and the task at hand.

25

ACTION IN THE NIGHT

They waited for the blanket of night to be complete before the men streamed out of the Keep. All of them were awake, all of them engaged in some form of activity.

Stars twinkled above them, a nearly full moon glowing and shedding light upon the castle. Sam worried about it. It was so bright he could make out the men standing next to them and the expressions they wore.

It was so bright the Belmarch might see them, and decide to investigate.

The group of men split into two. Bill took the majority of the masons to the wall, while Sam led the rest up to the unfinished tower and the waiting carpenters.

"Ready?" Kerien asked.

"Yes." Sam pulled out his hammer and got to work with the rest of them. He knocked free the final pegs holding the jib beam of the crane. The men holding it lowered it gently to the stone.

"Quietly," Sam said as they dropped it with a louder thunk than he wanted. "Your lives depend on it."

The rebuke did its job, and the silence that reigned among them was solemn and sacred. There was a tension in the air. Men looked over their shoulder at the Belmarch fires glowing outside their former homes, and twitched if anyone made more than a small noise.

One of the masons assigned to their group was struggling with the rope and a knot. Sam went over to him and laid a hand on his shoulder. He looked up, a look of fear on his face.

Sam knelt beside him, taking the tension on the rope and giving him some slack. "Deep breath."

The man followed his advice, and was able to loosen the knot free. There was no wind, but the night was getting cold. Sam's breath came out in streams, and steam rose from the men as they worked.

Pieces came off the crane. Not as fast as he'd like, but fast enough. Soon men were taking them down the stairs, some too heavy for one man to take and some lighter.

The jib beam they left for last, set off to the side. As the heaviest piece of wood, it was the last to go.

Sam and five other men surrounded it. "Up to the stomach first, then the shoulder, just like we talked about."

They nodded, each one ready. Sam gave the order, and they knelt down and picked it up. It was heavy enough to take his breath away, but with all of them they soon had it onto their shoulders.

A man waiting farther down the stairs lit his candle, and they started down. It was too important and heavy to try and do without light, and it helped Sam see.

He led it down the spiral staircase, keeping the front of it as close to the wall as possible. It was long, almost too long, and he remembered the problems they had bringing it up.

After a few rests they made it to the door at the bottom. More men waited, and took positions on the jib beam, easing the strain on his shoulder. His legs were burning now.

But now they were to the first test of the night.

The door stood open, but its frame was small.

"Turn it down, and aim for the bottom left corner." Sam tried to move the beam into position, but either because he wasn't clear or they didn't know what to do it wasn't working.

"Bring it down," Sam said.

"We're trying." He looked back. Arms were in the air, but they couldn't raise it far enough up.

Sam crouched down instead, lowering his end and tipping it forward. The front of the jib scraped against the ground and the wall behind him.

he moved forward, pulling the beam with him. The front of it wobbled, moving precariously.

An inch more and they were at the threshold of the door, but the beam stuck on the inside of the jamb.

"Back up. Forward now." Sam shifted his shoulder, pulling it right. Then, the tip was through and into the hall.

Sam breathed a sigh of relief, stopping to take a rest with everyone else in the hallway. They took it through the castle with no other problems, soon coming into the yard with the night sky up above.

The cold was biting now. Sam's fingers were cold, colder than they had been. Other men had the tips of theirs turn black, losing all feeling in them.

They tramped across the courtyard and up the stairs of the wall. The others were standing by as the masons were disassembling the merlons, about a quarter of the way down each one.

This was the part that Sam was nervous about. The stones had to be taken off one by one, lest they drop the whole merlon into the rocks below.

"Are you sure this is the best way?" Ned asked, taking up a position next to him.

"Bill thought it was the quietest." It certainly was the slowest method.

Sam wondered why, but a few minutes watching them made it clear to see. The stones were subjected to the wind and the coldest part of the night, and it was difficult for the masons to work with them.

Even with hands covered in clothe they had to keep taking turns. It seemed like with each stone they removed another mason took a turn.

It was slow, agonizing going. The moon rose higher into the night sky.

Sam huddled with the others, keeping close to share each other's body heat. He wanted to yell at them, urge them on, but he knew that would only make things worse.

He couldn't work the hammer and chisels with the skill that they did, and had to keep watching helplessly. Bit by bit the merlons came down.

And bit by bit the masons' slowed down. The breathing became labored, even when they were resting. Sam wanted to help them, but couldn't.

Their movements grew more erratic. Chisels slipped, hammers rang against the stone instead of the chisel heads, and stones clattered to the battlement floor.

Sam winced at each one, but he couldn't stop them now. They were running out of time.

Then, he watched with horror as a young mason wen tot remove a stone, and accidentally knocked it over the edge of the wall.

26

A Letter

Evan woke, a gentle tapping on his door. The night was cold outside his generous covers, and for a moment he almost went back to sleep.

Then, memories of the day before came to him, and his eyes were open.

"Come in."

Rhys entered, fully clothed with a makeshift pack in his hand. Evan threw off his covers and sat up, dangling his legs just above the ground.

He hadn't got much sleep, and a fog seeped through his brain. He had spent too much time last night thinking, unable to fall asleep.

"It looks like tonight is it then."

"They are finishing up the crane as we speak," Rhys said. There was a weight over his head, Evan could see it. This was not going to be an easy day.

"I've thought about this. No matter how I look at it you are the best choice." Evan pulled on a shirt, helping to keep the cold off his goose-bump ridden skin.

The room was musty. He didn't remember the last time it had been cleaned properly. Even his clothes had some of the smell on them. He should have asked for them to be washed, but until now it had slipped his mind.

He had so much more to think about lately.

"What will happen to me?" Evan asked.

"Only you will be able to answer that question," Rhys said.

"And if I go out now, to see you off?"

Rhys shifted his weight, but didn't say anything. Evan suspected as much.

It wasn't fair, he thought at first. But, having thought about it, he wasn't sure he would do anything different. They deserved someone who could lead.

"And what about Sam? Would he let them..."

"I suspect not. It seems I was wrong about him. He has more backbone than I expected." Rhys pulled his pack in front of him and rummaged through it. "But let's turn to happier things, shall we? I didn't come here just to say goodbye."

Evan asked for a moment to get dressed, and Rhys obliged by going into his study. He took some time to do it, selecting the uniform of the Hornblood line.

Before he put it on he stared at it. Evan had seen his father in it too many times to count. It was his standard wear, even though he did wear other outfits on occasion.

And now Evan was putting it on, perhaps for the last time. What would his father think of him? What would his father do in his situation?

He had grappled with it most of the night, but couldn't see any better option. This was his castle, this was his duty. He couldn't let it fall to others to shoulder the responsibility.

He had allowed that to happen for far too long.

The Overseer was waiting. Evan let out a wry chuckle at that. In a few hours he wouldn't be the Overseer anymore. That too would fall on his shoulders.

The undershirt was rough, and cold from sitting out all night. It scraped against his skin as it went over his head. The pants were no better.

Each successive layer added more cloth, and more weight. When he clicked the belt together, the sound echoing in the empty room.

It was done. He only had to add the coat and he was ready to leave his apartments.

Evan walked into his study directly. Rhys was waiting patiently and Evan bit him to sit.

"Thank you." He had something in his grip, but it was hidden in his pack.

"Before you go, I would like you to take a message." Evan joined him, sitting across from hi at his desk. The parchment he had been working on all night was still out, a pen and inkwell ready to be unstopped for the final touch.

"Certainly. Two whom?"

"To my father." Evan felt a wave of emotion. Fear, anger, sadness, desire. He fought it down. This might be the last time and the last chance to speak with him. "I've tried to detail what I've done here. And what I haven't."

He picked up the pen, the feather of it tickling his hand. Rhys was silent, and reverent. Why Evan unstopped the ink Rhys lit a candle for him to see.

"Thank you." The tip dipped into the black liquid, and it pulled as he brought it back to. A few drips came off and rippled the surface.

No more waiting. There wasn't anything else he had to add at this point, even through the struggling and the pain of the previous night.

The pen scratched against the parchment as he signed his name. He pulled it out of himself, and looked away as soon as he could.

A sweep of sand, a quick shake, and he rolled it up. A few drips of wax from the candle sealed it, and his ring left its imprint.

The Tree of Everling. *May the curse be lifted.*

Evan held out the roll, and Rhys took it carefully. "I will do everything in my power to make sure it gets to him."

Evan let go.

He took a deep breath. He had done wrong for so long there was no way to make up for it.

But he could try.

Rhys put the message away, and in return pulled out a small, red book. "I've had this for many years. It is fitting it falls to you."

Evan took it. The cover was soft, some sort of velvet. He dragged his thumb across it.

"Wait until I'm gone to read it," Rhys said. The darkness was overwhelming, but Evan knew the sun would come soon.

Rhys stood, and Evan followed. "It is time."

It was time. Evan knew it. He went around the desk, and grasped Rhys' hand.

"Go with the blessing of the Duke, and the fate of the castle

27

THE CRANE

Sam watched in horror as the mason grabbed for the rock and missed. The few moments it was falling felt like an eternity.A nd then it hit, clattering against the rocks below until it finally splashed into the river with a resounding plunk.

Bill was on the young man in an instant, beating him across the head. "Fool, you've ruined us all."

Sam was there, struggling to pull him off. The mason was whimpering and crying, blood trickling from cuts on his lip and the corner of his eye. "Bill, calm."

Bill almost turned on Sam, but he regained his composure and stopped. Everyone froze then, turning to the south.

Sam felt his heart beating fast, and blood was in his ears. He felt hot and sick. This was it. This was the end."We must move faster," Sam said in a whisper. "Set up the crane, now."

That sent them into action. The masons returned to their work, trying to take out the last remaining courses as quickly as they could."The next person to drop a rock over the side is going after it," Bill said. The warning didn't need the ominous growl he added, but it certainly cemented his seriousness.

"Bring over the braces, work around the others." Sam took one, setting it into the space they had made in the top of the wall. The other carpenters led the rest of the work.

Cold mist curled from his mouth. Sam hoped the Belmarch hadn't noticed or heard, but he knew they probably wouldn't miss it. The sound still rang in his own ears.

"Trent," Sam said as soon as he was done with a brace. Trent was at his side in a flash. "Warn the sentries. Get them ready for an attack, and make sure they have enough bows."

Trent nodded and then was gone. They still had to assemble the crane, and dawn wasn't far off. *We aren't going to make it.* The masons, as fast as they were going, were too slow.

"Bill, can we get away with not having to take them all down?" Sam pulled him off to the side.

Bill examined the wall, then looked back down at the boat. "With the swing of the crane, I don't think we can. We'll need to take them down to the floor."

Off in the distance, a drumbeat sounded. Bill cursed, and Sam couldn't help but do the same.

"We're out of time.""I'll knock them over," Bill said, picking up his hammer and pushing a mason out of the way.

Sam let him work, turning his attention to the crane. He knocked pegs into place, urging the others to work faster.

Kerien was supplying the parts as fast as he could. There was an urgency in everyone's actions that hadn't been there before.

Sam caught movement out of the corner of his eye. Forms were spilling out of the Keep. It was the women and children— all the men were already engaged with the wall work.

"Can they help?" Ned asked, seeing him looking."Have them ready to tie up the boat." Sam looked to the horizon. The sky was lightening.

And the Belmarch were assembling. Sam could hear their shouts carrying from their camp, helped by the calm stillness that still hung in the air.

Men were sweating and grunting. Hammers knocked and chipped away.

A loud crash behind him made him jump. Bill had cut loose a merlon, and it had crashed into the rocks below. He moved on to the next one. Four more to go, and two of them were already almost disassembled.

They might get away with it if they could get the crane assembled. Precious moments slipped by as the wooden structure took its form, a skeleton in the pre-dawn light.

They were able to work faster, though, with the lighter sky."Careful, a mistake now will cost us dearly," Sam said as a hammer accidentally hit the frame instead of the peg it was aimed at.

They were down to the jib now, but they were going to have trouble raising it and keeping out of the masons' way.

Bill sent another pile of rock into the river and moved to the next. He worked like a machine, cutting away the bottom mortar joints as deep as he could get them. Every so often, he urged the others to push it off, judging his progress by how much it moved.

Sam was seated now, and he was so tired. His fingers were clumsy, and he noted how discolored they looked.

They rang the bell. There was no use trying to hide it now. The Belmarch knew, and they were coming.

Sam wished they could have tied up the boat earlier, had it ready for the crane, but they needed it built before they could loop the rope through the pulley.

"Pick it up from the right side. We'll come in through the top." Sam crouched next to it, fingers scraping against the stone-covered rock of the battlement. Together they lifted the beam.

It wobbled, off-balance from the awkward loading position. "Hold fast," Sam yelled, feeling it tip.

Bill dropped his hammer and was on the other side in an instant. The beam righted, then they pushed it into place. Kerien was at the peg, slamming it home.

Sam stood back to catch his breath, muscles drained and energy gone from the effort. Defenders had taken up their positions on the south wall, bows strung and arrows at the ready.

The Belmarch streamed across the plain in a disorganized rush.

But the rope was through and fed down to the men and women waiting at the boat below. The Overseer was helping, tying it up in a four-pointed harness Sam had never seen.

The crane was finished, the boat almost at the ready. Only two merlons remained.

But the Belmarch were coming.

28

THE EASTERN WALL

The soft peals of the bell echoed in his study. Evan opened his eyes and took a deep breath.

On the outside he may have appeared calm, but beneath he was a roil of conflicting thoughts and emotions. There was no better time than now.

He stood, clipped on his sword, and adjusted his uniform. People were shouting outside as he swung on his coat, buckling it beneath his chin.

His helmet lay on the desk. Evan looked at the crest of the Hornbloods and said a small prayer to his ancestors to give him strength.

He took it up and left. The corridors of the Keep were silent. His footsteps echoed as he walked the halls for the first time in weeks—perhaps months.

On the other side of each door, he expected to see someone waiting with a sword or a dagger, but with each door he passed, there was no one.

The Keep was empty.

Soon he was at the entrance doors, and he stopped before them. Cold crept in from the cracks between them and at the jambs, and some light.

Evan put his hand on the door, the rough wood cold beneath his fingers. The smell of outside drifted to him—a strange and intoxicating smell.

He was filled with fear, but he pushed open the door anyway.

Light stung his eyes, and Evan blinked back tears that welled
up from the cold that stung them.

The courtyard was a chaos of action, most of it at the eastern wall. Men were shooting arrows on the south battlements,
some flying back in return.

When he caught his breath and bearings, Evan examined
the situation with a pounding heart rate.

Men were struggling with ropes and a boat by the eastern
wall. *That would be the responsibility of the Overseer.* The
south wall, however, looked like it could use some help.

The men on it were disorganized, guards were yelling and
shouting. Evan's feet seemed frozen in place. He couldn't
move.

He felt the presence of Yand at his back. Silent, imposing,
always looking on and judging him without showing it.

Evan mustered his courage, swallowed his fear, and walked
to the southern wall.

Sam couldn't believe his eyes. There he was, the Duke of
Hornblood walking across the courtyard. He didn't run, he
didn't falter, but he walked with a purpose Sam didn't expect.

"Sam," Ned said, breaking his concentration. He had one
hand on the rope, and realized that he needed to focus. With
one last look he turned back to the task at hand.

Another crash, and a cheer from everyone on the wall.
Another merlon had seen its demise in the river.

And only two more remained.

Kerien was wrapping the rope around the pulley, and Sam helped feed the slack through.

Below them the ropes tightened as they pulled the ropes up. A large knot lifted into the air, then the slack was gone.

Ned hammered the final pin in place.

"Pull," Sam bellowed, pushing his shoulder into the capstan. It didn't move, but more men threw their weight behind it, until at last it lifted with a creak.

Shouts from below cheered them on. The boat tipped and wobbled, but then was in the air. It broke free of the snow that had piled up on it and swung.

The Overseer was running up the stairs, and reached them as the boat did. Hands grabbed and pulled at it, swinging it over the wall.

The crane stuck, lodged on some projection. Sam called for a halt, and they pushed the boat back far enough for Kerien to smash the offending bit of wood free.

"Get in," Sam said. Rhys, with the help of a few people boosting him, climbed into the boat.

There was still one merlon in the way. Bill was yelling, and more than a few masons were chipping at the base of it.

Sam pulled at the boat with the others, and it swung back over the middle of the wall. They held it there, giving the masons enough room to work without getting in their way.

There were Belmarch soldiers at the eastern wall now. Sam could see the archers leaning out over the wall and firing at them.

A man was hit by a Belmarch arrow and tumbled off with a scream. Sam winced when the sound was cut short.

"Bill, you need to hurry." They hadn't come around the eastern wall yet, and Sam wondered what they were seeing and thinking.

Could they see the boat from their vantage point? They had to have seen it, otherwise they wouldn't be attacking.

The snow had slowed them down. The first rays of the sun were striking the cloudy sky. Sunrise dawned on the castle.

And still the boat sat, waiting to break free from the wall. Sam checked the distance again, careful up against the now open wall.

It will make it. His heart fluttered and his head spun. Sam leaned up against the frame of the crane and waited.

29

ATTACK OF THE BELMARCH

The stairs were icy and slippery, but Evan took little time to mount them. He kept his head up, his gaze fixed to the top.

The defenders on the wall were still in organized chaos. Bowstrings twanged all around as Evan got to the top, men shouting for cover and pointing out where the enemy had gone.

For a second Evan stood helpless at the top of the stairs. Then, someone noticed him, taken aback.

The man's mouth dropped open, and his eyes widened. "D-Duke," he stammered.

The words caught the attention of others, and the surprise spread like a ripple in a pond, disrupting the defenders from shooting arrows.

There was a bow leaning up against the side of the wall. Evan walked over and took it, testing its strength. It had been a while since he had shot one, but he picked up an arrow and nocked it to the string.

His coat was in the way, so he pushed it off to the side and leaned over the edge of the wall.

Attackers swarmed up the plain to the wall carrying ladders, but there were only a few of them.

Evan pulled the bow back, struggling against the weight of it, and set the feather of the arrow against his cheek. It tickled his skin, but he ignored it as he sighted down the bow.

He released. The arrow flew with a whisper, finally striking the leg of an attacker.

Evan frowned and turned back to the others. Men were staring at him. Some had looks of horror, most of surprise, and there were some hard looks of anger spread among them.

"We must buy them time." Evan picked up another arrow. "Keep them from the east wall."

Evan turned back to the attackers, feeling a pricking in between his shoulder blades. This was the critical moment, and his stomach turned knots with fear.

He didn't want to die, if he could help it, and the thought of his death at the hands of his own subjects made him squirm even more.

"You heard him," a guardsman said. "Keep them busy." Men responded, and turned back to their defense.

Evan sighted, then let fly. This time his aim was better, taking a man in the chest. Around him the others fired on the lead attackers, trying to keep them from rounding the corner of the wall.

Evan looked back to the boat. It was dangling precariously over the wall. He hoped they had enough time, but turned his attention back to the attackers.

He would buy them as much time as he could.

A crack rang out. "Push it!" Bill screamed. They pushed with all their might.

It gave.

The stones crashed to the ground, and the way was clear.

Sam's heart soared with hope. "Hold on Rhys." He leaned against the boat, urging the others to do the same.

As it swung, slowly, Sam caught sight of Belmarch attackers rounding the corner of the east wall.

The defenders were trying to stop them, throwing down arrows and stones. Duke Hornblood was in the lead, hair disheveled and looking harried, pouring on as much damage as he could.

The Overseer was clutching the edges of the boat, leaning over.

"Lower him down!" Sam pulled at the capstan brake, letting it free. The weight of the boat helped them, and the rope sang out as it fell.

"That's too fast, slow it!"

Hands grabbed at the rope, then let go as they burned. Sam couldn't feel his fingers, but clutched at it.

He feared it wasn't enough.

The boat hit the water with a wrenching crash, waves spreading out from its sides and splashing up the rocks.

Sam dashed to the edge, examining their work.

His heart soared. It was in the river, caught by the current.

Overseer Rhys was sawing at the ropes. He cut the boat free and took up the oar, pushing the prow of it further into the river.

But the Belmarch were close enough to fire on him now, and were sending arrows his way.

"Stop them, we must stop them!" Duke Hornblood was calling to all of them.

It spurned them to action. All the men on the wall rushed to help, picking up stones and blocks and anything they could get their hands on.

Arrows and rock rained down from the wall, falling upon the attackers like rain.

They wilted from the attack, and seeing the boat was too far into the water, they fell back, slipping and sliding over the blood covered snow.

Sam's heart thumped, and a lump formed in his throat. Tears formed in his eyes and fell. They had done it.

A cheer rang out from the wall, and the defenders shouted and whooped as the Belmarch ran out of bowshot and back to their camp.

They left more than a few bodies behind them, and even more limping, injured by the failed attack.

Sam watched Overseer Rhys paddle out to the center of the river. He held up a hand to signal he was unharmed. Behind him the dawn exploded in a cacophony of color.

They had a chance. It was a small one, but it was still a chance.

Sam leaned on the ruins of the wall and watched the sunrise, hope blossoming in his heart.

Epilogue

Evan gulped down the fresh winter air, trying to recover. Cheers surrounded him, but he could not partake in their joy.

Rhys was gone now, a speck that had disappeared on the river downstream. He felt some of his fear go with him, but not all of it.

When his heart had calmed and the cheers had died down Evan still faced the river, afraid to turn and face his subjects.

But face them he must.

Squaring his shoulders he turned. Eyes stared at him, all faces turned his direction. Sweat trickled down his brow and he wiped it away, but it wasn't sweat. It was blood.

He felt the wound. It was a graze, from an arrow, most likely. He didn't remember how he had gotten it, but it didn't matter now.

Evan was near the edge of the wall and suddenly became extremely aware of it. Forty men faced him. All it would take was one little push. They could claim it was an accident.

"You did well today," Evan said. He wasn't sure what else he could say. "I haven't..." he trailed off.

The wall was silent. Evan lowered his head. "I like to think I'm a different man than I was."

Sam Freeman was before him then, ripping a strip of his own ragged coat off. "You're hurt, Your Highness."

"I don't deserve that title."

"Deserve it or not, we'll get you patched up." Sam turned back to the others. "Isn't that right?"

Murmurs ran through the crowd, but there wasn't the same hostility Evan had known before. He let Sam wrap his head.

"Thank you," Evan said.

Sam smiled. "You are welcome. On a day like today, we should celebrate." Sam turned back to the crowd. "This day we will remember to our last breath."

They cheered again, smiles appearing on faces. Evan wasn't sure if he was out of danger, but he knew that he was safe then.

He couldn't help but smile.

Branch of the Everlong

Epic of Hornblood Castle #3

Eric Kercher

Paper and Sword, LLC

To Nina, a wonderful and loving mother who always believed
in me.

1

HUNTER FOR THE HUNTED

Scritch, scratch. Little legs pattered by in the darkness. Sam waited patiently, even though his mind was telling him to move.

Small squeaks echoed in the room, the dark hollows of the castle basement.

It was getting closer. It scuffed and shuffled. He smelled horrible, covered in refuse and his unwashed scent from weeks of the same clothes and no chance to get them clean.

Behind the creature water dripped in a slow, steady flow. His belly gnawed at his ribcage, almost on fire.

He had to wait.

It got closer, and then it was there. Sam lunged.

The rat tried to move, but his blade found it faster. Red, glowing eyes stared at him as it hissed and spat, trying to scratch him.

He was breathing hard, even though he hadn't moved more than a foot. This was a big one, and he was pleased.

The movements died, the screams of the rat slowing and then dying away.

Sam panted in the darkness. Warm blood covered his hand. He pulled his prey up and slung it over his shoulder.

Up the stairs he climbed, one foot in front of the other. Like every day he wondered whether Rhys had made it. Not knowing ate at him more than the hunger.

He stopped at the top of the stairs to catch his breath and slow his pounding heart, leaning against the cold, hard wall.

Sam put his head against it, letting the rough, cool stone suck the heat from his head, and coughed.

It was a dry, rasping cough. His leg throbbed, the old wounds coming back to him. When he had recovered enough, he opened the door.

Blinking against the light, Sam stepped out of the dungeons of the Keep and into the hall. He was still inside, but light trickled in from the rooms up ahead.

Voices drifted in, and he shuffled to them. He took a look at his blood-drenched hand, already drying off, and thought about washing.

He winced, thinking of the freezing cold water against his skin. That they still had plenty of, if they could break the ice off the top of the well.

"Sam!" Martha exclaimed, cutting off her conversation with Belinda. "What happened to you?"

"I've killed the thing eating our food." Sam dropped the rat on the counter. Its tongue rolled out of its mouth, but the rest of it was going stiff. "I know it isn't appetizing, but I thought we could eat it. I thought it fitting."

He slumped into a chair. So little strength, there was too little of it left in his body. He eyed the rat, thinking of how its flesh might taste.

Warm and succulent, roasted over a nice, crackling fire. Dripping with fat. Sam's mouth watered.

"I'll do what I can," Martha said.

Belinda was staring at him, a hint of a glare subdued by her exhaustion.

"Give it to the boy," Sam said. He was getting so thin it broke his heart every time he saw those little cheeks.

Beady little eyes poked out from the blanket at her chest. He moved, coughed, then started crying.

Belinda turned and comforted him, rocking him back and forth and shushing him. She shot him one last glare and walked out of the kitchen.

The rat wouldn't last. They would eat of all it, that he knew for sure, down to cracking the bones to get to the marrow. They needed the meat.

He felt a wave of sadness wash over him that this is what it had come to. Sam tried to control it, but he was so tired.

How long has it been since Rhys left in the boat? It was all a haze now, the fog that never left his brain seeping through his body.

Sam sniffed. He averted his gaze, aware that Belinda didn't take too kindly to him. His heart ached at that too, wished he could do something about it, but he knew that her sadness and grief overruled everything else. She had gone so long with hate in her that he wasn't sure it would ever go away.

And that ate at him too, gnawing worse than the hunger did.

He wanted to make it go away but knew that she was in total control of the situation.

"That is… kind of you," Martha said, snapping him out of his thoughts and back to reality.

"I hate to see him like that. He should be fat and happy, not sticks and bones poking through his skin." His own skin felt tight, as he suspected everyone else's did. Fat was in short supply within the walls of the castle.

"I'll see what I can do about cooking it." Martha stared at the dead rat. She pushed up her sleeves and took out a knife, sharpening it with quick, efficient strokes, only expending enough energy to get it sharp enough to slice underneath the matted fur and skin, parting it from the muscle with quick slices.

"I can bring you something to burn." There wasn't much left, but he could find scraps to use. A few sticks might do for a fire. His mouth watered just watching her cut the measly strips of meat from the tiny bones.

A few moments of work and the rat was dressed and ready to eat, organs and all. "I'll put it into a stew." Martha looked around and pulled out a small pot. "This will do."

Sam eased himself into the corner, sliding down the stone until he was supported by the floor. It was cold too, no way to escape it. The smell of the rat, blood and bone and meat, drifted over to him and tortured him. His breath was coming in short gasps. "Let me rest, and then I will go out to the workshop."

His eyelids felt heavy and tried to drift shut, but he didn't let them. After a few minutes, and while Martha prepared everything, his breathing steadied, and Sam got back to his feet. He nodded in her direction and walked out to the workshop, bracing himself for the cold before opening the Keep door and walking out into the snow and wind.

It wasn't as cold as it had been, but it was still brutal on his body. He was shivering within a few seconds, and his hands fumbled when he finally reached the workshop and pulled out the smallest scraps of wood he could. The wood pile was down to almost nothing. They had burned almost everything else and were scavenging beams from the castle when they had the strength at the beginning of the day.

He couldn't get Archie's face out of his mind as he worked, and the faces of all the others that had died. They walked in a long, sad line through his mind, just staring at him. It was enough, and he felt a mixture of shame and sadness as they did.

After that, and while he walked back to the Keep, came the worst of it. The children, emaciated and thin, still living, but only just, came to mind. He wanted to close his eyes when he got inside but didn't. A few of them peered out at him from the pile of bodies, watching him cross the room with curiosity until he slipped out of view and down the hall.

They were all counting on him to survive, and there was nothing he could do about it now. Their fate rested with Overseer Rhys and his luck, for better or for ill.

"This is all I could find that was handy," Sam said as he entered the kitchen. Martha looked at it with tired eyes and nodded. He got to work lighting the fire under the pot, a strange sight in a fireplace so large to be confined to such as small fire. They could have thrown in a quarter of the tree and burned it, and probably would in the future.

If they survived.

The fire caught, and smoke filled the kitchen. The tiny amount of heat coming from it was a blessing, and Martha pressed up beside him to share in it. Soon they had a small fire, and the pot pressed against it.

She was so close, and warm. *It feels nice, in a way*. That strange fluttering feeling came back in his stomach, pushing aside the hunger for a few blessed moments.

He knew he should say something, but he wasn't sure what. He was keenly aware of every part of her touching him. She moved, reaching out a hand to stir the pot with a long spoon. That side of his body was chilled, used to the warmth of her skin, wrapped up in all the clothing she could find.

Sam cleared his throat. "What do you think we will do in spring?"

Martha looked at him. A lock of her hair fell down over her eye. "What do you mean by that question?"

"I'm not sure." Sam looked away. "Trying to pass the time, I imagine."

"I pray that we make it to spring." He looked back at her, but she was staring at the fire. It was dancing, sending up small tufts of smoke that curled up the chimney. Sam wanted to reach down and hold it in his hand, bring it near to his bosom to suck up its warmth, but he restrained himself and savored the momentary feeling of warmth it gave him, little as it may be. "I'm afraid the food will be gone next week."

He knew it was coming, but it still hit him in the stomach like a punch to the gut. All their rationing and scrimping, all of it was for nothing. "It will run out when it runs out. We'll have to go on after that."

"Until when? When we die?" She had tears in the corner of her eyes. "The children..."

"If there was anything you could do for them you would have done it already." Martha bit her thumb and squeezed her eyes shut. She looked so vulnerable, so frail.

Sam wanted to reach out and take her hand, sweep her into his arms and hold her. For all her iron appearance, her harsh way with the other girls in the castle, this was another side that he had never seen.

A breeze from the window gusted through the kitchen and the fire sputtered dangerously. Sam reached out his hands to shield it. The pot hadn't boiled yet.

What am I supposed to say, what am I supposed to do? Sam chewed at his lip. Martha wiped her eyes.

"Here I am blubbering when there's a job to do." She stirred the pot again. "What must you think of me?"

"I think you care about everyone around you." Sam swallowed. "I... admire you for it."

Their eyes locked. Sam felt his face flush, steam rising to his cheeks. Martha was searching his eyes, looking for something, but he wasn't sure what. "The soup is ready."

His heart was pounding. He could still feel the heat from her body on him, but it was gone an instant later when she stood and took the pot from the fire. It had been boiling. For how long, he wasn't sure, but the fire was dying down and the wood had been almost all consumed.

"Did I say something wrong?" Sam stood too.

"Will you get Belinda for me?" Martha poured the soup into waiting bowls. She refused to make eye contact with him, but worked with a steady, practiced hand.

His mind was a rush of emotions and thoughts tripping over each other. What had he said to make her act this way? Was it him saying she cared about everyone? *I can't see why that would make her angry.*

All he could do was turn and leave, searching for Belinda and her child. He found her in the great hall, huddled up against the mass of bodies, and signaled for her.

The confusion was still in him, but there was also a strange sense of anger with it. It must have shown in his face, because Belinda looked at him with a soft expression of alarm and clutched her child closer. Still, she followed him into the hall, away from the others.

"What is it? What have I done?" she asked when they were out of earshot of the others, in a hissing whisper.

"You've done? Nothing you've done." Sam took a deep breath, calmed himself. "I'm sorry, it's just...you wouldn't understand."

"Hold on." Belinda had been following him, but at the words he turned to see her stopped. Gone was the expression of concern, now replaced with one of anger. "Have you hurt her?"

"Hurt who?" Sam took a step back and raised his hands.

"Martha. Have you broken her heart?"

2

SHIPWRECKED

The harsh wind blew across the river. Rhys, trembling with cold, hunched down in the boat to protect himself from it.

He kept his eye on the river, watching for snags and banks hidden just under the surface of the water. There was no fear of being caught by the Belmarch by now. He had left them behind days ago, but he had no help if he ran aground, and the water was freezing. Splashes of it, and spray, flew in his face and froze into thin icicles off his eyebrows and his beard.

The current was swift and was sweeping him downstream at an astounding pace. Using an oar as a stiller, he turned the boat around the river bends.

As he turned the small amount of water in the bottom of the boat sloshed and splashed at his feet. His legs were getting tired, he was propping them up out of the water. Every so often he had to stop and scoop a few more inches out of the boat to toss over the side with a small bucket.

The boat was leaking. There wasn't anything he could do about it now, it wasn't fast and he didn't have any way to repair it. The sawdust stuffed into the joints held up somewhat, swelling to fill the void, but the pressure of the water beneath the boat was pushing it out. He was having to do more bailing and less watching, and it made him nervous.

And the wind wasn't helping. It pushed the surface of the water up into waves that rocked and cracked against the boat's hull, setting him on edge. His teeth clamped together tightly, his hand white, gripping the edge of the oar.

The bank was covered in forest, but the river was high and the edges of the bank jagged and rocky. He had thought about stopping and walking the rest of the way, but each time he thought of the others waiting for him, starving to death, he kept going.

With a plish, a clump of sawdust gave way. Water streamed into the boat. Rhys cursed, looked up at the stars, and wondered where he was.

Sweat broke out on his brow, making him even colder, and he bailed furiously. It wasn't enough though, he couldn't keep up.

Just one more bend, then I'll have to get to the bank. It had been so long since he had been on the river, years if not decades, but the moon glimmering in the reflection shattered into a million pieces by the wind.

His heart was beating a mile a minute and thundered in his ears. His shirt and coat were wet, and he shivered with the cold. He couldn't wait any longer and aimed for the bank.

A ripple, a hump caught his eye, and he reacted without thinking. Rhys turned the boat back into the middle of the river.

Something scraped against the hull, then popped as it reached the back of the hull. The boat lurched rightward, tilting so much it almost threw Rhys off.

He couldn't control it. The boat was listing heavily to the right, and a quick glance told him it was over. The hull had a deep gash ripped in it below the waterline.

All he could do now was pray and bail, hoping it would hold up enough to make it to the bank.

Rhys bailed furiously, his arms protesting against the use. The flaps of skin on his arms jiggled in his sleeves.

The boat struck the bank. Rhys lurched forward, falling into the water with a splash. His entire skin contracted it was so cold, and he came out of it spluttering and splashing.

He reached back, grabbed his pack, and struggled to get out onto the muddy bank. The river roared in his ears, and the boat started to creak and groan.

He made it, scrambling up the bank on his hands and knees, and stopped at the top, gasping for breath. It was colder than ever, and he knew he was in danger. He was starting to feel sleepy and struggled to his feet.

Leaving the boat behind, Rhys turned south and walked, forcing each leg forward even though they protested.

He wasn't sure how long he walked, but the sky was beginning to brighten. His mind was a fog, and he couldn't think well. Had he gone far enough downriver to Jareth?

There was shouting, or something like it, in the distance. Rhys kept walking, trudging, and stumbling. He kept getting back to his feet, and his lips were moving.

Hands grabbed at him, pulled him up over shoulders. Someone was looking at him, talking to him, but he was so far away.

Rhys wanted to close his eyes and go to sleep, but rough hands shook at him.

A door opened, light flowing out of it, and Rhys passed through. It was warm inside, but it made him shiver more. Something was at his lips, and he drank of it. It wasn't cold, but it wasn't hot either.

They laid him down, and then, at last, Rhys slipped off to sleep.

⚬

"We should move now and risk the river." General Granb stared over the table with a glare, daring others to speak.

"You wish to throw away our fighters? Waste them without purpose?" Sable sneered. "It is no wonder we've had such a hard time lately. No, we know the siege is strong and the castle is weak. It would be prudent to invade later, once the river subsides."

Raltone rubbed his chin, then let them bicker for another few minutes, enjoying the back and forth.

Granb was getting quite worked up, his face red. The scars stood out even whiter than usual. They were shouting at each other now.

"Enough," Raltone said, waving a hand. The noise died down. He couldn't hide the irritation in his voice. "The castle was supposed to be mine months ago. That was your responsibility, General Granb."

"It was Shigon that failed you," Granb said, the color draining from his face. "He was too weak to overpower a minimal amount of troops and a bunch of tradesmen."

"Silence," Raltone hissed. Granb shut his mouth quickly, almost taking a step back. He wouldn't let this ruin his plans. "These Chathem will pay for their resistance, and they will serve as an example of what happens to those that resist us."

He slammed a fist onto the table. "For too long you have all failed me. I grow tired of it."

Silence fell, a deadly silence. Raltone scowled at them all. "Chathem will be ours."

Rhys awoke to the sound of voices, hushed and low. When he opened his eyes, he was confused. This was a strange place, a place he did not know.

"Where-" he coughed at the effort of trying to speak, his voice catching in his parched throat.

His body wasn't responding how he wanted it to.

"Drink this," a woman's voice said. Something hard was held to his lips, then clear, sweet water flowed into his mouth. "We almost lost you to the cold stranger."

Rhys sat up, with some help from the woman and a man next to her. He was in a bed in a small cabin. It smelled of fish, in a good way, and woodsmoke.

A fire crackled merrily in the corner fireplace. The sight of it almost made him cry. The cold that settled in his bones was gone, and he soaked up the heat.

"Where am I?" he asked.

"Greenport," the man said. His eyes were hard and piercing, a strange contrast to the woman's warm gaze. "Who are you?" he demanded.

"Poppy," the woman scolded. "We talked about this. The poor man's almost up and died."

"I understand. I'm Rhys Clayton, once courtier to the King and Overseer of Castle Hornblood's construction." The words sapped the strength out of him.

Poppy's eyes didn't unharden. "Never heard of no Castle Hornblood around here, or any castle."

"Excuse my husband, dear. You came in looking like a ghost last night, and you don't look much better. Would you like something to eat?"

The mention of food made his mouth water, then he smelled it. Butter. Real butter, and milk. Fresh bread was mixed in with it and nearly drove him crazy with desire.

"Yes, yes!" Rhys cried.

They helped him to the table, and he fell upon the bowl of butter. It melted in his mouth, rich and creamy, sliding down like smooth silk into his ravenous stomach. When he had emptied the bowl, he turned his attention to the milk.

They stared at him like they would a wild animal. He didn't care at first, but when his appetite began to fade, he slowed and tried to regain his composure.

He looked around for something to wipe his face but found none. Something dribbled down his beard, so he tried to wipe it away.

Watching his saviors, he felt a sense of shame come over him at his actions. "I apologize for my rudeness. It's-" he started again. "The castle is starving. I haven't had a good meal in weeks." He tried to sound nonchalant, but he hid the fact he hadn't eaten since he boarded the boat days ago. He couldn't bear to take anything else with him, even though they had packed food with his supplies. He had left it in the kitchen when no one was looking.

"I see," Poppy said, even though he didn't look like he saw at all. His wife elbowed him in the ribcage.

"We forgot to introduce ourselves," she said. "My name is Pike, and this is my husband, Poppy. I function as a sort of healer in the village, so it was no wonder they brought you to my doorstep."

"Pleased to make your acquaintance," Rhys said. "How far are we from the capital?"

"Ironwood? Ain't much more than a few days' ride in good weather," Poppy said, scratching his chin.

Rhys tried to stand, but he was weak and fell back again. Pike let out a small cry of alarm and rushed to his side.

"What are you doing? You'll hurt yourself." They eased him back into the chair, stiff backed and hard.

"I have to get to the capital," Rhys said. "You don't understand, I have to get there as soon as I can." He clutched at their arms, looking from one to the other. "If we don't send help, they're going to die."

"You're in no shape to be going anywhere," Poppy said, pulling him over to the bed.

"You need your rest, dear," Pike said, eyes creased with concern. Rhys struggled, trying to break free, but he was too weak. His breath came short, and he started coughing again.

They eased him back into the bed. Rhys gripped at Pike's arm, his thin fingers clutched around her wrist. "I have to make it there, tonight, as soon as possible."

She gave him a pained smile. "That won't be possible. It's snowing now. A big blizzard is moving in."

He stopped and listened. The wind was howling outside, and there were drifts of snow spilling through cracks around the door and oilcloth windows. He hadn't realized it until then, the sound of the fire had been too loud.

The thought of going out into the cold again, after being so warm, made him shudder, and brought with it a heaping of shame.

He should go anyway. Everyone in the castle was going to have to deal with this, why should he be any different?

Rhys took a deep breath. The smell of dinner was still thick, but his stomach was so full he feared eating anything else would cause it to burst. That satisfaction brought more shame with it, piling on more.

"Is there no one who could take me?"

"I don't think you'd get anyone tonight," Poppy said.

Rhys worked his jaw, finally speaking at last. "The more time I take, the more people die. I must reach the capital. Will you help me?"

3

COLD WATER FISHING

"Will you tell us about them?" Pike sat down on a stool next to the bed. Rhys let go of her arm and put it over his eyes.

"About a hundred men, women, and children are stuck, trapped in a siege. We've been building a fortification for over three years at the headwaters of the Golden River, a bastion to protect us from Belmarch."

He couldn't meet their eyes. "But we weren't fast enough. They came on us in the night, burning and looting, and we were forced to retreat into the castle. They tried to take it, and we repelled them time and time again, and now they seem content to starve us out. They sent me, risking all, to get help."

The house was silent except for the wind and fire. There was a tapping on the side of the door, a rattle of wood on wood.

Pike sat, chewing her lip. Poppy took out a pipe and slowly packed it, getting up to take a stick from the fire to light it. He stood there, puffing out great plumes of white.

"You bring us ill news," Pike said, breaking the silence. "We haven't heard of any of this."

"Will you help me? I have friends, well-connected friends, that will reward any who help me. Belmarch is on the rise, and if we don't stop them, we could be swept away." Rhys was feeling his strength fade away. They were right, he couldn't leave tonight if he wanted to. "I'm in no shape to travel, I agree with you, but it might be that there would be someone who could take me as far as Jareth."

Poppy cleared his throat and looked at Pike. No words passed between them, but he turned to a peg on the wall where his coat and hat hung and put them on. "Stay here, I'll ask around."

"In the meantime, you need to get some rest," Pike said. "I'll make you some tea to help you get to sleep."

As she got up to put the kettle on Poppy knocked out his pipe into the fire, red ash that licked up like a fiery snow. He opened the door, a wild wind bringing with it gusts of snow, struggled outside, and slammed it shut behind him.

Rhys let go of Pike and slipped back into the bed. His thoughts and emotions churned like the blizzard outside, tossing this way and that.

What am I going to do? He wanted to go out into the cold, continue his journey. He needed to, the weight of it hung on his shoulders like irons.

But he couldn't make it like this. He knew that, and so did they. Now he was reliant on the kindness of strangers to accomplish his mission.

Do I need to do it? Would anyone fault me for giving up? Rhys turned uncomfortably at the thought.

He could do it, go south and drift into obscurity. He might spend his next few months running, but there were places beyond the reach of the Chathem King. Many places, and no one knew he had escaped the castle except the defenders inside.

It would be so easy to run from his duty, to let the burden slip off and fall into the river. They were almost dead anyway, and he owed them nothing.

"What is it?" Pike asked, at his side in an instant. "You seem so troubled."

"Nothing," Rhys said quickly.

"I saw it in your eyes, tell me." She was young, the wrinkles not touching her eyes yet. They looked at him, first at one eye then the other.

"I think of my companions, that is all." *You didn't tell her that you were thinking of abandoning them to their fate, did you? You're a weak man, unworthy of any title.*

"Why does it trouble you so?" Pike was staring at him, like he was emitting some kind of strange light.

"Are they your friends?"

"Hardly. A man of my station-" What station was he now? An Overseer who abandoned his post? Royal blood without any prospects? "I'm tired. I must rest now." Rhys turned away, pulling the thick, woolen blanket up around his shoulders.

Pike respected his wishes and left him alone, but it didn't make Rhys satisfied. His exhausted body, finally filled with food for the first time in months, forced him into a fitful and troubled sleep.

Rhys woke guilty and in a strange place. It was daytime, or just barely, a tinge of red cast on the log wall of the cabin. Someone was at the fire, poking it and bringing it back to life, even as the wind howled through the eaves.

He was hungry, but somehow warm. Rhys sat up, letting the thick blanket slip and a tinge of the cool air in the cabin touch him. He quickly wrapped it around his body.

"Good morning," Pike said, smiling. She was busy in the small kitchen near the fireplace, mixing something in a big wooden bowl. Her arm moved furiously, but she seemed completely serene otherwise.

"Good morning," Rhys said, swinging his legs over the side of the bed and touching them to the cool floorboards.

"Morning," Poppy said, stirring the fire and adding another log. It smashed into the ashes, sending up a flurry of red and yellow that burned out immediately.

"Are you feeling better this morning?" Pike asked. She spooned out a measure of the mixture into a pan and set it on the coals that Poppy had revealed.

Rhys examined his body, and tested his muscles. Everything seemed to be in good working order, if not a touch sore. Other than his hunger, which wasn't sure he could ever satisfy again, nothing seemed out of place. He had even slept better than he had in weeks, even distressed as he was.

"I'm much better, thank you." Rhys winced. "I apologize for my ill manners. I wasn't... myself yesterday."

"You've had a dreadful burden to carry, dear. Don't worry your head about it. Once we fill up your belly with my flatcakes you'll feel right as rain."

"Is there any word on the...help?" Rhys asked. He stood, moved closer to the warmth of the fire, catching a glimpse of outside.

It was covered in snow, still and quiet except for the wind. The world was hazy through the oilcloth covering the openings, even though ice crept in the corners. He was grateful of the fire as soon as he saw it, and the snow at the edges of the door. It was impossible to keep the weather out, and was a reminder of the castle and the people depending on him.

"Are you sure you're up to traveling?" Pike asked, brow creased and wrinkled.

"I don't have a choice. I have to go. I must go." Rhys sat at the table.

"Joe's got a sled and horses. He said he could do it, but didn't seem keen on it." Poppy joined him at the table and took out a pipe, packing the bowl slowly.

"Do put that away, Poppy. Let him alone."

"I don't mind," Rhys said. "Please, go ahead." *I won't be any more of an inconvenience than I already am.* Pike took out the first of the cakes, golden brown and smelling wonderful, and added another batch. In another pot she dropped a few eggs into boiling water, watching them almost as much as she watched Rhys.

"We've managed to find some clothes your size," Pike nodded to the foot of the bed. "You'll have to excuse them. They aren't in the best condition, but you need them."

They looked tired and worn, but far warmer than what he had on now. While breakfast was cooking he put them on. They were a little large for him in his current condition.

"Thank you, these are an improvement. I don't deserve your kindness," Rhys said, joining Poppy as he puffed on the pipe and sent lazy spirals of tobacco smoke wafting around the small cabin. Half of it was sucked out of the cabin immediately through the drafts, but the rest hung to the rafters above.

Pike announced breakfast, and Rhys licked his lips. His mouth had been watering the entire time she had been cooking, and he tore into the food as soon as it touched his plate, although with more restraint than he had the previous evening.

"Slow down, you might choke," Poppy said with an arched eyebrow.

"Let him be. He's still almost half dead," Pike chided. The food was delicious, the flatcakes warm and fluffy, a crunchy crust with a soft, puffy inside, and the eggs were cooked until they were firm but still soft.

Even as he ate it and enjoyed it, a wave of shame washed over him. Here he was, stuffing his face, while others starved.

But he had to eat. He wouldn't have strength for anything if he didn't. Like it or not, he had to do it.

"When is the earliest he can leave, this Joe?" Rhys asked between bites. He knew it wasn't proper of him, but he couldn't help it. He had already wasted too much time as it was.

"I don't know." Poppy was short and to the point. "He didn't promise he'd do it. It would be mighty inconvenient for him to do it at all, let alone now."

"I have resources."

Poppy's eyebrows raised. "Do you now?"

"Not with me," Rhys confessed. He could convince them to empty the treasury, if it would stop the Belmarch at the border. *I think*.

"That makes it a might harder to take you seriously, then." Poppy took a bite of his flatcake. "And Joe a lot more reluctant to go."

"The Belmarch have already invaded," Rhys said, wiping the last of his plate clean with a piece of cake and devouring it. "When they sweep through here, killing and burning, will Joe take that as currency?"

Pike looked at Poppy. They exchanged an uneasy glance, and Poppy returned the pipe to his mouth with a click of his teeth. His smoke cut through the smell of breakfast.

"I've no reason to lie about it." Rhys stood up, rolled up his sleeve, and grabbed a bit of his hanging flesh, pulling it so tight they could see the bone underneath. "Do you think a man wants to be like this for pleasure?"

"We don't think you're lying," Pike said. "It's just that we're a simple folk in a simple place. What you say is... complicated."

"It'll be simple enough when the blood starts flowing." Rhys sat back down. "This isn't something you can avoid, and you know it."

"They've never come down this far before," Pike said, but there was a hint of concern in her voice.

"I'll take him," Poppy said.

"Poppy, you can't do that."

"Someone has to. I don't see Joe doing it anytime soon without payment up front. That only leaves one other option."

"Whoever takes me, we need to leave soon. The sooner the better." The food had given Rhys some of his strength back.

He thought he could make it now, provided he would still be able to eat. *But what about them?*

"I don't like it." Pike shook her head. "Not one bit." She sighed. "But I see you've made up your mind. Easier to break a rock than change it. I'll help you get ready."

Poppy nodded and tapped out his pipe into the fire. "I'll get the sled ready."

4

AT THE MERCY OF OTHERS

A few hours later, and after a hearty lunch that continued to restore him to health, Rhys found himself atop a homemade sled in two feet of snow. A brown mare was hitched to it, breath streaming out her nostrils like smokestacks.

It was another cold day that took the breath away, but Rhys was better protected now with thicker clothes and a warmer, if worn, coat.

"Take care of him," Pike called, waving from the doorway, a shawl wrapped around her shoulders. Poppy nodded, but Rhys wasn't sure she was talking to Poppy or him. He had thanked her for her kindness, and for saving his life, but he wasn't sure it had been enough.

He was still feeling weak, and coughed as he eyed the horizon and sky. It was clear, but this was the time of year where that was little solace against the winter snowstorms that came in without notice.

"We'll be fine," Poppy said, taking up the reins. Rhys nodded, and the man whipped the mare into action. The sled groaned, then skimmed over the snow as the horse kicked great gouts of it up with her footsteps.

"To Jareth, then the capital," Rhys murmured.

"Unless we cross now, head west."

"We? I couldn't ask you to do that. I'll find a way when I get to Jareth," Rhys said, bumping along with the rest of the supplies. Pike had loaded them down with enough to last for weeks, as well as enough firewood that it almost over-burdened the horse. Poppy had removed some, despite her protests, but there was plenty left.

"Do you think there's even enough snow to make it the whole way?" Rhys asked. The sled skimmed over the surface of the fresh snow, the mare struggling through the deep piles of it.

"More than enough. I know a way." Poppy barely held the reins, twitching them every so often if the horse strayed from his intended path.

"I told you; I can find a way myself." The last thing Rhys wanted to do was find himself more in debt to these people. They had saved him, kept him alive, and now were willing to take him where he needed to go.

The sun came out, sparkling on the snow like stars. It was so bright it hurt his eyes, so he hid them.

"And how would you do that?" Poppy pulled out his pipe and put it between his teeth, keeping it unlit. His hood was so big it nearly touched his mustache. "Exchange your non-existent coin for a ride?"

Rhys stewed it over in his mind. He hadn't been prepared for this, or not nearly enough. All that time he had thought the biggest problem would be getting out of the castle.

He sniffed. "I see your point. I'm reliant on the kindness of strangers."

"Is that what we are now?"

"That isn't what I meant. I-" They passed by a copse of trees, then entered a meadow. The snow was shallower here, and the horse snorted and pulled ahead at a faster trot. "You've already done too much for me. It isn't right to ask you to do more."

"Good thing I'm not asking." Poppy leaned back, pulled his hat almost over his eyes to block the glare. "Besides, Pike needs some things we can't get out here. A trip to Ironwood wouldn't hurt. And I have healing tonics she needs to sell."

He motioned behind him. The tinkling that Rhys had heard was a group of bottles in a straw filled box at the top of the supplies.

Rhys looked back at him. "You talked it over with her, didn't you?"

Poppy shrugged. "You were sleeping all night and half the morning. We had to talk about something."

"And I suppose you said I wouldn't make it on my own."

Poppy shrugged, took his pipe from his mouth and tapped it over the side of the sled.

"Well," Rhys said after a while. "Thank you."

The air was cold, almost frighteningly so, but he was warm. It felt like a miracle. The wind from the sled whipped across his cheeks, providing a light sting, but it almost felt refreshing after spending so much time outside. Rhys lifted his head to the sky and closed his eyes. He let the sun soak into his cheeks, counteracting the tinge of cold with a tingle of warmth. His lip twitched, and he almost smiled at it.

There was a good chance he could do it. With Poppy to lead him they would make it to Ironwood, and then Whitehall.

He could picture it now, the great gleaming walls of mottled white stone rising higher than any building in the building, supported by massive blocks of stone at the base that got progressively lighter as they went up. The King would be standing at the lattice windows, watching him coming, his court surrounding him, vying for attention.

And Rhys would be back in his element.

He almost shivered at it, thinking of the intrigue and drama that must have exchanged while he was gone on his exile to the northern lands.

That small thing came back into his mind, a mere trifle that threatened to overpower everything else. He could let them go, let them meet their fate. He could return to his riches, his satin and down pillows, warmed for him by servants.

Another nagging through pricked at him, the memory of faces. Sick, cold faces half-starved, some of them children. It overpowered them quickly.

Each face was a chain, fastened around his neck. Each one weighed him down, returned him to his duty.

He had taken the position of Overseer of the Castle Hornblood unwillingly, forced out by chance and machinations of others. However, he had sworn an oath to do his duty and execute the will of his King and people.

Rhys shivered and pulled his coat tighter around his neck. The sled bumped over something harder than the snow, making a heart wrenching grating noise.

"If you've got something on your mind best let it out now," Poppy said beside him. The reins were in his lap now, the mare seemed to know the way on her own. He was calmly filling his pipe full of tobacco leaf. "We've a long road ahead of us, several days."

The cold in his heart overwhelmed the warmth of the sun and the sparkle of the snow. The landscape looked fresh and clean, but his heart was too full and heavy.

"Given enough time, yes. Right now..." Rhys shrugged.

"Suit yourself." They traveled over the snow, out of familiar lands. The sound of the river had long faded away, only the sound of the sled and the jingle of the harness on the horse made any noise now.

Rhys leaned back, closed his eyes, and slipped off into sleep.

—◆O◆—

His face was cold when the sled pulled to a halt, waking him. Rhys opened his eyes, blinking in the light of the late morning sun.

The landscape had changed. The rolling hills and spindly trees had given way to plains. Looking closer, Rhys realized that there were houses dotting the horizon, and barns.

"Where are we?" His voice cracked, unused to going so long without use. Poppy reached down beside him and pulled out a waterskin and handed it to him.

"Drink up. We've left the river lands behind. Now we're in the heart of Chathem, farmland and plains as far as you can see." Poppy turned and dug around in the supplies while Rhys drank greedily.

The second it hit his lips the water shocked him with how cold it was, chunks of ice mixed in. He drank it, feeling relief from the thirst that had shown itself when he had recovered from waking. It gathered in his belly until it had warmed.

"This is the Chathem I'm most familiar with."

"Oh?" Poppy turned, a lump of cheese and some bread fished from behind him. He handed it off to Rhys and took a small carrot and bag of grains to the horse, who was breathing heavily.

They were beside a small creek, frozen over in the winter air, and after a few kicks from Poppy's boot, accessible to the horse to drink from.

"I grew up in a place like it."

"On a farm?"

"No." Rhys stood up, stretching the soreness out of his muscles. His joints popped as he did, and he groaned. "Not a farm. Where did you grow up?"

"Right near the river," Poppy said. "My father was a bargeman, did some time traveling, and settled down with my mother where we live now." He peered up into the sky, then crunched across the snow to take the rest of the food.

It was good, and the cheese went well with the bread. Poppy tore off a piece of bread and popped it into his mouth.

"You stayed."

"I had to. The river is in my blood, in many."

"You couldn't leave if you wanted to. Even to take a poor beggar halfway across the kingdom." Rhys spread out his hands.

Poppy smiled. "You might say that. I've done my fair share of traveling too. Can't say I like it as much as staying home." Poppy went back to his side of the sled. "Well and good. Ready?"

Rhys nodded, then sat back down as he flicked the reins. Butter, the mare, took off at a light trot. The snow was thinner here, but still came up above her ankles.

They didn't talk much the rest of the day. Rhys watched the world go by, watching the farmers come to their doors and look back at them.

Their stoves sent white spirals of smoke up in the air, eventually mingling with the clouds up above.

Rhys thought. He wondered who he would go to first. He thought about what he would say. He thought about who to avoid.

There were all too many of the latter. Oh, if he could go back in time and do it all again, he would, and better.

Much better.

"We'll stop for dinner," Poppy said.

"How long will Butter go?"

"She'll go for a while. Don't worry, we'll get there in time."

"I'm not sure we will, even if we travel all night." The wind was harsh against his face, and there was no protection here, no groups of trees to break it, even if it was poor cover. The gaunt faces, the thin as reeds arms and legs lingered in his mind.

Poppy looked at him with a searching eye. "No use to worry about what you can't change. You'll doubt yourself to death if you think that way."

Rhys furrowed his brows. "I'd rather not speak of death."

"Ah, but death will come whether you speak of it or not." Poppy clicked and pulled up the reins. "Here is as good as any."

Rhys stewed in his own thoughts as they ate, hating that there wasn't more he could do. The meal was brief, and light, and left him wanting more.

The sun was going down now, slipping beneath the horizon without a hint of sunset on a cloudless sky. After so many days of winter, it was a relief to have so little cloud cover.

They started back again, with the horse going at little more than a brisk walk. Rhys couldn't get out and pull it himself, but he felt like if he did it wouldn't be much slower.

They made light conversation, talking about the weather and the river. Boats were a common topic for both of them, and Rhys remembered enough about them to keep the conversation flowing.

"You seem to know a lot about boats for a man who grew up on a farm."

"Near farms, not on one," Rhys said. "And I didn't say I stayed there, only that it was where I grew up. I felt a calling to the river and ended up at a port town of some importance."

"Jareth?"

"No. It doesn't matter. I learned enough to keep me in knowledge until now, apparently, but not so much to make me a master at it. Life circumstances changed, and that road led me here."

5

At the Edge

Evan considered himself in the pale reflection of the mirror. He touched his cheeks, sunken in more than he'd ever seen them.

His stomach growled at him, the constant nagging hunger that seemed to gnaw him from the inside ever present. Evan coughed. The cold hadn't eased up in weeks, and the wind howled around the Keep outside.

He pulled his coat tighter and left his room and the Keep. Along the way he greeted the few who were up and about. They bowed and gave him deference, but not like they used to.

Evan hurt inside each time it happened. *Who am I, that I deserve it though?* He was lucky to still be alive, considering everything that had happened.

The wind bit his nose and face as the door to the Keep almost flew out of his hands. Bracing himself, Evan walked out into the cold.

A foot and a half of snow coated the courtyard, in the places it hadn't drifted up against the walls and the buildings in the castle. The sun, obscured by the clouds, cast little light. They were coming off the shortest days, but not by much.

He should be walking among the garrison, inspecting his men before they took to the walls for duty. Instead, few men dotted the walls, too few, but there was too little food to expect them up there in this weather.

The snow squelched underfoot as he walked through the path that others had trodden down. He had a destination in mind and walked with determination.

The guards in the guardhouse tried to snap to attention when he walked in, and it pleased him, but their movements were weak and they barely rose from sitting positions, or leaned up from lying.

"Duke, good morning. I wasn't expecting you," Mathew said. He wasn't Evan's first choice, but Rhys had vouched for him, and it was enough to give him a chance.

Not that Evan had much of a choice.

"Please, as you were," Evan said. Looks of relief flooded faces, and they sat down with a groan, as if there was a big rush of air in the building. It was surprisingly warm inside, except near the door, and Evan moved into the room to escape the cold.

How he wished for a fire again. "I've come to see how everyone is." Evan walked along the rows of bunks. Faces stared at him, exhausted and gaunt. Arms were thin, and so were legs. Mathew followed him nervously. "Relax guardsman, I'm not here to throw you out."

"I know that, Your Highness." Mathew glanced at his fellow guardsman and the workers that were slated for sentry duty. They were a pitiful lot. "May we speak in private?"

Evan completed his lap, surprised at how winded he was from his short excursion in the snow. He dreaded going outside, but there was nowhere more private at the time.

"They look tired," Evan noted.

"We're sleeping all the time. The rations are too low, we need more food." Mathew spoke with boldness, his clothes hanging off his body. "Some of the men are grumbling. They don't think Rhys survived the attack, they say he was killed by an arrow."

Evan was swept back for a moment, to the moment he saw Rhys and his boat slip out of his sight. The man looked alive but bent down to avoid the very fate Mathew mentioned. "Have faith. The trip downriver was a few days, and a week or more to get to the capital. Rhys will do his duty and bring us help." Evan spoke with more conviction than he felt, another doubt that seemed to gnaw at him. *Should I have gone myself?*

He imagined himself riding into Whitehall, astride his steed. He would have dismounted and swept into the throne room, to the surprise of all those in attendance, and demanded an immediate audience with the King.

The vision dissolved and vanished. That was not to be, it was never to be.

"It's just..."

"Go on," Evan urged.

"They should have been here by now, if they were coming." the capital was a few weeks away by foot, but he was right. Had they moved immediately they would have been here.

Weeks ago.

"Have faith," Evan said, repeating words he had heard his father say during difficult times. "We will see the end of this." *True words, however they turn out.*

"You're right, Your Highness." Mathew seemed mollified, if for the moment. Would this conversation spread?

"Send word if you need any help." What he meant went unspoken, of course. They needed help, lots of it. Whether it would come or not, Evan could only guess. "I will be up on the wall for the next few minutes."

Mathew acknowledged and saluted him, then went back inside.

Evan turned back to the wall. The steps were mostly free of ice, but there were some trickier parts that required extra attention. He had been doing rounds of the battlements ever since Rhys had left, and it seemed to be helping.

He was getting to know them men, at least. Their names, for starters, something he never would have thought about a few months ago, but something his father had urged him to do.

"Get to know your men and they will fight harder for you. Show that you care." Words spoken long ago, in what seemed like a different life.

Time seemed to rush by and creep slowly all at once. One minute he was thinking how slow the day was going and then the next minute a week had passed.

Not having enough food had contributed. His training sessions had shortened, then stopped. Now he spent most of his time reading through the library of books, even the boring ones, and walking through the castle.

He did the same today, stopping at each sentry to see how he was doing and if he had seen anything of note. Each man, and there were about five in all, said no to the latter and put up a good show about the former, but they all shivered and didn't have enough clothes for how cold it was.

They shared the coats. Evan had found that out quite by accident one day. He wished they didn't have to, and had demanded his servants search the store rooms for extra clothes, but there was none to be had. Most of them were lost in the initial attack, leaving little for the others to wear.

He should have thought about that when he came up here. He should have planned better, made them bring everything inside the walls.

Yand had urged him to do it, and he let the Overseer's worry about moving everything slowing down the construction overrule the good advice. He was hoping Rhys would make up for it now, but that nagging worry that he was already dead filled him with dread.

Evan pulled his cloak closer, painfully aware of how much more it protected him than the other men on the wall. He gazed out toward the smoke of the Belmarch camp. They were warming themselves around the fire, laughing and talking as if they were having a feast and not conducting a siege. Their voices drifted up to him over the cold, snowy plain that separated them.

The ruins of the village were hidden by the white blanket that covered everything. They still sent sentries to the woods every day. The Belmarch weren't letting their guard down at all.

But Evan felt like theirs was slipping. While he was up on the wall another batch of men came out of the guardhouse and up the stairs, taking the watch from the freezing men and transferring bows, arrows, and coats.

Another thing to worry about, the supply of arrows and bowstrings. Evan chewed his lip as he watched them carelessly transfer from frozen fingers to frozen fingers. One slip and the strings would be lost in the snow and ruined.

He couldn't do anything about it. *What would I do, yell at them?* They fumbled, exhausted from lack of food, but none were lost in the exchange. It was a small miracle.

Once more he looked to the south, straining his eyes on the horizon, hoping and praying he would see an army marching through the forest on their way to rescue them.

For a second, he could almost hear the tramp of feet, hear the cadence being called out and repeated.

But it was all in his mind. There were no troops. There might not be anyone coming.

Are they waiting for spring? The snow would pose a challenge to any force big enough to bring them what they needed. Food, supplies, clothing, arms, Evan had no doubt Rhys would have them bring what they needed.

If Rhys even made it. Evan blinked as the sun came out from behind the clouds, bringing a hint of blessed warmth but shining bright in his eyes. Evan couldn't stand being up on the wall and walked down the icy steps and back to the Keep.

No longer a prisoner in his own quarters, Evan didn't feel like he had free rein of the castle.

He didn't want to go back, but the wind was too harsh and the cold too biting to do anything but seek shelter, so Evan slunk back to the Keep and slipped inside.

It wasn't warm or cozy, but inside he was able to get out of the wind. It helped. Evan rubbed some life back into his limbs and went back through the corridor to the great room, pausing to look around.

Over in the corner someone coughed. Evan frowned at it, and how ill it sounded. He hoped it wouldn't spread like the plagues he was reading about.

When his eyes adjusted, they were met with a sad sight. The mattresses, or what served as the mattresses, were pushed together in a big heap. Bodies piled up against each other to conserve warmth, and the coughs ran through the pile.

Forms shifted, eyes peered up at him. Faces, gaunt with hunger, seared into his mind. Some of them were children.

They had lost a little boy last week. Evan had watched them carry the body out into the cold to be set to freeze. The ground was too hard to dig into even if they had the strength. It joined the growing pile set aside for warmer weather to deal with.

How much longer will they last? Evan looked away, unable to bear it, knowing that he bore the brunt of the responsibility. He should have anticipated this better and pushed for a stronger garrison when he had the chance.

Now all he could do was sit and wait, hope that Rhys had made it.

He returned to his study, and stood beneath the large crest above his desk. It wasn't the best he had seen, there were craftsmen in the capital that would make a wooden bird seem real, but it was honest and well made with an even hand.

Unlike himself, it represented the best of his line. The Tree unbroken by winter and wind, an ever present landmark on the horizon. He recalled how it swayed and moved in the summer breezes, and towered over all other trees in winter, thick and fat in comparison to the twigs around it.

He took out the Histories and grabbed a blanket, wrapping it around himself as he sunk into the chair.

It creaked and protested, but not because of his weight. Something about the air seemed to suck the strength out of everything, living and unliving, in the castle.

He tried to read, but his mind wandered, distracted. Evan got up and walked around, pacing his room to get his blood flowing, until at last dinner was brought in.

Barger had brought it, and after a pleasant greeting stood waiting for Evan to dismiss him.

For some reason he couldn't. Evan caught sight of Barger's wrists in his sleeves. They were so thin and bony he mistook them for twigs.

"Is everything all right, Your Highness?"

Evan stared at the wrists, then back to his plate. It was the usual, mush heaped up in a little pile, but something kept nagging at him.

He felt his own wrists, poked at them with a bony finger. He had never been plump himself, but he still had muscle to spare.

All at once he made the connection, and it angered him. Evan pushed away his plate and turned back to his servant.

His eyes burned with passion, his sadness consumed. "You have been giving me more than the ration, haven't you?"

6

THE SECRET

Barger stood, eyes wide, before an angry Duke of Hornblood.

"Yes, Your Highness." He bowed his head, answering Evan at last. He didn't want to , Evan could see it in his eyes.

"Who gave this order?" Evan stood, almost knocking back his chair. The little one had died of hunger, of that he was sure, and here he was eating more than his share.

"The Overseer told us to. He said you needed your strength for what was to come."

He had a fair point. If Evan wasted away, who would be left to lead them? Thinking about it sent a sharp stab of shame.

After all he had done, he deserved no special treatment. As he turned it over in his mind, he wondered if he didn't deserve less for all his inaction.

"Rhys," he growled, pacing the room. "I should have known." A thought came to him. Evan spun on his heel. "What else have you been hiding from me?"

"I hid nothing, Your Highness," Barger said, his tone conciliatory. "The Overseer never told us to lie either."

"But you did."

"No, Your Highness."

Evan wanted to shout at him, he wanted to hit him, he wanted to do something to the pitiful wretch, but the more his passion flowed the more he knew he couldn't. This wasn't Barger's fault. It wasn't even Rhys' fault.

It was his own.

The food seemed like a curse was on it. *How am I supposed to eat it now?* He wished he had never seen it, never thought about it.

But that wasn't right either. The stores were getting so low they were down to the moldy and rotten dregs of the harvests. They had weeks, at most, left, perhaps even less.

Or that was what he was told.

Fear crept up his spine. A deep dread crept into his soul, and he wondered if the inventories he had been given were right.

"Take it back, give it to the most needful." Barger started to protest but Evan cut him off. He picked up his cloak and fastened it back on. "I'm going to the cellars and I don't want you or anyone else to stop me."

Evan marched out of the door and down the hall, but then his steps faltered. He hadn't been down to the cellars since he arrived. He didn't know where they were. *Are they behind the great hall in the kitchen?*

Chewing his lip, Evan slowed his pace to a crawl. He had never taken the time to explore the castle before, not beyond the easy and obvious places. The kitchens, for instance, he had never been to.

He could ask, or he could find his own way. Evan thought of the looks he would get asking for directions for the food, so he made up his mind to find it by himself.

The obvious place to start were the stair towers, and so he went to the one nearest to his room and study, cracking open the door and heading down instead of up. It only went down one level before it ended, spitting him out into a dark, dank hall that was surprisingly warm through a small doorway.

His feet thudded on the rough stone floor, echoing in the empty hall. The walls were tight and there was barely enough room for him to move. It was hard to see and he let his eyes adjust to the light.

Evan wrinkled his nose. The smell down here was awful, a mixture of sewage, rot, and mold that he could barely stand. He covered his nose and moved forward, tracing one hand along the wall to keep from running into the wall.

His hand went over rough stone until it hit wood. Fumbling around, he finally found a metal door handle and pushed.

He realized why they hadn't been bringing him reports now. It was almost impossible to see anything but a big black shadow. It could have been a small room, a huge room, or anything in between for all he could tell.

I have to check. Evan held his breath and went in. He stumbled around in the dark, hoping his eyes would adjust, but the best he could see were strange shapes and the outline of the door he came in in gray.

"What am I doing here?" Evan stopped stumbling around the room and slipped to a sitting position. He was in an empty cellar in the unfinished castle his father had tasked him to complete, and all his subjects were starving to death.

He couldn't have messed it up any worse if he tried. All those years, all those lessons, all the harsh words, they were all for nothing. He banged his head against the wall, feeling the sharp lance of pain as it struck. *At least I feel something.*

His stomach growled at him, demanding more. Evan clutched at it with two hands. How many children felt the same, or worse, because he hadn't thought of asking a simple question? Or maybe he knew the whole time, deep down, and didn't care.

That would have been the old him, the Duke of Hornblood known for his carousing and lack of morals. That Duke wouldn't have cared, not a single bit.

But he did. He felt shame, and sadness, that he hadn't seen earlier, hadn't asked earlier. It hurt. *Is this something I'm supposed to always feel?*

It was a burden, like a weight that had settled over his shoulders. It was crushing.

He wasn't sure how long he was down there, but Evan didn't really care. He went over his life, where he had gone wrong and what he could have done differently and wanted to.

Scenes of his youth replayed in his head. Nights he was ashamed of, that made him cringe inside even to this day. Guilt, shame, sadness, it all poured through him, infused into him.

He licked his lips, tasting the remnants of his morning meal, and it made him even more ashamed. The others hadn't had as much as he did. All those years he had wondered what it would be like to a commoner, and now, in this dark cell of a dungeon beneath a castle that was to be his, he felt it.

Hungry, alone, and guilt ridden, Evan mourned for a life that could have been.

He was roused only by the sound of the alarm bell, distant and distorted as it echoed through the halls and the stairs until it finally reached him. A stab of panic ran through him, and he jumped to his feet, tripping and tumbling in the darkness until he finally found the door.

We don't have the strength to resist them. Rough stone guided him left, then he saw the light from the stairs and rushed up it and back into his room.

His armor was ready, as it always was these days, and he rushed to put it on. The others would be manning the walls already, but it could be too late already.

Fatigue sapped him of his strength. The armor felt heavier than it really was, but there was nothing he could do about it now. After he strapped on his sword and took up his helmet, Evan ran to the door and out into the hallway.

There were still people asleep or huddled in the great hall as he passed it, but he paid no attention to them. The cold draft greeted him at the entrance door, and it was just as bad as he pushed them open into the dazzling light of the day.

When his eyes adjusted, he rushed over to the wall. He was right, it was lined with men. They looked tired, leaning on spears and against the walls, but all had their eyes trained on the enemy encampment to the south.

And they were all grouped on the southern walls.

Is it a feint? A surprise massing? Dread came up and filled his stomach as he took the stairs two at a time. It was still winter, and the Black River looked impassable to him, but there was always the chance the Belmarch would muster their forces and cross with an army that could crush them beneath their boots.

And it seemed that day had come.

"What's going on?" he asked as he got to the top, almost out of breath from the short journey. Mathew was standing near the gatehouse and was the only one to look back. Another pointed to the south.

Evan followed his hand. A lump formed in his throat, and his eyes burned.

He expected the sound of fighting, the twang of arrows, the clash of steel, but it had been too quiet. He realized that now and knew the reason.

The enemy camp had been deserted.

He blinked again, breath held, trying to fathom it. *The Belmarch had left.*

But that wasn't all, someone had taken their pace. Ranks of soldiers marched through the ruins of the makeshift village. Fifty, sixty, more. The sound of their boots reached them now.

"We're saved," someone said. The spell was broken, and reality acknowledged. The Tree of Everlong was held high on banners over the forces, and behind it looked to be wagons.

"Open the gate," Evan ordered, snapping out of his dream-like state that had come over him at the sight of it. "Everyone get to the gate."

He wasn't sure how they were going to open it, but he thought they might find a way. Cheers went up along the wall, men waving and shouting.

Then Evan realized it might be a trick. Men were already pouring down the wall though, eager to welcome the incoming forces. "Hold, don't open the gate," he yelled, going back to the edge of the wall. "Hold I said. Wait until we confirm."

That put a damper on the celebration. People were streaming out of the Keep, eager to see what the commotion was. Evan returned to the edge of the wall, casting a more dubious eye on the situation.

He cursed himself, not thinking of it sooner. It would have been like the Belmarch, devious and evil, to do something of the sort. He shook his head.

They had come so close to lowering their guard, letting them in without even checking. "Where are the sentries on the east and west walls?" Evan asked, turning back to Mathew.

"I-I don't know."

"Send men to them now, check to make sure we aren't being lured into a surprise attack." Evan caught himself, realizing that he wouldn't have even thought of this a few months ago, but he had read every book in the library now.

And more than one was about military tactics. Tactics such as fooling your enemies, posing as friendly forces to carry out sneak attacks.

But the more he looked upon the forces approaching the less he thought it was the case. He doubted himself, but the crest of the Hornbloods emblazoned on their banners were accurate, down to the branches on the tree.

"Sentries have been stationed on the east and west walls, Your Highness." Mathew had returned and was at his elbow now.

"Where is Freeman?" Evan asked.

"I haven't seen him."

"Get him up here." Mathew nodded and was off. Evan needed someone else with him who knew of this kind of thing. "Ready your bows, keep on the alert."

Bows were strung, and arrows readied, but the closer the soldiers got the more Evan thought that it really was them. They marched in ordered lines, each carrying a large pack on his back and enough armor to keep his vital organs covered but not too much to weigh him down.

He scanned the faces, but Evan didn't recognize anyone in the front ranks. They were looking up at the walls, and saw doubtful eyes looking back at them.

A man shouted an order, calling a halt. The group of soldiers stopped at once, in time, and stood. A tickle of some familiarity pulled at Evan, and he hoped beyond hope.

Was it him?

"Here, Your Highness." Sam Freeman was at his side now. "You wanted me?"

A quick glance caught Evan by surprise. Sam looked horrible, withered and pale. He quickly recomposed himself. "What do you think?"

A figure stepped out from the side of the group of the soldiers, head shrouded in a helmet. "They're well-armed," Sam said. "Over a hundred, I'd estimate." The figure approached the wall, tramping through the snow.

Evan kept a close eye on him. "Hold your arrows. He wants to talk." Bows lowered, arrows un-nocked. The figure stopped on the road below the gate.

"Since when was the Duke of Hornblood and his Captain so cautious?" The man yelled up to the wall. Evan let out a sigh of relief, hope and joy flowing through him now.

The man unfastened his helmet and took it off. Evan laughed at the confirmation, recognizing him immediately, then called down to him, "What a relief to see you, you old hound!"

7

A Welcome Caravan

"You recognized me, I'm impressed." A grizzled face looked up at them, the hint of a smile playing at the corner of his mouth.

Evan laughed. "You know I'd recognize that voice, and who could forget a face like that?" A scar ran down the center of the man's face, not quite perfectly vertical, a souvenir from a dead general. "Open the gate," he called back.

"Glad you finally decided to show me some hospitality," the man said.

"Your Highness?" Sam asked.

"This is Captain Silverthorn, one of my father's oldest captains," Evan said. Sam nodded. Movement near the village caught his attention.

Wagons. And more than a few, there had to be a train of them. "Ah, I see you spotted the reason it took us so long to get here," Silverthorn said, his booming voice echoing against the walls of the castle.

Hope upon hope swelled within him. Evan smiled, and the warm sun on his face more than made up for the cool breeze that cut through his clothes and nearly into the core of him. The tip of his nose was cold and had lost all feeling, but he knew the men around him were far worse off.

"Bless you Silverthorn, and the one who sent you," Evan said.

"Your father gives his regards," Silverthorn said, and Evan wiped the corners of his eyes. Giddiness ran along the men, and conversations broke out.

The gate took more effort to open than Evan originally thought. The braces were easy enough to move, but the remains of the battering ram had to be pulled out and it had bent the portcullis terribly.

When they had opened the inner doors, and not without a fight and the sweat of many men, they were left with a gate that wouldn't raise more than a few feet before it was stuck at the top.

"May I suggest a solution?" Bill asked as Evan and Sam stood looking at the conundrum.

"Please," Evan said.

"Force bent it, perhaps force can bend it back?" A few of the thick, iron bars were almost broken, and one had snapped clean through and through.

"Dale," Sam said, then turned to a few men waiting. "Go get him and his hammers."

A few moments later the blacksmith had appeared. They had lowered the portcullis back into place, and the newly arrived soldiers were milling about.

A quick explanation of the situation was in order, and after that Dale examined the gate.

"I built it, I can put it back aright." He scratched his beard. "It won't be easy though. Give me a few minutes and I'll figure it out. Issac, give me the big hammer."

While he thought and prepared, Evan met Silverthorn off to one side, clasping hands through the portcullis.

"It's good to see you. It's good to see all of you." Evan was grinning from ear to ear. "Please tell me you brought food."

"More than enough to keep you fed until next year." Silverthorn nodded back toward the wagons. "And once we get it inside, we can enjoy some of it."

"I'm afraid it can't wait, and we need something to cook it with. We've been without firewood for a few days now." Evan wasn't sure why he didn't tell him the truth, that they had been cutting off pieces of the castle keep to burn for fuel for weeks, but it slipped out so smoothly it surprised him.

Silverthorn gave the order and food was brought to the portcullis. While Dale hammered at the bars in strategic places, the sound deafening in the small tunnel, they passed food through the bars. Men were dispatched to the forests to bring back firewood and the crack of a tree falling sounded beautiful.

It took them longer to get the tree cut up and transported back. By the time they had, Dale had beaten the portcullis into enough shape to raise it enough for men to come through crouched over.

Everyone was out in the courtyard, eyes gleaming and bright, laughter and shouting in the air. The mood was ecstatic. After such a long, hard winter Evan couldn't blame them.

Food wasn't the only thing Silverthorn had brought. Clothes, coats, and shoes were passed out. Thin hands clutched at them, pulled them under the gate, and wrapped them around thin frames.

Silverthorn watched them, a curious expression on his face.

"What is it?" Evan asked, after they were far enough from the others.

"They look too weak to have made it."

Evan felt a pang remembering those who didn't. Including the young boy, there were at least twenty in all. "We all made it, somehow." He stared off into the distance, until Silverthorn touched his elbow.

"Sorry, I lost myself."

The old captain scrutinized him with a searching look. "You've changed, my boy. No longer a boy, I see."

"No. No longer a boy." For all the desires he had of growing up, now that it had happened…

"Your father will hear the report. He will be pleased to hear that you all did so well."

Evan snorted. "Father pleased? Doubtful."

"Ah, you give him too little credit. The Archduke is a generous man, and he watches more than you think."

"Generous with a sharp tongue and a hard word." Evan looked down and ground the back of his boot into the rock hard soil. It had started to melt at the top, warmed by the sun and the constant tramping of boots. The white snow had turned a dirty brown now. "I don't want to talk about him though. What news of the King and his fighting? The last we heard there were raiders in the east giving him trouble."

Silverthorn looked like he was going to say something else about his father, but then reconsidered it and arched an eyebrow. "He's raised the armies and called the banner-men to him. They marched last year and were caught at the river crossing in an ambush." Silverthorn shook his head. "It was all they could do to keep from drowning in the river."

A chill ran down his spine. "You bring us ill news in difficult times."

"I can't help that it happened. Your father is with the King now, and most of his forces."

"He...wasn't in the battle, was he?" They continued offloading supplies, a barrel of cheese and butter was opened and spread among them. The carts were emptied now, barrels rolled under the opening and a long line of supplies waiting to get by. The first of the men who had gone into the forest were coming back across the plains, dragging corpses of trees to be cut up and burned.

"He was, and survived. Kept the left flank from collapsing and kept the retreat orderly. They set up on the bank in a defensive position, picketing as far as they could against surprise attacks." Silverthorn shook his head. "What a time for the Belmarch to regroup and come back."

"This was an advance party," Evan said. He licked his lips and eyed the cheese. The defenders were gorging themselves on it. Silverthorn motioned and one of his men brought some over. Evan took it and thanked him. "Who knows what they mean to do."

The first bite flooded his mouth with flavor, soaking in saliva and going down like butter. Evan devoured it as they looked on.

"Careful not to eat too much too fast. In your condition it will upset the stomach." Silverthorn motioned over to his sergeant. "Slow them down, will you? Order them."

The soldiers sprang into action, restoring order among the crowd that had gathered and was pressing in, hands reaching for food. It took a few minutes before order was restored. The soldiers got the starving defenders into a line and passed out food.

It was the smell that had brought them, and not just of the cheese and butter. There was meat, raw and salted, and biscuits and hard tack, and raw ingredients from the southern lands of Chathem. Silverthorn confided in him that there were even raisins, a present his mother had slipped in.

His mother thinking of him once again. They had been his favorite as a child, a delicacy that others couldn't afford.

And a reminder of what he had that others didn't. His thoughts must have shown through to his face, because Silverthorn dropped his voice and spoke in his ear.

"What bothers you?"

Evan realized the corners of his mouth had pulled down into a frown. He still had a block of cheese in his hand half eaten the rest of it a solid form in his stomach.

"How is my mother?" he asked, words stilted and too formal.

"The Archduchess is well, although she has been fraught with worry these past few months. After we lost contact with you..." Silverthorn shrugged. "You can thank her for convincing your father to send us, through correspondence of course. With the Archduke away she's had to bear the burden-" he cut off.

"That should have fallen to me." Evan held the cheese in his hand. He knew if he took another bite it would taste like ash.

"That's not what I meant," Silverthorn said, almost seeming flustered. His iron face had a tinge to it.

"I haven't been a good son, and I've been an even poorer duke." Evan held up a hand to stop Silverthorn from protesting. "I know what I was like, but now I have something else to live for, a purpose that I have been avoiding all my life. It falls to me to lead these people, and I intend to follow through with it."

Silverthorn said nothing, but watched him with pressed lips. Men were cutting up the timber now, hacking off branches and stripping away the sticks. The young children were picking them up by the bundle-full, laughing and smiling and taking them up to the Keep to be fed into the fire.

"You have grown more than I ever expected," he said at last. The smell of fresh cut wood drifted with the cool breeze, blessedly soft compared to the harsh winds they'd had. "Is this Yand's doing?"

"In part. Captain Yand died a few months ago, killed in an attack we were able to repulse."

"I'm sorry to hear that. He was a good man and a good friend."

Evan looked to the north. "Yes, he was."

"You two were close. You have my condolences."

"Thank you. Another thing I'd rather not talk about." Silverthorn nodded.

"My men can take care of the rest of the supplies. Shall we go in and discuss other matters?"

Evan nodded. "How rude of me not to invite you. Please, come in and join me in my study." He was feeling better, if not a little lightheaded, and finished the rest of the cheese as they walked across the courtyard.

Silverthorn filled him in on the trip, how many men he had brought, and the plans to bring up more workers in the springtime to bolster the ranks.

A fire was crackling in the fireplace when they entered his study, and Barger was feeding it logs. He rose and bowed to the Duke, then continued his task.

"You were saying?" Evan asked.

Silverthorn looked at the servant pointedly.

"Tell me what you can, it's been a while since we've had some warmth in this room and I don't intend to stop him." Evan stamped the snow off his feet and took his seat, offering his other to the old captain. "Besides, he isn't too bad once you get to know him."

Silverthorn's eyes widened, and he stared at him. Seeing him in such shock, after knowing how much it had taken to do it, gave Evan some amount of pleasure.

"May I offer you some wine?" Evan asked. Silverthorn nodded, and Barger got up and poured a glass, handing it over, then went back to the fire which was by now crackling merrily along and finally filling the room full of heat, and a good bit of smoke along with it.

Silverthorn took and drank. The smoke stung Evan's eyes, but it felt so good to be warm he didn't care. He sunk into his chair and sighed, but kept his coat on.

"Are you not going to have wine as well?"

Evan opened one eye. "Not anymore."

The corner of Silverthorn's mouth twitched, but his hand went to the sword at his side. "What have you done with Duke Hornblood?"

8

PASSING OF A FRIEND

Martha was hard at work in the kitchens, which were alive and lively for once. It had been so long since the fire was crackling and roaring in the fireplace that it brought a wave of emotion in Sam that threatened to overwhelm him.

She bustled around the kitchen, giving direction and laying a hand where needed. The chatter of the women was muted, damped by sheer hunger and exhaustion, but still there, nonetheless.

And the smells, oh the smells! Sam bathed in it, luxuriated it in, drank it all in. The smell of meat cooking, and smoke. Bread, long forgotten, now tickled his nose with its wonderful fluffy smell.

"Sam Freeman," Martha said, stopping in front of him with her hands on her hips. "If you keep standing there getting in the way with that loopy look on your face, I'll remove you myself."

Sam almost blushed. "Just here to help. What do you need?"

She arched an eyebrow, but then pointed over to a pot. "You can help by filling that up for me."

Others crowded at the door, enticed by the smells of food. They were going to have a real feast tonight. Sam took the cold pot by the handles and lugged it out to the well.

The snow didn't feel as bad with shoes on his feet that kept out the worst of the cold, and the new coat he got kept him mostly warm.

They had extras, the Hornblood supply train was expecting over a hundred defenders and twice as many family members, but the winter had taken its toll and starvation had claimed its victims.

Three bodies were hauled from the mass in the great hall once they were emptied out. Ned had been one of them.

Sam had kept that thought as far away from himself as he could, but his path took him by the bodies, and he couldn't help but look at him.

Cold and blue, devoid of the charm and life that had once filled him, Ned lay with the others in the snow. The other two were on top, not covered in snow like the rest that had died earlier.

There were too many of them. His heart wrenched, and he kept going with his full pot of water, trying to concentrate on it enough not to spill it.

Instead of thinking of those cold, lifeless eyes, Sam looked to the sky where the smoke from the fires inside the Keep rose. Three distinct plumes, one from the kitchen, one in the great hall, and one in the Duke's quarters, were swept away in the brisk winter breeze.

Clouds were coming behind it, another threat of snowstorm that lingered in the pale, blue sky.

Let it come. They were prepared now, able to access the forest for fuel that would burn away the worst of the cold.

It was good to get into the Keep and out of the elements, and the door slamming shut was a welcome tune since he was on the other side of it.

Laughter and voices drifted from the great hall, and Sam glimpsed them as he walked by. The Hornblood troops were arrayed along the tables, separated from the workers who were too tired to help or were eating to regain their strength.

Silverthorn was in the place of honor. Sam had seen him in action and approved of the man. He led his troops with discipline and sharp eye, not letting them get away with anything and keeping order with a soft word.

It was, Sam felt, a relief beyond measure. Of a quality of Captain Yand, Captain Silverthorn would relieve him of his burden and prove a good leader and adviser to the Duke.

Then, he was gone, back into the raging kitchens, and sought out Martha.

"Put it there." She had somehow re-acquired a spoon. Sam looked closer at it. It looked like the same one she always had in the kitchen, and she wielded it like a sword, smacking hands and fingers that tried to sneak and disrupt.

Careful not to spill, Sam put it on the hook by the fire. Martha swung it over, near enough to be licked by the three foot high flames that burned like beacons. "Now off with you," she said, shooing him away like a fly.

Did I detect a hint of a smile? An unruly lock of hair covered her eye. He fought the urge to push it away and listened to her direction.

The woman was confusing, and set his heart a-flutter. He was too old to be feeling this way, too far past his prime to prance and romp like a young stallion.

And yet, he held his head high as he walked out, aware of the glances and giggles of the other girls as he left.

Sam wasn't sure what to do now. He could wait for the cooked food or eat some of the dry rations they had out. He wasn't sure how long it would take to be ready, and he had filled up enough to beat back most of the painful hunger in his belly already.

A hint of guilt pulled at him, and he knew where he had to go.

Adjusting his coat, he marched past the great hall and back out into the cold of the courtyard.

A blast of cold air greeted him, and he turned back to the dead, stopping in front of Ned's rigid body.

Sam felt numb. He hadn't believed that Ned was dead, not really. Even now he thought those eyes would open under the bushy brows and give him a wink.

But that was not to be, and he knew it. Sam knelt down next to his friend. He was at a loss, unable to do anything and choked up.

Should I say something?

He reached out and touched Ned's hand. It was ice cold and felt like stone. He shrank back from it, unable to keep from shivering.

Would this be his fate too? Would he lay cold and dead?

The Keep was even less finished than it had been before the siege started, parts of it demolished to burn for the cook fires. From the day he had arrived it had been in a perpetual state of incompletion.

Will I leave it unfinished?

The thought of it scared him the most. Just another thing destroyed in his life, or left unfinished.

He hadn't promised he would finish it.

He slipped into memories. Meeting Ned for the first time, times of laughter, times of sorrow. How the man had imparted his wisdom.

It was all such a waste. A good man lay dead before him, his entire life gone in an instant, all so that someone else could steal, and take, and plunder something that didn't belong to them.

"Take care of them." He remembered the words on the wall, the promise that Ned made him make.

How he wished that he could go back and take those words back. They were a curse, spoken by his own mouth.

He sat and longed for the days of sweat and heat, for the time of building and creations and not destruction and death.

He wished to go back, to keep on working, shaving after shaving, plank after plank.

But it was not meant to be. He realized that he mourned for that dead time almost as much as Ned, and it brought great shame upon him.

Sam hung his head. Ned lay cold and lifeless before him, and he couldn't take it anymore. There was no time to bury him, no way to break the earth as hard as rock, just like all the others.

"Perhaps it's a time to build then," Sam said. He released Ned, let him go off into the afterlife, and rose. Another grave, another death in a long line of them.

A loud cheer from inside the Keep distracted him. *They must have served the food.*

His mouth was watering, and the smell of food mingled with the smoke from the Keep. Sam turned, gave one last look at his dear friend, and went inside.

The feast was in full swing, and a great cloud of humidity rolled out of the doors as he entered. Sam breathed deep and licked his lips. His stomach grumbled watching the food platters run round the room passed from hand to hand.

There were heaps of it, more than he had seen being cooked, and the most that the hall had ever seen.

But it was Martha who captured his attention.

She directed the food, standing over the doors to the kitchen with her spoon as a scepter and a cudgel, a trained eye on all that surrounded her.

She still looked tired, and starved, but some food had brought color to her cheeks again, a hearty rose red.

It gave him some measure of joy to see. He wanted to talk to her, to understand how she was feeling, but there were so many people around he didn't think he would get the chance.

She looked at him then, and their eyes met. A quick glance away, and her eyes were back on his. *Did they linger?*

"Sam, pull up a seat and join us," Bill said, coming up behind him and clapping him on the back. Sam's gaze was broken, and when he looked back Martha had moved on.

He was torn for a second, wanting to go back to the other carpenters and sit with them, but with Ned being going he was left with Kerien and Trent, who looked like they were having a good time, but something didn't sit right with him. Would they accept him now that there was no Ned to soothe over the wrinkles in their relationship?

So, Sam turned and went with Bill, who was holding a big mug of ale, a ruddy complexion in his cheeks. He looked so merry and happy though that the twinge of apprehension boiled away within Sam.

The masons made up the bulk of the seating, and Bill took his place at the head of the table, but ordered room made for Sam. He put Sam at his right hand, shifting Barry down a seat. Sam gave him a glance, remembering the beating he had helped enact, but Barry didn't seem to remember, or didn't look like he harbored any ill will.

Plates heaped with food were passed around, carried out of the kitchen like treasure chests. A large deer, set on a spit, carried by the Duke's own servants, came out as the crowning piece, tender and steaming and giving off waves of a delicious aroma.

Then, the Duke arrived, Captain Silverthorn at his right hand. The conversation died down and the laughter stilled as he stood just inside the doorway.

His eyes flashed around the room. Sam hadn't expected him to come out, that he would be locked away within his tower.

Screams echoed in the dank, dingy tunnel. Raltone frowned at a drip of water from the ceiling, taking care to step well around it. "When they die make sure you keep their heads for display. Put them in a prominent position, but well below the Salz men. I wouldn't want the wrong message sent to the men."

"Yes, mi'lord," the gaoler mumbled. His face was so round and misshapen Raltone was surprised he was able to talk, but the strange accent that came with it made it almost impossible to tell.

Still, he was a master at what he did, and talking wasn't the reason he kept him around.

Sable walked behind him in the small corridor, following him up the winding halls and steep staircases back into the castle proper.

"The army is ready, we can move as soon as you give the order," he said.

"I know that isn't the reason you're here." Raltone gestured to his right as they emerged back into the ground floor. A servant ran over to brush off his boots, taking care to get every hint of dirt and mud. "You have something to ask, I presume?"

"Let me lead the army." Sable looked pale, deflated even. He still hadn't recovered from his previous experience. Neither, as Raltone had found out, had the other men. Those that had survived, that is. "I'll sweep through Chathem like a driving wind and reclaim the glory of the Belmarch."

It was slightly chilly in the hall as they entered, and Raltone snapped. A servant appeared, wrapping him with a cloak. Raltone sniffed. "Stoke the fires."

The new throne was ready, and Raltone gazed at it, ignoring Sable and the other men who gathered around. Vultures, every one of them. They wanted him dead, would pick at his corpse the moment they could.

They would take his hard work and shatter it. He wouldn't allow it though.

"You will command," he said, turning back to Sable, well within hearing of the others. This would travel faster than the winter wind that howled outside, the blasted weather that kept him pinned here in his seat of power.

Sable smiled, knowing that he was trapped. Raltone had spoken in public, quite clearly.

But the trap had been laid, and Raltone took his seat, admiring the plush arms and the comfortable cushion of it. The back, however, was so straight it almost leaned forward, a constant reminder of how fragile his hold on power was.

"But," he said, holding up a finger. "It will be a joint command. You will command half the forces, and General Granb will command the other half."

The smile was wiped out in an instant, but it was replaced. Raltone detested the young man, unable to hide his own emotions. A fool, but a useful tool to keep Granb in check.

"We move as soon as the passes are open. Prepare your men well." Raltone waved his hand. "Dismissed."

Sable bowed, spun stiffly, and marched off.

"And Sable." The man stopped and turned. "Don't fail me." Sable walked off, a hint of fear in his step.

Raltone leaned back, bumping into the throne. Chathem would fall, after so many years of effort by his predecessor, it would fall to him.

9

FEAST OF THE LONG WINTER

"To the men who came bearing gifts and life." The Duke raised his glass high into the air, then drank to their health. The toast was repeated, then the sound of a great cheer echoed through the hall. Backs were slapped, men were embraced, and the Duke slipped through the crowd to take the place of honor at the head table.

Sam watched him nimbly avoid notice. He looked so young but had grown up so much in the past few weeks. *How old is he, I wonder?*

Bill turned and whispered in his ear. "Looks like the Duke is back in the good graces of his subjects."

Sam turned back to see a sly grin on his face. "What are you planning?"

"Not a thing." Bill's look turned into one of complete innocence. Sam knew there was more, but he didn't care, and he didn't want to be swept up in it.

Despite the food and drink, he wished to be outside, back among the forest. He imagined himself there for a moment, running hands across bark, selecting the best trees to be felled. The cold breath of the winter still on his neck.

And then he was swept away, pulled into the rejoicing and merriment of the night. The ale and wine flowed, and the food seemed endless.

Sam found himself sneaking glances over at Martha through the night. The warmth of the kitchens had touched her face, giving it a warm glow, and the food had banished the worst of the darkness that had overtaken her. She was still a long way from healthy, but she didn't look so close to death now.

One of the younger girls swept up to her and placed a sprig of holly in her hair. Martha blushed and tried to take it out, casting a furtive glance in his direction, but the girl put it back in and scolded her.

The interaction, and the funny feeling in his stomach, made him reach for his ale, taking a deep draught of it. He imagined taking it out of her hair, brushing it back behind her ear, and kissing her.

He knew he shouldn't think of that, and he squeezed his eyes shut, draining the entire mug. Another was in his hands seconds later. There was an underlying sense of fear, one of dread, that this was not everything it seemed to be. Silverthorn laughed and drank with the rest of them, more grim than others, but joyful nonetheless.

What would it be like to let him take control, to lead the training sessions with the tradesmen who weren't cut out to be soldiers? He imagined that now that there was a professional fighting force he would no longer be needed.

Then he glanced at his side. Bill was leading the conversation surrounding him, so intent upon himself he didn't notice Sam watching. Was this in Bill's best interest, now that there were others with more power in the castle?

It all made his head hurt, and then another glance at Martha made it all the worse. He didn't know what to think about her, but deep down he knew that she was off limits. It wouldn't be right to her dead husband, a good man taken by sickness and tragedy to swoop in and steal her from his memory.

Or was that even a possibility? Was that something he was just pretending to want, that he thought about to make himself feel better?

As far as he knew Martha didn't like him much, if at all, let alone love him.

Love.

Thinking the word made him squishy inside. It was too much to commit to, too dangerous of a concept. After all, wasn't he the one who had killed and murdered less than a few months ago? What kind of man like that deserved love, let alone the love of a kind and generous woman like Martha.

Someone bumped into him, spilling his drink all over the table. The group surrounding him roared with laughter.

Sam didn't find it funny, licking the liquid off his lips and trying to find something to wipe his dripping face off.

"Here, drink up," Bill said, pushing another mug of beer into his hand. Someone else threw him a small towel, and he used it to mop himself off.

"I shouldn't have anymore." It was going to his head, which was already lightheaded, but it did have a relaxing effect on his muscles.

"Come on, what will it hurt? This is a day to remember, let's make the night to match." Bill grinned at him, like a coyote over a rabbit.

"You're right. I should lighten my load a little." He took what looked like a long pull, but was only just a small amount out of the mug. Whoever had poured it had left little head on it, but it still got into his nose and tickled.

"Lighten your load, and loosen that belt." Bill slapped him on the stomach, almost making him spit out his ale. Sam glared at him, but he had moved on already, telling a bawdy tale to his drinking companion next to him.

It devolved into something that made his ears burn, and he wanted to curl up and leave, but instead he contented himself to turn to the mason next to him, Barry.

"Pass me the bread, will you?" Sam held out his hand, and he handed it over.

"What's got into your pants tonight?" Barry squinted with one eye. "Not grateful enough to the others around us? Seems to me there's plenty of reason to be happy."

There was something about the tone in the older man's voice that set him on edge, and put his teeth together in a clench. Sam still remembered the night in Bill's cabin and hadn't forgiven him for it.

Not that they had asked forgiveness anyway.

"I'll get my strength back and then feel grateful." Sam bit into the bread, warm and delightful. It had cooled some, but was almost fresh out of the ovens.

"You'll get more than strength back if you keep this up." Barry leaned in closer and leered at him. "She's been watching you all night. A little more ale might bring her to your bed for a rough and tumble."

Anger rose in him, at his bad breath, at his crude language, and what he could only assume was directed at Martha. Sam breathed through his nose, trying to contain himself, but Barry continued.

"What? Not interested? That's fine by me, give me a few minutes alone with her and I'll be the one enjoying myself." He laughed crudely. "Saggy tits and all."

Sam felt the thing locked away stir, but he couldn't help it.

It purred, slinked around his mind, and he felt his vision haze over. It wasn't just the alcohol, although that was catching up to him now too, it was more than that.

And then he saw Martha, hazarding a glance in her direction. She wasn't looking at him, caught in a conversation with the girl next to her, but she was chatting away.

All he had to do was walk away, or tell a quick joke to diffuse the situation. He thought of one, flashing through his mind, but out of rage and spite he discarded it.

This may be a night of celebration, but the man had gone too far.

Sam stood and turned to him. He didn't know what he was supposed to do, but he reached out and poured his ale over his head.

Barry fell back, sputtering and spitting curses at him, then banged his head on the ground. Others were up around him in an instant, surrounding him.

All Bill's men.

Sam threw down the mug, and the handle broke as it hit the stone floor with a clatter. The laughter in the room continued, but there was talking and whispering near him.

"I'll kill you for that," Barry said, wiping his face and rising.

Bill was in between them, before Sam could even take a step forward. He didn't say a thing, but fixed his eye on Barry.

"Get him out of here," Bill said. "What's gotten into you?" he shouted at the retreating man. "Treat Sam with the respect he's owed."

But Sam's rage had not died down, and a simple act such as that wasn't going to satisfy the thing inside him.

This is why I'll never create, why I'll never finish.

"Talk to me Sam." Bill was in his face, and Sam blinked. The room had gone quiet now, and everyone was staring at him.

Martha and the Duke included.

Sam licked his lips, tasting the remnants of the ale. *What was I thinking?*

With so many eyes on him, he was able to suppress the thing and drain the rage inside him, replacing it with a heavy dose of shame.

"Just a tumble, that's all," Sam mumbled, feigning drunkenness. "I must have had too much to drink."

"That's so." Bill turned to the crowd. "We've all had a little too much to drink tonight, haven't we? I'll drink to that!" He raised his own mug and downed it in a few seconds, then raised it high.

The masons cheered, shattering the tense air that had pervaded the room, and the cheers spread to the others. The ale kept flowing, and mugs were drained, but Sam didn't know what to do.

He sat back down, easing off his wobbly legs. All of his energy had deflated, leaving him feeling empty and lightheaded.

"Why did you do that to me?" Sam asked.

Bill turned his chair to Sam, sitting beside him. "Whatever do you mean?"

"You know. Don't play dumb with me now."

"I haven't done a thing, Sam. I'm sorry that you have lingering resentment to Barry." There was more than a hint of danger in Bill's eyes. "As for me, what's happened in the past between us is all water under the bridge as far as I'm concerned."

"Water under the bridge?" Sam echoed, then shook his head. It was clearing, and he was regaining his focus. Every fiber in his being wanted to look at Martha, but he resisted.

Instead, he looked up toward the head table. The Duke was watching him, and they locked eyes. What was going on behind them, Sam couldn't tell, but it wasn't joy or mirth.

It was altogether something different.

"I don't want to play these games," Sam said, rising again sharply. "You can if you want, but I refuse. Now, I still have a job to do and a castle to finish, which I intend to do, so if you don't want to help me then you keep out of my way."

His voice was raised, and he knew it, but he couldn't help it, the words seemed to flow from him in his exhausted and drained state. Sam had eaten all he really needed anyway, and he avoided the sudden stares and sharp eyes that watched him as he turned and walked away.

"No, let him go," Bill said as he walked away, probably to one of his henchmen.

With friends like that I'd rather take the Belmarch. He stomped out into the cold of the courtyard, looking up into the sky and wrapping his hands around himself. Stars twinkled in the clear sky, and the moon hung in a half round lower on the eastern horizon.

Sentries patrolled the wall, actually walking where before they had not enough strength to move, but every now and then one of them cast a look in the direction of the Keep. Sam didn't blame them. The sounds of joy and laughter drifted out of it.

As his body cooled his head cleared. The anger dissipated into the cold night air and the thing coiled deep inside him went back to sleep. He urged it there, calmed it where it had been riled up, and was grateful that he hadn't gone too far.

He was within a breath of stabbing the man with the knife that lay gleaming on the table beside his plate. He wondered if that wasn't the point of Bill inviting him to eat there.

Sam shivered. He knew he couldn't stay out much longer, but he didn't want to go back inside and face the others. *I couldn't control myself.*

Before he turned to go back in, he cast one last look up into the sky. One day he would be free of the shackles that bound him, that forced him into a life he hated.

One day he would be free to build and not tear down. To create and not destroy. "One day I will be free," he whispered.

10

OLD WOUNDS

Evan watched Sam leave the great hall with interest. He moved like a fighter, unable to mask it in the pure emotion that overtook him. The Duke glanced back at Bill, who seemed pleased with himself.

What game is he playing?

"Who is that man?" Silverthorn asked, keeping his voice low enough so that only Evan could hear it.

"The master carpenter, Sam Freeman." Evan took up his goblet, filled with pure water. The smell of wine and ale tempted him. He wanted to taste it, to drain the cups of it until it poured out oblivion into his soul.

But he had duties and obligations tonight and would for the rest of his life.

Conversation returned to the room, which had fallen in a hush. The newcomers made mention of the incident, the mason that had been humiliated now dusted off and been sent off to bed with by few of his companions.

"And what do you think of him, Silverthorn?" Evan asked, poking at the meat on his plate. "Given your... short amount of time that you have known of him."

"A dangerous man." Silverthorn looked at the door. "But he seems to garner respect among these men."

Evan smiled and recounted the stories that had been told to him. The beating back of the attacks, the slaying of the giant.

He left out the part about him crafting the crest above his desk. He wasn't sure why, other than it seemed a trivial matter.

"And what do you think of him, Your Highness?"

Evan considered the question and rested his head on his hand. *What do I think of him?*

He was conflicted. By what, Evan didn't know, but he had seen others in the same way, sometimes himself.

"There is more to him than meets the eye," he said at last.

"A bland and trite response. That is the Duke that I know." Silverthorn took a sip from his goblet, ignoring the scowl that Evan shot his way.

"You better still have the ear of my father, otherwise I'd have you punished for that."

"Your father pays me to tell him the truth, and I'm not about to stop for some snot nosed son of his who can't bear it." The last Evan knew as an intentional tweak, pushing him to do something he would regret.

"I regret to inform you that I've grown up past those immature ways," Evan said. "Now I find myself in charge of an entire castle's worth of defenders and their families. You won't get the rise out of me that you used to Silverthorn."

Silverthorn matched his gaze with one that was more steely and filled with danger. Evan was more than a little scared of the man and had been since he was younger. "Besides, it wouldn't be right to beat the old." Evan let the insult slip out smoothly.

It lodged deep, only the slightest narrowing of Silverthorn's eyes giving him away, but give him away it did.

Finally, after what seemed like an eternity locking eyes, a half-smile crept up the edge of his face. "You have grown up."

"Not as much as you think."

Silverthorn laughed then, a big, hearty laugh that drew Evan in and forced him to join in.

It felt good. He couldn't even remember the last time he had laughed so well or so long, and his insides started to ache because of it.

But, eventually, the laughter died down. Silverthorn clapped him on the shoulder and lifted his glass.

"I drink to you, Your Highness, and the man you have yet to become."

"And I drink to you, and the man you once were." Evan winked at him, and, exchanging grins, they both drank up from their cups.

The rest of the night passed quickly, the merriment and happiness unleashed from months of hardship all the more pronounced. Soon couples were retiring to nooks and crannies of the castle, openly displaying their intentions to those around.

Not everyone had a family though, and Evan could sense the divide that opened between those with families and those without. Jealous, alcohol induced glances were shot at the pairs as they tripped and wobbled through the doorway.

"Give them some time," Silverthorn said, when he noticed Evan watching. "The night is young, and the times are evil."

"They aren't the ones I'm worried about." Evan chewed on his lip, and clasped his empty cup tight. "Not that I'm not jealous of them, I could use the arm of a good woman around me right now, but I don't know…" He struggled to find the right words without sounding petty, or childish.

"You have no women of the night to satiate the needs of the men," Silverthorn said.

"You always had a way with words, always dancing around what you wanted to say."

Silverthorn shrugged. "For all the time you've spent running around chasing my shadow and training with me I thought you would appreciate the bluntness."

Blunt was exactly what the man was. "A few days ago I was trying to think of ways to keep them alive." Evan looked around at the dwindling numbers still in the great hall. They were almost all drunk lingerers, without the strength to pull themselves back to their own beds, or men bedding down for the night.

A pair came back, looking disheveled. "Now they have other needs that I didn't even consider." A thought struck Evan, one that he hadn't even considered before then.

"How does my father manage it?"

Silverthorn drained his cup. "He's had a lot of practice, and he has progeny to think of. How he does it?" He shrugged. "That lies far above my realm and pay. But I suspect his father was hard on him too, always preparing him for what was to come."

Old wounds were coming back to the surface, and they stung. Evan wanted to push them away, but at the same time this was the first time he had Silverthorn's full and undivided attention. Few men knew his father better.

"You speak as if my father cares about me," Evan said roughly. He took up his knife and stabbed half a loaf of bread, bringing it to his lips and tearing off a chunk.

"Your father is the Archduke. He must be above reproach, show no favoritism. Or that's what he always told me." Silverthorn turned his chair, facing Evan.

"Did you know that he asked me to teach you, long before Yand?"

"You? He couldn't do that, he would be lost without you leading the guard." Evan was aghast at the very suggestion of it.

"Your mother was against it. She said I was too rough and would break you. Like a ship against the rocks, she said. So, deferring to your mother's wishes, he appointed Yand." Silverthorn watched him with a stone face. The room was quiet now, just a few whispers and murmurs and snores from the side of the room where the beds had been shoved up against the wall to make room for tables.

"I think now that they both were wise. From Yand you learned a great deal more than you would have from me, and it will serve you well far into the future."

"I don't believe you." Evan shook his head. He set the bread back down. He didn't feel like eating anymore, his stomach finally satisfied for the first time in weeks. "You've been one of Father's favorites ever since I've known you."

"Or I've known you." Silverthorn dipped his head.

"So why would he waste your talents and your loyalties on me?"

He didn't say anything for a while. Silverthorn had always been cautious, decisive when he did act, but cautious. Father said that's what made him such a good guard.

"That is a question only you and he can answer." Silverthorn stood and stretched, his joints creaking as he did. "If you'll excuse me, Your Highness, the road was long and the travel cold for a man of my age. It is far past time I should have retired."

Evan returned his bow, and the man walked away back to his room. The fire had died down in the great hearth, but a young girl was at it now adding logs. Each one she tossed made embers dance and fly, and Evan stared into the red, flickering glow.

His mind was a mess of questions and confusion, things he had thought he knew now cast in doubt. For so many years his father had been hard on him, abused him, was cold to him. How could he possibly have wanted what was best for him?

And yet, here he was sending one of his most trusted men north during war with the eastern raiders. By all accounts Silverthorn should have been right by his father's side and should have been.

Evan shook his head. No, it must have been that the fighting had died down for the season, that the raiders had retreated east like they always did and that there was another explanation for this.

And he thought he knew what it was.

The Archduke didn't trust him. He was still the young boy who didn't know his way around anything, and he needed looking after.

Silverthorn was here as a minder, as a spy. He was here to report on how Evan was faring and what other mistakes he had made, like usual.

His hand tightened around his cup, and he glanced over at one filled with wine. It would be so easy to reach out and take it.

That's what my father would expect me to do. To take the easy way out, drown myself in alcohol once again. Evan gnashed his teeth, railed against the feeling of desire that welled up inside him like a river about to overflow its banks.

But still, he wanted it. It would make all his problems go away, for a moment at least. Or, for a night.

Who would he be in the morning? And what would he feel? He knew.

Evan couldn't take it anymore, and pushed away from the table and almost ran out the door into the hall. A few more steps brought him out of the Keep and into the courtyard.

He took a deep breath of the cold, night air. It burned his lungs coming in, but he felt it and rejoiced. It was something different, at least, than to fall prey to the temptation that waited inside.

Despite the cold, he decided to go up to the walls and see how the men were doing. He wished they could have joined in, but they had been fed before they left, or had been relieved of their watch to join in for a few minutes or so, coming and going with the crowds.

Now, they walked on the walls, finally showing some sort of life. Evan shivered, but took care on the cold steps. They were icy and dangerous, liable to send a man over the edge to his death.

"Good evening, Your Highness," the sentry closest to him said upon seeing him emerge from below. He tipped his head and held a fist to his brow, open to show it was empty.

Evan greeted him and returned the salute. His breath made gusts of fog. "Have you seen anything unusual?"

The sentry smiled a sloppy grin, which surprised Evan. "Nothing outside the walls, if that's what you mean. There have been quite a few... couples taking their leave though."

Evan couldn't help but feel a sense of squeamishness. Not that he cared much, but there was something about the night that made everything seem like it had been held back for too long.

The castle was like a kettle boiling, and had been for some time, but tonight the steam was coming out. *I wonder how mine will show?*

"If they aren't too loud, let them have their fun," he finally said in response. He was getting too cold to stay up here, and the night breeze was chilling him through his clothes.

It was a reminder of what they had gone through, and Evan stared up to the north, as a reminder of what was going to come.

Evan bid the man good night, making his excuses, and turned. Something caught his eye, however, and he stopped.

It was a flash, or so he thought, somewhere far into the distance. *Near the tree line.*

"What is it, Your Highness?" the sentry stood at his side.

He peered into the dark. *The river was too high, too rough to try and cross this time of year. It couldn't possibly be the Belmarch, could it?*

But at the pit of his stomach, a lump of dread was spreading.

11

AT THE WALLS OF IRONWOOD

The days passed quickly on the road, and Rhys felt his strength returning with every meal. He didn't feel the need to gorge himself with food now, like it would be gone when he turned his head, and the travels even started to feel pleasant.

The weather was nice, the sky clear and sunny with a crisp chill to the air. The snow was fresh from the storm that had come in before they had left, and made for good sledding.

"We're making good time," Rhys remarked as they set off from their lunch time stop.

Poppy made a sign and spit into the snow, then mumbled underneath his breath.

"What was that?"

"You bring ill fortune speaking in that way."

Rhys was shocked. "What? Just by commenting on how well our progress was?"

Once again Poppy made his sign and spit. "There it is again. Don't you know you don't ask for sun when it's raining and ask for rain when it's sunny?"

"Why not? Wouldn't that make the most sense? You won't want or need rain if its already raining."

"You inlanders, always wanting and hoping for things. You should be grateful for living in the present, in the now." He took out his pipe and lit it with a quick strike of his tinderbox, then gave his horse a gentle flick.

The sled jerked forward, then slipped into cutting a groove in the snow. Rhys reflected on the words, not happy about being called an inlander.

"You have a point, but I'm not appreciative of how you said it."

Poppy gave a small chuckle, which inflamed Rhys even more. He knit his brows and sunk into the seat. "How long do you think we have until we get there?"

"Depends on the weather. A few days, maybe more." Poppy shrugged. "Or it could take weeks."

"Weeks? Surely you can't mean that?"

"If we get caught in a blizzard..." He clicked the pipe between his teeth. It was hand carved, with a fish on the bowl, and he wrapped his dark hand around it.

He let the matter drop and Rhys contented himself to watching as the landscape changed on their journey.

The farms continued, for what seemed like forever, until the flat lands started to hump and heave into rolling hills.

The journey was harder now, with the horse having to pull them uphill, but the lightening of their load by eating and burning helped.

Rhys retreated into himself, content to let Poppy smoke his pipe and lead the horse on with careful attention to the reins but only a light touch.

They passed into lands that Rhys was familiar with, stopping for the night in a farmer's barn to keep warm from the biting cold.

Meals were simple, but filling, and after a quick breakfast they were off once more.

To pass the time he worked through the list of people he should visit first, and who would be less likely to help.

His recent fall from grace had hurt his standing in the court, but Rhys thought that Tabitha might be his best bet. She still owed him for getting her out of that tight spot.

He chuckled to himself. She should have been more careful, or taken less lovers. One or two were easy enough to hide from her clueless husband, but five was a bit much.

"What is it?" Poppy was staring at him, smoke drifting from his pipe.

"Nothing."

"Laughing by yourself when no joke is told might be considered something where I'm from. I don't know what it means to you."

The sun was splashing a dazzling display of colors on the low clouds. Rhys caught a whiff of pine beneath the pungent odor of manure and horse.

"Palace intrigues, and a long forgotten memory." *Had it been that long?* He wracked his brain, trying to pinpoint when it was. Not more than a few years ago.

Poppy grunted. "Sorry I asked."

"Not in your boathouse?"

"Not even remotely." The man looked straight ahead, pipe firmly clamped between his teeth.

But Rhys was tiring of the long silences, and his regains strength had renewed him more than he thought. He couldn't bear to take more miles in quiet.

"What would you do, if you were in my place?" Rhys asked. He scratched his chin, hanging loosely and filled with stubble. How he wished for a warm bowl of water and a sharp razor again.

"I don't envy your task, not one bit."

"That doesn't answer my question." Rhys looked closer at him, searching his face for a tell. "Anyone with eyes can see you're well thought of in your village, and I'm guessing it wasn't by accident."

Poppy glanced over at him. "Are you asking for my advice?"

"I am."

He sniffed, then blew a smoke ring that was split apart and blown away by the wind almost as soon as it was out of his mouth. "Things have changed in the court, from what I have heard. The King is far more worried about the eastern raiders than the northern ones."

"The Belmarch are far more dangerous than the eastern raiders."

"That may be, but it has been years since the Belmarch posed any real threat to us. The raiders, on the other hand, have invaded once a year for the last decade."

"And then they leave. Everyone knows that they aren't here to stay, only to pillage and return."

"But they haven't."

Rhys sat upright. The implications of that one little sentence ran through his mind like lightning. "What do you mean they haven't?"

Poppy shrugged. "They've been staying for the last few years, getting a foothold. And the King has been having a tough time getting rid of them. One of his most troublesome problems, I'd say. The southern lords have been clamoring and complaining non-stop since it started."

"And so that's why we've been neglected for so long."

"It's hard to listen to a boy when the wolf's at your doorstep."

It all seemed to make sense now, the ignored pleas for help, the dwindling resources sent their way. It seemed like only the Hornbloods had been sending supplies north for the last few months before the siege and now Rhys suspected that was the case.

So why hadn't his sources told him? It set a troubling spike deep in his heart, and shook him to the very foundation of his being.

Things were far more grim for Chathem than he originally suspected, and Poppy seemed to sense his discomfort.

"It isn't all bad. The King has raised his armies and marched east, expelling them for the season. He's stationed a large garrison on the border of the Golden River, and I suspect the raiders will have a harder time getting across this time."

"How many years has this been happening?" Rhys asked quietly, secretly counting the time.

Poppy didn't say at first. The sled scraped over the snow, the old mare pulling quietly along. "Three years."

Just about a year into the castle's construction. And a few after his fall from grace.

"We'll stop for lunch in a few hours." Poppy squinted against the sun, watching its height up above. Clouds were gathering in the east, but it was calm and clear where they were.

For now.

There was a burden in the air, a heaviness that went into his bones and troubled him. Some of it was the weather, the rest...

Rhys wasn't feeling well, not well at all. Whatever would come of his journey, he wasn't sure that he could help Castle Hornblood now.

And that hurt him the most.

The promise he had made, the look in their eyes as he splashed into the river and broke away, the cheer going up on the castle walls.

It might all be for nothing.

Rhys swallowed, choking back his feelings. He wanted someone to yell at, to scream at, and berate.

But there was only him, Poppy, and an old mare in the rolling hills of Chathem.

So, all he could do was hold it in and hope that there was a miracle waiting in Ironwood.

———◦———

Then, there it was. He saw it emerging from the hill as they crested it, a long way off but shining in the sun and the fresh snow brought the night before.

The great white walls of Whitehall glimmered, reflecting the sun from the snow like diamonds.

The road had been well traveled the last day of their journey, and the track trodden well. The road was straight now, leading to the Northern Gate set into the wide walls of Ironwood.

As they approached the guards on the wall were more visible, sentries set to watch for threats seemed so laughable this far into the center of Chathem, but Rhys knew how quickly those enemies could travel.

"Here we are," Poppy said. "I'll take you as far as Whitehall and no further."

"You don't have to do that, I can make my own way from here."

"Nonsense, I have business to attend to. I told you as much before we left."

Rhys murmured his thanks, grateful for not having to walk in the snow. The boots they had given him didn't fit quite well enough, and were too loose, but he wasn't going to complain in front of him.

Not after all their kindness.

In his heart was a big knot though, and a lump of dread resting in his belly. There were so many questions that he had to answer and had no good answer for them.

Whatever the case, he had to remember the defenders of the castle. They were relying on him to do his best.

But he wasn't sure it was going to be good enough.

The pit deep in his stomach wasn't going away. Rhys had hoped with the sighting it would, but it had only grown larger.

They joined a small caravan on their way to the gate, the road turned somewhat muddy. Poppy kept off the road and in the hard-packed snow and ice just off to the side.

The wind blew their direction, taking the smells of the city with it. Rhys wrinkled his nose at the smell of the filth layered into the smoke and baking bread. It sparked a familiar note though and brought up memories he wished had laid dormant.

They stopped in the line waiting at the gate. Traffic had slowed to a crawl as the guard questioned those entering the city.

"Why are they doing this?" Rhys asked. Poppy only shrugged. They seemed to be stopping every cart and traveler, uncharacteristically since the last time he had been in Ironwood.

Another troubling sign.

An old woman carrying a basket was next. The guards lifted the lid, peering inside. A few words were exchanged, and the woman passed into the city.

Men were watching from the battlements, spears in hand. Rhys noted the bows, strung and at the ready, and wondered what kind of fear had overtaken the city.

"Waste of time, wish they would hurry up," the man behind them said. He was carrying wood on his back, straining against the weight of it and crouched over. Rhys commiserated with him privately, then a thought struck him and he turned.

"Say, friend, it's been a while since I've been in the city. What's all the fuss about?"

The man looked at him with one lazy eye, the other staring off into the distance. "You haven't heard about the attack?"

A stab of concern struck him, but he kept it out of his voice. "Attack? No, not at all," Rhys said.

"Eastern raiders came up last harvest, went undetected through the border and all the way to the city." The old man sniffed, and the line moved forward as another was admitted into the city. "Scaled the walls in the middle of the night and made it to Whitehall. Almost killed the King, I hear, but he fought them off and killed them in his nightclothes."

"I didn't know." Rhys exchanged glances with Poppy. "No wonder they've increased the guard."

"Increased? The King is going to wage war on them when spring comes, take every fighting man he can, or so I hear."

"He's already called in the southern lords," a young woman said, breaking into the conversation. "Aunt Jamy said so last week when she was here."

"And the northern lords have pledged their troops too," her companion said, a much older middle aged woman. "He'll save us from them, make sure they can never do it again."

Rhys turned his attention back to the guards, they were next in line. "This doesn't look good," he whispered to Poppy.

"It doesn't look good for my sled either." He pointed to the road up ahead, a pile of mud instead of fresh snow. "I'm not sure I can get through."

Rhys looked up. The guards were staring at him, or behind him. He looked back, but he couldn't see anything of note.

A rough hand grabbed his shoulder and spun him around. An equally matched guardsman, with a chipped front tooth looked him up and down. He turned back and bellowed to the others "That's him, take him."

12

ALONE AGAIN

"You could stay longer." Evan watched Silverthorn packing, taking what little he had and returning it to his trunk. He had the biggest room besides Evan. It had belonged to Overseer Rhys when he was still here, but his rank had meant it was left open.

Now, Evan leaned against the door frame. A tweak in his memory made him stand up straight, the look of Yand from far ago and a simple rebuke of not standing up straight. *Even now he haunts me.*

"I must return. I have my orders and they are to go back as soon as everything is seen to here."

"But it isn't. You know that the Belmarch can return."

"They won't be here this winter, I can tell you that much. You couldn't move an army in snow like that, and it'll be worse north of the river."

Evan knew he had a good point, but he didn't want to be left on his own again. The man had just gotten here less than two weeks ago, and now he was set to leave.

Leaving him alone once again.

He had grown used to the conversations, of not having to hold himself back like he did among the others. It was... good to have someone closer to his own rank that he could talk with.

Of course, his father had ordered him back again.

"Levitus is a good man, and a good commander. He's a solid choice and will keep the men in line."

"He isn't a tactician, or a trainer like you. He doesn't know how to take the men and turn them into a fighting force." Evan chewed his lower lip. "And neither do I."

"I thought you trusted this man of yours, the carpenter." Silverthorn tucked the last of his clothes into the chest, then shut and locked it. He turned back to Evan to give him his full attention. The case smelled like horse leather and steel, things Evan had always associated with the guard. Now, he knew why.

"I had to. He was the only one with fighting experience. Father didn't send me his brightest and most experienced fighters, and the men the King supplied didn't know much either."

"It sounds like you're complaining, Your Highness." Silverthorn wore his iron mask, but the hint of disapproval was evident. *Still treating me like a child.*

"He's proven himself, but I don't think I can rely on him." Evan sighed and sat in the chair. Silverthorn motioned to the one across and Evan waved, giving him permission to sit.

"I can't tarry any longer."

"Even though the roads are snowed in and hard to travel?"

"Even so. More-so. I have to get back to your father. You're Duke Hornblood and bear the title and his blood. You will do fine here, and you will hold the castle."

"With what forces? A few dozen more men?" Evan shook his head.

"You survived a siege." Silverthorn shrugged. "I will speak to your father, give him a message."

"What good will that do? He has no time for me."

"He set you in this place, a place of honor and one of challenge."

"Honor?" The word rang cold against the rough stone walls. A fire crackled in the fireplace, keeping back the worst of the cold, but the walls were leaky and drafty. "What honor is it to stand here in the north, in an unfinished castle, and with not enough men to hold it?"

"Your Highness, you were given one hundred men."

"Ninety-nine," Evan interrupted.

"Myself not included, more than enough to keep an invading army at bay. You have archers aplenty, and with enough arms to keep you supplied in the event of an attack. But yes, your father considers this duty one of honor."

The anger that was creeping in while Silverthorn was talking had burned in his insides for years. A hatred, on the verge of love, that he didn't know existed.

It made him want to drink, and drown the anger in a flood of wine or ale.

Instead, Evan took a deep breath, trying to restore himself. It wasn't working.

"Then a message to him I will send." Evan tried to keep the bite out of his voice. He wasn't sure he succeeded, but Silverthorn showed no emotion in his face. He bent his head in a bow of acknowledgment.

Evan worked his jaw, holding back the worst of his words. He stood and paced around the small room. "Send this message to him. Father, it is your son. I have held the castle despite the winter and a siege by the Belmarch. They intend to send more than what they tried to take us with when the weather clears. I will try my best to reinforce the defenses but am lacking in men to build as I have lost over half my working men to hunger and cold.

"Your son will stand alone in the north, and he will live or die trying to fulfill his duty." Evan bit back an insult that he wanted to hurl, wondering if Silverthorn would faithfully reproduce it word for word or if he would blunt the anger and the hatred that leaked through. "I expect nothing more from you than what you have already provided. I may live to see you again. With deepest regards Duke Evan Hornblood."

"Are you sure you don't want to write that down?" Silverthorn asked.

"I don't have anything to write with," Evan lied.

Silverthorn got up, moving to his chest, but Evan stopped him. "I wouldn't trust myself to keep a civil hand if I did."

"As Your Highness wishes."

The anger had fizzled somewhat but was still a cold ember. Silverthorn threw another log on the fire. It spit and hissed, still green from being freshly cut.

"I'll take lunch and then set off."

Evan didn't have the heart to argue, but he wanted him to stay. Once again, he would find himself alone in the world, no familiar faces to keep him company and talk to. Just a group of soldiers and builders, and no real way to control them.

On the other hand, with the reinforcement of his own men Evan was now more secure that the castle wouldn't rise up against him and kill him.

They ate in Silverthorn's room, waited on by Barger and the rest of the servants. Evan ate it and conversed politely, but it felt like sand in his mouth with no flavor at all.

All too soon Silverthorn was dressed and ready, his chest loaded up on the cart with his small entourage of two other men at his side.

He was here less than a month, and the winds were getting warmer. A few more months would see spring start to come through, and the snow would melt.

Evan felt it was bittersweet, finally seeing an end to the worst of the weather, but now he would face the threat of an invasion head on.

And they couldn't stop an army with a hundred men.

"Your Highness. You will do fine here, don't fear." Silverthorn reached out a mailed hand and grabbed onto his shoulder. "I will do what I can, and inform your father of the situation. I know there will be more help on the way."

"Travel safely Captain Silverthorn." Evan embraced the man, his strength nearly crushing him. *Oh, to have him at my side in a fight. What I wouldn't give to have an army of him.*

Then he was on his horse. With a final salute Silverthorn clicked his heels and set out. The horse turned and rode, with the cart trundling behind him.

Evan felt worse than he ever had, and more alone than he had since he learned of Yand's death. The small band of men passed through the open gates and into the road beyond the castle, stopping the line of men bringing felled trees and stone into the courtyard.

The sounds of hammers rang around the courtyard once again. Evan wasn't sure if it was the blacksmith or the masons, but it had been a long time since he had heard that. He didn't want Silverthorn to go, not just because he was a competent soldier and capable leader, but he knew there was something more to it.

So, he crossed the yard and ascended the wall, watching them disappear into the woods with an ache in his heart.

Perhaps it is because he is the only connection I had to my family. He didn't like thinking of it, but he knew it was probably true. How was he supposed to bear his family name and do well of it, when he had so little skill and experience to speak of?

As he stood on the wall, feeling the cold wind on his body, Evan cursed his past self. Always shirking responsibility, always trying to get out of everything just so he could feel better about himself.

The drinking, the carousing, the foolish play. It was all an attempt to escape something bigger, something stronger than himself.

And the desire to drink came back upon him in force. It burned in his throat, itched his lips. Evan licked them, feeling his mouth go dry.

A little drink would cure it, bring back the moisture he needed. And it would drown out the problems that seemed to keep piling up. It would be a way out, and a way out was what he needed right now.

"Everything in order, Your Highness?" Sam asked, from behind him.

Evan hadn't heard him come up behind him but turned now. "Fine. How are the carpentry supplies?" he asked awkwardly.

"The Belmarch burned the best of it while they were here." Sam spat the words out, then realized how he sounded. "No offense by my tone."

"None taken. You are a foreigner, are you not?"

"I am."

"Where do you come from?"

Sam shifted. "I'd prefer not to answer, if you don't mind."

Bold. A small hint of anger came up inside him, but Evan stifled it. What right did he have to demand anything of him?

But he was still the Duke of Hornblood, and he could not tolerate this. He had to do something. His father would have had the man whipped for insubordination, but he wasn't sure that would work.

And he wasn't sure who would do the whipping.

Evan frowned. "I should have you punished for that."

"Go ahead." Sam didn't even bat an eye. He seemed to know what kind of predicament Evan was in. Or, he didn't care. "While we're fighting among ourselves there are others out there who would gladly come and slit our throats."

"You think they'll be back?" Evan didn't know why he asked it. He knew the answer.

So did Sam, but he turned back to the courtyard instead. "I need your blessing to build what I had in mind before, with some changes."

"What kind of changes?"

"Dangerous changes." His face was tight, lips spread into a fine line. Age was showing at his temples, graying that once before had been brown. "And ones that will make more work for the masons."

"So, this is what it is about." Evan crossed his arms. The man hadn't even given him a few moments peace by himself before coming with his demands.

He had seen it done many times before but had never been the one taking the full brunt of it. He wasn't sure what to think, other than that he didn't like it.

"I need to do this," Sam whispered, staring at the Keep. Evan faltered, following his gaze. He expected something there, something bad that had pulled Sam's attention.

But it was nothing, just the unfinished Keep. A testament to what could be, given enough time.

A place for defense of Chathem and the hope for his people.

Sam's reaction had ignited his curiosity. "What is it you hope to do?"

Sam blinked, then shook his head as if waking up from a dream. "Spring is coming soon. I can smell it in the air. We need to hurry before they come back. Will you give me what I need?" He turned back to Evan, imploring him.

So much of this man was a mystery to him, so much needed to be told. He wasn't comfortable not knowing, and remembered the advice of his former tutors and teachers about trusting those who would betray him.

But Sam hadn't betrayed him, not yet at least. He could have done it, taken him out at every opportunity. Evan shivered, remembering being surrounded on the wall.

Sam had protected him. He owed him his life, and a debt of gratitude that went far beyond it.

Still, he was hesitant to give him complete control, and was still stinging from the lack of an answer to his own question. "I will think about it."

13

A Fresh Supply

Sam bid the Duke goodbye but stayed on the wall thinking about what he said and the plans for the future.

He looked back at the unfinished Keep. She was a shell of what she had been, scavenged bones that were picked over like a vulture's meal.

It was a shame, and made him close his eyes, but when he did, he could see it complete, shining in the sun with the banner of Hornblood flying and flapping in the summer sun.

When he opened his eyes again it was gone, a leaf in the breeze.

What would it take to make it a reality? Something stirred inside him, but it wasn't the violent, angry thing that resided deep down inside.

It was something different. Almost...excited.

He glanced back over his shoulder, watching the logs dragged one by one along the road and into the castle, swallowed up through the gate.

A pang of regret for everything that they had lost in the attack, and one final look out to the north, then Sam left the walls into the castle courtyard.

As agreed upon, they were taking them next to the makeshift carpenter's workshop and cutting off the branches with axe and hatchet. Since the trees were bare from autumn they had no mess of leaves to move out of the way, but there were twigs and shards of wood everywhere.

Keiren was directing the flow of wood, rejecting the worst of the logs for the fires and keeping the best for the timber pile. The rest he was putting in a separate pile.

The men were looking healthier, no longer emaciated after a good night of feasting and a few days of eating well.

Sam hadn't expected Captain Silverthorn to leave at all, let alone so early. He didn't know what to think of that, other than that he wasn't sure who else would be able to train them other than himself.

"What do you have?" Sam asked.

"These would make good timbers, except there are a few questionable places that might not work well that I wanted you to take a look at. Ned or Archie would have known." A flash of sadness, or anger, went across Kerien's face.

Sam made a mental note to check the ones Kerien had cleared earlier, not wanting to do it in front of him. The man had been through enough that he wasn't sure how he would react to Sam going back over his work.

He was just glad that Kerien had expressed some doubt up front, glad that he hadn't overestimated his abilities.

"Good, if you can start dressing them into beams I'll take a look at this. Trent." Trent stopped chopping off branches and came to his side. "Help me with this."

Sam was glad for the work, something to keep his mind off the sinking feeling he was having that he would be back in charge of the training in less than a day or two.

The training sessions, after they had recovered enough to do so, had been short but intense. Captain Silverthorn was no stranger to training new recruits, that Sam could tell right away, but they had advanced beyond that designation a while ago.

Now, in addition to being masons and carpenters, they were proficient fighters able to handle the end of a sword and spear.

He thought about it in between logs. Most were good and sound, straight enough to be massaged into a beam or a column brace once the sapwood was trimmed back.

A few, however, had checks that were too big to overcome, or knots that ran too deep, and had to be cut up or sent to the firewood pile.

It was less than he was expecting though. Kerien had done a good job, considering the speed at which the logs were flowing. Every so often he would hear a distant crack, another tree falling in the forest.

It had taken them months to find the logs that had been lost in the fire, and most had been drying for a year. They didn't have that luxury now, and Sam didn't like it.

But did it really matter? The castle walls were built and firm. The gate was well constructed and just needed a bit of patching, and the Keep was finished enough to keep out any invaders who made it past those defenses.

"What will we use these for?" Trent asked as the timber piled up higher and higher. They had a few that were strong and long, promising for large beams or columns.

The question echoed his own in his mind. "I was planning on using them for the Keep."

"The Keep? We can't put them in this wet, can we?"

"The winter has dried them some, and they will yield most of their water within the next few months." Sam looked back up at the Keep, thinking of all they had pulled out and was lost.

Good, dry wood that had taken months to dress and install.

"Master Freeman, I don't understand." Trent's eyebrows were knitted in a furrow. "When will we use them?"

"Not until they are ready." Sam paused, wiping the bark from his hands. The movement of wood had made him warm, and he almost stripped off his outer coat. Sweat trickled down his back, tickling him all the way.

"But that will be years."

"For some, yes. But we must plan for the future."

"What future?" Sam's eyes snapped to Trent's. They were ablaze.

"The only future we have."

"If we stay here the only future we'll have will be death and blood." The vehemence in his tone surprised Sam.

"No."

"I've seen it, and I know it to be true." His own emotions roiled inside. It would be so easy to leave now, to slip out into the night and be gone.

It had been on his mind ever since the Hornblood soldiers had arrived.

"That may be true," Sam said, keeping his voice low. Trent had attracted the attention of the others and they were staring at them. "Do you want to be here, Trent?"

"I-I don't know."

"An honest answer. Here." Sam tapped a log. "Take this with me to the workshop. I've got a plan for it."

Trent nodded, then took his position on the other end. They pulled it into the workshop, wrestling it across two workbenches to prop it up.

But most importantly, to get out of earshot and prying eyes.

"I share your concern, and with what we have I wouldn't be sure we could stave off another siege." Sam sat on his stool, easing the pressure off his aching feet. His body wasn't used to the work and was still trying to recover. He took a swig from his water skin, refreshing water pouring down his throat.

"I've lived my life afraid of the Belmarch," Trent said. "But now that I've faced them in battle..."

"You aren't a soldier Trent, you're something else. I see it in you as I see it in myself."

Trent drew a deep breath, agony flashing across his face. "I didn't like killing them. It was..."

"No one should get used to it. I wish we hadn't been put in this position, but I've seen firsthand what these Belmarch can do, and I know why they chose this place to build this castle." Sam stood and picked up his hatchet, starting to cut the bark off the log.

"If we don't build this, what will happen to the rest of Chathem? Would they survive the onslaught of bloodthirsty men willing to do whatever it took?"

"No," Trent said, joining him. Their blades scraped against the wood. Fresh sap filled the air with its fragrance. "I have family to the south, my father and mother and sisters." He shook his head.

"There are things here that we love." Martha's face came to mind, then he shook it out of his vision. "There are men and women we have to protect here."

"I don't know if I can do it. I want to run."

"As do we all. You aren't the first to consider it, and you won't be the last, but this is our land and our home." A fire burned in his stomach, filling his body with its warmth. It counteracted the chill in the workshop. "I have a plan, and I think it will give us the best chance for survival."

"I'm sorry, I wish I wasn't so weak." Trent was holding back tears.

"You aren't weak," Sam said. "I've seen you up on the wall, standing your ground when other men would have fled. I've seen you build when it was too hot and cold, gone on when others would have quit. I see the strength that was in your heart and in your soul." He put down his hatchet and squeezed Trent's shoulder.

"I've seen weak men abandon their brothers on the battle-field, or leave before it even starts. No, you are not weak."

"You're one of the only reasons I haven't run away yet." Trent rubbed his eyes with a sleeve.

Sam was taken aback. "Me?"

"After all we've been through, you're still here and willing to do anything. I see it, the Duke sees it, and the Overseer saw it."

"You give me more credit than I am due."

"I've learned more than how to hold a plane and saw, or a sword."

Sam didn't like the way this was going, was uncomfortable with what seemed like high praise to him. He shifted, letting go of Trent's shoulder, and returned to his work.

The hatchet handle was warm, oiled after years of work by hands. Freshly sharpened, it cut through the bark like a hot knife through butter.

"I'm sorry if I said the wrong thing," Trent said, turning to the log as well.

"No, it isn't that." Sam shook his head, then held it with a hand. "I never set out to do this when I came here, to train someone I mean." He reflected for a moment. "But the more I think about it the more I realize how much of a blessing it has been."

The bark was scratchy and rough beneath his hand. The last few months had been so hard, and now this. He didn't know how to react or what to think, so he didn't.

Together, in silence, they finished de-barking the log, then returned out into the courtyard with the others in the fading light of the day.

Raltone savored the fresh spring air, delighted at the change in weather. Gone were the cold days of winter, and all the snow and ice that came with it.

"And a good riddance too," he said.

"What was that, mi'Lord?" Sable asked.

"Nothing, are they ready to move?" He cast a sneer in his young compatriot's direction, lest he think him weak.

"Ready for your order," General Granb said. He had been subdued and put in his place. Raltone smiled, this one he actually felt as the once favored General squirmed.

"And you, Sable?"

"Ready for your order." He didn't glance at Granb.

Good. They have grown even more distrustful of each other.

With the sun shining, and the snow melting, Raltone gave a quick nod. "Then set them on their way."

He sat back in his chair, relaxing on the balcony as orders were given and relayed. Far back behind the troops in front, the horns sounded.

Men in rows of three stepped into formation, tight lines that would flash as they marched by. Granb did have his ambitions, but the man knew who to pick to keep the men disciplined.

They marched by, a thousand feet stamping in unison. The sound was music to Raltone's ears, and he plucked a bit of meat from the plate to chew on.

It was tender, cooked just the way he liked it, and juice almost flowed out as he took a bite. Paired with his dark red southern wine, it was a delicious meal and it got him in the mood to make a few decisions.

"Bring me my consort, and make sure she looks good." He stood, raising his glass. Others on the balcony scrambled to join him, Granb and Sable included. "Today marks the day we finally rise up above our squabbles and infighting to take what is rightfully ours.

"We scrape and dig in the hard dirt and rock, barely eking out a living here only to have it taken by the early snows and harsh storms of winter. But now, we will take Chathem and their soft lands and soft people and make them our own as it is by right."

"By right," echoed the others, the anger he felt at it being taken away from them in their voices.

"So, drink up, and drink hearty, for we march not to battle, but to a war that they have been owed for generations. To the Belmarch!"

Troops tramped by, a seemingly unending supply of them, and Raltone drank deep, imagining the glory to come.

14

DESTINY

"Why did you bother me with this?" Evan rubbed his forehead, trying to massage away the headache that had developed there.

"Your Highness, how are we to do our best work with the ground so cold? It freezes the men's hands and makes it impossible to quarry."

"What happened to the stone that we had piled up in the courtyard? I seem to remember large stacks of them lining up along the eastern wall, and the western wall."

Bill smiled a greasy smile, but it didn't fool Evan. He had spent enough time in taverns and inns to know when men were trying to shirk their duty or weasel out of a gambling debt. He never thought that would come in handy when he was having his...fun on his nightly escapades.

"Not much of it is worth anything. Too cracked for foundation stone and too jagged for anything other than infill."

"I see." Evan sat back, glancing at the bar in the corner of the room. It might have been emptied long ago, but it never seemed to escape his notice.

Particularity in times like these.

"How long is it taking you to dress the stone then, if it's too rough to use in the walls?" *Had Rhys had to deal with this many excuses? Or is it just me?*

Bill's eyes widened, just a touch before he recovered. "Too long, Your Highness. And with the state the men are in, it's worse than quarrying new stone."

"Then you've solved your dilemma." Evan took up his pen and dipped it in the inkwell. "Quarry the stone, as cold as it may be, and continue the supply for the new defenses as directed." He wrote it down before Bill could recover and make more excuses. "I'll expect everything to be on schedule and as promised." Evan looked up, arching an eyebrow. "Unless what you promised wasn't right to begin with. That would be...unfortunate, as I see you're a man well respected among your peers. It would be a shame to demote you after such long service to my family."

Bill's eyes wandered up above him, exactly where Evan had hoped. It made him hate himself a little, relying on his family's weight, but what else could he do? He didn't have many choices out here.

"You're right, as usual, Your Highness." Bill bowed, scraping back and out of the room as quickly as he could while making his niceties.

When the door shut behind him, Evan sighed and slumped back. The ink had stained his finger, and even though he tried to wipe it off, it was still there, stinking of it too.

He rubbed his eyes, trying to clear his head. No wonder Rhys had wanted to get out of here, and no wonder he was so far behind. He hadn't believed the poor man before, that he was under-manned and low on resources, but now that they had to do this himself, it was exhausting.

And nerve-wracking.

Spring was just around the corner, and warmer weather would clear the passes in Belmarch and leave them vulnerable to attack. Like last time, he wasn't sure they would get any help from anyone down south.

He picked up his book on castle construction, thumbing through the masonry chapter again, trying to see where it had said anything about rough stone being useful for anything other than infill.

He had to read through the whole chapter to reassure himself that it wasn't true, that it didn't say that anywhere.

The question was if Bill said it because he was incompetent, or if he was lying to cover something else up.

It was hard to decide, but he couldn't well throw him over the wall. He was honest when he said he was held in good regard among the men, almost too good. He had cultivated his loyalty well, and the masons were thick in it.

It would have to be a hard fall from grace to drop his standing, and Evan thought of different ways of doing it.

Each time, he came up short.

Barger knocked at the door, a quiet rapping that was perfectly spaced. Evan bid him enter, then stood to stretch.

"Is it dinner already?" Evan asked, after greeting the man and receiving one in return.

"Yes, Your Highness." Barger set the meal on the table, a stew based on the smell coming from it, then went to tend to the fire.

"I wonder, what do you think of Bill?" Evan walked up to the table, but didn't sit at it. He kept a close eye on Barger out of the corner of his eye.

"The mason?"

"Who else?"

Barger poked at the logs glowing in the fireplace, shifting them around to make room for more. They hissed and spat at him. "What would you like to know about him?"

"How did he manage to earn his position?" Evan pushed away the irritation at not getting a good answer from him, and took off the cover. He was right, stewed vegetables and what might have been meat, but with a nice, fat, crusty roll alongside. "Seems young for a master mason."

"No one else wanted the position, from what I have heard." Evan took a bite as he listened, the roll crunching. Inside was soft and fluffy.

"No one?"

"No one who valued their life." With a careful touch he added a log, making sure it flared up before he stood. "Bill is a violent man, quite difficult to see unless you catch him at the right time. He tends to have others do his dirty work for him now."

"I see." Evan made a mental note to watch him more carefully. Barger stood, clasping his hands behind his back, then cleared his throat. "Go on then, as distasteful as I find it."

Barger slipped out a piece of paper and started going through the inventory. It wasn't as bad as Rhys had been, that man could have put a bear to sleep, but he still wasn't used to it.

Evan finished his meal and sat back, listening to the long list of supplies that had been brought in and added to the little they had.

By all accounts they were in a good position, plenty of arms and food, and well supplied for a garrison. The only problem was that they weren't a garrison.

"Thank you, and thank the cooks for me." Evan stood, pacing around his room, as Barger wrapped up his tallies and put them back in his pocket.

"Do you require anything else, Your Highness?" Barger had cleared the meal while he was pacing.

"No, nothing." Barger turned to leave. "Wait, there is something." Evan had been turning it over in his mind for quite some time now, a thorny problem he couldn't seem to put a finger on. "Why is it that Sam Freeman is in the position he's in?"

"Similar circumstances to Bill, I'm afraid. The previous master carpenter died in the same sickness that took the head mason."

"But he doesn't seem that...old."

"He isn't, from the rumors I've been told. Late thirties or early forties. What is the reason you have for this question, if you don't mind my asking, Your Highness?"

"I'm troubled. I don't know where he came from, or where his loyalties lie. He's a proficient fighter and a good leader but refuses to tell me or anyone else why that is."

"Perhaps it is because he does not want anyone else to know."

"And that's what troubles me." Evan stopped, turning short and pivoting on his heel. A log shifted in the fire, spitting and cracking. "Men who hide secrets are not to be trusted."

"Quite so, Your Highness." Barger was standing, heels together, watching attentively.

"I don't know why I brought you into this mess. You really shouldn't have anything to say on the matter." Evan sighed. "To be honest, I'm at a loss for advisers ever since Overseer Rhys left."

"Your time with Captain Silverthorn was not...productive?"

"Too much so." Evan walked to his seat, then slipped into it, leaning on his desk. "He gave me a long list of things to watch out for, things to do." He held up a note scribbled with markings and writing.

"It is the duty and honor of the Duke, I'm afraid." Evan knew that Barger was only humoring him, listening was his own duty. What he said or did afterward, Evan wasn't sure.

"Dismissed." Barger turned to go. "And Barger, thank you." He gave a deep bow, considering his package of dishes, and left Evan alone.

He sat, watching the fire for a while. Seeing the red and yellow battle with each other, tossing and lancing at one another in their quest to consume. The thick smell of pine smoke was in the air and curled up around the chimney, not all of it escaping up and out of the room, but Evan didn't mind. It had been too long without for him to not like it.

But his eyes kept wandering down to the note, a list that he appreciated and detested all in the same breath. He sighed, hoping the weight would roll off his shoulders and onto someone else.

That isn't my destiny. He rolled the word around in his mind, wondering what it really meant. *Destiny.*

Something he hadn't spent a lot of time considering, something barely spoken of in his childhood. A path that was chosen for him.

A good word for what I live. All the things he had given up, been forced to give up. A childhood alone, a youth spent the same way. Always wanting to be accepted, to have a friend, and always being told you were above them and must lead them one day.

It was no wonder I was driven to the drink. The hatred inside his breast grew and worsened then, a life of ease not so because of what he was called to do.

He wished he was back in the slums again, accepted by the very bottom members of society, or among the houses of ill repute. The women there didn't care who or what he was, only the color of his coin. He could buy friends for gold, and they would make his night shine.

That's what he'd told himself, but deep down he knew it was a lie. Those men and women were just as empty as he was, on as much of a search and journey as he.

Evan buried his hands in his head, staring at the words on the page.

"Train constantly for attack. Make sure the men know how to use the bows in the dark. Keep all openings shut and locked unless directly used for access."

All simple things, all things that had been drilled into him as a child that he had long put aside. Silverthorn, or his father, was always trying to remind him of his past.

Something he always wanted to forget.

Evan's throat was so dry every time he swallowed it was like sand scratching his throat. It wouldn't be much to summon Barger, to tell him to bring the wine. There was still a little bit left in the casks he had brought, and more that were sent with the arms. Not good stuff, from what he could gather, but enough to drown these problems for a night.

Just one night. Just one sip. After that it would be easy to stop. He had already done it for weeks now.

It was tormenting him, calling to him. Evan stood up, his hands shaking trying to hold it back.

He was going to fail. He was going to do it. Then, his eyes chanced to look upon his sword.

It too had been a gift from his father, along with the duty that was bound like a millstone around his neck.

Well balanced, sharp, a delight to hold, he was by it in an instant, holding onto it like a drowning man clutches at the tree branch floating by.

It was cold in his hands, soaking the warmth from his fingers, but it felt good. So good.

He drew it, the rasp from the scabbard ringing in his ears and filling the place the drink wanted to go.

He turned back into himself, losing himself in the forms. It had been too long, and he stumbled at points in the harder forms. So, he continued, starting over.

It wasn't much, but the pain of the workout reminded him of what was real, of why he couldn't regress. He couldn't drown his sorrows in wine, but he could drown them in his own sweat.

Soon, it came pouring out of him as he moved faster and faster, thrust after parry, swing after charge.

When he finished the last form, he stood gasping. His heart pounded, and he could only lean on his sword and stare up at the crest of the Hornbloods hanging above his desk.

"I will show him that this Hornblood still has life left in his veins. I will not give up."

15

THE MANTLE

As soon as Evan said the words he realized that had been in this place before. Alone, afraid, no knowledge of what to do.

But that time he had survived, managed to make it out of his room and into the world that surrounded him.

He took a deep breath, breathing in the smoke and the smell of ink and paper all rolled up into one. His hands brushed the leathery parchment, then grasped it.

It was a long list, and some of them he could never really be finished with.

"Always be vigilant?" It felt a bit silly talking to himself out loud, but he was alone in his room with no one to overhear.

Making up his mind, he tucked the paper into his pocket and sheathed his sword. He had caught his breath, and his heartbeat had slowed enough to be at a quick pace instead of pounding. It was time to make another visit.

Evan swept on his coat and strode out the door. Sounds of the cooks echoed down the corridor, through the open door at the end. They were talking, giggling, and laughing. It was a good, solid sound, and strengthened his resolve.

he passed by the kitchens, getting a glimpse in and sampling the wonderful aromas drifting out of it. There was meat, spiced heavily it smelled like, and cracking with fat. It made his mouth water and he swallowed it back.

No one gave him a second glance. *They are relying on someone to protect them.* His mother's face swam to his mind, and it brought a faint smile to his lips.

She was south of here, and to the west, deep in Hornblood territory and the Hornwood. She had slipped in a package for Silverthorn to deliver.

It was still in his room, a bundle that felt suspiciously like books. Another gift to strengthen him, or so she would have said.

The sun was sinking as he entered the courtyard, and the chill of the night was blowing in from the north. Evan kept one hand on the hilt of his sword but tightened his collar and turned to the carpenters' workshop.

He wasn't sure why he had to go there, other than that's where he thought Sam would be.

He was right, but the other two were there also. Evan wasn't sure of their names, but they stared at him as he opened the flap and strode inside. In the distance the masons' hammers rang and sang.

"Good evening, Your Highness," they said when they had recovered from their shock. Evan returned their greetings and turned to Sam, who still had a plane in his hand.

"I wish to speak with you." Evan glanced at the others. "In private."

Sam nodded, and the other two packed up their tools and left them. Evan waited until the sound of their boots was gone, taking a seat on a stool that was covered in wood shavings, after cleaning it off.

"To what do I owe the pleasure?" Sam smiled, more baring of teeth than a real smile. He tried to cover it quickly. "I apologize for the...tone. It's been a long day."

"It's been a long year," Evan said. "And what I'm about to ask for will make it longer, for you."

"Me only?"

"If you agree to it, I suspect it will affect a great many more." Evan leaned forward. "Why did you come here?"

Their eyes locked. Something passed over Sam's face, and through his eyes. Evan couldn't put a finger on what it was. It was emotions, but what emotions?

He wasn't going to let him get out of this question and stared without blinking.

"That's... a good question." Sam brushed at the section of wood before him. Shavings fell to the floor, added to the growing pile.

Evan was uncomfortable but had to know the answer. The silence stretched on as Sam dropped his gaze to the table before him, working out the answer to the question.

"In some ways I think it is a way to atone for what I've done." Sam shook his head. "But I'm not sure about that anymore either. I have this...this urge inside me that I can't seem to satisfy. I thought coming here would help."

Evan wasn't sure that was what Sam was going to say, and he scrutinized the man further, but no additional explanation was given.

"You signed up for this, you know what you owe."

"I do."

"Then I would ask that you function as the Overseer, in Rhys' absence."

Sam's eyes flashed back up. "Your Highness, I couldn't. I don't know how to build a castle."

"Neither, I suspect, did he," Evan said. "And neither can I. If you don't do it, take up this mantle that I've laid upon you, then who exactly will?"

That caused him anguish. "I know many good men that could, and all of them are in the ground."

What should he do? Evan saw the conflict in the man's eyes and in his heart. His father would have counseled a heavy hand, perhaps, to order him to it.

But he wasn't his father. He wasn't his mother. Evan had to accept that he had to be his own man.

"I've woken up in too many ditches to count, done things to fritter away my youth that would make a woman of the night blush," Evan said, capturing Sam's attention.

"Your Highness, why are you telling me this?" It only added to the man's visible anguish.

"I'm no better than you. I happened to be born to a certain man and woman and that gives me the right to rule. The duty," Evan spat, "to rule. But I don't know how to do that, and I've spent years trying to run from it. So, you can either help me learn, or you can watch as the Belmarch wash over us without stopping, burning and killing everything and everyone we ever loved."

Sam stared at him, eyes wide and jaw dropped.

"What do you have to say?"

"Your Highness, I -" Sam snapped his jaw shut, then turned away from him. "I don't know what to say."

"Say yes, and then we can be done with it."

"It isn't that easy."

"No, I'm afraid it isn't." The fire was dying down, but it still gave its heat and light to the room. Evan waited for Sam to continue, examining everything else while he did.

It was a place of work, that he was sure. There were no frills or art to speak of, it was a plain as a monk's room, but everything was solidly built. The workbenches were stout and had good, thick legs, and were filled with tools of all kinds.

"When I came to this place, I expected to be a simple laborer." Sam spoke, his back still to him. "A way to...get away from what I had become. And what I was going to be."

Evan leaned back, the stool creaking under his shifting weight. It wasn't the most comfortable, far more spartan than his own carved wooden chair with cushions, but it beat being on his feet. The light from the day was dying, not as early as it had been.

The bell rang then, calling everyone to evening formation.

"It is time to make a decision, Sam Freeman." Evan stood, tightened his coat about him again.

"It's all so much to think about." Sam turned back to him but didn't meet his eyes. He put away his tools, and the tools of the others, walking around the workshop and doing anything but consider his proposition. "I have to admit, I'm overwhelmed. Will you give me some time, to think about it?"

He needs time. Didn't I need time too? Evan suppressed the bit of vexation he felt. It was an honor, one that should rightfully go to nobility. *Can't he see what kind of risk I am taking?*

"A night. No more. Think about it and give me your answer tomorrow." Sam had finished with the tools, everything in a place that had some sense of order, even if Evan couldn't figure out what it was.

"You are too kind, Your Highness. I will think on it, and I will think well." Sam clutched his hands.

Evan waited for him to go, to leave the workshop and enter the courtyard. "Aren't you to help lead the exercises?" he asked, when it was clear that Sam was staying.

"Yes, yes of course." Sam pulled his coat from a hook near the entrance flap, fumbled with the button at the top, and then finally managed to get it fixed. "They will be back, won't they?"

Evan chewed on his bottom lip, then stopped as soon as he realized he was doing it. "Every day I wonder if they will be on the horizon. When they come back, it will be with an army."

Sam let out a deep breath. "I was afraid I was the only one who thought so." He gave a simple bow, but one well practiced. *A clue to his past, perhaps?*

"Goodnight, Duke Hornblood." And when Evan had returned the greeting, he was gone.

Evan followed, breathless into the evening twilight. The sunset had faded and the gloom of the night was nearly complete, but there was still the haze of glow spread out over the castle walls that made everything hard to see.

He crunched through the thinning snow, listening to the sounds of men assembling and talking in the yard. The clink of practice swords, a laugh here and there, and the squad leaders yelling at them to get into their positions all echoed around the courtyard, bounced from wall to wall.

The smell of sweat would soon be filling the air, mingling with the woodsmoke and hint of spring on the fading evening breeze. Evan stopped in the shadow of the Keep to watch them, keeping well out of sight in order to observe and think by himself.

Silverthorn had given a few pointers to the guards that made up the squad leaders, and they soon had all the workers assembled in nearly straight rows and columns. From there pairs were divided and set against one another.

They practiced sparring forms as Evan watched. His mind wandered to the south, to the fertile lands that they protected that had long ago been stripped of forest and tree.

Were they too soft from years of peace? Did they not see the enemy that was on their doorstep?

But Evan had to be honest with himself, neither did the Hornbloods. His father had sued for the right to build the castle, but from what he remembered it was only a precaution. He thought the internal power struggles and infighting would keep them at bay for years.

And so, Evan had believed so too. Maybe that's why his father had sent him here to be in charge, to be safely out of the way while the King called for his forces to be sent east and south to fight those raiders.

He turned the thought over in his mind, unsure of what it meant or why it mattered. His conversations with Silverthorn returned to him, time spent listening to words from a trusted adviser to his father that seemed to mean little to him.

Particularly his parting words.

He tried to dismiss them, to focus on observing the men. At first, he was successful. The steam was rising off them, and they were shedding outer garments as they trained. They had shifted from sparring practice to full-fledged fighting, striking and kicking and punching in order to bring the other man down to his knees.

And they weren't holding back either. It looked like some were locked in mortal combat, but as soon as a squad leader came over to finish the fight they released each other.

Evan was surprised at how much better they were than when he first came. Those first nights, where he had watched Yand train them surreptitiously from the shadows, were an abomination.

Now, however, they looked as though they might have a chance to stand their ground, given the right protection and advantage. They were still far from professional fighters, but they wouldn't be useless in battle.

Battle. *Is that what is coming?*

There was something on the night air, now still. A force of some kind was growing in the north, he could feel it. A storm was brewing, and it meant to come south and sweep them from their position and into Chathem.

And the only thing standing in between Belmarch and Chathem was this castle.

Evan looked to the north, shivering in the night air, and was afraid.

16

A MEETING IN THE KITCHENS

Sam attacked Trent, pressing his advantage in arm reach with powerful strokes. Each one knocked Trent's sword away, but somehow he managed to bring it back into blocking position before the next one landed.

There was fear on his face, a real fear, which made Sam realize what he was doing. His muscles were starting to regain their former strength, and he stopped as the end of the round was called.

Sweat trickled down the side of his nose and he wiped it away as he made his bow. Trent's eyes were wide.

"Did I do something wrong?" he asked in a whisper.

Blood was pounding through his ears, fed by the thing that waited inside and the anger that was brought up by the Duke. "No," he said curtly. "I'm sorry, I should have held back more, but you did well."

That thing wanted to crunch and snap, and was almost awake, but Sam had managed to control it somehow.

Mathew was up now, calling an end to the night's training. His blood still roared in his ears, even though he had managed to get some control of his breathing, and Sam didn't feel like sticking around to talk with any of the others, as they were apt to do following the training sessions.

"Keep working on the forms," Sam said, clasping Trent's arm and trying to smooth out his rough treatment. "You've done well to improve, but there is always someone stronger and faster that will end your life if you let them."

"I will."

Sam nodded, then caught what he had said. He gave a curt good night then turned and walked back to the Keep. His mind was ablaze.

Overseer of the castle? I couldn't do that. He knew someone else should have the position, would do a better job, but when he tried to think of who he came up short.

Bill was too power hungry. Mathew too green. None of the carpenters were even remotely ready. Dale wouldn't care.

He had to talk to someone about this, and Dale first came to mind, but when he went to the forge it was empty and cold, so he trudged back to the Keep.

The only other person he wanted to talk to about it, who was still alive, he thought might be in the kitchen.

But he was too strung up and angry to go see her first, so he paced the halls and stairs, going up and down and around where he knew he could find her.

As his heart rate slowed and his breathing normalized, Sam soon found that he wasn't walking to calm down any more, but out of nervousness.

What will she think? What will I say? Sam clasped his fingers and put them behind his head, trying to rationalize the state he was in.

"Don't be a coward," he said to himself, "Just go see her." Squaring up, he marched through the empty great hall and down the corridor to the kitchen.

And then stopped just outside the door.

He couldn't do it. It felt like there was a chasm between him and the door. He tried to raise his hand and open it, but it wouldn't respond.

Sam was just about to turn around and flee when it banged open, making him jump.

"What are you doing out here, sneaking around?" Martha was waving a spoon in his face, but then stopped as soon as she saw who it was. "Sam! I thought you were a little one trying to sneak a midnight snack."

"Sorry to disturb you." Sam swallowed, then stuffed his hands in his pockets. *It's done now, no use trying to run away.* "May I... join you?"

"Come in," she said with a smile, and he followed her in, checking the corners. They were alone and she pulled out a little stool for him to sit in by the fire, getting another for herself and bidding him sit.

His senses were assaulted by the thousand and myriad of smells and tastes that lived in the kitchen. Breads, meat, vegetables among all the herbs and spices that were shipped in with the resupply. It helped distract him as Martha offered to make him something warm to drink.

"Now then, what brings you to see me?" Her eyes twinkled in the low burning light of the fire, banked down for the night. Sam felt warm inside and was warmed by its heat.

"I had to talk to someone, and I was hoping to catch you."

"Whatever is the matter?" Her smile slipped as she watched him. "You look-"

"Martha, I've been asked to do something that I don't think I can." His face felt tight, and he tried to relax it. His entire body felt strung up, like a string stretched tight. "I don't know what to do."

"What have you been asked to do?" Her voice was quiet and soothing, and she leaned forward.

What am I thinking? I can't tell her. He was in agony, and she looked so beautiful in the soft light that it made it worse.

She's no longer a wife. The flash of a thought made him squeeze his eyes shut, then put a hand over them. He took a deep breath.

"The Duke asked me to be the Overseer." It was out, there was no taking it back now.

He wanted desperately to look at her, but he couldn't bring himself to.

"How do you feel about that?" He glanced up, met her eyes. She didn't seem surprised, or even disgusted like he thought she would. There was no disapproval in those eyes, only reassurance.

"I couldn't do it."

"Why not?" she asked, voice soft and low. So different from the commanding voice she yielded like her spoon with the other women.

He thought she would have been judgmental, that she would have agreed with him and urged him to say no, even though he didn't see a way how. This, though...

This was not what I expected. He didn't have an answer for her and struggled to find one. She waited patiently. "I don't know how."

"So, learn."

"It isn't that easy."

Martha shrugged, then captured a stray bit of hair that had come loose, brushing it behind her ear. "I didn't say it would be easy."

"But don't you see how impossible it is?" Sam stood up and turned away, stroking his chin. "I can't be in charge of the castle, that should be someone else."

"Should it be me?" He spun at her question, a hint of undercurrent in her tone. He dare not think of what it was.

But she was smiling a half smile, hiding it well. "Or should it be... Bill?" she asked.

"You know that would be a disaster, and its exactly what he wants. I think that's the reason he chose the Overseer to leave."

Her eyes widened in real surprise. "He chose the Overseer?"

Sam stepped back, bringing up his hands, and stammered "I didn't mean to say that. Promise me you won't tell anyone else about it."

Her eyes were narrow now, and she was almost out of her seat. White-knuckled hands clenched around her spoon. "What have you been up to?"

"It was the Overseer's choice, but Bill wanted him gone too. He wouldn't help me with the boat unless I agreed to it."

"That dirty, rotten scoundrel." Her smile was twisted into a scowl now. "Always scheming and scraping about. What else did you agree to?"

He had shrunk back, but now that he had gathered his wits Sam straightened. Martha was half his size. *I shouldn't be this afraid of her.*

"That's not what I came to talk about. I'll tell you later, another time, when I don't have the weight of the castle on my shoulders."

Her scowl faded at the reminder but didn't disappear. "You take my advice Sam Freeman, you be careful around that snake." She sniffed. "And as for you feeling like you can't do this or that I want you to stop it and start acting like a man."

Martha rose and advanced. It took all he had to stand firm. "If you can think of someone else who can do it tonight, then you tell him no. If, however, you come up short like you have for however long you've been thinking on it then you know the answer you have to give."

She was next to him now, near enough he could smell the sweat and cooking on her, and the unique smell that only she had. "But I don't know how to do it."

"And you'll learn, just like everyone else learns when they don't know how. I didn't know how to bake and cook or lead a kitchen, and now see how the girls are in their place."

"Martha, half those women are your age or older."

"Which makes it worse. They should know what to do and how to do it without my direction, but still, they need it." Her face softened. "Just like all those men out there need someone to lead them."

"I'm no leader either."

"Which makes you the best man to do the job." She was so close, he could almost feel the heat coming off of her. Her eyes were so soft in the light, her lips looked so supple. Martha reached up and smoothed a wrinkle in his shirt. "Sam," her voice was almost a whisper now. "I have to tell you something."

His heart was pounding. She hadn't taken her hand off his chest. Her touch was so soft, and he wanted to reach up and take her hand, lift her chin.

He cracked open his suddenly dry mouth. "What is it?"

"I-" She blinked, peering up at him from underneath her lashes.

He was drawn down to her, felt lightheaded and anxious. The lock of hair fell back over her eyes.

Sam reached out and brushed it back behind her ear.

The door slammed open, two girls bursting in laughing and giggling. Martha's head whipped around, and she snatched her hand away.

Sam pulled back too, heart pounding and breathing heavily. The two girls went silent, the air filled with an oppressive awkwardness.

"We're sorry mistress Martha," one of the girls murmured. They were clasping arms and looking down at the floor.

Martha looked as if she had seen a ghost and busied herself with putting her hair up. "What are you two doing down here at this hour?"

"We came to put away the vegetables for tomorrow," the younger one said, holding up a basket filled with dried potatoes and turnips. "We didn't mean to..."

"I'll have none of that," Martha marched up to them. Sam wanted to crawl into a hole and die somewhere, anywhere but here.

The door was still open and called to him as a possible means of escape, but all three of the women were in between it and him.

"Sam and I were just talking about something that need not concern you," she continued, rummaging around in the basket, then finally snatching it from them. "Now, go on and get gone. Off with you." She shooed them away, and they made a short curtsy and turned to go, but they kept sending darting glances his way.

Sam wasn't sure what to do, his hands itched, and his feet didn't seem to want to move. "Yes, Martha and I weren't doing anything," he said, then started to blush at how bad it sounded as it came out of his mouth. She turned slowly and stared at him, eyes almost bulging.

The girls were fighting to keep smiles off their faces as they turned and left in silence. The tension didn't leave with them though, it lingered.

"I'm sorry I bothered you so lately," he stammered, making for the door.

"You don't need to go," Martha said, reaching out for him. Sam couldn't stand being inside the kitchen for another minute though and made a beeline for the door. "Wait, Sam!"

He stopped in the doorway, grasping the rough wooden frame for dear life, holding onto it to keep him afloat. "I'm sorry, I shouldn't have caught you up in this. It was my burden to share, not to give to anyone else, and it will be my burden to bear."

"You put too much of it on your shoulders," she said, voice cracking. "You don't have to try and bear it alone."

He wanted to turn, to catch her up in his arms and hold her, wipe away the tears that he knew were streaming down her face.

But, he couldn't. "Goodnight, Martha," he said, then left.

17

CHILDISH DREAMS

Evan watched the men finish their training for the night and slipped into the Keep before they returned. Back in his room, he went through his new evening ritual.

First, he took out his sword and practiced each of the forms Yand had spent so many years teaching him. By now he was smooth with each one, and was tempted to go through the motions, but something in Yand's training kept him from doing that.

It must have been Yand himself, and how he always seemed so intense when he was training, completely focused on one movement after the other.

His muscles felt better afterward, the kinks worked out of them, but he was tired. He selected a book, the Histories again, and sat in his chair next to the fire to read.

It was his fourth time reading it, at least, and he finished a few chapters before putting it away.

He fingered the spines of each book on his bookshelf, but glanced at the package from his mother he still had yet to open.

She had known him so well, he wondered what she had given him. *Why have I waited so long to open it?*

He suspected there was news from home, and that was what kept him away. What could possibly be so bad that his mother would send to him?

Or perhaps it was a letter from his father, finally disowning him after one too many failures. Evan shivered despite the pleasant temperature of the room. There was a pit in his stomach, a feeling of dread.

But it might be good news for all I know. Curiosity grew, bigger than his fear, and finally he could take it no longer.

Evan crossed the room and picked it up, the smooth oilskin wrapping left residue on his fingers. With one pull he tugged open the string and let it fall, revealing the contents inside.

There was a letter at the top, folded neatly into four and a perfect square, his mother's handwriting spelling out his full name.

She rarely used his full name, but in official correspondence she was a stickler for protocol. The dread grew.

He pushed it off to the side and picked up the plush red leather-bound book, and its mate underneath.

There was no title emblazoned on the front, or the side, but when he opened it, there was a beautiful scribe's handwriting. *Tales of the Eventide.*

The second was its companion, a second volume. Evan had never heard of them, and was completely befuddled. *Why these?*

With a glance back at the letter, which he let lie, he took his two new books back to the fireplace.

Starting at the beginning, and placing the second volume off to the side, Evan took up the deeply leather smelling book and started reading.

Pages turned with a simple rustle, complemented by the gentle murmur of the fire as it pulled air up the chimney with it. Evan fell into those tales, and didn't come out until the very last page.

When he did, he blinked. The fire had burned low, almost out, and Barger was standing at his side.

"Is everything all right, Your Highness?"

"Yes," Evan said, shutting the book softly. His eyes wandered over to the second volume, wondering if they told of the same great heroes from old. "Confused, that's all."

"It is late, I was wondering when you would retire."

"Is it now?" Evan glanced at the letter on his desk. "I think I'll go to bed then and save this one for tomorrow."

Barger nodded, then banked the fire down for the night. Evan watched him, in a daze, and as he was about to go grabbed his arm.

"Do you believe them?"

"Believe what, Your Highness?"

"Any of the old stories?"

Barger shook his head and smiled wanly. "I was never fond of them, and no one really told me any."

"Surely that couldn't be true," Evan said, letting go of the poor man. "Even my mother told me stories when I was younger, of knights in shining armor coming in to kill the beast guarding the princess and win her heart."

Barger stood stiffly. "Not all men are given the opportunity, Your Highness." His voice was calm, but empty of emotion like he had squeezed a sponge out.

"I want to think they are true, that they could be," Evan said. "But I gave up hope that I would be that knight long ago."

"Childish dreams die when you grow older," Barger said. Evan felt the exhaustion flood over him then and noticed it in Barger's face too. The man was worn out, and not just from the winter.

"I don't understand why my mother sent these to me." Evan picked up the books and presented them. He waved over to the bookshelf. "She sent so many practical books, things that I suspect she thought I would need, but these are meant to be told to children."

"I would not know the mind of the Duchess, Your Highness."

"I think you do, and I think you would. So many times you know my mind better than I know myself that it scares me. Always there with the right thing at the right time, ready without my asking."

"I have been in your service many years," Barger said, still cold and toneless.

"And you have seen me with my mother those same years."

"Your Highness, I should leave." Barger made a motion to go to the door, but Evan stopped him, rising from his chair.

"Now then, you're here now and I need you. Why would my mother send these?"

Barger held up his hands in defeat. "I couldn't say."

"Make a guess."

"The Duchess may have told you why she did it."

Evan cocked his head to the side. "What makes you think that?"

"The letter, Your Highness." Barger motioned to the desk, pointed it out. Evan narrowed his eyes, and examined Barger closer. That letter had only been there this night.

"If you like, I can stay here while you open it." Barger relaxed into a more natural position as Evan considered it.

An owl hooted outside. "Yes," Evan said, knowing that it meant he would be forced to open it.

He wasn't sure why he was so reticent. It was his mother, not his father, or so he hoped.

Evan slowly went over to the desk as Barger patiently waited. He picked up the letter, turning it over in his hands. The Hornblood seal was pushed into the wax, a light touch of his mother's ring.

He brushed his thumb across it, smooth and waxy. The ridges were stark in feel against the rest of it.

Glancing up at Barger, who stared at him with a blank face, Evan took up his knife and cut it in a swift strike.

It was open now, and he unfolded it, relieved to see his mother's writing.

Evan sat back in the chair and read.

"What is it, Your Highness?"

He glanced back up at Barger, who wore a look of concern. "My father's been wounded."

It was so strange to think of him, so strong and able, now confined to a bed.

Evan felt lightheaded, and leaned back. His world was spinning. He had never even considered his father could be in such a position.

"I'm sorry to hear that."

"I-I'd like a drink."

"At once." Barger was gone in an instant, out the door, leaving him alone.

Evan clutched at the letter, re-reading it twice more. It was true, it had to be. That was her gentle handwriting, her graceful signature.

The door creaked open, a soft tinkling as Barger entered carrying a tray with a cup on it. Steam rose, obscuring the fire, from the lip.

"Here you are." He set the cup in front of him, but Evan was distracted, carried away in his thoughts. "Would you like me to take it away?"

"What?" He noticed the cup then. "No, thank you." Evan's shaking hand hit the side of it. *What if he dies? What would I do then?*

"She wants me to stay here." The cup was warm, almost too hot for his hands.

"Careful, Your Highness, that just came from the kettle." Barger was still staring at him, waiting on him.

Evan realized he was about to take a big mouthful of it and stopped. It smelled of willow bark. It must have been the tea that came with the soldiers.

He took a sip, scalding his tongue in the process, but the tea brought him to his senses. "Thank you." He blew on it to cool it down, taking another smaller sip that only flooded his mouth with warmth.

The feeling traveled down his throat to his stomach, which by now was turning upside down. "What if he dies? What would happen to me then?" Evan put the cup back down and rose, pacing around his room at a furious pace.

His exhaustion was gone now, he couldn't sleep. She had tried to make it gentle, soft even, but he could tell that he was hurt badly. Too badly.

"May I suggest that it might not be as bad as it seems?"

"You don't know her like I do." Evan shook his head, wiping back his hair. He wanted something stronger. He needed a drink. His throat felt like sandpaper.

But there was none in the room, and he knew that Barger wouldn't go get some.

I could go myself. "I'm not ready to be the Archduke. I can barely function now. I can't even keep the castle safe."

"Was there any other news?" Barger was following him, at a loss for how to help him. Evan didn't know what he needed himself, other than a cool glass of wine.

No, get hold of yourself.

"I need to go." Evan grabbed his sword and coat and headed for the door. "Don't wait up for me."

He walked down the corridor and through the Keep, turning left intentionally to keep away from the stairs that led to the cellar.

They kept the alcohol down there, at his request, and he wasn't sure what he would do if he went down there, but he knew he wouldn't be able to resist it if he saw it.

He almost stopped at the kitchen, knowing there might be a stray barrel or two, but pushed by, going out the door into the bitter cold of the night.

Snow was falling, soft flakes that stuck in his hair and on his shoulders, and he took a moment to wrap his coat around his shoulders.

He wandered listlessly around the courtyard at first, then up to the walls. He touched it, feeling the cold soak up the warmth of his body, the roughness of the rock, and stared up at the top of it.

They aren't protecting me, they're trapping me inside. His entire life he had been trapped, no choice of friends, no choice of profession, not even a choice of who he would one day marry.

Everything was prescribed for him, a path that was laid out before he was ever born.

And now that path might be even closer than he realized. His entire family was counting on him now.

With a chill, he realized that his father might be dead even now, and a strange feeling of sadness accompanied it. He thought for a long time that he would be relieved when his father was gone.

Now, he was realizing what that would mean. It would mean an end to his simple life and the start of one much bigger. One filled with endless drivel and pressure too powerful to resist.

Evan pulled out his sword, turning back to the courtyard and the training grounds. He slipped into the first form, using it to clear his head.

Thrust. Parry. Strike. Thrust. Parry. Strike.

The sword was an extension of his body, another part to manipulate, just like Yand had taught him.

Thrust. His father was going to die. Strike. He would become the Archduke. Parry. He would be in charge of all of Hornblood.

The Ironwood. The Tree of Everling. Everything.

He broke out in a cold sweat, pushing away the thought even as he continued with his training.

The moon glinted off his blade as he spun. The forms melded into each other, and he sped up, trying to keep hold of his sanity.

He didn't know where he was going. He didn't know what to do.

And there was no one to guide him.

He kept going until his muscles ached and his lungs screamed, until his arms were shaking with the effort of holding up his sword, and then he pushed harder.

Legs shook, numbed by the cold, until he could finally hold it no longer. The sword clanged in the snow.

And Evan fell to the ground after it, eyes staring up at a cloudy night sky.

18

DEVOURING TREE

Snow fell around him, blanketing the courtyard in a silent, soft deafening. Evan blinked as a solitary snowflake fell in his eye and quickly melted.

His breath rose in big, white clouds that seemed black in the light of the moon, and he wondered what he was going to do.

When he caught his breath he got back up, out of the freezing snow, and went back to his room.

The Keep was quiet, almost everyone asleep by now, and he met not a soul on his way. He went to his room, stripped off his wet clothes next to the crackling fire that filled him with heat, and went to bed.

That night he had strange dreams, that he was at the Tree of Everlong leading the Midnight Watch, his mother and father standing with his grandparents that had long passed from this earth and watched.

He had no voice, but everyone seemed to be listening to him, and when he tried to turn around the great tree had turned into a monster, a gaping wide maw filled with rows of wooden fangs waiting as a tree branch arm grabbed him around the waist and pulled him inside to eat him.

Evan woke up in a sweat before the monster could kill him, heart pounding nearly out of his chest.

The fire had died down, leaving his room chilly, and he gathered the blankets back up around his body.

It was another day, another step closer to the duty he had spent his whole life running from. The sense of dread that his father might be dead hung on him, clung to him like a bad smell, and he found he could sit in his bed no longer.

Cold stone sucked the heat from his feet when he stood, and he jumped over to dress and get ready for the day.

There was no sign of Barger, and a quick glance told him it was still dark outside. It had been a short night.

And he felt it.

His body was still tired from the late night training session, but his eyes were bleary and heavy from the lack of sleep.

Evan went back to his study to re-read the letter, hoping everything from the night before was part of his nightmare, but it was still true.

The books seemed like some kind of sick joke now that he looked at them. He still had no clue why his mother had sent them.

To remind me of something? To teach me something? If so, what could a group of stories ever teach him?

He spent the time until breakfast reading his books on military tactics. When Barger entered the room, he wasn't sure how to treat him.

"Good morning, Your Highness." Barger was perfectly cordial and seemed to show no hint of the awkwardness that Evan himself felt.

He pursed his lips, unsure of whether he should bring it up or let the ruse go on. "Any word today?"

"The inventory is in progress, and we should have updated numbers this afternoon." Barger made his place at the table and stood by while Evan took his seat and started eating. "If you mean did anyone notice anything last night, I do not believe so."

He turned and tended the fire as Evan crunched on some toast, a small portion of butter covering it. It was crispy on the outside, but a bit burnt along the edges. Evan frowned at it, but then let it go.

Barger poked at the fire, getting great leaping flames working at the unburned portions of the logs, and soon had it crackling merrily. It warmed Evan from its heat, but it didn't banish the feeling of fear from his nightmare.

"We aren't ready." Evan stared into the flames, watching them shake and dance. "And we need to be."

"Your Highness?"

"Bring Sam Freeman to me. I want to speak to him." Barger nodded, then bowed.

Evan finished his meal while he waited, but he didn't have to wait long. A few minutes later the door opened and Barger admitted Sam, who greeted him and stood in front of his desk.

"You were supposed to give me an answer." Evan walked to his desk and sat, leaning back under the crest.

"I still feel that I am not the right man for the position," Sam said.

"My father is dead."

"The Archduke? I'm sorry..."

"Or might as well be, and we have the Belmarch breathing down my neck on their way to destroy everything. I don't have time for your self-doubt," Evan took a deep breath, calming himself. "We don't have time for your doubt now. Either take the position or leave."

Anguish played across Sam's eyes, but Evan thought he was going to say yes anyway. He finally nodded.

"Good. Now that we've got that out of the way we have some planning to do." Evan motioned to the chair, and Sam sat. "We have a lot of work to do, and I want to be ready. The Belmarch are going to remember who the Hornbloods are after they meet us."

The look of concern faded from Sam's face, and a hint of a smile played at his lips. "Very well, Your Highness. Where do we start?"

"You can get started on the work immediately." His chair creaked as the Duke leaned forward.

"Before we go further, Your Highness."

"What is it?" The Duke had reached out and was about to pull his book back.

"How long will you expect me to perform this job?"

The Duke paused and looked up. "I imagine if Rhys comes back, you would be released from it. Or, if a suitable replacement is found."

"That is my concern."

"Ah." The Duke put the book back, then reconsidered and shut it. "I can't say for sure what I think happened to Rhys, but in the event that he...hasn't survived, I give you my word that I will have a replacement sent. My father will know someone, or have one in mind, to take the position."

Sam exhaled, relieved that this would not continue in perpetuity. "I'm not sure where to start."

"Take Rhys' office, look through what he left. He gave me some instruction that I can pass on, but a bulk of his work is in the records there."

"His office? I couldn't do that."

"You'll have to. After lunch we'll go over what I know. You can meet me here." The Duke took up his book again, and Sam happened to catch a glimpse of the spine.

Boat building? He could have used that a long time ago. *What is the Duke of Hornblood doing with a book on boat building?*

"Is there anything else?" The Duke was peering at him from over the cover.

Sam swallowed. "No, Your Highness." he was dismissed, and started to leave.

"Wait, you'll need his key." The Duke rummaged through his pockets and produced a large, brass key. Sam went back and took it. It was cool, and smooth.

He left with it in hand, and stared at it out in the hallway. This was a place he never expected to be in, a situation beyond all imagination just a few months before.

But there was little he could do about it now, and Sam went there reluctantly. He stopped outside the big, brown door, remembering that he helped build it.

And now, his new task lay within. Fear and dread ran through him. He didn't know how to oversee anything, let alone a castle, but then he had not been a carpenter before either.

Nor had he always been a fighter.

He slipped the key into the lock and turned. There was resistance, and he pushed, then it was through as the lock clicked back.

He pushed the door opened and went inside. It was dark, and quiet. A layer of dust had accumulated on the ground and his feet left prints as he fumbled about.

Finally, he found the tinderbox where he remembered Rhys had kept it and lit a candle. There were no windows in this place, and it had a dank, musty smell. Water dripped down the chimney, from melting ice perhaps.

Sam examined the room. Rhys had left it fairly well cleaned up, with a stack of papers tied with string on one side of the desk. His possessions were still strewn about the room, but in their places in cupboards and shelves.

I won't be touching those. It felt eerie and oppressive. He kept glancing to the desk, and what would certainly be the records.

"Sam?" He turned. Martha was in the doorway, arms across her chest. She was peering in, squinting into the dim room.

"Martha." He didn't know what else to say.

"I thought you would be here, after what you said last night." She stepped one step into the room. "I hope..." Her face was drawn, and she looked older than she was.

"No," he said, looking around the room. "No, not at all. I mean, will you have a seat?" He found a chair and pulled it out for her.

"Yes. I'd like that. We've been so busy with lunch." He set it out for her, and she slipped into it. "I brought some wood. I wasn't sure if anyone had refilled it since he left."

Sam was touched. *Had she thought of him, or was it a habit, always making sure everything was in its place?* He tried to get a good look at her face, but it was hidden in the shadows.

She told him it was in the hall, and he brought it into the room and filled the fireplace. He cut a few starters off and coaxed a fire up, feeding it carefully and keeping it away from the drips until it was big enough to turn them to steam.

With some effort he soon had it burning, and added a few more logs until it burned strong and bright, casting an orange glow into the room and banishing some of the dank.

Water dripped down and sizzled, turning to steam to mix with the sweet smelling smoke that was sucked up the chimney and out of the room.

Martha was watching him, now lit up by a healthy glow. She had gained back some weight, and he was glad to see how much healthier she looked.

And there was something about her face as he watched it in the soft glow. It turned his stomach into knots and dried out his mouth.

"I should-" he stammered, wanting to continue, "about last night, I mean-"

He felt lightheaded and giddy. *I'm not a boy of fifteen anymore.* "What I mean to say is..."

"You aren't good with words?"

"No, that's not it." His head shot back to look at her. She had a hint of a smile. It melted the stern look she usually wore and made her seem about three years younger.

Then, as he stared, she furrowed her brows. "What is it? Is something wrong?"

"Yes. I mean no-" *Come on, Sam, you've been in dangerous places with less fear than this.* He took a deep breath, trying to calm the flutter in his heart. "What happened the other night. I didn't mean to take advantage of you like that. It wasn't right, and I wanted to apologize."

Her eyes opened wider. *She isn't going to forgive me for it, I knew it.*

"Take advantage of me?" she whispered.

"I won't do it again, I swear."

"Is that what this is about? Why you've been avoiding me all this time?"

Sam hunched over, preparing for a strike, but the blow never came.

"Sam." She stood and glided over to him. With a tender touch, she lifted his head. The flames of the fire licked up. Their eyes met, more than words passing between them.

Sam was more lightheaded than ever, but she was there, mere inches from his body. He reached out a trembling hand, and she took it, lacing her fingers through his and holding onto him fiercely. She looked up at him with those soft eyes, and her soft lips parted.

"I have been a fool," he said, mouth dry and cracking. He moistened his lips.

"No more a fool than I."

Gently, he wrapped an arm around her hips and pulled her in close, pressing her body up against his. Martha's eyes closed, and he leaned down.

Lips touched, and they melted into each other's arms.

19

New Walls

"What if they make it through, or what if they never even take the gate?" Evan paced with his hands behind his back, then went back to the book. "They're going to have the advantage of numbers and we have to negate it."

"We still fall back to the Keep, but we can harass them as they come." Sam pointed to the sketch, drawing a line down the new walls that he had suggested long ago. "As long as we have holes to shoot from, we stand a good chance."

"We'll have to reinforce the northern wall." Evan tried to think of every angle they might take. "It will bear the brunt of the attack."

"Agreed." It was the shallowest point on the Black River. Anywhere else would be either too deep or take too much time to build rafts. The Castle was well positioned to oversee it though.

"And you think you can finish the norther tower defenses?"

"Once we get the interior walls finished, I think so."

"Then we have a plan." Evan stopped pacing and joined him at the desk. He looked down at their overhead view, and a strong memory of Yand took him.

He had been too dense to see it before, too naïve. Evan shook his head. He learned his lesson, though, and now he was not going to make the same mistake twice.

"You'll have the support of the masons, I'll see to it. Bill might not like it, but there will be no excuses this time."

Sam was silent.

"What is it?" Evan asked. The faint smell of lunch hung in the air, a hearty stew and freshly baked rolls.

"Just something Bill said." Sam shook his head. "Never mind. It isn't worth mentioning. It will be a lot of work, and I can't see it being done before spring comes, or even summer."

"It will have to be sooner than that. Early spring will be the latest I expect the Belmarch to march." His muscles were still sore, but he would get a chance to limber them up after they were done. "We can't wait for spring to start, let alone wait for it to finish."

"We're up against time. The soldiers will have to work, too."

"You'll have them."

"It will take a miracle to survive, or an army," Sam said, putting his hands on the desk and leaning over the sketch.

"Since we don't have an army, let's hope for a miracle."

Sam traced the new walls. "What do you think happened to Rhys?"

The question caught him by surprise. "He made it to the capital and sent us help."

"That's what I thought too, but Silverthorn left before Rhys could have had the chance."

"Where did you hear that?"

"The soldiers. I've been talking to them. They left two months ago and had trouble in the snows."

Evan did the calculations in his head, thinking back to how many weeks ago Rhys had left. Sam was right. It couldn't have been him.

"It doesn't matter what happened to him." Evan shoved aside the fear that the thought brought with it, adding to the fuel of the nightmare. *I could use a drink.*

"You're probably right. I just hope he made it...to wherever he was going."

Evan leaned over and blew out the candle. They were done with it now, and habit forced him to conserve it. He smiled.

How differently he acted. Just a few weeks and months in brutal conditions and he was thinking of things like saving a candle.

"He's more tenacious than he looks, and he can handle himself." Evan glanced at his mother's letter. "And he'll need it in the King's Court. Never has there been a larger gathering of snakes and backstabbers."

Sam frowned. "You seem to have some experience with it."

"Experience?" Evan said through gritted teeth. "I was forced there every summer for the first few decades of my life. It was horrible, but I managed to sneak away at night and make things a little more interesting." His snarl turned into a more natural smile as he thought of the better times.

But then the shame came with it, and the smile faded.

"I can't say I'm jealous of your situation," Sam said. He stood, stretching his legs and arms. "You couldn't pay me enough to take it away from you."

"You wouldn't make a good court attendant. They're all so filled with themselves and desperate for power they'd do anything." Evan furrowed his brows, remembering some of the least desirable. "And I mean anything."

Silence grew between them. Voices, muffled by the distance and the door, drifted down the hallway. Then it was gone.

"Surviving might be a worse situation than the alternative," Sam said. "I hope..."

"Yes."

"Well, no use dwelling on it now. We've got a castle to fortify and an angry horde of Belmarch to prepare for." Sam bowed and gave him a proper salutation, and Evan dismissed him.

He shut the door with a gentle click as he left. Evan was alone once again.

Instead of dwelling on it, he picked up his sword and worked through the forms once, letting them flow through him until they had loosened his muscles and brought him to a short breath.

The next few days passed quickly. They made good progress on the modifications since the snow had stopped and began to melt.

Sam led a group out into the forest to pick up as much leaves and kindling as he could, and they piled some next to the workshop while the rest were dumped over the side of the north wall.

The walls were laid out, and the foundations dug into the softening ground. Everyone pitched in, despite their desire not to, and Evan saw to it that no man shirked by getting down in the mud himself and taking a turn.

After that, no one complained. Bit by bit, the forms began to take shape. Evan started to see how the walls would go up side by side.

And as he stood over it in the warming sun, water dripping from the eaves of the roofs, the hard knot in his stomach grew even harder.

"Don't be daunted by the size," Sam said, coming up from behind him. "Bill and the masons may not look it, but they can work when they have to. Now that they have some clear direction and a purpose, you'll see that it goes up quickly."

"I hope you're right," was all he could say in return. As he watched the progress, which seemed slow in comparison to what they needed, he wondered if he should call off the nightly training and focus all efforts on the construction.

He pondered it, thought about it, agonized over it, for hours that day. In the end he decided it was better to have a group of fighters ready and prepared than a few sets of walls.

They wouldn't be much good without the skills needed to survive.

So, Evan let the training continue, and attended when he could, working on his own forms when he tired of watching the others spar and train.

He thought about joining them, but knew he would outclass them and didn't want to embarrass any of them. Those lessons he had paid attention to and could see that Sam knew what he was teaching.

It roused his suspicion even more and became something of a thorn in his side. *Where did this man come from, and why is he so adept at fighting?*

Evan set Barger to find out as much as he could, but the servant came up empty-handed every night.

Then, one night, Barger came in with a hint of a smile on his face.

"What is it?" Evan asked. There was something good on the plates he carried, but he was more interested in what Barger had in his head.

"I've found something out about our friend, Sam Freeman."

20

THE ROAD AHEAD

"It's no good mi'Lord, the pass is too wet to get through." Raltone stared down at the quagmire of men and arms. Thick, brown mud covered every one of them up to their knees. His own steed, a great black stallion, shied away from the road below, backing up from the squishy grass. "We must turn back," Sable said at his left.

"General, what do you think?"

"I think we need to wait until it dries for us to get the baggage train through. If we don't, the men will starve."

"It could be a risk I'm willing to take." Raltone looked up to the mountains beyond, the pass rising to their blue base that was still frosted with white. A few more miles and they would be over it, a few days travel in good conditions.

"Turn back to the last dry encampment. We'll wait." Raltone turned his steed and kicked it into a trot, not waiting for the others to join. If he had to wait here, he might as well do it in style.

Winter still clung stubbornly to the mountains, even though the valleys were long ago melted and covered with new growth. It was always a risk, but he'd thought they could make it.

Sable caught up to him, bringing his own horse in line. Raltone noted that he almost came fully abreast.

"We could go around them to the west," Sable said. "It would take less time if we used it. We could catch them unaware."

"Since the failure of my previous men, I'm sure they are well aware we are coming." Raltone thought about it, then pulled up his short.

A sly smile crept across his face. "There is something you can do for me Sable."

Sable swallowed. "Yes, mi'Lord?"

Sam helped wrestle the stone the last few inches, sweat pouring down his back. It slid into place as they tipped it off the roller and sank into the mud at the bottom of the hole.

"There. Not the best conditions for building your wall, but it will have to do." Bill wiped off his hands, then walked back to the long row of masons dressing stone.

Sam leaned back to rest and catch his breath. The first of his improvements was in full swing now, a new set of walls that led from the gate up to the Keep.

They were no ordinary walls. Each was actually a set of walls, forming a hollow channel in the middle. This was going to be key to their use, once done.

And when the gate was breached, which he was planning on now, they would prove a nasty surprise for whoever came in.

When he had recovered, Sam walked back to the workshop. Trent and Kerien were working, with another small set of hands helping. Sam frowned at the young boy who kept his head down as he darted about the workshop.

"Almost done with this one, then we have a few more to go." Kerien patted his timber, a relatively short beam that would help tie the two walls together. They had enough lumber, but it was so green.

Sam didn't like using it like this, but they didn't have much choice.

It wouldn't play well with the stone, as wet as it was, and he wasn't sure how well it would hold up.

Would it shrink too much and pull the wall over prematurely? Or worse, right in the middle of an attack?

He hated the thought, envisioning an opening in their defenses and the enemy seizing on the advantage.

They wouldn't stand a chance.

"Good. Well done," Sam said. Kerien stopped what he was doing and swiveled around with wide eyes. Sam rubbed at a spot of mud on his trousers and walked to his workbench.

He wasn't sure why Kerien was giving him the look, but he let it pass and slumped onto his stool to recover. The stone was heavy and had taken a lot out of him, but he was grateful it was in. The rest of the wall would be built now, and none too soon.

Fresh air was bringing with it the warm smell of spring, and they had thrown the flaps of the workshop open to let it in. Sam breathed it in, grateful for the increase in temperature but wary of what it might bring.

The rivers were still swollen, fed with the snow melt high up in the north. It would protect them, for now, but come the end of spring it would die down and recede, leaving the river passable once again.

Trent was busy with his work, but once Sam recovered he went over to inspect. The cheeks of the tenons were smooth and fairly flat. Not perfect, but they didn't have time for that perfection. He checked them for square, and they were good enough.

"Better work on the sides, although you can clean up the shoulders more here."

"I thought about that but didn't have the time. Won't it be covered up in the wall?"

"Yes, but it has to be flat enough to seat properly. See where it waves here." Sam traced the center, which was bent out in a u shape. "That will stop the tenon from going all the way through. If you have to make a mistake, make sure the edges are the highest points." Sam walked Trent through some pointers, showing him a few different ways to make the cuts.

"Try one on the next few. Don't give up on it until you've gotten the hang of it. After that, if you prefer another way, do it."

"Thank you." Trent gave a little nod, then took up his chisel.

"You're welcome." Something about Trent's tone made him warm inside, like he had lighted a fire within him. This time, though, it was good.

He wanted to tell someone about it, but then realized that he didn't have anyone to tell. Martha wouldn't look at him it seemed, let alone give him the time of day to talk to him.

"Go ahead and keep working." The feeling inside was suppressed, and Sam moved on to Kerien.

His work was solid, but not perfect. Sam complimented him on it, and Kerien gave him another one of those looks.

"What's gotten into you?" he asked.

"What do you mean?"

"You aren't insulting me, or telling me everything I do is wrong."

That stung a little. "I don't think that is fair," Sam said, crossing his arms. "You have always had potential in there somewhere, and I'm glad it's coming out. That's it."

Part of him remembered Ned and the advice he had given him, how he opened his eyes to what was right in front of him. Another part of him knew he was down to two carpenters, and there was a lot of work still to go on the castle. He was going to need all the help he could get, and if it meant making them feel a little better, he would do it.

"You're just different, that's all I'm saying." Kerien returned to his work. "Not that I want you to go back."

Sam snorted. "Give me enough excuses and I'll leave in a heartbeat."

Kerien smiled, but his pace of work picked up.

Jospeh, the youngest addition to the crew, was busy sweeping up, and Sam stopped him, kneeling down to see him better eye to eye.

"How is your mother?"

"Good."

"Getting enough to eat?" Joseph nodded. "Good." Sam mussed his hair. "Make sure you get into all the corners. Collect everything, we're going to need it for later." He had plans for this.

Joseph nodded, and went back to sweeping. Sam watched him, wondering what it would be like to have a child. The thought of it, and who he might like to have one with, made his cheeks flush and he turned away quickly back to his own work.

No time to think about foolish thoughts like that.

Sam threw himself into his work, keeping going night and day. He tried to get as much done as he could, but the days seemed to fly by without stopping.

Logs rolled into the courtyard and into the workshop faster than they could process them. The resulting timbers were sucked up almost as quickly as they touched the finished pile, straight into the wall that was going up faster than they could keep up.

Bill was driving the masons now, with Evan standing over his back, watching almost every waking second.

Time in the workshop was split up by meals and training, with a few hours to sleep each night, but Sam and the others worked by torchlight far into the night.

The days went by. The work started taking its toll. Sam was sleeping less and less, dreaming up new defenses and different ideas of what could be done to strengthen their position.

Most of it he discarded. Some of it was good enough to take to Duke Hornblood, and a few of those were debated and implemented.

If the Belmarch were coming back, they would be met with some nasty surprises.

He was so caught up in his work he almost forgot about Martha, or meant to. He would see her almost every meal and think about her every night before he went to bed replaying that scene over and over in his head.

By the time he drifted off to sleep he wanted to pull his hair out in shame. When he woke up the next morning he would always resolve to find a way to make it up to her, to make it right somehow.

And every day he ended the day having not done so. But he felt that there was no one to confide in, no one he could talk to about it.

Ned was gone, and he wasn't comfortable talking to Dale about it, if he could find the time. Dale was more overworked than he was, constantly working to repair the tools of both the masons and their own, in addition to all the other work that demanded iron around the castle.

They hadn't gotten a new shipment of ore with the last supply, so Dale was forced to have his apprentices scrounge and scrape up anything they could. Nails from old boxes in the basement, old horse shoes stuck in the mud revealed by the warming weather, and he was forced to do most of the work himself.

Sam commiserated with him from time to time over a meal, but by the time it was over they were both whisked off to their respective duties and never had time to breathe.

All of this was in addition to training the men in combat and war fighting. That took almost all his energy alone, and Sam was beginning to tire of it. He started snapping at anyone who complained too much, or didn't do as he said quick enough.

Men were starting to avoid him, to shy away from him, but he was so tired he didn't care much.

There was something far more important on his mind, and something far more pressing to deal with.

He was feeling the effects, though, his movements becoming sluggish after a few weeks straight of the intense schedule. Sam kept telling himself it wasn't happening, that he was just fine, even though he was making more and more mistakes.

Finally, it caught up to him at one evening dinner, when he fell asleep and drenched himself in the evening stew. That woke him up faster than anything else.

"Sam, we need to get you to bed." Martha was at his side somehow. He hadn't seen her come over. The stew dripped off his face and soaked the front of him. She tugged at his arm.

"I'm fine. Leave me be." He tried to pull his arm away, but she kept a hold of it with a surprisingly strong grip. "There is more to do."

"And there will be more to do tomorrow. Come on, up with you." She nodded to Kerien at his side, who helped him to his feet.

Sam blinked away the sleep and told them he was fine to walk. Everyone in the great hall was watching him, silent over the sound of fire at the far end of the room. Sam felt it, but he was too tired to feel shame.

"Go, I've got him," Martha said when they were in the hall.

"Are you sure?" Kerien asked.

"My legs work fine," Sam said. "And I'm right here, you know."

"He might need some help down the stairs." Kerien had bags under his eyes too.

"Go get your dinner," Martha said, and shooed him off. She wiped down Sam's front with a handkerchief as Kerien left.

"Thank you for your help, but I can manage from here."

Martha stared up at him through narrowed eyes, a hand on her hip. "No, you don't, Sam Freeman. I know what you're going to do the moment I'm out of sight."

21

Movement

Evan watched from afar as the castle defenses took shape. The work he had done was long over, but it had its intended effect.

And he was sure his father wouldn't have approved of his actions, but that was only at the back of his mind. Even now, he thought of the lessons Yand had taught him, of how to treat those below you with respect.

Evan found himself outside, watching the work progress, as the warm, spring sun shone down and glinted off the chisels of the masons. Hammer blows rung out, a simple melody that echoed around the courtyard and bounced back and forth. Small shoots of green were coming up in the less heavily trafficked areas of the yard, and at the base of the walls, a hopeful reminder of the season to come.

Nearly all the snow had melted, except the most stubbornly deep drifts in the shade, and the last snowfall had been weeks ago. That made Evan think of the lands to the north, and how they too would be thawing and melting.

Feet squished through the resulting mud, a thick, brown paste that seemed to be everywhere and get into everything. Long streaks of it were trailed into the Keep, much to the chagrin of the ladies, and it was ever present.

"It's coming along, isn't it?" Sam stepped up beside him, stopping to rest before he took another load of beams to the half-finished walls. They had most of the lower courses complete, laid out in the straight lines that would eventually be above their heads, and it was clear what it would look like at this point.

"You look horrible," Evan said, looking the man over.

"Thanks," he said dryly. His hair was unkempt and looked like it hadn't been cared for in weeks, and his eyes were red and bloodshot. "If you can imagine, it was worse yesterday."

"I heard about that."

"Ah." Sam licked his lips but kept his eyes on the masons. Bill was keeping them working, and in line, and they seemed to be working efficiently. The horses that Silverthorn had left were essential to keep the rock flowing from the quarry now that they had run out of what had been stored within the walls.

"I would like to rest more, but..."

Evan shook his head. "Say no more." He, too, had been up countless hours. It was difficult to sleep. "With the sword hanging over your head, it is hard to sleep."

Sam nodded.

"On the other hand, the training seems to be going well. I've heard the soldiers remark on the improvement in the few weeks they've been here," Evan said, watching for a reaction.

He didn't get one. Sam only seemed to stew in his thoughts. *Should I reveal it now?*

"If you'll excuse me, Your Highness?"

Evan nodded, and Sam picked up his pair of beams, setting off for the far end of the wall. He watched from afar, leaning against the side of the Keep in the sun.

Trent joined Sam with another pair after a few minutes, and together they pulled them up the nearly complete wall. The masons had left notches at the top, and the two men made some final adjustments to the beams before dropping them into this space and hammering them home with an oversized mallet. Evan had seen this happen more than a few times and knew that the masons would come behind and lay the final few courses on top to complete the wall, tying them together.

That left a space wide enough for a man to draw an arrow in, both to the interior path that led directly from the gate to the Keep, and the courtyard on either side.

Evan still wasn't sure it would work well, but he had to trust Sam's instinct. From what he knew about him now it would be a good idea to do so.

Eventually the noon bell rang, and Evan reluctantly left the warm, sunny courtyard to retreat back into the Keep for the meal.

It was nothing special, drawn from the supplies that had been brought up, but included some berries that a few foraging parties had stumbled across in the wood. They were red and sweet, a type of strawberry that grew in the forest, and complemented the fresh bread that the women had prepared.

Whoever made it knew what they were doing, for day after day it came out light and fluffy on the outside with a wonderfully crisp crust on the outside. It was good enough by itself, which was good because their supplies of butter and cheese had run out. Anything that remained was carefully locked away in the cellar in the emergency rations.

Evan distasted even the thought of it. A whole cellar set aside to feed the castle in the event of another siege. He wasn't sure what they would do if it came to that, but was certain that the enemy army coming would have no patience for it.

And that was what scared him the most.

They would have the advantage of numbers, not some small raiding party like the last one. He would do the same in the Belmarch leader's place, and he hated that there was nothing he could do about it.

But he had sent his message south with Silverthorn, to be delivered to his father, if he still lived.

That brought a grimace to Evan's face, so much so that Barger asked about it as he was clearing away the remains of his lunch.

"I'm not ready."

"Ready for what, Your Highness?" Barger worked smoothly and methodically.

"To be Archduke." Evan stood up, irritated at the thought of it, and started pacing around his room. The old thirst returned to him, and Barger seemed to notice.

"I understand. I was not prepared to come here, and yet the task came to me."

"You didn't have much choice, did you?"

"I did have a choice."

Evan froze. That wasn't something he had ever thought about, and he turned back to Barger. "What?"

"I was offered a different position. One with less...honor and opportunity for advancement. However, it was tempting in its own right."

"Someone...gave you the chance to not come here with me?"

"Yes."

"And you didn't take it?" Evan drilled into him with his eyes.

"After how I treated you all those years?"

He was ashamed of it, and it leaked into his voice. His old self had been horrible, hadn't even known Barger's name or even noticed him.

"Correct."

"Why?"

Barger's lips pursed ever so slightly. "That is a question I asked myself for a while," he said softly, careful with his words.

"I won't take offense," Evan promised. He might not have been the best master, but he could make up for it now if just to hear Barger out.

"I made a promise." Evan wanted to urge him on, but he saw that the man was thinking, considering what to say next, and he waited until he continued. "To Captain Yand. When I was younger, he made me make a promise to take care of you when he was gone. He said you needed solid men around you to keep you out of trouble."

Despite the sadness that the words stirred in him, Evan couldn't help but feel a small smile creep onto his face. "Well, he was right, wasn't he?"

Barger's face reflected the smile. It improved the man's appearance, and Evan realized it might have been the first time he had ever seen it. "He was right, Your Highness. Although, I think he would have recognized the man you are as who he thought you would be."

"I'm a long way from that," Evan said, a hint of sadness coming back into his voice. Yand had always treated him better than he deserved, always expected him to be a better man than he was.

The loss pained him even more. Evan wished he could take Yand back to the Hornwood and bury him as he deserved. He was better than the shallow grave he'd been given.

At that moment, Evan resolved to do it. "When we get out of this I'm going to lay Yand to rest as he should be."

Barger nodded, sensing his sadness. "I'll take my leave, Your Highness, and take these back to the kitchens."

Evan nodded and bid the servant a good day. The pressure hadn't been relieved, but it had helped to share a smile. Evan never expected it would have, and then realized how fond he had grown of Barger.

The man has been with me for years. How had the servant found his way into the Duke's service? Evan couldn't remember, for that matter, he couldn't remember selecting any of his servants.

His mother? That would be the most logical choice. She always had a keen eye for servants, who was the best and where to place them. Her lady-in-waiting had been at her side for decades, ever since she had married his father or longer, or so he heard.

How does she do it? Evan wondered as he went through his afternoon training, sliding into the forms that came easier and easier every day. They were starting to flow like water now. He entered one, and the motions rippled and cascaded over his body, then he was done and out the other side, breathing deep with his sword still outstretched.

With little else to do, Evan finished another set and then read through another book on warfare. The new books caught his eye as he finished, and he took one out with him to the wall, intending to watch the progress.

The rivers were raging, flooded with the melting snow farther to the north, each lapping at and spilling out of its banks. Evan guessed they had to be five feet higher than normal, and a hearty moat to keep out any enemies.

He dwelled on what it meant to set the castle here, right at the most defensible position between Chathem and Belmarch. Whoever had chosen the spot had been wise, with the rocky shoreline a good foundation to build upon.

There were no other bridge between the two countries. If they had they had long ago been destroyed in the generations of fighting that had been exchanged, the Belmarch almost always the assessor.

He examined the other side, just as covered in trees, that extended out and up to a mountain range off in the distance. Its craggy peaks pierced the green tops of the trees, then rose to white caps that looked difficult to traverse, a perfect wall to keep out any that tried to invade Belmarch. Evan suspected those mountains and the hard packed earth beyond them were why the Belmarch always desired Chathem lands. All that came out of them was metal and dust, little in the way of food and sustenance.

However, Chathem was a land rich in soil, good for growing crops and timber. He imagined he would desire them if he were in the Belmarch's place, not that it excused their blood-thirsty actions.

He blinked. Evan found that time had gotten away from him in his thoughts. The spring wind had died down, and with it the warmth. A chill was on the air, even though most of the land surrounding the castle was starting to turn green. Shoots of grass poked up through the tiny bits of snow still left in the shadows and blossomed everywhere else.

Behind him, the work had progressed. It looked like the carpenters had put up another few beams, and the masons were finishing the last few courses of the stone beneath the connectors. Small windows looked out over the courtyard, big enough to shoot an arrow through but a challenge to try to shoot back in.

Forms passed through the two walls, masons carrying stone most likely, but it was difficult to see them from this far away on the wall. Evan examined the new defenses, thinking as he would if he were the enemy.

The Keep was solid and well built, designed and construct-ed with one entrance that was now flanked by two walls. Going through the side might be a tactic they might take, but Evan wouldn't. The door looked to be the softest spot.

And now it was hardened with extra fortifications. Evan hoped that it would be enough, but after the siege he wasn't sure. That hadn't been a whole army.

Evan looked back to Belmarch, squinting in the late after-noon sun. Something about it didn't feel right.

Out of the corner of his eye, he saw movement on the opposite bank. Evan bolted upright and stared into the trees at the spot, waiting for movement again.

He didn't have to wait long.

22

A Pledge and Oath

Then it was gone. Evan thought it might be a mistake, a strange daydream, because no matter how hard he looked he couldn't make out that form again.

The shape of a man, brief and darkened in the shadow of the trees, but a man nonetheless.

A chill ran down Evan's back, and the ramifications hit him like a rock. He glanced back to the new fortifications, and the new surprises they had in store.

Soldiers and workers were toiling, moving rock and wood and metal as fast as they could, but it wouldn't be enough. They weren't finished, they weren't ready.

But it seemed that time was up. After the long days of preparation, the hard work that had gone into this already. It was too late to do any more.

There was another sentry on the wall, farther down to the west, and Evan approached. "What did you see?"

The man clutched at his spear. Evan had seen him working rock often, a mason. He looked down. "I thought I saw..."

"A person, on the other side of the river?"

The man nodded. Evan breathed deep, the smell of spring fresh in the air, a contrast to what he was feeling deep inside. "I saw it too."

"It wasn't real, was it?"

Evan looked back across the river. It was quiet. "Keep a close eye on that bank. If you see anything else, don't hesitate to raise the alarm." Evan clapped the man on the back. "Stand firm. These walls were well built, and thick. They will stand."

He wondered how often his father had spoken words he wanted to feel but didn't. It didn't feel good, but he believed them, or at least he told himself that.

The stone walls were thick and firm beneath his feet, more than just a few inches wide, and had already withstood a beating.

But there was so much of it, and too few defenders to properly defend it. Not for the first time Evan wondered why they had made it so big, but put it out of his mind.

He left the sentry and went to the northern tower, climbing the steep, winding stairs around the circular tower to the top where he could get the best view.

Another sentry was there, watching Belmarch. "Have you seen anything?"

The man started and whirled around to face him. "No, Your Highness," he stammered.

Evan squinted and looked as far as he could into Belmarch. No smoke, no fires, not even a cloud of dust, but since it had been so wet he didn't think there would have been. It was quiet, empty. Not even a flock of birds flew there.

Perhaps it was a figment of his imagination, but then why had the other man reported the same thing?

Evan kept calm, trying to not let the raging emotions inside him show, and left after an appropriate amount of time. His footsteps rang on the stone stairs as he descended, his heart pounding in his ears.

He went first to the guardhouse, finding Mathew and telling him to double the guard.

"Double, Your Highness?" Mathew asked.

"And prepare the arms for distribution."

"You know something then." Mathew's brows furrowed.

"Do as I say, but do it quietly. No need for alarm yet, just caution."

Mathew saluted. Levitus was next, and Evan found him working with the other soldiers hauling rock. Evan pulled him off to the side and told him what he'd seen.

"We will be ready, Your Highness." Levitus bowed in obedience, unfazed by his words. Solidly built, he seemed to exhibit that in every aspect of his nature. "I will get the men ready now."

"No, keep them working." They were at the top course. Evan wasn't sure how critical it was. "Might as well use the time we have."

The dinner bell rang then, interrupting his plans. Evan dismissed Levitus but told him to send a messenger for Sam to meet him in his study. A light drizzle from blue clouds above dripped down, soaking him. He smelled rain in the air as soon as he realized what was happening and hurried back inside.

Dinner was waiting for him when he arrived, and he stripped his coat to dry by the fire. Evan glanced at the food but was so consumed with worry that he couldn't touch it, no matter how tempting it looked. Venison on a bed of potatoes.

Instead, he paced round the room until Sam knocked on the door and entered at his command.

"You wanted to see me, Your Highness?"

Evan bade him to sit, but continued pacing.

"I'm afraid were' out of time." Evan again recounted the story, bringing a thundercloud to Sam's face.

"We knew they would come," Sam said, face taut. "I wish we had more time."

"As do we all, but will what we have work?"

"No." Sam slowly shook his head. "Bill needs to set that final course for it to work as intended."

"How long will it take?"

"Another day or two, maybe longer. He wasn't sure the last time I asked him and I was so caught up in my own work." Sam spread his hands. "We needed the arrows, and we only have four of us."

Evan stopped and spun on his heel to face him. "Have you had anything to eat?"

Sam shook his head.

"Then take mine. Go ahead, I can't eat it."

Sam looked exhausted, even after getting some rest. Evan suspected he had been up, despite his desire that he sleep more. "You haven't been sleeping well?"

Sam crossed his arms and looked at the food.

"Go on, have it. It will be thrown away if you don't."

At last, and with great reluctance, Sam picked up the silver fork and started to eat.

"I'm having nightmares. It's hard to sleep."

The man was almost twice his age, or he looked like it. Evan saw something in his eyes, a hint of the past life that he kept locked away.

"I'm going to need fighting men, Sam." Evan clasped his hands behind his back, and spoke barely above a whisper. "I don't know why you want to hide your past from us, or what you feel you did that was so bad, but the time for building has come and gone. I need a destroyer."

Sam's face flashed, a myriad of emotions playing over it. "I don't think you understand what you ask of me."

"I understand completely. It isn't just our lives at stake here. If we don't hold this castle, you know where the Belmarch will go, and what they will do. Our lives will be forfeit if we can't find the will to stand up and fight." Evan saw that he was too conflicted, like so many men that were drinking in the taverns. Hard lives they wanted to escape, like the lonely one he wanted to leave. "I'm not asking you to do this for me. I'm asking you to do this for them."

Evan pointed beyond his door. "For the ones who have already sacrificed their lives. For the ones that survived. The children that will become young men and women, the families that would be torn to shreds if we didn't stop them. The friends you hold dear, the men you work beside and sweat beside and bleed beside. I'm asking you to do this for them, not for me."

"There is a beast within me," Sam said, his face finally calming. He looked peaceful. "A monster that consumes and destroys. It isn't what I did that I'm running from." His eyes flashed to Evan's. "It's who I am."

There was a danger lurking there, not hidden well. Evan wanted to draw back, suddenly afraid of this man sitting before him, but he ignored it. He had confronted men who had wanted to take his life and lived to tell the tale.

"Who are you, then?"

Sam drew back his head in surprise and blinked.

"Are you not Sam Freeman? Master of the carpenters at Hornblood Castle, Overseer, trainer, lover?"

That last got to him, and Sam's mouth parted. The danger in his eyes was gone, replaced with embarrassment.

"Who you are is not who you were." Evan held out a hand. "It is not who you have to be."

Sam considered his hand, agitated and fidgeting, a strange condition for Evan to see him in.

Finally, after what seemed like minutes, he stood and took his hand. His grip was powerful, hard and firm, but his hand was warm.

"Tell me, if I fight for you, what will happen?" Sam looked deep into Evan's eyes. "Will you be the man who came here?" Something was bubbling between them, and Evan wasn't sure if it was a test or something else.

"No. That man is gone, drowned in his own ego."

"Then we will go as two men of our own, not what we were, and fight together," Sam said.

"Together." Evan nodded.

"And will you be the Duke of Hornblood?"

"I will."

Sam smiled then. The tension that had been building between them evaporated.

"Then I will go, make as much progress with what little time we can, and live up to what you expect."

Evan watched him go, then stopped him as he opened the door. "The ending."

"What?"

"Sometimes the endings don't always turn out right."

Sam turned back. "I'm not sure I understand."

"In the books." Evan went to his desk and picked one up. "Most turn out happy in the end, but not all."

Sam gave him a half smile, then left.

Evan slumped into the chair by the fire, letting the tension flow from his body and forcing it to relax. They might not have much time, but this was going to be his last peaceful night in a long time, of that he was certain.

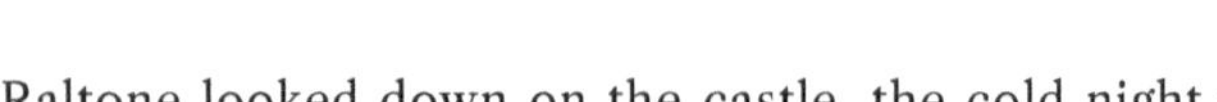

Raltone looked down on the castle, the cold night wind rustling his hair and stinging his cheeks.

He wanted it burned. It was an affront to him and his people. "For too long we've been seen as backward, unable to take care of ourselves, and savages. That ends now."

A murmur ran through the group behind him. His horse whinnied and Raltone pulled up the reins, backing it up from the edge of the mountain.

Behind him his troops flowed through the still-soggy pass. "How long until they are through?"

"About five more hours mi'Lord and everyone and everything will be on the other side," Granb said.

"I was asking Sable."

Granb frowned, then hid it and bowed. He pulled back.

Sable looked uncomfortable, sickly, but he pulled up. "He speaks the truth. They should be over tonight while the darkness still holds."

"I want no fires, not a hint given away. Not even a scout." He got no response and stopped staring at the fires through the windows of the castle to turn back.

Both Granb and Sable shifted in their saddles.

"What is it?" His voice carried a hint of warning.

"We had sent a scout already, mi'Lord," Granb said after a long, uncomfortable silence.

"Who gave that order?" He was barely whispering, and both of them leaned forward. Neither answered at first. "Shall I have both of you removed and imprisoned?"

"It was I," Sable said, looking down. "I had no idea that wasn't what you wanted, mi'Lord. I would not have done it."

Raltone frowned as he stammered. "When we get there, I want you to lead the attack personally. From the front."

Sable's eyes widened, but he swallowed and wisely kept his mouth shut. Raltone took one last look while they had the advantage of elevation, scanning the swollen river for any sign of stopping, then turned his steed back down the slope and onto the narrow path.

The others followed, and they descended the mountain. As they did the castle was obstructed by the trees, but inside Raltone was starting to feel the excitement build.

The entire land of Chathem lay before him, and with the eastern raiders paid off to invade they wouldn't be prepared for attack.

The time was finally right for him to claim what was rightfully theirs.

23

ALL IS WELL

Evan wiped the sweat from his brow and paused to catch his breath. Men kept moving, carrying stone from the masons down below up to the wall above in the torchlight.

The night had a warmth to it, the hint of spring in full bloom. Evan squinted against the darkness, trying to see how much longer they had to go.

He couldn't make it out, and ended up giving up until he could get back to the top himself. His coat had been shed long ago, like the others, his body warm enough from the work.

Evan went back to the line, waiting to get another block. He didn't have long to wait, the masons were carving at a furious rate. Soon they handed him a roughly shaped stone, good enough to get to the top, where Bill was directing the final finishing and placement.

The stone was large, and heavy, and weighed him down, but Evan went to the makeshift ladder and tied it to the rope. With a quick jerk he signaled the men at the top and mounted the ladder, racing to get up it before the stone was off the ground.

Two men heaved at the rope, exhaustion straining their muscles and showing in their face, and he grabbed onto the rough, fibrous rope and helped. In a few pulls it was at the top, and Evan regained his load and walked carefully across the stone wall down to the end.

"Put it here," Bill said, pointing beside him, then turned, "Your Highness," he added, belatedly and with a toothy smile.

Evan let the rock drop into place. It sank into the prepared mortar, which dripped out the sides and flowed down the wall. He stepped back to let Bill examine it. "Good enough without dressing, on to the next one." A mason followed him, scooping out more mortar from his reed bag and working it between his stone and the ones next to it to fill the gaps. He wasn't thorough, but pushed with his trowel until most of the gap disappeared.

"How long do you need?" Evan asked, coming up behind Bill.

Bill squinted, then licked his thumb before holding it up before him. "A few days and we'd have it finished at this rate."

"Is there any way to go faster?"

"Yes," Bill said, staring at him. "Give me more masons."

"That's the one thing I can't make."

"One?" Bill smiled, but Evan wasn't concerned at it, and even had to smile back. Bill was like many men he had wasted nights with drinking and carousing, and had a familiar spirit that resonated with Evan.

He wasn't sure why, given the man's past and the things he had done, or was accused of at least. For the moment, Evan wasn't concerned. He might need men who were prone to violence and was glad it wasn't going to be directed toward him for a change.

"You being out here has helped," Bill said, pausing to sit and rest. "I have to give you credit for it, and I'm not sure I would have believed it had someone told me you'd be willing to work alongside us a few weeks ago."

"We all have our...quirks, don't we?" Evan joined him, looking up at the clouds that drifted over the face of a nearly full moon. The smell of wildflowers was in the air, but the sound of the river had lessened.

Only in the moment of peace did he notice it. The one thing that stood between them and Belmarch, and it was dying down like it wanted to invade.

Soon it would trickle to a stream as the majority of the Venti shifted to the Golden River and open up its path to man and beast. Evan wished its bottom would stay mud, that it would suck at their feet and drag them down, but knew it was a useless hope.

In a few days it would practically be a road to an army, with them sitting in a castle right at the end of it, flat and ready to be plucked like a goose.

"Back to work. You've had enough rest," Evan said, rising to his feet. Bill joined him, with grumbling that he couldn't hear.

Evan spent the next few hours helping until Bill called an end to the shift for everyone to get rest. He stayed for a few more rounds of stone hauling, then was too tired to go any further and slipped away to his bed.

It welcomed him like a warm glove and, before he could even dream, the morning light woke him again.

Evan sat up and rubbed the sleep from his eyes. Someone knocked at his door and through a yawn, he invited them in.

Barger walked through carrying a tray of food. "Good morning, Your Highness. I thought you might like something to eat."

Evan's stomach grumbled. It had been a while since he had eaten dinner the night before. "How long did I sleep?"

"Not long past breakfast, only a few hours."

Evan cursed and threw back the covers. He sprang out of bed onto the cold floor and started to dress. "Why didn't you wake me?"

"You needed the sleep, and it's quiet outside." Barger tended the fire, adding another log onto the banked ashes.

"You mean..."

"All is well."

"For now," Evan said, but inside he was elated. Another day, more work done. Sam and the carpenters were working on arrow shafts, and Dale was finishing as many heads as he could. They could sharpen the tips in a bind, but this was good news.

His mind was abuzz with thoughts, what they had to do, where they had to build, and Barger had to remind him to eat once the fire had begun to lick into flames at the fireplace.

Barely chewing, Evan gulped down his food. He wasn't sure what it was, but he had dressed and was out the door in less time than it took Barger to get the fire going and collect his dishes.

The sounds of construction grew louder the closer he got to the exit of the Keep. Hammers were ringing on chisels, and men were shouting and talking. There was little laughing, there wasn't enough time for anyone to get distracted that way.

Evan realized he'd forgotten a coat at the entrance door, but pushed it open anyway. It was warm outside, almost too warm for so early in spring, but he welcomed the feeling on his skin and would have breathed deep if he weren't so worried.

He went up the ladder and straight to the northern wall, watching Belmarch for any signs of the enemy. It was quiet, but Mathew was there too, watching.

"Good morning, Your Highness."

Evan gave a quick greeting. "What have you seen?"

"Nothing. It is quiet."

Evan breathed a sigh of relief. "Good."

"No, it's too quiet." Mathew looked to the other side of the river, staring intently into the forest. "Not a hint of wildlife, and no bird all morning."

The dread that had been reduced as soon as he saw Belmarch quiet started to grow again, and Evan reached for his sword, wrapping a hand around the hilt for reassurance. The cool of the leather felt good, solid.

"What are they waiting for?" Evan whispered, mostly to himself. Mathew had been stiff, and Evan wondered why.

Now, he knew. He felt it too, the keen edge that his body was prepared for something. Without knowing what it was his body was ready.

"Night," Mathew whispered. "They're waiting for nightfall."

In darkness they can hide. "Of course. Then we shall give them a night they will remember, won't we?"

Evan sat at his table, staring up at the Hornblood crest hanging over his desk. The sunlight was still coming in through the window, but it had turned a vibrant shade of red.

There were many things on his mind, and it seemed like a whirlwind. Was his father still alive? What was his mother doing? Would there be reinforcements sent as he'd asked?

He closed his eyes and put his head in his hands. He wished Yand were still here, a guiding hand and a wise counsel. He wished Silverthorn was still here, a fighter and a leader that would put everything right and make sure he knew what to do.

A part of him even wished his father were here, to take away this burden and lead the defenders how they should be led. He was realizing how much burden the Archduke had, and how it must make him do things he did not want to do.

Evan looked up, realizing the old hatred had been relegated to something far smaller than it was. It was still there, and he imagined it always would be, but he held something else bigger.

Respect.

Respect for what decisions his father had to make, for the actions he had to take to keep his family safe and his subjects protected. Evan had thought him cold and distant, but realized why he had been that way.

It was not an easy burden to bear.

A soft knock at the door disturbed him. Barger came in, as requested, but without a sound. There was too much heaviness in the air for words.

Evan stood and walked to the center of the room. Barger brought him his armor, piece by piece, and helped him put it on. Each added more weight to his body, but Evan took it in stride.

He took the helmet last, but did not put it on. It was cold on his fingers, a decorative Tree of Everlong worked into the crown. The roots traveled down the side of the helmet, a reminder of who was the root of the Hornbloods.

The last of the light was dying, and twilight was upon them. Barger stepped back, waiting as straight as an arrow, and Evan nodded to him.

He went out into the courtyard where the others had assembled under the cover of darkness. They were quiet, but ready for a fight.

Evan was the last to join. All eyes turned to him as he stepped into the yard. He glanced up at the wall.

Only two sentries walked it, watching in the night. Two, when there should have been more for an invading army on the horizon.

If they knew the army was there, that is.

Now was not a time for telling the enemy they knew they were coming, despite what he would rather have.

Evan turned back to the waiting group and examined their faces in the fast fading light.

Some were too young, some were too old. All of them were scared. He saw it in their eyes, felt it in their gaze. He felt it in his own heart, beating loudly in his chest, constricted by his breastplate.

"For Chathem." His words were merely a whisper, "and the defenders of Hornblood Castle."

His father would have made a bigger speech, a grander speech. One that would inspire them to fight harder than they ever could. He had to settle for the only words he knew to say, and to hope that they would be enough.

But as he looked out, and as the light faded, he thought he saw some ease to their fear. He didn't feel it himself. His hands trembled.

But he was going to have to lead despite it.

And then the sentry on the wall screamed out in pain.

Evan turned, careful to stay calm, as the others shied back. Sam stepped up beside him, and he was glad to have someone, anyone, there.

He froze. The man's scream cut off into a gurgle, then a death rattle. Something was up on the wall, a shadow against the moonlight.

His heart beat louder, faster. It was not an ordinary man, but worse.

24

A Feast for Vultures

"Archers!" Evan pulled out his sword. By the time he could point it at the figure, twangs from behind him were sounding, the whistle of arrows flying overhead close behind.

The figure moved. Arrow flew past where it had just been and over the wall, harmlessly sailing by it.

Evan blinked. It had moved so fast he couldn't believe it, but there it was again. Only this time it wasn't moving out of the way.

It jumped off the wall, charging straight for them, straight for him, a blade glinting in the moonlight like a silver crescent streaking through the air.

Evan had no time to react, no time to think, but somehow his body moved to meet it. He brought his sword up and to the right, and it connected with the sword.

His hand almost spun back as the force of the monster knocked away his sword.

No, it can't be. Whatever it was didn't expect such power and jumped back.

But it was too late. Evan had seen it in the torchlight and had been overcome by fear.

An arrow flew by his ear. This time, it found its mark in the chest of the man-shaped monster.

It looked down and growled, then reached up a hairy claw and snapped the arrow in two. Black blood oozed from the wound, but it didn't seem to notice any more than that.

Men gasped behind him. Some cursed. Prayers were said, cries to gods that went up into the night sky.

The words shook him from his shock, and Evan emerged as if from a dream. The monster was moving again, coming for him, and he slipped into the forms, letting his body take over.

He ducked. The long, sinister blade swept over him, missing by an inch.

Planting his foot, he shoved forward with a thrust. All his strength went into it.

And his blade found flesh.

The thing roared, deafening him and almost driving him back by the sound alone. A sickly vomit smell washed over him, laden with death and decay, and the monster's fangs dripped with the blood of his victim.

It reached down, lightning fast, but Evan was already moving, setting his sword against its hamstring and pulling as he dove to the side.

He wasn't fast enough. It clipped his shoulder, knocking him off balanced, and he hit the ground hard.

Before he could get up the thing roared again. There was shouting now, a din of chaos. Arrows were flying.

His right shoulder was hurting, but Evan rose and turned to face it. Sam was holding it at bay with his spear while the others peppered it with arrow and strikes.

One man darted in with a sword, but the monster swatted him away. He flew up in the air and crumpled a dozen feet from where he'd started.

Evan ignored the blood pounding in his ears and his heart pounding in his chest. He couldn't wait for it to kill more.

He charged it, attacking with a vicious downward cut, but it was met with a counter.

The force of the monster's blade shook through his arm, rising almost to his head.

Evan pulled back, then tried again. Sam struck with the spear, distracting the monster, giving him enough of an opening to duck underneath it.

There was no time to wear it out, and Evan saw only one option. He struck at the unprotected neck, drawing a long line along it.

The monster roared again and stepped back to clutch at his neck. It was too much and too long, and it toppled backward.

Evan stopped, leaning on his sword to watch.

But he couldn't believe his eyes again. There, in a pool of its own blood, the body...changed.

"What is it?" someone asked.

"Devilry!" cried another. A murmur ran through the men.

All that was left of it was a dead man, sunken and shrunk, no sign of life.

Evan walked to it with a trembling hand, reaching out to touch it.

It was solid, no ghost, but there was no strength in those arms.

"Whatever it was, we killed it," he said.

"We can't face an army of those." Bill strode into the firelight. "The Belmarch have discovered evil powers. They've changed themselves to demons."

"We do not need to face an army of them," Sam said. He was farther back, his face obscured in the shadows. Whispers ran through the group.

Evan's shoulder was hurting more. He tried to look at it but couldn't see much under his armor. There was no blood. "Everyone to the wall. They will know that we won't be caught unaware."

They hesitated, but he turned and strode to the wall. He took the steps two at a time and found his place between two merlons.

The river was talking, not in the roar that he had hoped for in the rush of water that would keep it unpassable, but in a lighter hush.

Even in the night he knew it was possible to cross. Boulders that were near the bottom shone white as the water parted around them.

But there was no army crossing. Yet.

Levitus was shouting at the defenders, berating them for their fear.

Fear was great within him, though, and he kept replaying the fight in his head. It felt like it had gone on for so long, but he knew it was only moments.

Someone came up beside him.

"How do you know?" Evan asked.

"Whatever drove that man to do what he did, it was beyond painful to his body," Sam said. The dead man's face flashed in Evan's mind, the mouth twisted and contorted, the eyes wide in horror. "Even if they do have some ancient power, not all of them will be willing to use it. They are just as superstitious and suspicious of powers like that as we are."

"But we have no counter to it." Evan shuddered to think of hundreds of them climbing the walls, and he leaned over the side to check. They were empty. "There are two men dead to one, and there would have been more if we had to face them on our own."

Sam stared out over the river, then his hand tightened on his spear. "They come." As men filed by behind him, horns sounded across the river.

Evan looked to the tree line, just in time to see it stir.

"Bows at the ready," he called. The order went down the line, and arrows rattled. Those that had not strung them did so now.

Figures emerged from the shadows of the forest. What looked like the entire tree line moved out now, and men approached the shore.

The army of the Belmarch had come.

Evan started counting, but soon gave up as dozens turned into hundreds. They could not stand up against this many.

But if they did not, then he had no doubt they would kill and murder. Dread turned into outright fear, and only his hand on the merlon beside him held him up.

"There are so many," someone said.

"We could flee," another said.

"There will be no escape," Sam said, raising his voice. "They will come after you and chase you down. They would kill everything you ever loved and then move into the country, murdering and pillaging as they went."

That silenced some of them, but the chatter continued. Evan wasn't sure he wanted to stay behind the walls, but he touched them to reassure himself.

They were thick, made of rock many feet thick. They were strong, and difficult to climb.

Even though that monster had made it.

"We can hold them back here, and wait for reinforcements to arrive," Evan called out. "You are men of Chathem and will stand strong." Out of sheer luck, his voice didn't waver and break.

The army continued to pour out of the trees. They lined up, fierce eyes watching the defenders on the wall.

Then, out of the center, a group on horseback emerged. Evan's eyes were drawn to the man in the lead as he took his horse up to the river and splashed into the shallows.

There, horse up to its knees, he stopped.

"If you surrender now, I may let you live," the man on horseback called.

It was silent, except for the flow of the river.

Evan wondered if he was telling the truth, wondered who this man was. He didn't look particularly impressive. He wasn't large, or muscular, or even that tall.

But even from this distance he could see something in the man's eyes. A fire, a terrible ability to do whatever he needed to do for power. An unquenchable thirst for it.

And in those eyes Evan found a strange kindred.

It made him uncomfortable, it made him squirm. Was this the kind of man he would be? Willing to lead an army to take whatever he wanted by force?

He thought about surrendering, how much easier it would be. He could finally give up his titles, finally be rid of the responsibility. Evan looked up and down the line of men.

And then his eyes met Sam.

A man not even of this land, and still willing to stay and fight when he could have run. He owed no allegiance to Evan or the Hornbloods, but had sacrificed to train the others and to build this castle.

Even now, he saw Sam was tired. They all were.

From the men on the wall to the women and children inside, they wouldn't survive if the Belmarch got inside these walls, no matter if it was by surrender or force.

So Evan decided. He sheathed his sword.

"Your Highness, what are you doing?" Sam asked.

"Giving him an answer." Evan walked to the nearest archer and took the bow from him. The man gave it up, wide-eyed in surprise.

He took up an arrow, fitted it to the bow, and raised it. The feather tickled his cheek, and Evan breathed deep, remembering all his training.

He let fly the arrow, and it whistled into the air. It splashed into the river just before the horse and rider, making it shy away and whinny.

"This is Chathem land. As the sworn protector, I will give you one chance to go back. Any invasion of these lands will be met with force." Evan handed the bow back and watched the man.

He had regained control of his steed, still in the shallows. Tension crackled in the air.

"You will regret this." He turned and walked back into Belmarch, but only to talk to the other men on horseback.

Evan wanted to breathe a sigh of relief, but knew that it wouldn't be that easy.

The men scattered, kicking their horses into action and traveling up and down the bank. Orders were passed in the Belmarch tongue, and a great cry rang out from them. It billowed across the river, impossibly loud from the great army.

Evan could only watch, helpless, as the infantry waded into the river and began to cross.

25

Fire

Sam watched the enemy advance, exchanging his spear for a bow. He wished Ned was beside him, he was so much better of a shot than he was, but as he looked down he almost chuckled.

There were more than enough targets down there. If he missed there was something wrong with him.

"Archers, ready." The high walls extended their range well into the river, but not all the way. The enemy troops splashed into the shallows where the river was the narrowest.

Just as they'd planned.

Sam joined the others, nocking an arrow to the string and pulling back.

"Fire!" Levitus yelled.

He sighted at one soldier wielding an axe above his head and let loose. A hundred arrows flew into the air, louder than a flock of birds and deadly.

The first rank was carrying ladders, hastily constructed in the forest beyond. The arrows landed, almost half on their mark, and men screamed and shouted as they dropped.

The defenders didn't have time to celebrate though, because they kept coming on, augmented by archers of their own.

"Aim for the ladder carriers," Sam shouted. The second volley wasn't as strong, nor was it as effective, and the bow firing dissolved into individual shots.

Sam ducked as a return arrow flew over his head, whistling by his ear. He went back up, aiming for the enemy who shot it, but couldn't find him. He shifted his focus to another and let loose.

Bodies started to pile up in the river, hampering the advance of the Belmarch. Splashes mixed with shouts, and the smell of death quickly started to blow over them.

He was using arrows too quickly and soon found himself down to three. "Arrows," he called, joining in the chorus that ran down the wall.

Men and young boys scrambled up the wall, bringing what they could. Dale was one of them, no archer himself, and brought Sam a bundled.

"How goes it?" he asked as Sam took them and stashed them at the base of the wall.

Sam hazarded another glance. "They're making it to our side," he said with dismay. He had hoped that they would have slowed them down more than that, but a few ladder carriers were already scrambling up the rocks.

Down the wall a man screamed and tumbled off the wall, smashing on the rocks below. His scream ended abruptly.

"Tell me you have something that will make them unwelcome," Dale said.

Sam grinned and smacked him on the shoulder. "Better get back to it."

Dale tipped his fist at him, then scrambled off, ducking down low to avoid the arrows flying overhead.

He was breathing hard now. The air smelled of blood and sweat, and sounds overwhelmed his senses.

He glanced over to the Duke. He looked untouched, and Sam was glad. The man had taken a heavy blow earlier, but he wasn't even favoring his right side.

Maybe it wasn't as bad as he thought.

An arrow clattered on the wall next to him.

Sam flinched. A few more inches to one side and it would have found his head.

He pulled back his bow and hopped up, taking aim at a ladder carrier below. His arrow found its mark, and the man crumpled to the ground, the ladder clattering back into the river.

It started to get washed away, but another group of men grabbed it. Up to the east of him ladders were going up to the wall.

"They're going to get up!" Sam pointed to them, and the Duke saw.

"Torch," he commanded. "Light them."

The order passed down the wall, and torches were lit and passed along. The first ladder hit just as they threw the torches over the side.

Sam threw his own, and counted to three. The sound of the brush and dry leaves they had placed and hid beneath the wall catching flame came a second later.

His heart pounded as he waited, hoping that it would work.

Then, another monster was there, on the wall.

Sam jumped up, grabbed at his spear as it killed a soldier near him.

Another was able to cut at it, but then it turned on him. It moved like lightning, it was so fast.

But it was distracted and had its back to him. Sam thrust with the spear, catching it just below the nape of the neck.

He pushed with all his might, and it went through reluctantly. The thing went limp, taking his spear with it.

Sam scrambled to grab at it, was just able to pull it free before the body tumbled into the courtyard.

Behind, Trent stood wide eyed. "Thank you."

"Back to the wall," Sam said, wiping the blood off his face. Was it the monster's or his own?

His body felt fine.

The base of the wall was glowing, smoke coming up like a curtain. The ladders they were using had gotten wet on the trip over, but they were smoking now.

And the base of them were on fire.

Sam kicked one over, pushing it back with the butt of his spear, and it toppled backward. "Brush, bring up the brush."

He tossed one bundle they had staged up on the wall, a mixture of brush and shavings from the workshop.

They caught fire quickly, adding to the conflagration below, and it drove the Belmarch back. More bundles of them came up from below, and the defenders started being more selective with their targets.

Bowstring still twanged, and arrow still flew, but they were targeted at the enemy archers, who were starting to trickle down as the flames pushed them back.

Sam watched them, just peeking over the edge of the wall. With the Golden River to the east and the northern wall aflame, they only had one real choice.

Trumpets sounded again. Men burst from the trees carrying a large log by the cut down branches. The front had been sharpened to a tip and they had makeshift shields above their heads.

They splashed into the river, but headed west, downstream.

Just as we thought. Sam added another bundle to the fire below, taking pleasure as it whooshed into flames.

The leader was smart, and he understood the castle's weakness. While they tried to keep the ladders from the wall the battering ram crossed behind the attackers.

They were headed for the gate.

They were doing it. Evan looked out over the wall and watched them going for the gate.

Behind the battering ram streamed the rest of the army.

There were so many. Too many to count. Evan felt the rock in the pit of his stomach grow harder and harder.

How are we going to survive?

They were less than two hundred, and thousands were crossing. All they had were bows and a few small arms, but they had the arms of thousands.

Evan swallowed but ducked back behind the wall to think. Up and down the wall men were still fighting, firing arrows or pushing off the remaining ladders, or throwing more bundles over the wall to add to the fire burning beneath them.

It was too much. Evan closed his eyes, let the shouts and screams and sounds of the fire and death fade away.

He was back with Yand, looking over the low hill, the first moment he had seen the castle. It was smaller than he expected, but even from the distance the walls seemed big and solid. Men streamed over the construction, working to raise the fortress up out of the earth from where it slept.

It was always a fool's errand, to build so close to the Belmarch and their warlike ways, but it was not his position to question, only to obey.

His father had taught him that lesson, or tried to. Over and over he resisted, and now Evan knew why.

For one day, after he had taken his proper place, he would lead the Hornblood lands in his father's stead.

Evan's eyes snapped open, and he sucked in a deep breath. It had all been for this reason, all the years of disobedience, the nights in the taverns, the misbehavior when he knew it would embarrass his family.

The curse that he had brought about himself would cause the downfall of his house and all the people he cared about.

But it wasn't going to happen in the future, it was happening now. Even as he looked, men were dying. An arrow took a man to his left in the neck, and he crumpled up against the wall clutching at it until his blood was drained and his life over.

Haml, a young mason. Barely twenty summers old, and a long life ahead of him.

His blank, lifeless eyes stared up at Evan, who scrambled back to try and escape that accusing gaze.

It was his fault. He touched what was forbidden, he brought this down upon them.

And now there was no way out. The gate was barred, a long line of enemies behind it ready to rush in.

They would destroy it.

They would make it inside.

They would kill him and everyone else, and then they would sweep south, spoiling the land and desecrating his home.

Blood would well up from the ground, and the last of their people would either flee or be enslaved.

Evan hung his head in shame. He had brought this on them.

"Duke Hornblood." Someone grabbed his arm. "They are at the gate now. You need to give the order."

"Order?" Evan was in a daze. He could barely think. There was no use in trying, they would still kill them all.

Sam knelt down in front of him, eye to eye. "You are a Duke of Hornblood. Look at these men."

He followed Sam's finger. To the west men were still fighting, firing arrow after arrow with grim looks on their faces.

One of them had a bandage wrapped around his left eye, but he still fought on. Another was handing arrows out, cradling an arm smashed to bits.

"You don't understand, I'm cursed."

"That's enough out of you. On your feet like a man." Sam pulled him up.

Evan stared at him, shocked at how he spoke.

"You can either die here as a sniveling coward, too afraid to lead your men, or you can choose a different path."

Anger, anger at the words brought him back to his sense. The way he insulted him, a Duke of Hornblood, how little he knew him.

"What will it be, Your Highness?" Sam spit the word out like it was a foul taste. "A cursed coward, or a true leader?"

There were men here, men that deserved to live. He didn't deserve anything, not to be a Duke or the future Archduke, nor had he earned their respect.

And yet, they still gave it. They could have killed him long ago, but they chose to listen to him.

Like the men in those stories his mother had given him.

"I can't let them down." Sam smiled as Evan spoke. "Are we destined to the path that was laid before us?" Evan asked.

Sam wavered, looked away. Even though the fire beneath the wall cast an orange glow on him, his face fell into shadow.

"I can only hope that a man can change." Evan sensed more desire in Sam, a desire to say something else, something deeper, but it came and went.

I'm not the only one fighting a destiny.

"Then, if we can change, let us change together." Evan held out a hand. Sam looked up, then took it. "Tonight is the last night I ever pitied myself. Tonight is the last night I didn't think of myself of a Duke of Hornblood."

He looked back out over the raging river of men passing through the river. "This may be my last night alive. I don't want to live with any regrets."

"Nor do I," Sam said. Evan realized the kinship that lay between them, a man so easy to talk with him as an equal.

"Then I would ask a former prince and knight to fight with me, by my side," Evan said. Sam's eyes opened wide in shock. "Whatever man you used to be, whatever the reasons you left that life, we need you for who you are, not for who you were."

"I was never a prince," Sam said, eyes glistening in the firelight. "But I hated the killing. It seemed so senseless."

"If we don't stop them, there will be more killing. Surely, you can see that?"

A boom sounded at the gate. Sam turned to it. Another one followed, and then they were coming at a steady pace.

Evan clasped his shoulder. Sam nodded. Evan rose his voice and shouted, "To the gate!"

26

WELCOMING PARTY

The group of men waiting in the courtyard sprang up and sprinted to the southern wall. Another band rose from their hiding positions on the east wall and started firing arrows into the attackers.

Evan nodded to Sam, then ducked down and sprinted to the gatehouse. He passed by men doing their best, and he gave them what little encouragement he could, all the while knowing it wouldn't be enough.

But in every eye he saw there was a hardened resilience, a desire to fight ingrained deep within. No one doubted the fight would be difficult, but they knew that it could be done.

A random stone on the battlements tripped him, and Evan almost stumbled over the side, but at the last minute he caught himself, slamming into the hard rock. His right shoulder screamed in a pain that flared and traveled down his arm, but he picked himself up, brushed off his scraped hands, and kept going.

The Belmarch were not going to let up with a little bit of archery and were returning fire where they could. The fires along the north side helped, blinding them, and most of their arrows went high or low, clattering harmlessly.

But not every one.

A man twirled in front of him, clutching at an arrow sprouting from his shoulder. Evan caught him and laid him against the wall, wishing someone else would come to help. None did. His breathing was labored as Evan propped him up and told him to get ready.

"This will hurt." Evan grasped the rough arrow shaft, and the man closed his eyes with a grimace. With a quick motion, one he had only seen once but read about, Evan snapped the shaft of the arrow. Blood spurted from the shaft, and Evan held his hand against it.

The wounded man groaned, and clamped down with gritted teeth, but Evan couldn't stay with him. He called another soldier over. "Put a bandage on that and make sure the bleeding stops."

Evan made sure one more time that he was taken care of, then kept going.

The percussive sounds of the battering ram had changed. It was no longer a thick, hollow sound, but there were tiny hints of splinters. Smoke rose from the gatehouse, a good sign, and Evan took a peek over the side before he went in.

Soldiers were lined up below, makeshift shields of wood and mud held above them. One archer spied him and sent an arrow his way, so Evan ducked back behind the wall and into the gatehouse.

The smoke from the fire made his eyes water, and he crouched down to avoid being overwhelmed by the smell. "Is it ready?"

"Yes, Your Highness," Levitus said, waiting by the pot stirred by a younger mason.

"Good, do it now." Each boom made him wince, the sound getting hollower and hollower. It took three men to pick up the pot and carry it to the hole, a great cloud of steam rising off it as they did.

An arrow found its way up the murder hole, almost making them jump back, but momentum carried them on. They tipped and a great gush of a waterfall came out, leaking steam that mingled with the dark black smoke already hovering at the roof.

Men screamed below, scalded by the hot water, and ran out. The booms stopped for a blessed moment, but Evan knew that soon they would return.

But, in the meantime, the Belmarch were stopped and exposed. Other men brought in chunks of rock, cut from the masons to be as jagged as they could get them.

Evan took up one too, almost cutting himself on a sharp edge. One by one they lined up to toss them below, another delaying tactic.

But what are we delaying them until? Evan was next, and he threw down the rock before sliding out of the way.

The water and rock were having their intended effect though, and the battering ram lay abandoned on the ground. Evan could see it through a corner of one of the murder holes.

It moved as more Belmarch soldiers tried to pick it up, but another pot of water was already boiling and was added to discourage them.

Now the smell of blood mixed with smoke and water, and it was starting to make him sick. Evan gave them some encouragement but went back through the gatehouse door to get some fresh air and see how the rest of the defenders were faring.

They were putting up a fight and wearing the Belmarch down. More rocks were being thrown outside, since they was easier to access.

Evan stole between merlons until he was next to Levitus. "How bad are the losses?"

Levitus fired off an arrow, grim-faced as there was a scream off in the distance. "Not as bad as I expected, worse than I hoped. Keeping them off the wall with that fire was a neat trick, but I'm not sure it will last that long."

Evan looked to the northern wall, where he had assigned Sam to. "Every second counts." He glanced into the sky, a great cloud of smoke filling it and drifting, obscuring the stars.

The night had brought a chill, one he hadn't felt while he was moving, but now made him shiver as it dried his sweat. *What am I waiting for? Help from my father?*

"We could use some reinforcements, if you were planning on a miracle," Levitus said.

Evan snorted. "If I could produce it, I would have already." He snuck a glance over the wall. The steady stream of soldiers had lightened, and there were no archers in the immediate vicinity.

With the momentary lull, Evan was able to get his first good look at the Belmarch army. That they were fighters, he had no doubt.

Every one was clad in fighting leathers, and every one had a weapon of iron. Most were simple swords, curved but wicked looking, but there were a few spears thrown in for good measure.

They crossed the stream even as he watched, forming a cluster at the trees to the west. He had a glimmer of hope as he watched them mull about, trying to keep out of arrow range.

They might be able to make it after all. The thought caught in his throat, made him almost breathless.

Then, the steady pounding of the battering ram began again.

27

THE BEACON

The fires were dying down on the north wall. They still sent up great plumes of thick, black smoke, but the heat Sam once felt from them was getting less and less.

Despite their attempts to keep it going, they were running out of the tinder and wood shaving bundles they had made and had burned through all of the fuel they had placed there beforehand.

And the rate of fire they were taking from the Belmarch was getting worse. Sam took a peek, then ducked his head back as three arrows clattered around him. The ladders were back too, smacking against the wall even though the fires still raged.

"They're wetting them," Trent said as he fired off another arrow. "It's protecting the ladders from the fires."

Sam grimaced. He hadn't planned on them finding a way of protecting the ladders, and cursed himself for not thinking of how easy it would be to wet them sooner. Despite it, they were falling into his trap.

"Start bringing the men in, two at a time, from the outer edges. Pass the word, we need to fall back."

"Already?" Trent asked.

Sam jerked his head to the wall and popped up to get another shot off. An arrow flew by his cheek, but he was able to aim at an attacker in the river.

He never knew if he hit the man or not, though, because he had to fall back down under cover as soon as he could. *There are too many of them.*

Trent was wide eyed. "I'll pass the word."

He turned and did it as quietly as he could. They had a plan, but Sam wondered when it would fall apart.

The sounds of battle helped hide the word being passed, and since they were taking so much fire, it felt more natural to have fewer men. Their absence would be felt less, and Sam knew the only way this would work is if they had the element of surprise.

At the end of it, however, he wasn't sure what they would do.

A ladder fell onto the wall in front of him, spraying him with ice cold droplets of water. Sam jumped back in surprise, then readied to push it over with his spear, but a man was almost at the top.

Or what used to be a man.

Sam had to choke down his fear, despite seeing them before, and pushed with all his weight against the ladder, but the monster grabbed onto the shaft before he could do so, and wrenched.

The spear flew out of his hand, and his shoulder and arm almost came with it. His heart leaped into his throat as Sam pulled his backup sword like lightning.

The monster was up and over the wall before he could finish, its own blade singing a deadly song as it struck at Sam's throat.

He dropped, twisting and sliding his blade across the monster's abdomen, bringing a spray of blood as it cut below its meager armor.

Sam didn't even have time to shout for help before it was at him again, sword flashing so fast it was a blur.

He tried to keep up, backing away as he parried, the monster snarling at him. Froth dripped from its fangs, breath worse than a rotten carcass.

Sam lost ground, until Trent flew in with a thrust from over his shoulder and a deafening battle cry. Cut all over, Sam still turned to help, pressing the attack.

At first, they struggled to get in sync, so much so that the monster rigged a gash down Trent's leg.

When his blade whistled by Sam's throat, his mind cleared. The vision of him being a few inches closer was all he needed.

"Left," Sam said, lunging to the right. Trent, barely a hair behind him, cut from the left.

The monster parried Trent, but couldn't get to Sam in time, and leaped back with a hole in its leg.

They moved together, Sam not needing to say anything. He could sense Trent out of the corner of his eye.

Perfectly in sync, they became a whirlwind of death. Cuts bloomed on the monster, who could barely keep from a mortal wound, backing up one step at a time.

Behind it, another ladder had appeared on the wall, with Belmarch soldiers pouring over it. Someone behind him was yelling for a retreat, almost distracting Sam.

But he remembered all those who were locked away in the Keep, safe for now from the murderous hands of their enemies.

The women, the children. Belinda and her child. Joseph. *Martha*.

He couldn't lose, not now. With one last battle cry Sam sprung forward, rolling underneath the monster's grasp, and hamstringing it.

Seconds later, its head fell to the floor, rapidly changing back to that of a man, helped by a dripping blade in Trent's hand.

Sam gasped for breath, the adrenaline pulling back long enough to let him realize what kind of situation they were in.

Men were retreating, running back down the stairs, as the Belmarch gained more and more of a foothold on the battlements. A group of five or six were coming for them now.

"Sam," Trent warned.

"Go." He scooped up his bow and turned. He followed Trent to the stairs as more and more ladders sprung up.

They were ahead of them now, but Sam couldn't stop now. They attacked, setting the attackers on their heels.

They were savage fighters, inflicting more wounds on the two defenders who by this time were the last on the wall, but Sam and Trent had the upper hand in skill, and overwhelmed them.

With a few new wounds, they made it to the stairs. Pain was catching up to Sam now, the ache of battle and the fatigue of swinging his sword setting in.

But, one foot in front of another, he descended the stairs to the courtyard, until soft earth was once again beneath his feet.

He took one glance behind him. Belmarch attackers were streaming over the walls and following them into the courtyard.

A hundred feet away, the defender's ladder up the wall shone like a beacon, the only way to safety now.

Sam gritted his teeth and ran through the pain.

28

Unraveling Plans

Blood streamed down Evan's head, warm and sticky. His hand went to the wound, expecting the worst. No arrow, nothing lodged in his skull.

Only a flesh wound. He breathed a sigh of relief and returned the favor, catching an enemy archer in the eye.

"There are too many," Levitus said. "We need to fall back."

"No, it's too soon."

The dread in the pit of his stomach still hadn't gone away. They had a plan to fall back to the Keep, but afterward...

And now, it was coming faster than he wanted. Mathew ran up to them, ducking for cover as he went. "We've lost the northern wall and are retreating from the west."

Evan whirled, dismayed to see the northern wall almost completely filled with Belmarchers. Not a single defender was left on the wall, at least not any that were still alive. A few bodies were visible between the legs of the attackers.

More dead. *How many more need to die?* Evan wanted to sit down, to go back to his home, to be done with this.

But here were two men right beside him who needed him, eyes boring into his soul.

And the men on the west wall were retreating back to them, eyes on the attackers as they rounded the corner.

They could put up a fight for a few more minutes, but not much longer, and the multitude outside the gates was growing.

"Give them one last bath, then we'll go." Evan reached down deep, trying to tell if it was the right decision, but there was only silence and the deep well of self-doubt.

But he was a Hornblood, a branch of the family that kept the Hornwood alive and thriving. Protector of the Everlong.

He tried to run through the old sayings, hoping that they would make him feel better.

Somehow, they did. He remembered his ancestors, and the men in the stories, how they overcame monsters and storms, traveled across seas and came out of deserts to triumph on the other side.

"One more, yes, Your Highness." Mathew was wearing a big grin, and sprinted back inside the gatehouse.

"Start getting them into the walls, let have them attack, and pull up the ladder. We don't want any unwelcome visitors," Evan said.

Levitus saluted and disappeared, running to the west and shouting as he did. His voice was enveloped in the din and clash of the fighting.

They were making an orderly escape, and holding their own against the Belmarch, on the west wall. Evan drew his sword and advanced across the battlements, smelling the ash and smoke of the fire and urging it on.

It took him no time to round the corner, passing a stream of men who glanced at him with exhausted faces covered in blood and ash.

He could taste it in the air, bitter and sour, and wished again for the clear air of peace.

Then, he was in the thick of fighting and advanced through the wavering line.

"Fall back," Evan ordered, even as he pushed through to attack. He struck out, catching a Belmarcher in the gut, whose eyes widened in shock as he clutched at his belly.

Evan kicked him back, using his body to knock over another few attackers, and slipped into the forms.

His mind went blank, and all he could see were the weapons and movements of the men he fought.

Swords flashed at him, but he parried them or dodged, and struck back with lightning speed.

He felt no exhaustion, felt no weight, but let himself go. *This is what Yand was trying to teach me.* The thought floated in his mind, like he was looking down on his body.

They could only come at him two at a time, and he used it to his advantage. Bodies started to pile up as he killed one after the other.

The attackers were bogged down and had to climb over the dead bodies of their friends and countrymen to reach him, and Evan kept up the fight, making them pay dearly.

His lungs burned, his heart pounded, but the forms came like water.

Strike after strike, blow after blow, he flowed. Evan was aware that he was getting hit, but nothing was serious enough for him to stop.

Then, one last man charged, swinging an axe down from over his head.

Evan sidestepped, clipped him with his foot, and pushed him over the edge of the wall and back to the outside.

His scream was cut short a second later.

The Belmarch stared at him, stopped on the wall.

Exhaustion caught up to him like a wave, smashing into his body, and he almost crumpled over, but still they just looked at him.

Someone was yelling his name. He looked back for just a second. It was Levitus calling him.

Evan realized he alone was left standing on the west wall.

The Belmarch backed up, looking for the nearest stairs, and none would go forward.

Evan saw they were trying to cut him off and turned and ran back.

His feet slapped against the hard stone, legs protesting and screaming, as Levitus waved him over to the trapdoor.

The ladder they had put into the courtyard side of the newest walls leading to the Keep was gone.

But there were men at the stairs, barely a few feet in front of him, and Belmarch archers were shooting at him.

Evan wasn't sure he was going to make it before they would, and tried to increase his pace, but his legs felt like stone.

He was only a few feet away when a Belmarcher jumped up on the wall, blocking his path, and turned to face him with sword and shield at the ready.

It was too late. He wasn't going to make it.

29

AN OPPORTUNE TIME

A sword blossomed from the Belmarcher's throat, and he slipped to his knees.

Sam pulled his sword free of the man and kicked the body back down the wall.

Evan staggered the last few feet, taking Sam's hand, and he was almost pulled down the trapdoor ladder.

It slammed shut with a bang, and Sam slid the locking bar in place.

"Glad you made it," Sam said as pounding started on the trapdoor. "It might not take them long to get through it, even though it's four inch thick oak."

Evan recovered his breath. "How many made it?"

"I'm not sure." Men were lining the hollow wall, shooting arrows into the courtyard attackers. They had nowhere to go and were trying to stay out of range.

Evan peered out an arrow hole. Belmarchers were clustered up at the entrance to the stairs, and all along it.

Their numbers were working against them now, just like Sam had said.

Evan leaned his head against the cold stone and took a moment to recover. His body was beaten, and he hadn't realized how badly his right shoulder hurt.

As he stood it lanced with pain, and he involuntarily cried out.

"Your Highness!" Sam was by his side.

"Just my shoulder. How much time do you think we have?"

Sam watched him warily, examining him for major injuries, then glanced at the trapdoor. "An hour, at most. Probably less."

"Well then, let's give them something to think about." Evan smiled but knew that he couldn't pull a bow back now. Not with this pain.

He also had a big gash near his knee, but it had clotted over and wasn't bleeding, so he put weight on his leg.

It didn't hurt that badly, and he could walk well enough. Evan walked down the small corridor, pausing as defenders drew back their bows to shoot.

The supply of arrows was low. Dangerously low, and they had only the reserve in the Keep left.

"Make them count," Evan said. He watched an older mason sight, breathe deep, and loose.

Outside, he was rewarded by a shout of pain.

The Belmarch were trying to shoot back, but the arrowslits were doing their job well. Nothing was getting through.

The pounding started back, and Evan turned to the gate. He hadn't realized it had stopped.

One final parting gift. He hoped it had killed as many as possible.

Evan was at a loss for what to do now. He couldn't fight back, not now, and he couldn't stop them from coming in the gate.

They were going to breach it soon, if they didn't find a way into their hastily constructed tunnels, and there was nothing he could do but listen to the mayhem and shouting around him and smell the blood and excrement of battle.

Then, the gate gave way. He winced at the sound of the crunch, then splintering, and the great cheer from the Belmarch outside.

Thousands of them raised their voices in victory, the blood lust thick.

Evan glanced down at his blade. It was dripping blood into the dust. He swung it, trying to get most of it off, and stalked back toward the entrance.

Through the arrowslit, he saw the Belmarch ripping back the remains of the gate and portcullis.

They were eager and overcome with the heat of the battle.

"Divide, half take the left, the other focus on the right," Evan ordered. His command was passed down the tunnel. "They are coming."

Then, the gate was breached, and Belmarch climbed in between the walls.

They were confused to find no one there, until the arrows started.

The first attackers died quickly, but more took their place. They stepped over the bodies of their comrades and rushed forward.

Some stopped, trying to slide spears and swords through the arrowslits.

Evan rewarded one of them with a sword to the throat. He fell back with a bubbling gurgle and back into the dust.

It was the most Evan could do. He felt powerless now, as the Belmarch advanced in the courtyard and through the gate.

"We don't have enough room to avoid them," Evan shouted, jumping back as a sword poked at him.

He trapped it with his foot, then slashed at the attacker holding onto it.

"I was hoping we could hold out longer," Sam said, grimly firing arrows out towards the men in the courtyard. He picked up his last one. "It might be time to get back into the Keep."

Evan didn't want to give the order. A man down the tunnel screamed, his voice echoing severely, and slumped to the ground, a spear in him.

He couldn't see the sky, but it was dark even with the torches lining the tunnel.

"Fall back to the Keep." The flow of arrows had trickled to a stream, and the Belmarch in the courtyard were advancing to the wall without fear.

The words were bitter in his mouth, like he had failed once again. Only this time instead of him waking up in the gutter they would all be dead.

Every one of them.

Men shuffled back, a few of them wounded enough to be pulled, and the tunnel emptied into the Keep.

"Sam, you first." Evan pointed down the tunnel.

Sam nodded, then followed the others.

Evan took one last look, then joined him.

The Keep was filled, men standing at the entrance door that had been blocked and reinforced. Even though it was going to be a struggle, Evan knew that their enemy would get the battering ram through.

"Is everything ready?" Torchlight flickered over the group of them. Bill had been leading the group in the other tunnel, and he stepped forward now into the orange glow.

"It is ready. At your command."

Evan glanced at the two open doors. If they waited too long...

But they couldn't do it too early. The Belmarch were at the door, pounding on it in vain.

They shouted back for the battering ram.

Men shifted in the hallway, an uncomfortable silence taking over.

The Belmarch stopped pounding, and Evan stood and watched the door, his entire world narrowing to it.

"Not yet," he whispered, dry mouth cracking.

30

THE RED DAY

Men stood in the quiet of the night, breathing heavily. The torches flickered and consumed their fuel, shedding a small amount of heat on the wounded and broken gathered there.

Evan felt himself pulled into a sense of peace, even though they could hear the scraping and shouting of the Belmarch attackers.

Three ways in, and soon it would be none. Evan licked his lips, tasting sweat, blood, and ash all mixed together.

He thought he should say something, and gathered his words. His father would know what words were needed.

But I'm not my father. He was his own man, and in this moment he had to act like it.

"No matter what happens," he hated how final the words came out, but pressed on, "I can die well knowing we did our best."

"The night is not yet over," Sam said, stepping out of the shadows. He was covered in cuts, and his left eye was swollen shut. He looked like walking death. "We have hope yet."

"Hope for the morning, hope for a new day," Evan said. The gloom of the night was indeed lifting, the blackness he thought would go on forever turning to a light gray as the light of morning twilight streamed in.

"A better life," Bill said.

"And time with those we hold most dear," Sam whispered. The tone in the hallway had changed.

Inside Evan, the fear melted away. He wiped off his sword and sheathed it, straightened his back, and turned back to the door.

"Let them come and meet the men of Chathem."

He waited, with all the others, as the Belmarch shuffled the battering ram in through the broken gate and down between the walls they were trapped between.

Men still beat at the trapdoors, but had not gotten through.

Feet tramped close, then orders were called, and with a great shout they came.

Boom.

The first blow echoed through the hall. Dust shifted and fell from up above. Evan felt it through his feet.

"Hold." Men were pressed up against him, waiting in anticipation thick like a morning fog upon the river.

They brought the ram back, then rushed forward again.

Boom.

The braces held, the door shivered.

They went back again.

Boom.

Evan looked to Sam, who nodded. "Take them down."

Bill slipped into the east tunnel, Sam the west, carrying their large, wooden mallets.

Evan watched the door.

Boom.

It had given more than the last time. The wood wouldn't hold up forever.

Boom.

Now there was another sound, a knocking hollow sound, drifting through each door.

The Belmarch didn't seem to notice, but the energy in the hall heightened.

Evan held his breath.

Bill reappeared, rushed through the door, and slammed it. Sam followed a few seconds later.

Boom.

Evan frowned, his entire face tightening. He glanced at Sam. "I thought it was supposed to fall right away."

Sam's lips tightened. "The other beams might be holding tighter than I anticipated."

"Your Highness, they might be at the walls," Levitus said. "We should take the men up." His left arm hung at his side, unnaturally limp.

"Sam, make this work," Evan said, grasping his arm. To the others, "To your stations."

He turned and led his third of the men up the stairs to the right.

Sam didn't know why it wasn't working. They had notched the beams right, the masons had put in the wall the way he had asked.

But nothing happened.

Boom.

The sound rattled his skull. The walls were still standing. They shouldn't be.

Boom.

Sam realized what had happened, and then the weight of how to fix it fell upon him.

Bill was still here, and Trent. "The walls need to be pushed."

"Pushed?" Bill asked, eyebrows drawn down.

He thought it could be just one. "Lock the door behind me if I don't make it."

Sam strode through the door.

"Sam, no," Trent said, trying to hold him back. *He was a smart man.*

"I'll just start it, I'll be back through before you know it."

"You might not make it, you might..." There was a real fear in Trent's eyes.

"I know." Emotion choked at his throat. "Take care... I am proud of you."

He broke away from Trent's grasp and was in the tunnel of walls a second later. Sam collected himself, looked up at the wall, and put his hands against them.

The stone, rough and jagged beneath his hands, was cold.

Boom.

He couldn't wait any longer.0020Sam dug his feet into the dirt, squatted, and pushed.

It was too big, too heavy.

Try as he might, Sam could not budge it. He strained, he struggled.

Then, two more pairs of hands joined his, Bill on his right and Trent on his left.

"No, go back," he gasped.

"You need the help," Bill said.

"I'm not leaving you," Trent said.

Feeling a mixture of relief and sadness, Sam bore down and pushed again, his feet digging into the earth.

The wall budged.

Evan was the first onto the wall, the sky a light gray and a fresh breeze blowing from the south.

The sight made his heart drop. Belmarch filled the courtyard, were assembled all along the outside of the southern wall.

And the battering ram was ready for another hit.

"Aim for those on the ram," Evan said. The twenty or so men who could still shoot arrows fired.

He put his hands on the edge of the wall, watching the clouds up above turn orange. There was no escape, there was no way out.

And the Belmarch still came, down to a trickle of horses and carts, across the river.

They were invading.

The man on the horse had taken up position with the rest of his leadership on the plain outside the walls.

Evan could feel his eyes on him, and the victory he must be pleased about.

They even had reinforcements coming up, a great army emerging from the forest to the southwest.

All seemed lost.

Still, he was at peace. They still had to get in the Keep, and it would cost them dearly, maybe enough to slow them down enough so that the others could flee.

He turned his attention to the walls, watching them closely. Nothing happened.

Men were setting fire to the trapdoors now, trying to weaken them enough to get in.

"Come on," Evan whispered. The defenders peppered them with arrows, but there were too many to make much of a difference.

Belmarch invaders surrounded the newly built walls. He couldn't ask for a better time.

Then, the left wall leaned in. Evan leaned in looking closer.

It teetered, then started to topple.

Just like Sam had said, the walls collapsed, first the right side, then the left.

The Keep rumbled, the sound like rolling thunder. Men screamed and were silenced, great clouds of dust rose.

Evan felt the tremor through the stone and struggled to stay on his feet.

He coughed, trying to keep the dust out of his lungs, and the others on the wall fell back.

When it cleared, the courtyard was chaos. None of the Belmarch in between the walls had survived, and now stone blocked the entrance.

A good portion of those on the other side hadn't been able to escape either, and the attackers were in a state of total confusion.

"It worked," Evan whispered. Horns sounded, but they were not the horns of the Belmarch.

They were the horns of Hornblood.

Evan looked to the south, where the sound had come from.

The army was charging, but they weren't from Belmarch.

It was the King of Chathem, the banner of his own father flying by his side.

Already confused, the Belmarch were unprepared for the attack on their flank. The man on horseback struggled to form up ranks, but it was too late.

Evan watched as the Chathem army slammed into the Belmarch, ripping them in two, and pushing them to the Black River.

He sank to his knees, overwhelmed at the turn of events. His death was no longer inevitable.

Evan Hornblood looked to the light of the morning sky and felt peace wash over him like warmth.

Epilogue

Evan felt his legs shake as he walked down the stairs to the entrance of the Keep, the feeling and sounds bouncing around inside those of joy and exuberance.

Word had spread of the King's arrival, and women and children rushed past him to see.

At the entrance the left most door was open, blocked with rubble.

Sam, Trent, and Bill were inside being seen to by Martha and a few others. They were bruised and beaten, black and blue on anything that was visible, and Sam's left leg was broken.

"It worked." Evan knelt down next to Sam, clasping his hand. "They're routing the Belmarch, who are fleeing back to their own land. I hope that they will stay there."

"I hope for peace," Sam said.

"Excuse me, Your Highness," Martha said. Evan rose, gave her his place, and sat to rest.

His body ached, and his shoulder shot pain down his arm anytime he moved it.

But they had made it. They had survived the attack.

And he had held. He had been a man of Hornblood.

When they were finally able to clear the rubble enough to get outside it was after noon.

Evan was the first to greet the King, who strode into the Keep with flashing eyes and teeth. Evan's father, the Archduke of Hornblood, was at his side, still bandaged from his previous wounds, and Rhys was smiling behind them.

Evan couldn't believe his eyes, but Rhys just motioned to him and kept smiling.

The King commended Evan on his work holding until they could arrive, making mention of being held up by eastern raiders.

"It was not me, Your Honor," Evan said. "These men fought bravely, valiantly, and built well. They are the ones who should be commended."

"Well noted." The King waved to an adviser and whispered in his ear.

The Archduke pulled him to the side and asked for a word in private. Evan nodded and led him to his study, catching Rhys by the arm before he went.

"Was this your doing?"

"It's a long story, I'll tell you about it another time," Rhys said, "but I still have friends in Ironwood."

In Evan's study, his father looked first upon the crest on the wall, a slight smile on his lips. "You have done... more than I ever thought of you, my son."

"I wasn't ready to take your place," Evan said, startling him. "And I spent so long trying to run from it. I never really knew that was what I was doing all these years."

The Archduke studied him, his face turning tender for what seemed to Evan to be the first time.

"I know. You will be ready, when the time comes." The Archduke smiled and embraced his son.

Sam and Martha wed the next week, and the defenders took a well-deserved feast to mark its occasion. Belinda stood by Martha's side, baby in hand, and although he could still see grief in her eyes, the hate was gone.

The King and his army returned to the south, leaving a hefty garrison and promise of provision.

The workers returned to work on the castle, and additional workers were sent to bolster their efforts.

Bill remained master mason and grew into the role.

Kerien became the master carpenter as Sam was occupied with his work as Overseer. No replacement was offered to Sam, and he settled into the work.

Two years later Sam stood on the Keep, repairs to the gate and wall complete, as Bill set the final stone.

He pulled Martha close in a hug as the cheer rang out around them.

The castle was complete. He looked on it with satisfaction, and the knowledge that something of him, and everyone who worked to build it, would remain with it while the walls stood.

ECLECTIC STORIES

Thank you for spending your precious time reading this book.

If stories make you salivate, learn more about lore, take an exclusive sneak peek behind the scenes, and get writing updates in my newsletter, Eric's Eclectic Stories.

As a bonus you'll get *Stories from the Deep*, a Patmos Sea Fantasy Adventure anthology that gives a glimpses of lore, extra prologues and epilogues, and character backstories.

If you aren't satisfied, unsubscribe at any time.

Join at erickercher.com.

-Eric Kercher

ALSO BY ERIC KERCHER

Patmos Sea Fantasy Adventure Series

Fathomless Pursuit
Architect's Prize
Ironbound Path
Sunken Prey
Unanswered Prophecy
Hardened Pilgrim
Final Peace

Seventh Hall Chronicles

Seventh Hall
Ode to the Survivors
Bastion of the Deep

Epic of Hornblood Castle

Siege of the Unfinished Keep
Winter at Hornblood
Branch of the Everlong

Castlebound Adventures

Rats in the Cellar!

Anthologies

Red Eagle Anthology
Searchlight Anthology

About Author

Eric Kercher was born and raised in a small town on the Great Plains on good books. After attending a small state school on the east coast he joined the US Navy to serve his country and explore the world. He worked on submarines, and the world beneath the waves captivated him with all its mysteries and wonders. After spending time in larger cities, he's settled down in a quiet town with his wife and children. When not on an adventure in a good book the author enjoys creating dust woodworking, architecture, and spending time with loved ones.

Find out more at www.erickercher.com.

www.ingramcontent.com/pod-product-compliance
Lightning Source LLC
Chambersburg PA
CBHW061029310726
48969CB00004B/886